# UNBROKEN SPIRITS

ANNA ANDERSON

*For information, contact:*

***Boundless Book Publishers***
*1301 Fannin St*
*Houston, TX 77002, USA*
*www.boundlessbookpublishers.com*
*Email: info@boundlessbookpublishers.com*
*Phone: +(833) 506-1149*

***Published by Boundless Book Publishers***

***ISBNs:***
*Paperback: 979-8-9929978-1-1*

# DEDICATION

To my parents, who have been my biggest supporters and cheerleaders throughout this whole journey. Without you, this book wouldn't have made it this far.

# ACKNOWLEDGEMENTS

Eight years ago, I started writing this story in a black spiral bound notebook in the middle of my American History class. I don't exactly remember what sparked the idea, but I do remember clearly starting this story. Since then, this story has gone through so many changes. As I read through the very first drafts in that notebook, I nearly didn't recognize the plot or some of the characters. Each draft, however, has brought the story closer to its final product, the book you hold in your hands.

Publishing this book has been such a long process, and a very exciting experience. This opportunity wouldn't have been possible without the guidance hand of my Heavenly Father helping me know where I needed to be and what I needed to do. He has been the main reason this book is here today. It's been a learning curve but I am grateful for everyone who's helped me along the way. There were so many people that helped me with this, and this book wouldn't be the masterpiece it is today without the amazing people that helped me along the way.

First and foremost, I'd like to thank Jason Cole, who has been my main point of contact and has helped me understand each part of this process. I am so grateful for his help and all the work he and his team have put into this book.

I'd also like to thank Isabella Winnow, my editor, for helping me refine and tweak my book so that it is the best that it can be!

I, an un-artistically gifted writer, would not have been able to finish this book without the help of Axel Stone who did all of the cover design. I cried when I first saw the cover.

There were so many of my friends that helped me with this, making sure things made sense and helping ground me when I felt like I was losing my mind, and pushing me to take the next step in my career.

Last, but not least, I'd like to thank my parents, Jon and Brandee Anderson, for their unwavering support and love through these past eight years. Without their constant asking to read it, I never would have finished as soon as I did. They are who this book is dedicated to and who I will always be grateful for.

# ABOUT THE AUTHOR

I have been telling stories since I started talking. Stories are a way of learning about life and understanding the difficult and hard things that happen. I started seriously writing in my early teenage years, following a blossoming story of injustice and finding courage within yourself. I love to travel and I love pulling ideas from the areas I see, adding a sense of realism to the fantasy. Unbroken Spirits is my first novel, and it is the dream of a young girl made real.

# PART ONE

# PROLOGUE

Trey had a feeling that the night was too quiet. Light from the moon sparsely made it through the dense trees, which made it hard to see what was going on outside. This was Trey's third night this week on night patrol for the park. His wife had not been thrilled when he left, even less so when he explained that he would be on duty tomorrow night as well. With a sigh, he sunk into a chair and pulled out his dinner.

"What's for dinner tonight, Jefferson?" Carl asked, startling Trey as he slid down in a chair next to him.

Trey glanced up mid-bite at his partner. The younger man had blonde hair that was flat from wearing his hat all day. "Ham sandwich. Courtesy of the wife," he said around a mouthful of food.

Carl pulled out his own dinner. "That's a mighty fine sandwich."

Trey nodded. "I've got a mighty fine wife."

*"We have a problem, Jefferson. Rock slides near the Taylor trail,"* Peter said over the radio in Trey's pocket.

The two men shared a look before running to their jeep. Trey climbed into the driver's side while Carl climbed into the passenger seat. "On our way. Is Boyd with you?" Trey's half eaten sandwich is left on the table, along with the book he was reading. The rockslide was probably nothing, but the sinking feeling in his gut didn't disappear.

*"Come quick. It's not a normal rockslide."* A pause. *"Hey, boss,"* a younger voice said over the radio.

"Good. We're nearly there." The jeep's lights illuminated a large part of the road as the vehicle bumped over the various rocks and a few tree branches.

A large *boom* shook the ground. Carl grabbed onto the handle while Trey wrestled with the steering wheel, knuckles white.

"What was that?" Carl asked as he looked out the window at the darkened mountains and trees nearby.

Trey shook his head, not fully understanding what just happened. Rock slides don't cause earthquakes. "Let's just get to the boys, then we'll figure it out." With the windows down, they heard the distant crack of rocks hitting each other. Peter's jeep was already parked at the trailhead. Carl and Trey quickly jumped out of their vehicle and started running down the trail. They didn't have to run far before they came up on the two men. Peter and Boyd stood in front of a large boulder, flashlights pointed at the boulder.

"I thought you said rock slide," Trey said to the tall redhead.

Peter turned around. "Rocks are sliding, just only off this boulder."

Trey turned his light to the large boulder, studying it. There was a perfect rectangle etched into the surface and rocks littered the ground around it. "Did this have anything to do with the earthquake?"

"It happened at the same time that the rectangle appeared," he said.

Trey took one step towards the boulder before the ground shook again. The four men thrust their arms out for balance and gripped onto low hanging tree branches. Water sloshed in the river behind them. Light emerged from the etched rectangle, blinding the four men. A sound like thunder boomed and rocks sprayed in every direction, sending the men scrambling for cover. Trey was knocked to the ground by a large object barreling into him.

"Is everyone okay?" Peter asked as the light faded.

The groans from the three men were his answer. Trey blinked and sat up, then stilled. Lying on the ground beside him was a young man in nothing but shorts and giant silver bird wings trailing from his back. He shakes his head, blonde hair obscuring his eyes. The giant wings moved sporadically as the young man pushed himself up. The young man stood a few inches taller than Trey's six foot two, the wings making him seem more imposing.

Trey's hands flew to his gun, resting on the handle. "Who are you?" he asked and turned his light on the man.

That caught the other three men's attention and they made their way towards Trey.

The young man blinked and stared at the four of them with reflective silver eyes. *"Enta?"* he asked in a strange tongue and accent.

"Do you speak english?" Peter asked.

The young man turned his bright gaze on the redhead. "English?" he asked, stretching out the word. "Human tongue?"

Peter nodded. "Our language, yes."

The wings behind the young man fluttered as he shifted back and forth on his feet. He looked back toward the boulder and his face fell. The rectangle seemed to be cut out, and the young man ran towards it, placing the palm of his hands in the center.

*"Nag, nag, nag!"* he shouted. A light started to emit from the young man. With shoulders bent inwards, he turned back towards Trey and his team. The four men backed up and Trey raised his gun. The young man looked at them, tears brimming his silver eyes.

"Apology," he whispered as the light grew brighter.

Boyd fell to the ground, clutching his chest. Gurgling sounds rose from his throat as he tried to breathe, and the river started flowing faster and faster. The once calm waters rose up and down, forming white tipped caps that sloshed over the rocks nearby. Carl rose from the ground with a scream. He grasped at the trees as he floated up and up, rising past the tree tops.

Trey pointed his gun at the strange young man. “Stop whatever you’re doing, now!” he shouted.

The winged man stared at him and tears fell from his eyes. “Apology,” he whispered again. The silver wings behind him dropped so low, they nearly touched the ground.

“Trey, stop!” Peter shouted. “Don’t shoot him!”

The ground shook, knocking the two men to the ground. “Tranq him! Make him stop!” Trey screamed.

The young man seemed unaffected by the events happening around him. The silver wings behind him spread and fluttered as Peter pulled out a tranquilizer. From his place on the ground, he fired, hitting the man in the middle of his bare chest.

The young man stared at it before collapsing, his wings spread wide across the ground.

The earthquake did not stop, and Carl’s screams eventually faded into nothing.

# CHAPTER ONE

# 732

The end of the world started with fireworks. Reds and blues, greens and purples, oranges and yellows. People outside were shouting and laughing, most of them probably drunk, celebrating the end of the year and bringing in the new one. Nobody was prepared for the fires that started.

I watched with my older brother, Jake, out his window that night, originally enjoying the fireworks. We hadn't realized how late it was, and we were startled by the sound of his watch beeping.

"Midnight," he whispered. Jake glanced over his shoulder at the door. The small strip of light shining from the hallway lets us know that Mom and Dad are still up. "We better get to bed. Mom and Dad will be upset if they find out we're up this late."

We took one last look out the window before we closed it. That's when the screaming started. Jake and I froze with the window half open, the night air wafting over us. That's when we saw the fire. We watched with wide eyes. And then we felt something within us stir. Jake was the first one of us to figure it out. He hesitantly stretched out his hand and golden light shot into the sky. We both jumped back in shock. After a moment, we started giggling. I decided to try it out. I closed my eyes and focused on the new feeling and then I opened my hand and a warm yellow light pooled in my palm. Jake and I spent hours exploring our new power, doing our best not to wake our parents. We would periodically glance back at the small strip of light under the door, waiting for footsteps walking by. I was ten years old when magic entered our lives, changing them forever.

The next months were spent learning how to master this new power of ours. Jake and I often would get together with Colton, my best friend, and discover new ways to use it. We would make objects float, or cause a light show to go off in the living room. Our magic didn't hurt anyone. It seemed like it was there for entertainment.

I was fourteen when the announcement came, further altering our lives. It was a few days before Jake's sixteenth birthday and we were all lounging in the living room, the TV playing softly in the background. Jake and I were trying to see who could make the coolest animals out of our magic as Mom and Dad sat on the couch talking softly. Dad then turned up the volume on the TV. The two news anchors sitting behind their table were talking casually, discussing the current standing on magic.

"Studies have shown that there are two different magic types," the woman said. "A harmless type that seems to only affects children, and a second, more dangerous type, that only affects some adults. We still do not know the source of this strange power, nor why it has come into our lives."

"My kids love their magic, regardless of where it comes from," the man replied, chuckling to himself. "What have we been told about the situation with this more dangerous magic?"

The woman took a deep breath in. "There are programs being put in place, a testing center if you will, to test for magic. It manifests itself starting at age sixteen. These programs will be a center to help control this new magic."

Jake stared at the TV, then looked at the animals on the ground. "Dad, will I have to go to that testing center?"

My dad peeled his gaze away from the TV. "I'm sure it's nothing to worry about, bud. We'll figure it all out," he said.

Jake's birthday was a day of nervous excitement. Mom made his favorite breakfast, chocolate chip pancakes before she and my dad took Jake out for the day. Jake had given me a hug that seemed longer than normal. "I love you," he whispered. "I'll see you soon."

I nod into his chest. "I'll see you soon," I whispered. I watched them drive away from the front window, our black van getting smaller and smaller as it traveled down the street.

It was hours before they came back.

At the sound of the garage door, I jumped off the couch and ran to the door, flinging it open. Mom and Dad were still sitting in the car. I didn't see Jake through the windows. I hesitantly walked down the steps and closer to the car. Dad saw me and smiled, opening the door to greet me.

"Hey," he whispered, his voice soft.

"What's wrong?" I asked. "Where's Jake?"

My dad let out a deep sigh. "They said that they are going to help him control his magic. He has to stay in their program until he's gained control."

I shake my head. "No, he said he was coming back."

My dad stands up and pulls me into a tight embrace. I feel tears prick my eyes. My dad's arms around me are the only thing grounding me as my world felt like it was falling apart.

I didn't use my magic again after that.

I was sixteen when my parents took me to the testing center. I picked at a loose string on my shirt as we drove down the highway, my heart pounding. The testing center was a large, rectangular building that reminded me of a DMV. The parking lot was half full of vans, sedans, and SUVs of all different colors. My parents turned around and gave me a smile.

"Ready?" My mom asked.

I nodded, shoving back the fear that tried to climb its way up. I was the last one out of the car. My parents walked on either side of me, my mom's arm around my shoulders. It felt like I was moving through thick molasses as I walked closer and closer to the beige building. I started to fiddle with the string again as we walked through the front doors.

Inside the building, people were lined up with their children. Some families were all together. There was one couple who walked out holding each other close. The wife was crying and her husband had his arm around her, leading her out of the building. Another family was hugging their daughter close and smiling, laughing quietly as they walked out. I felt my heart start to pound as we approached the desk. My parents checked us in and then we were led to a small room to wait. The room was plain with beige walls and black cushioned chairs. When the door opened again, two men dressed in all black walked in.

"Good morning," the man with blonde hair and a large tattoo on his arm said. "We've got one test for you today."

I met his eyes and nodded. The man pulled a chair closer to where I sat and pulled out a small black box. My mom rubbed my shoulder as he strapped it onto my arm.

"What is that?" I asked, feeling something within me swirl. *What is that?*

The man glances up at me. "This is a device that will check if you have magic," he explained. "It doesn't hurt and the test is very quick."

I watched him as he pressed buttons on the device. It lit up and started flashing a blue light. I held my breath as I watched. The thing inside me continued to swirl and seemed to get angry. I squirmed in my seat, feeling uncomfortable. That swirling grew and grew until the small black box exploded. I jerked backwards, forgetting that the device was strapped onto my arm. The tattooed man flinched before he fished in his pocket for something.

"Requesting assistance in room 5," he said into the radio on his shoulder.

I stared at the remains of the box, sitting very still as my pulse skyrocketed. That swirling settled down and seemed to rest inside my chest.

Something clanged on the ground. The blonde man picked it up and held it out to me. "This is yours," he said flatly.

I started at the small metal item. It looked like a pendant that would sit on a necklace. The image on it depicted what looked like a flame behind a firework. I shook my head no. "It's not mine," I whispered.

My parents stiffened beside me. "Honey," my mom said. "It's yours."

I turned to look at her. "What?"

"You," her words were cut off by a small sob. "You have magic."

I looked back at the tattooed man who still held out the pendant. "Did I…?"

He nodded his head.

“What is that?” I whispered, looking at the pendant.

“Something created by your magic. It stays with you, no matter what we do with it, it will find its way back to you.” He pressed it into my hand before he removed the strap from my arm.

Another man clad in black walked in through the door, this time holding a pair of silver bracelets. I clutched the metal pendant in my hand and back up in my chair.

“Our program helps people like you learn control,” the tattooed man said. “These bracelets here are to help prevent any unnecessary accidents from happening.” He glanced down at the broken box and strap in his hands at that.

I looked at my parents. “Will I, will I get to go home?” I stuttered out.

“When you’ve learned control,” the man said coldly. He nodded pointedly at the man holding the bracelets.

“Jake, he…” I trailed off at the tears in my mom's eyes. “I’ll come back. I promise.” I straightened up and felt the weight of my words settle. I would come back to them.

The man with the bracelets clasped one around each of my wrists. “Come with me,” he said. I stood on shaky legs and walked towards the door, sparing one last glance at my parents before the door closed. The man switched the silver bracelets for thick handcuffs the moment the door clicked shut.

"What's going on?" I asked nervously.

The man did not answer me, instead, he pulled me along the hallways and into a small room. He shoved me into a chair where a woman with a tight bun tattooed a barcode on my neck. Without a word, he walked me to the back of the building, tossed me into the back of a van and locked the door. He left me huddled against the metal bench as the van started moving, cuffed hands pressed against my throbbing skin, taking me away from my parents and closer to their program.

I didn't know where magic had come from, but I knew one thing.

Magic was here to curse us.

# CHAPTER TWO

# 732

My head bangs into the van wall as it goes over a particularly large bump, forcing me from my restless sleep. After blinking, I lean my head back against the wall with a sigh, letting it bounce a few times. The chains rattle with the movement of the van. This wasn't a regular van with two rows of seats behind the driver's seats. This van was specifically built to transport people like me, people with magic. Its back is separated from the cab by a floor to ceiling metal wall. The two soft yellow lights on each of the walls do hardly anything to illuminate the dismal space. The bench I'm sitting on runs along the length of the wall, an identical one sits on the wall across from me. Five pairs of chains sit evenly spaced on each bench where the Workers, people who are in the Rebren Program for Magic Control, are locked in for transport. Three seats sit on the metal wall that separates the cab from the rest of the back. That is where the Handlers sit. Glancing around, I see the singular Handler staring at me from one of the three seats. His fingers flex on the gun in his hand, eyes are trained on me.

"Watching me to make sure I don't attack anyone in my sleep?" I ask with a smirk.

The Handler doesn't respond. They never do.

I chuckle and look away, idly rubbing the small pendant clutched in my hand. "How long have we been on the road? It's gotta be uncomfortable for you back here, watching me the whole time. You don't even get to sleep. Must suck," I ramble. "Me? I'm living the life of luxury here. I get to rest and not worry about anything. You guys take care of that for me."

The Handler still doesn't respond.

I sigh and raise my shackled hands to my face with a wince, rubbing my eyes, the action pulling at the long stripes that decorate my back. I had dreamed for the first time in a long time. I had dreamed about that day… I drop my hands, stopping to scratch at the Mark–the barcode they tattooed on me my first day– on my neck before dropping them onto my lap. I open my fist to reveal the pendant in my hand. Despite years of being shoved into my pocket, thrown, buried in the dirt, and the oils from my hands, it is still as bright as the day it was created. The fireworks and the flame are still etched into the metal, giving me an idea of what kind of magic I have. I let out a sigh and closed my hand, softly hitting my head against the wall a few more times. I let my eyes wander across the van's plain ceiling and count the screws holding the metal panels together.

Magic. The thing that got me, and countless others, into this situation. The pendant in my hand grows warm and I toss it across the van. It clunks against the walls, echoing in the small space. The Handler watches, but does nothing. I hear other Workers muttering amongst themselves sometimes. They talk about all the good that can come of

Magic if we stop shying away from it. Their words are always the same. Always good natured. But they are wrong. Magic has done nothing but tear families apart and bring out the worst in people since it arrived nine years ago. A weight appears back in my pocket and I let out a frustrated sigh, pulling the pendant out.

The van stops and the door to the cab of the van opens. The bright light from the cab hurts my eyes and I squint, raising my hands again to block the light. I blink a few times as I turn my attention to the door at the front of the van. A well dressed man in a blue suit walks through, closing the door behind him. He sits in the seat next to the Handler.

"Good afternoon, Evans," the man says to the Handler.

The Handler nods to him, finally taking his eyes off of me for the first time. "Afternoon, Johnathan," he replies.

The man, Johnathan, settles in his seat, setting his notepad on his lap and he knocks twice on the closed door. I feel the van lurch forward and we're moving again.

We're not at our destination then. I lean back against the wall, shoving the pendant back into my pocket.

Johnathan leans back in his seat. "732, how are you?" he asks, calling me by the number they tattooed onto my neck.

I roll my eyes, looking away from him. "I have a name," I say, staring blankly at the lock on the back doors.

"Yes, but you are no longer the person who deserves that name. Here at Rebren, you are now 2157732. We've been over this," he states, opening his notebook and clicking his pen.

2157732. The number they gave me four years ago as they etched it permanently into my skin. 21 to tell them what state I'm from, 57 for the city I lived in, 732 to replace my name. There were 731 people taken before me. 732 is what I am called most of the time, like some sort of sick nickname.

I sit up, resting my elbows against my knees, and look at him. My dirty hair falls around my face and I gently shake it out of the way. "We have, haven't we?" I agree. "If I remember correctly, and I usually am, I told you that I'm not going to answer to a number, Program policy or not."

He sighs, setting his pen down and staring at me with a bored expression.

"I'll even call you by your name, Johnathan. All I ask is that you do me the same courtesy," I say, pleading at him with my eyes. *I just need to know that someone other than me knows it. Someone who knows that I'm not just a number. Please…*

Johnathan's stare shifts to a tired expression before sighing again and adjusting his glasses. "You know I can't do that," he says softly.

I lean back against the wall, staring at the blank metal in front of me.

"Let's talk about what happened," he says, changing the topic.

"You mean the accident that happened because I can't control my magic? Sure. Let's talk," I mumble, looking down at my hands and picking at a hangnail on my thumb.

Johnathan rubs the bridge of his nose, then adjusts his glasses again. "You blew up a truck. How is that an accident?"

I close my eyes and focus on the magic swirling just underneath my skin. "I couldn't tell you. I don't know," I whisper, half lying to him. I know the explosion had something to do with my magic, but I didn't intentionally cause it. The wounds on my back itch, the result of using magic is twenty lashes. The pain hardly registers anymore, not after four years. What's more bothersome is the itching that happens when the blood dries.

"What was happening before it blew up?"

That was a new question. I open my eyes and face Johnathan. He's looking at me with a raised eyebrow. "Why?" I ask.

"Because I, and Rebren, are curious," he says.

"I got caught trying to sneak out," I say slowly. At a look from Johnathan, I continue. "I had nearly made it to the house when a Handler spotted me. He wrestled me back to the shed. I was scared and angry. I started pushing back against him when the truck blew up. I swear it wasn't intentional."

Johnathan scribbles in his notebook and nods. "I believe you," he says after a moment, meeting my eyes and closing his notebook.

I tilt my head to the side slightly. "You do?" I ask, confused. "Since when do you believe *me*? What did Stern Vern say to you?"

Johnathan furrows his eyebrows at the nickname. He opens his mouth to say something, but decides against it, shaking his head. "He told me you were trouble and to take you off his hands."

I smirk and rest my head against the wall again, letting the rumbling of the tires on the road sooth the pain that's starting to creep up from my back. "That sounds about right," I say.

"I do believe you, 732," Johnathan's says. "You strike me as sincere. And your story checks out."

The van slows to a stop and Johnathan gets up, taking his notebook with him. "We'll be arriving at Rebren shortly," he says before walking through the door, joining the driver in the cab.

# CHAPTER THREE

## 732

The van slows to a stop and the Handler stands up, walking to the other side of the van. The stationary vehicle shakes with each footfall, rattling the chains scattered across the interior. He turns to face me, his hand still holding his gun. I chuckle softly and shake my head. "You really think *that* is necessary with all of this?" I hold up my wrists, rattling the chains that connect the shackles on my wrist to the ones on my ankle and to the ones around my waist. "I, personally, think it's overkill. But, whatever you guys want, I guess."

A few uncomfortable minutes pass by before the back doors open. At that, the Handler walks to me and releases me from the chains securing me to the seat, leaving the shackles on my wrist. I glare at him as he does so, which earns me a hard shove, pushing my head downwards. I grunt as the Handler shoves me out of the van. I stumble and nearly fall off of the ledge. Catching myself on one of the doors, I jump down and am immediately grabbed by two different Handlers. One on either side, their grips like iron clamps on my biceps. I know that I'll have bruises later. The Handlers walk me into the large brick building in front of us. The size of the Rebren is one that I can never fully comprehend. This location has two separate buildings connected by a skybridge that casts a long shadow over the parking lot. How can something this big and popular be so bad? I feel the metal pendant in my pocket and the answer is clear: Magic. Magic corrupts people and has torn many lives apart. I keep my head down as we walk in, not wanting to see the large silver letters I've memorized that sit over the doors.

*Rebren Program for Magic Control: Chicago, Illinois Campus. Teaching your children since 2016.*

It makes my stomach turn.

A blast of air washes over me when the front doors open, aggravating the open wounds on my back. I breathe in through clenched teeth.

We don't have to go far before the Handlers stop at a desk. Johnathan appears from behind us and stands next to the Handler on my right. He pulls a few papers out and sets them on the desk.

"Identification and reason for return?" The woman at the desk asks, grabbing the papers and setting them next to her computer. Her curly red hair partially obscures her thick framed glasses as she types into her computer.

"2157732. Returned for unauthorized use of magic and destruction of property," Johnathan states. He glances at me before turning back to the woman at the desk. The woman waves the Handlers forward and grabs a scanner. I groan and look to the side. This always is the most humiliating part.

A hand is clamped on the back of my neck, fingers pressing into one of the open wounds there. I wince and breathe in sharply. My head is pulled to the side, exposing the black barcode. The woman quickly scans the barcode on my neck as if she's scanning an item at the grocery store. The scanner beeps and she pulls her hand back.

"Was anyone hurt?" she asks.

"No ma'am," Johnathan says.

She types something into her computer. "What was damaged?"

"The family truck."

"Extent of the damage?"

"Explosion. The truck will need replacing."

"What magic was used?" the woman asks, glancing at the blood smearing my clothes and skin.

"Magic caused the explosion, ma'am," Johnathan states.

I stare at my dirt stained shoes. The return process doesn't get any easier the more it happens.

"Was the proper punishment dealt out?"

"Yes, ma'am. Twenty lashes for magic use," Johnathan explains.

"The medic has been notified. Processing room 37 is open," she says and nods at us to leave.

The Handlers pull me away from the desk, leaving Johnathan there talking with the woman, and down hallways that all look the same. Past identical gray doors, the only difference in their appearance are the numbers on the plaques.

There are three main rooms at Rebren. The main rooms are viewing rooms. These have a few chairs, a desk, and a small bathroom attached to them. There are generally two to three Workers in each room. The large window looking into the room that passers by look in and see us. The second rooms are the small rooms where the Workers are sent to when Rebren closes. In those rooms are a bed and a small bathroom. There isn't much room to move around in and it's generally pretty cramped, even with one person. The third room is the processing room. This is where returned Workers are sent to be looked at, bandaged up, and cleaned up.

Shouting catches my attention. I snap my head up and look around. There is a girl a few years older than me being dragged by a Handler who is gripping her arm. "Please don't take me there!" She shouts. Tears stream down her face as she tries, and fails, to tug her arm out of the Handler's grasp.

The Handler, of course, provides no reaction. I can see a small glint in his eyes as he passes us.

Anger boils up inside me and I pull against the Handlers holding me. "Hey!" I shout. "Get off her!" Each tug pulls at the lashes on my back. I can feel fresh blood creating trails through the dried blood on my back. I tug myself free and run to the girl. "Get off her!" I pull at the Handler's arm.

He grunts and tosses me to the side. I grip at his uniform, leaving red smudges on the stark white fabric. The shackles on my wrists dig into my skin as my arms are stretched wide. He turns, letting go of the girl, and faces me. "Stay out of business that isn't yours, Worker," he growls as he stalks towards me.

I hold his gaze, heart hammering in my chest. The girl cowers against the wall, watching us with wide eyes.

"Greets," a voice behind me says.

He stops, looking at the Handler behind me. I turn around to see the two of them with their strange prod drawn.

"What is going on?" The Handler on the right asks.

"I was taking her to the Lab," Greets says. "Then this rat attacked me." He punctuates the word *rat* by shoving me towards the two Handlers. "Keep a better hold of your things, Richard."

The two Handlers grab me again. After nearly four years at Rebren, I've gotten used to people's hands appearing out of nowhere. "It won't happen again," Richard says. "Get your Worker and go."

The girl starts crying again as Greets grabs her. I catch her eyes as I am dragged away. "I'm so sorry," I whisper to her. Her only response is to look to the ground and follow Greets as he drags her away.

My Handlers are quiet as they drag me along. They shove me into a small room with a simple stone bench with chains and manacles resting on it.

"What was that?" Richard says, shoving me up against a wall, hands fisted in my dirty shirt.

My back lights on fire and spots dance across my vision. I flash him a pained smile. "You can't honestly tell me he was only taking her to the Lab, can you?"

Richard face softens ever so slightly and he lets out a small sigh. He eventually lets me go and looks to the side.

"Would you have done the same?" I ask, taking a step forward.

"Mind your tongue, 732," he says softly. He pauses. "Unfortunately, people like Greets get away with a lot of things."

I open my mouth to say something, but Richard cuts me off. He motions to shower in the corner. "Strip," he commands.

I hold out my hands, jingling the shackles. "Can these come off?" I ask.

Richard rolls his eyes but unlocks the metal and drops them onto the bench. I peel my shirt off, the fabric pulling at the freshly formed scabs along my back. The pendant hangs in my pocket as I shift my pants. I grab it out and hold it in a closed fist. After I finish stripping, I kick my bloody clothes into a corner and walk over to the shower. Richard grabs the shower head and, without warning, sprays frigid water at me. I sputter and blink against the onslaught of water.

"Was that necessary?" I shout, trying to block the stream pointed at me.

The water lowers until it's spraying on my feet. Richard shrugs and changes the setting to a calmer one. He motions for me to turn around. I do and he rinses the blood and grime from my body. I watch it run down the drain.

The water is turned off and I am tossed a rough towel. At the sound of chains, I turn around, towel halfway wrapped around my waist. Water still drips from my shoulder length hair, but I'd rather be covered than dry.

Richard motions to the bench, a pair of manacles in his hand. Those will be locked around my wrists, and an identical pair around my ankles, holding me in place and making sure I don't attack anyone when the door is opened again. They also prevent me from escaping.

"732," Richard says, pulling me from my trance. With a sigh, I sit down on the bench, slowly resting against the wall. Richard locks the manacles onto my ankles first before locking my wrists in a similar manner. I watch in silence, a familiar feeling of desperation rising up. For almost four years, I've worn more chains around my wrists than pairs of shoes. Richard tucks the key into his pocket and stands up. He meets my eyes before turning away and walking out the door. Was that sympathy I saw in his eyes? I watch them leave with my back straight and my head high. Despite what this place has tried to make me into, I haven't given up fighting back. Not yet, at least.

The lock clicks, echoing in the nearly empty space.

As I wait for the door to open again, I pick at my dirty fingernails. Despite the rough shower, there is still dirt and blood crusted underneath them. A camera blinks at me from a corner of the room. I glance at it every so often, counting the seconds between each flash of red, distracting me from thinking about how many times I've been in this situation. I'm starting to develop silvery lines around my wrists from the various cuffs I've worn. More marks that have been permanently etched into my skin to remind me of this terrible place. At the thought, I scratch at the Mark on my neck.

The sound of the latch retracting pulls my attention away from the camera. I straighten my back, wincing at the fresh pain, and train my eyes on the door. It swings open and a woman with her brown hair tied back in a bun walks in. She's got a large black bag with a red cross on it. The medic.

"Afternoon, Ma'am," I say, nodding my head to her.

She glances up at me with a raised eyebrow. "It's still morning," she states as she locks the door. Her black bag swings with her movements.

"Is it? I thought it'd been longer." I wiggle forwards, knowing she'll ask me to.

She sets her bag on one end of the bench and motions for me to turn around. Silently, I do, turning my back to her. She *tuts* quietly before ruffling around in her bag. She gently prods at my back and the wounds there.

"I know you have numbing medication somewhere," I joke through the pain blooming underneath her fingers. "I've also heard whisky does the job well."

"You're right, we have both readily available on hand. However," she starts dabbing and wiping away the fresh blood with a cloth. I gasp and drop my head, squeezing my eyes shut and gripping my knees even harder in order to keep still. "Neither of which are going to be spared on you. This is a punishment, remember 732."

*That doesn't mean the whole process has to hurt.* I don't respond, and she continues her work in silence. After she's cleaned the long wounds, she places bandages over them. Some of them wrap around my shoulders and up the back of my neck. What does she think when she tends to the Workers' wounds? Does she feel sympathy or apathy?

"Turn around," she says.

I do, adjusting the towel so it stays on. The medic has laid out a needle and a few tubes. She grabs my arms and examines them. She ties a blue band around my bicep and starts cleaning part of my arm with an alcohol wipe.

"What are you doing?" I ask. This is not part of the return process.

The medic glances up at me before grabbing the needle from beside her. She uncaps it and says "drawing your blood."

I squirm in my seat as she pulls the needle closer. I squeeze my eyes closed when I feel a pinch.

"You're squeamish around needles?" The medic asks.

"Seems crazy, I know," I say as my heart pounds. "Why are you taking my blood?"

"Because we need it," she states and switches out a tube.

I furrow my eyebrows. "Is something wrong?" I ask.

She doesn't respond. Instead, her eyes flick up to mine for a split second before focusing back on her work. "We want to run a few tests," she says and cleans up, putting a bandaid on my arm. She stands up, things shuffling behind her. "I'm finished," she says simply. Her hand is on the door handle before she turns around. "Keep them clean, and let someone know if they need to be changed."

I nod in understanding. "Thank you," I call to her as she leaves the room.

Again, I'm left alone, shivering in the towel. My hair has ceased dripping and now hangs in clumps around my face. I brush some of it behind my ear, wishing that I could shave it all off.

The door opens again and Richard stands there. I smirk. "Thought you'd forgotten about me," I joke and sit up. I hold out my wrists to him.

Richard walks forward, leaving the door propped open, and unlocks the chains around my ankles first. He locks handcuffs onto my wrists before removing the manacles. When he pulls me up, I have to grab the towel to make sure it doesn't fall down. I learned quickly that it's hard to get a towel on with my hands cuffed together, and I don't particularly like being naked in the middle of the hallway. Richard drags me past the processing rooms and to a stone door with the plaque *'24'* on it. He opens the door, unlocks the handcuffs, and lightly pushes me inside the small room. There is a singular light in the middle of the ceiling that does little to illuminate the rickety bed and small trunk at its base. I don't turn to face Richard as he closes the door, locking me in the small room.

I rummage through the trunk to find my size of clothes and a brush. The trunk is stocked with a few pairs of clothes in different sizes, toiletries, and bedding. There is nobody to clean up and get the room ready for the next Worker. I grab the clothes I need and quickly change, being wary not to tear open the bandaging or the wounds on my back. I brush my hair and towel dry it, brushing it again and tossing the towel into a corner of the room. There is a small mirror over the sink and I catch a glimpse of myself in it. It's enough to make me pause. My brown hair is halfway dry and resting on my shoulders. A small scar rests on my cheek from the tail of a whip at my first house. My green eyes look muddled and dull as if there is no life left in them. The black ink of my Mark is stark against my pale skin. I run my fingers over the tattoo, feeling the phantom sting of the needle. I look like little more than a shell of the boy I was. Tearing my eyes away from the mirror, I strip the bed of the old sheets and toss them with the towel. An unfortunate Worker will come by tomorrow to collect the laundry. I make the bed and sit on the edge, rubbing the pendant in my hand.

I won't be eating today. *Perks of being returned early in the morning*, I think. When a Worker is returned, they aren't put up for sale until the next day. It just so happens that Workers not brought to the cafeteria don't eat, and Workers not in viewing rooms don't get taken to the cafeteria. I asked a Handler about it once. The answer I got was something about letting the Workers rest and for the systems to fully process the return.

I lay back on the bed, listening to the groaning of the bedsprings. I crawl underneath the covers and quickly fall asleep.

# CHAPTER FOUR

## 54

"54, I've got a bag for you," the tall man with dark skin and long black hair says. He walks up and hands me the bag.

"Thanks, 12," I say as I toss it into the trailer. I reach up and wipe the sweat from my face, turning to face the crowd of men in dull brown uniforms. Handlers dressed in white line the perimeter. In my time here, nobody has tried to escape, although I'm sure it's crossed their minds.

A horn goes off, echoing from the speakers and across the clearing. The Workers trudge to the trailer and set their gloves in neat piles, making their way towards the lodge near the road. I follow them, setting my own gloves on the trailer. 12 ends up walking silently next to me. The silver chain around his neck glints in the sun, reflecting off the identical one around my neck. Robert Caulder, the man who paid for each of us, owns a logging company. He uses Workers to do the clean up jobs and allows his employees to go home to their families earlier. 12 has been here longer than me, coming up on nearly two years. I'm nearing the six month mark of being here, setting the record for the longest I've stayed at one house.

Cool air wafts over me as I step inside the lodge. The large group of Workers line up and are given simple sandwiches by the women Caulder has bought from Rebren. Nobody talks. Two Handlers stand by the doorways and the stairs, blocking the only way out of the building. I glance up the stairs as I pass by. Caulder's office sits right above the kitchen, and by default, Caulder himself. The food we are given is tasteless and bland, simply meant to give us the energy we need to continue working.

12 taps softly on the table when I sit down.

*It's hot today.*

I take a bite before tapping my reply back to him.

*It's hot every day.*

He smirks at that. When I first got here, 12 had pulled me aside in the shed. He's been watching the Handlers rotation and who keeps what keys. He wanted my help to try and escape and taught me Morse code. The Handlers only listen for talking, but don't watch our hands, letting us talk freely in front of them.

*The new one seems to be lax in his position.* He informs me.

I glance around quickly. *Red hair?* I tap in question.

*Yes. I want to see where they station him this week.*

I nod slightly. *Caulder has left security alone for the time being,* I say, recalling images of the map hanging behind his desk.

12’s eyes flick up to mine full of sympathy. Out of all the Workers, I’m in his office the most. He’ll take us individually and meet with us. Caulder signed up with Rebren to help Workers gain control of their magic and to train us to be obedient Workers. Due to my unique magic, as he likes to call it, I’ve spent the most time in his office.

*Anything else Caulder has been careless about?*

I eye a Handler walking towards me. *None yet. I’ll have a better answer soon.* I state as the Handler stops by our table. I look up towards him.

“You’ve been requested upstairs,” the man says in a gruff voice.

I stand, following him up the stairs. The wooden steps creak under our feet. Sunlight streams in from large windows and a green rug welcomes us into the hallway. The Handler grabs my shoulder and steers me towards a door on the right. He knocks twice and waits.

“Enter,” Caulders voice, even muffled by the door, sends shivers down my spine. I force my breathing to remain even as the Handler opens the door. My first few steps into the room are small. The Handler pushes my shoulder forward and I take bigger steps.

Robert Caulder sits behind his desk, white hair slicked back and glasses pushed up on his nose. His blue eyes are cast downward as he studies some papers on his desk, not looking up when we enter. I stop in front of his desk next to the chair, having learned my lesson about sitting down before I'm told.

Caulder shuffles his papers around before setting them down. He sits up and looks at me over his glasses. Even though I'm standing, his look makes me feel like our positions are swapped.

"54," he starts. "Please, sit."

I nod my thanks and quietly pull out the chair, sitting on the worn cushion.

"Any incidents today?" he asks me, following up on my magic. The reason I'm in this place is because I can't control it.

"No, sir," I answer, keeping my voice soft. Last time I spoke regularly, I got a beating for being disrespectful. My hands sit in my lap, cupped together.

"Good. That's progress," he says as he leans back in his chair. "We can get down to business. Tell me, how was your nighttime stroll?"

My blood runs cold as I meet his eyes. *Nighttime stroll?* Amusement is something I never want to see on this man's face, and that is exactly what greets me in his eyes.

"Yes, I know about you sneaking out last night. Tell me-" he leans forward, clasping his hands on his desk. "Did you act alone?"

My mouth has gone dry and I struggle to get the words out. "I, I don't know what you're talking about," I croak. My heart is pounding and the room seems cold, despite my uniform and the sun streaming in through the large window.

He raises an eyebrow. "Are you calling me a liar, 54?"

I shake my head. "No, sir."

"Then explain to me how you got out of the Shed last night," he demands, leaning back in his chair.

I open and close my mouth a few times, struggling to come up with the words. "I didn't leave the Shed, sir," I finally say.

Caulder sighs and turns his laptop around, showing me the footage of the cameras positioned at the Shed door. In the black and white video, there I am, walking around the yard before slipping back in through the door. The time stamp on the video says 2:17 AM. I blink a few times, unable to tear my eyes from the screen.

"Do you want to lie to me again, 54?" Caulder asks coldly.

"I don't know how that's possible," I whisper.

The laptop snaps closed and I meet Caulder's icy blue eyes. "Maybe you'll be more willing to tell me after your punishment." He nods to the Handler behind me. I stare at the desk as the man leaves the room, closing the door behind him. "Running is not tolerated, as you know. Nor is being in places you shouldn't be."

I clench my jaw, trying to still my racing heart. What will he do in order to get me to talk? To lie about something I didn't do?

The door opens again and the heavy footfalls tell me the Handler is back. I straighten up and face him. The Handler stands there, his hands clasped in front of him. He nods to Caulder.

"Let's get going, now," he says, standing. The chair creaks softly as he rises.

Slowly, I stand and follow him down the hallway, the Handler right behind me. Caulder opens the door past the last window, revealing a dimly lit room with tarps laid out on the ground. In the middle of the room hangs a chain where a young boy, barely sixteen, is being held up by his hands. He's trembling as he stares at the floor, rattling the metal. I turn back towards Caulder.

"Please, no," I whisper. "Hurt me, not him."

The Handler pushes me into the room and ties my hands behind my back, locking me to a hook on the wall. I grip the rope in my fists, feeling at the knot. Could I untie it and stop this whole thing?

"What would be the point of that?" Caulder asks as he strides into the room. "You and I both know you'd heal instantly. The point of punishment is that you learn that escaping of any kind is not allowed, not just to receive a slap on the wrist. Are you going to tell me how you escaped now?"

"I didn't escape! I'm not lying!" I shouted, tugging at the binds that hold me in place.

Caulder *tsks* before nodding to the Handler. The man strides forward, letting the leather in his hands uncurl. It slaps the ground and fresh tears run down the boy's face.

The boy meets my eyes. His tears have left streaks on his dirt caked face. I am paralyzed by his gaze. "Please," I beg. "Please don't hurt him."

"Tell me, 54. And I'll cut the count in half."

I lick my lips and stare at Caulder, pleading with him. I fall to my knees. "Please, I'm begging you! I…" I look at the boy strung up in the middle of the room, completely helpless. "I… I blocked the lock."

Caulder holds up a hand. "How?"

*Now what?* I swallow. "With a torn piece of cloth," I whisper the lie, lowering my gaze to the worn wooden floor.

Caulder is silent for a moment. "15, Handler Isaacs."

My head snaps up, watching Caulder walk to the edge of the room. I meet the boy's eyes. "I'm so sorry," I whisper.

Tears of my own fall when he starts to scream.

# CHAPTER FIVE

## 54

Blood soaks my pants where I kneel, tears streaming down my face. The Handler unchains the boy's hands and he collapses into a heap on the ground, sobbing. Red blood drips from the long stripes decorating his back. The Handler tosses the leather to the side, wiping the blood off of his face with a rag. Caulder walks the edges of the room, avoiding the splatters of blood, to where I kneel. He grips my chin in his hand, turning my head to face him.

"This is your punishment for sneaking out, 54," he says softly.

My eyes fall to the sobbing form. "Please let me heal him," I rasp, the sound barely audible to my ears.

Caulder jerks my head towards him. "Your magic is *mine* to use. You will not ask to heal anyone unless *I* give the word. Do you understand?" he hisses.

I stare up at him with wide eyes. "Yes, sir," I whisper.

He nods and lets go of me. My hands are unceremoniously untied and I am roughly pulled to my feet. The Handler shoves me out the door and quickly closes it. The lock clicks into place before I even have the chance to turn around.

The blood on my pants sticks to my skin as I walk down the stairs. I stare numbly at the ground as I step down. A few Workers look up but immediately go back to their food. I see 12 glance up at me before turning back to his food. The wooden bench groans as I settle into my seat.

*What happened?*

I push my food around on my plate, no longer hungry. *He said I snuck out last night.*

12 pauses for a moment. *What caused him to make that accusation?*

I force myself to take a bite. *Video footage from the Shed door camera.*

The man in front of me seems oddly stiff. *But you were asleep all night.*

I glance up at him, barely lifting my eyes. *So were you.*

*Touche.* He taps. *I had to use the toilet.*

*Ah.*

*Is the blood yours?* 12 asks after a stretch of quiet.

My knees feel sticky. *No.* My answer makes him pause. *We'll talk back at the Shed.*

Upstairs, a door slams open and the smell of blood fills my nostrils. I glance up and see the boy stumbling down the stairs. He makes his way towards the bathroom, sniffling. A small trail of blood marks his path.

*What happened?* 12 asks, staring at me.

I shake my head and turn back to my food. *My punishment.*

12 stares at me with wide eyes. He lowers his eyes as a Handler passes by, his heavy footfalls making the wood groan beneath him.

I can hear the boy's quiet sobs through the closed door as I walk away, following the other Workers back to the lumberyard.

* * *

At the end of the day, I am stopped by a Handler in the doorway of the Shed. He searches me, checking my pockets, waistband, and shoes, before I'm able to enter our sleeping quarters. Groans of tired men fill the large space, echoing off the empty walls and the tall ceiling. I spot the boy from earlier rifling through the trunk at the foot of his bed. Blood has stained his shirt and he's wincing as he digs around. I walk over to him and pause, watching 06 approach the dark haired boy.

"Are you doing okay?" the tall, blonde man whispers, sitting on the edge of the boy's bed.

The boy shrugs, causing more red to darken parts of his shirt. 06 rubs his shoulder gently. "Can I help with anything, 1048?"

The dark haired child shakes his head 'no.'

I breathe in deeply and step closer. "Hey," I start. "I'm 54."

Both 06 and the boy, 1048, glance up. Puffy green eyes meet mine as the young boy straightens, clenching his jaw. 06 moves from the edge of the bed to stand protective behind the dark haired figure, crossing his arms, his decorative tattoo showing.

"I'm so sorry," I whisper, feeling my throat close up.

1048 sets his things on his rickety bed. "Why did he do that?" he asks, his voice soft and small. There is a tremble to his speech. "What was that for?"

"It was a punishment," I whisper. My words are soft, barely audible to my ears.

He glances around. "Why didn't he whip you instead, then? Why did he whip me?" His eyes start welling with fresh tears. "What thing did you do that required someone else to take your punishment?" he pauses, blinking. Tears make fresh trails on his dirty cheeks. "Or have you gained favor in Mr. Caulder's eyes?"

I slowly shake my head. "My punishment was to watch him hurt you," I explain, softly.

“Why.” He clenches his fists at his side.

“Because I ‘haven’t learned my lesson’,” I quote. “Because Caulder thinks I escaped last night. Because physical punishments have no effect.” I sink down onto his bed, shoulders slumping forward. “You got hurt because of me and I’m so sorry.” I meet his eyes. “I want to fix it, to bandage your back, if you’ll let me.”

He stares at me, chest moving rapidly. “He told you not to heal me,” 1048 croaks, fists uncurling from his sides.

“I’m not healing you,” I say calmly, struggling to come up with an explanation. “Caulder won’t let me use my *talents* to help others. But he has said nothing about bandaging you up.”

1048 looks at me skeptically. “Fine,” he agrees before running off to the shower, his bundle of clothes in his arms.

06 watches him run to the bathroom. “Did you escape last night?” He asks calmly.

I shake my head ‘no.’ “He has video footage, and I don’t know how,” I explain. “I tried to tell him, I really did.”

The taller man nods. “I believe you,” he says flatly. “Next time, try not to drag others into it, okay?”

I nod and watch him walk off.

12 walks over to me and crosses his arms. “What is that all about?” he asks, cajun accent heavy.

I sigh, running a hand through my hair as I stand. "Caulder has video footage of me walking around the yard apparently," I state. I nod to the bathroom. "That was my punishment."

12 scratches his chin. "He didn't whip you?"

I shake my head.

"Why not?"

I cross my arms and breathe deeply. Caulder's threat runs through my mind. *"If you tell anyone what you can do, I'll make you watch as I hurt them, and then I'll lock you away with the knowledge that you cannot save them."* I choose my words carefully. "Physical punishments don't stick too well."

12 gives me a sideways look, but chooses not to say anything else on the subject. "How does this affect phase one of our plan?"

I rub my eyes and sigh. "I'm not sure. Give me a day and I'll figure it out."

12 nods.

The boy walks back to his bed, setting his things back in his trunk. He meets my eyes. 12 walks to his bed, leaving the boy and me alone.

"I'll go get the kit," I say softly. The first aid kit is against the back wall, right above the washing machines. The rumbling and rattling gets louder as I near them. The first aid kit is a large black box whose contents slide around when I grab it. I make my way back towards 1048 and set it on his bed. He's watching me from his spot on his trunk, shirt in his lap. The long stripes have stopped bleeding and most of the blood washed off in the shower. I examine his back. The long stripes are the only marks on his back and I pause, staring. Red seems to glare at me, stark against his flawless skin. These marks are here because of me, not because of anything he did. I gently apply the bandages, fingers brushing over his soft skin as I do so. I wish there was any sort of medication in the kit to give him. 1048 sits quietly, masking his sniffles, as I secure the bandages with tape.

"All done," I whisper to him as I stand up.

He's looking at his hands. His "thank you" is barely audible.

I can't seem to bring myself to walk away. I crouch down next to him. "What's going on?" I ask.

1048 finally looks up at me. His eyes are puffy and red. After a minute of silence, tears fill his eyes. I pull him close to me. "I have a project due today," he sobs.

I rub his back, confused. "A project?"

He nods. "For english."

English. *High school* project. I hold him tighter, careful of the stripes on his back. My magic pulses against the chain around my neck, trying to heal the boy in my arms.

# CHAPTER SIX

## 732

The cafeteria is full when I walk in after seeing yet another medic. They wanted to check something about my vitals, or my blood. This is the third time I've been brought to them, excluding my return at the beginning of the week. I'm more confused each time I go there. During this visit, they drew my blood and had me breathe into a tube, saying something about my lungs. I rub the band aid on the inside of my arm and walk towards the small line of people. The tray is warm when I grab it, nearly dropping it. The man in front of me glances back at me before turning forward again. He's in his mid-thirties and has been here for about a week. He was returned due to not enough work at his house.

"This is the first time you've been late to lunch, I believe," he says softly.

I shrug and place my tray on the metal shelf. "I would have rioted if they made me miss lunch," I whisper back.

He gives me a small smile. "Are you going to tell me why?"

I smirk. "Why would I do that?"

The woman behind the counter sets a plate of food on our tray and motions us to move along.

"Are we not acquaintances?" he asks on our way to sit down.

I shrug again and glance at him. His gaze is soft, reminding me of how my dad would look at me when we would talk. I quickly look away. "It's nothing," I say, clearing my throat at the sudden emotion.

"Kid," he starts, opting for the nickname he gave me when he first sat down across the table a few days ago. "We both know one of us will be gone in a few days. What's the harm in venting to a stranger you may never see again?"

I poke at the broccoli on my plate. "You don't need to worry about me," I say. "I told you, I'm trouble and they need to keep me in line." I give him a smile before stuffing half the bland sandwich into my mouth.

He sighs and picks up his own sandwich. "Tell me about life before Rebren," he says.

I pause, glancing up at him. "Why?" I ask around a mouthful of food.

He shrugs. "To distract you, make you feel human."

"I feel human all the time," I lie. A pit forms in my stomach at the words. I feel more like a caged animal than human lately.

His eyes are soft. "We all need to be reminded of our humanity every so often," he says gently.

I meet his gaze and feel, for the first time in years, equal with another person. Nobody is trying to command me, get me to obey orders, or punish me. I'm not chained up and the man in front of me doesn't hold my future in his hands. His gaze feels human and makes me feel oddly vulnerable.

"I've spilled plenty about my life, why not tell me about you?" I ask, pointing at him with my sandwich to break the thick tension that built in the seconds that passed, The man in front of me smiles and lets out a sigh.

A Handler walks past, glancing over at us, and we both look down. I lower my food and glare at him as he walks away.

"See, that there is why they think you're trouble," the man says with a smile.

I give him a confused look and go back to eating, picking up the uneaten half of my sandwich. "What is?"

"Glaring at the Handlers? Kid, you've got to cut the rebellious teenage act."

"It's not an act if I'm not a teenager." I pause. "I'm 19. I'm choosing to be a rebellious adult."

The man sighs and shakes his head. "You remind me of my daughter," he says. "She was in her rebellious teen phase last time I saw her."

I lower my sandwich. This man is a father, and this *program* tore him from that. "What is her name?"

"Marie," he says softly. "She looks just like her mother. Sadly, she inherited my stubbornness, but she has her mother's drive, and her kindness." He takes a deep breath and looks towards the windows near the ceiling.

"I have a brother," I say. The man looks at me with sad eyes. "He is the gentlest person I've ever met and yet, he still found ways to torment me." I smile, thinking of the days we'd spend chasing each other around the yard, or him trying to teach me sports. "He made people feel better just by being around them."

The man smiles. "What is his name?"

"Jake," I say softly. It's been years since I said his name to anyone other than my parents.

"Younger or older?"

"Older." My smile drops. "They took him years ago."

The man doesn't respond. There isn't much to say. We eat the rest of our meal in silence.

* * *

"732, welcome," a man in a white button up shirt says, stepping aside.

The Handler grabs my shoulder and shoves me inside. I stumble over my feet and almost fall down. The man in the white button up catches me. "Watch your step," he says gently.

I glare at the Handler. "Yeah, I'll be sure to do that. Thanks," I mumble as I follow the man into the room. This is different from the medical rooms they've taken me to. This one has more computers and vials, different jars and monitors everywhere. It looks more like a science lab than a doctor's office.

"My name is Sam, and I am one of the scientists working here at Rebren," the man says as he leads us to the back of the room. "Please stand here," he says, gesturing to a large mat. I step onto it and watch the man as he grabs things around the room. The Handler watches me, hand on his gun. He seems more tense than usual.

Sam approaches me with an armful of wires. "You'll need to take off your shoes for this to work," he says. "The Handler is going to unlock your hands and I'm going to trust you not to attack me, okay?"

I nod, kicking off my shoes and tossing them off the mat. The Handler unlocks the shackles, giving me a pointed glare as if to warn me against doing anything stupid. Sam attaches different pads to my chest and to my temples. "Now, 732, it is extremely important that you listen carefully," he starts.

"I have a name," I say.

Sam just smiles and tugs the hem of my shirt down, patting my shoulder. "You are in the Lab, 732. This is not a place where we partially care about names."

I glance at the Handler in confusion. "The Lab?"

"Yes. Here is where we figure out the details of magic, develop new ways of control and mastery of abilities, and develop new technology that will benefit all people" he explains.

"You brought me here because I'm having trouble with my magic?" I ask.

Sam shakes his head. "No, we have an easy solution to your problem. You are here, 732, so we can analyze your magic. It is quite interesting if I do say so. I haven't seen anything like it."

"So I'm a lab rat now?" A smothering wave of anxiety washes over me, threatening to choke me.

"Not yet," he says calmly, completely obvious to the panic radiating off of me, and steps back to where the Handler is. He presses a button on the wall. A glass pane lowers from the ceiling. I step towards them. They're trapping me in a glass box like an animal, to watch and study me.

"Stay on the mat 732," Sam says, his voice coming through an unseen speaker and echoing off the lowering panels.

I clench my jaw but don't move, glaring at them. *I hate that number. I hate this place.*

The panel fully slides into place with a soft *shrsh* of rubber against the glass. "Now 732, all I need you to do is aim at that black box on the wall there. Do you see it?" Sam asks.

I close my eyes and take a deep breath, turning towards the wall. *Calm yourself.* I think as I open my eyes. There is a large black box on the wall opposite me. I nod.

"Good. I need you to use your magic and aim there," he says.

I whip back to him. "What?" I ask. "You want me to do what?"

Sam nods. "I need you to use your magic."

I shake my head. "You've got to be joking," I say, running my hands through my hair. "I have no *idea* how to use my magic. You've whipped me enough times for me to learn how to not use my magic, that's for sure! If you've taught me anything, it's how to pretend it doesn't exist!" I pace on the mat, picking at the skin around my nails.

"You need to focus, 732. You've used magic before," Sam says.

"On accident!"

"Recall what you felt in those moments and try to do it on purpose. No punishments this time."

I stop pacing and stare at them. "No punishments? Do you swear it?" I step to the edge of the mat.

Sam nods. "I promise there will be no punishment for this use of magic," he says.

I take a breath, letting it out slowly, and nod. "I'll try," I say. I close my eyes and search for the…thing inside me. It's been there since I was ten. When I was ten, it felt like a warm light inside my chest. That light isn't there anymore. It disappeared the day I turned sixteen.

I breathe in and wiggle my fingers.

There is a slight buzz underneath my skin. The air smells of iron and of smoke. I focus on the buzzing. There was always that feeling when something exploded. With a similar black box that first day, with the truck last week. I open my eyes and focus the buzzing on the black box on the wall.

I breathe out.

The buzzing gets louder and the box smokes. I clench my jaw and block everything out except the black box. Heat radiates off the pendant in my pocket. More smoke pours out of it. I tilt my head to the side and breathe. It's almost like I can *feel* the box and what is inside of it. The buzz turns into a roar and the box explodes. I duck, shielding my head with my arms. The buzzing is gone.

There is clapping on the other side of the glass. "Well done, 732," Sam says.

I look at him, standing. Why is it hard to breathe all of a sudden?

"You did wonderfully," he says, pressing the button on the wall again. The glass slides up, freeing me from my clear cage.

"I destroyed the box," I say bluntly, glancing at it, chest heaving as I try to get enough air into my lungs. There are pieces of it strewn across the floor.

Sam walks towards me. "I expected something along those lines to happen," he says and adjusts the pads on my chest. Sam leads me towards a different area of the room where a long, stainless steel table sits. "I need you to remove your shirt, please."

I look at him through furrowed eyebrows. "What?" I ask, shocked.

He nods. "You did hear me correctly," he states, pulling over a rolling cart with lots of medical supplies. He fishes around in one of the drawers until he pulls out a long, large needle with a container attached to it.

I tense up and instinctively scoot backwards on the table.

"Please," he says and motions to my shirt.

I slowly do, eyeing the needle. I can feel my heart pounding and my magic thrumming. A familiar buzzing fills my head. Sam hooks the container and needle up to what looks like a pump.

"Lay down, please. And try not to squirm," he says and starts strapping my limbs down with leather straps that were hidden under the table. I flex my hands and close my eyes.

"What are you doing?" I ask, my voice shaking.

I hear Sam type on a computer and then start wiping my chest with a cold towel. My eyes snap open.

"We need a sample of your magic," he says. "After seeing some of the test results from your blood and different scans, we want to run more tests. There is something fascinatingly different about your magic." He brings the needle close to my chest and glances at his computer again. "Now I need you to breathe."

It seems that I can do anything but breathe. I squeeze my eyes shut and count backwards from one thousand. The pain from the needle isn't horrible. It stings, but isn't what I expected. I'm at eight hundred and seventy three when then the pump turns on, filling the room with what sounds like a pressurized vacuum. My eyes fly open and I gasp, my body convulsing. My magic flares and swirls around, moving towards the needle in my chest. When I get air into my lungs, I scream. Everything in me seems like it's lit on fire.

"Breathe, 732," Sam says calmly.

Breathing seems like the last thing I can do.

"Almost done."

My whole body shakes and strains against the restraints.

The pump is turned off and the needle removed. My magic calms down and I gasp for air, laying limp against the table. I feel something being placed over my chest and the restraints are undone. "You did well, and I got more than I needed. I hope we meet again, 732," Sam says.

I barely register his words. Everything hurts. I feel hands on me and I wince. The Handler tosses me over his shoulder and carries me out of the room and back to my room. He dumps me on the floor and leaves, locking the door. I pull myself into my bed and collapse, tugging the thin blanket around me.

*What just happened?*

# CHAPTER SEVEN

# 732

Rebren Employees walk down the halls the following evening, making sure everything is locked up for the night. I lean against the wall, still weak from yesterday, counting their steps. The walls are thin and I can hear the echo of their steps inside my room. I twitch my fingers, listening for the fading echoes.

The overhead light shuts off. I smile. Now or never. I focus on the lock. I made the box in the Lab explode, I can make a small explosion, right? All I need to do is get the inside of the lock to blow and the door should unlock. I focus on the door handle and breathe. My magic protests, but slowly enters the lock. The pendant heats up like it did in the Lab and it almost causes me to stop. The mechanism starts to smoke, taking my thoughts from the pendant, and I hear a small pop. I run over to the door and try the handle. It turns and the door opens. It's heavier than it looks and I heave it towards me, muscles straining. Giddy, I poke my head out. The hallway is quiet and I hesitantly step out of my room. Unsure of where to go, I turn left.

My footsteps are the only sound I hear as I walk along the tiled hallway. Locked doors line the walls and I glance at one of them. Underneath the number *19* is a sign that says 'occupied'. On the wall hangs a chart. I slow and grab it, silently sliding the clipboard off the hook. There is a picture of the Worker and all of her information. I glance back up at the door and then at the chart in my hand. I could get them all out, if I wanted. If I tried. If I planned and gave it enough thought. I pause in front of the girls door, looking down at the others lining the hallway.

What am I doing? I can get each of these people out of this place and I'm taking a night walk on my own for fun? I run a hand through my hair, looking at the green sign that says EXIT at the end of the hallway. If I were to get them out, where would we go? Chicago is a long way from home, especially on foot.

What about Jake? Would I even be able to find him?

"Hey!"

I snap back to reality and turn to see a Handler running towards me. I drop the clipboard and run in the opposite direction, away from the exit and deeper into Rebren.

My lungs burn and my chest aches. I haven't had the chance to run more than a couple feet in years. My bare feet hit the tiles fast and hard and my breath comes in gasps. I can hear the Handler shouting behind me, his heavy boots hitting the floor hard. He's gaining on me. I don't dare look back to see how much closer he's gotten. If I can go just a little faster…

The Handler grabs my shirt and yanks me backwards. I hit the ground and slide backwards, gasping for air. The Handler stands over me and glares. He yanks my head to the side to read my Mark. The Handler snorts when he sees who I am.

"I remember you," he says, bending down. "The trouble maker."

I glare at him. "Greets," I gasp.

He backhands me. I fall to the side, my hand flying to my face.

"I've wanted to do that for a long time. I'm always stopped by someone, sadly. But there's no one here to save you now," he whispers. "You are trouble, and deserve to be sent to the Lab." He straightens, grabs my shirt, and drags me up with him. "I have 2157732 in the hallway. Requesting back up," he says into the radio at his shoulder.

I use the momentary distraction to push myself away from him, causing my shirt to tear. Greets growls and pulls out his strange prod. Without turning it on, he hits me in the ribs. Gasping, I double over. Greets grabs me again and slams me against the wall, pressing his forearm to my chest.

"Oh no you don't," he says. "You're not going anywhere."

"What are you going to do?" I ask. "Are you going to take me to the Lab like you did with that girl?"

He tilts his head and presses his lips into a thin line. "Try me, I dare you," he whispers.

I smirk. My fingers twitch as I try to gather my magic. "How many people know about your little *detours*?"

He backhands me again. "I will gladly beat you senseless right here," he growls.

"Handler Greets," someone says.

I glance over Greets's shoulder to see two more Handlers and the Boss of the Rebren Program standing there.

"Please let go of 732 and step back," the Boss states calmly.

"Sir, with all due respect, he *ran*," Greets says through gritted teeth over his shoulder.

The Boss looks at his feet. I watch him, heart pounding, as he takes in a breath and shakes his head. When he looks back up he says, "I am well aware. Please let him go and step back."

Glaring at me, Greets reluctantly lets go of my shirt and steps back.

"732, I trust that you're not going to run, and we can go somewhere more private to have a chat," the Boss says.

I glance around to see Handlers filing in from both entrances to the hallway.

"Yes, sir," I say quietly.

The Boss nods. "Come with me," he says and walks down the hallway further in the direction I was running. Greets stares at us as we leave before he decides to return to his assigned post. The two Handlers that came with the Boss walk next to me, one on either side. The Boss enters a small room with a table and a few chairs in it. He motions for me to sit. I do, slowly, watching him slide into the chair across the table from me.

"I knew this was coming eventually, but I didn't expect you to wait so long," the Boss says with a smile.

I stare at him, not saying anything as anger builds in my chest. I've never met the Boss of the Rebren Program, but I have seen him in passing a few times. This man is responsible for tearing so many families apart. For taking my brother, and for taking me. He's responsible for all the pain and suffering that has happened across the continent. But he's also responsible for my fate at the moment. With a few words, he could have me beaten, taken to the Lab, or killed. What is there that I can say? "I figured it was time," I finally get out.

He smiles and leans back in his chair. "That makes sense. It has been a few years since you first arrived. I am curious how you got out and why you ran."

I glance at the Handlers before licking my lips. "I used magic to get out," I say bluntly. "And I ran because I don't like it here."

The Boss nods. "Honesty, I appreciate that," he says. He hasn't dropped the smile. "How did you use your magic to escape?"

My heart pounds in my chest. "I blew up the lock."

"Your magic is explosive," he whispers to himself. "And you were able to blow only the lock?"

I swallow. "I didn't exactly stop to examine my work," I point out.

The Boss nods, thoughtful. He taps his fingers on the arm of the chair. "I'm not going to punish you," he says after a while. The Boss looks back at me and, upon seeing my confused look, explains. "You have a buyer coming tomorrow afternoon. He's going to train you. I'll let him punish you how he sees fit then."

"Train me? You're sending me to a trainer?" I shout, leaning forward. The Handlers tighten their grips on their weapons. My heart pounds and my clothes suddenly feel restricted. They're sending me to *training* like a *dog*.

"He owns a business and needs Workers constantly. He just so happens to be the best person to teach you discipline," the Boss explains, his voice soft and gentle. "That is why I'm going to let him punish you instead."

I clench my jaw, hands curling over the edge of the armrests. "And if he can't train me? What then?" I ask.

The Boss nods again. "Good question. If you return untrainable, we'll send you to the Lab. Your magic is… quite interesting, to say the least."

My stomach drops. "That's fair," I say softly, leaning back into the chair. "Why don't you just send me there now?

The Boss nods once before leaning back in his chair. "As much as I want you back in the Lab, you're young. You're hard working. I tell you this in confidentiality, most people are having a hard time to get the new Workers to do what they want. They're either too inexperienced or fall ill too often. In truth, Rebren needs you working and not in the Lab right now," he pauses. "However, that is up to you if you decide to behave or not."

I lean back, processing his words. "Why are you trusting me with this?" I ask.

"Because I find you to be the type who can keep a secret," he says. "Is all of this making sense?"

Slowly, I nod.

The Boss smiles. "I knew you'd understand." He stands. "For now, you need to get some rest. You've got a long day ahead of you," he says. "Goodbye 732."

# CHAPTER EIGHT

## 732

"What did you do?" the man asks, setting his tray on the table across from me.

I glance up at him before looking back down at my oatmeal. I rest my hand on my cheek, covering the large bruise there. "Got into some trouble is all," I mumble.

"Why?" he asks, staring at me. He hasn't touched his oatmeal and his green eyes burn holes into my skin.

I shake my head, shoving another spoonful into my mouth. Tasteless mush. They don't flavor anything here. We're too unimportant for good food, apparently.

"732-"

"Don't call me that," I whisper, cutting him off.

The man sighs softly, slouching in his seat. He doesn't say anything more as he starts eating.

I sit up and lean back, setting my spoon down and shoving my bowl forward. "I tried to escape," I finally state.

The man looks at me and sets down his spoon as well. He shifts in his seat.

“I wanted to get out, wanted to go home,” I explain, my words getting faster. “But I hesitated because, if I got out, then so could all of you.”

The man's eyes are so sad, I can’t look at him. I turn my attention to the chipped edge of the table, picking at it. The soft wood flakes off as I dig my fingernails into it.

“Then the Handler found me and the Boss of Rebren wanted to have a talk with me.” I pick my spoon back up and shove the oatmeal to one side of my bowl.

“And you only got a bruise out of it?”

I nod. “I probably deserve it,” I pause. “They have a buyer lined up. He’ll be here sometime today. The Boss said he’d take care of the punishment.”

The man presses his lips together and nods, looking down. His voice is soft as he speaks. “A trainer?”

I pause, meeting his eyes. “How’d you know?”

“Lucky guess.” He gives me a sympathetic look. “I hope he’s not too hard on you.”

I shake my head. “You know these people. When are they ever easy on us?”

The man lets out a sigh and nods knowingly. “Just… don’t dig yourself deeper into this hole trying to crawl out of it, okay? Promise me that.”

His gaze pins me in place. "I can't promise that," I whisper.

"Kid, I know you're scared. Please, for your own good, don't make things worse for yourself."

I hold his gaze before nodding. He smiles sadly before we go back to eating in silence.

*   *   *

I pace in my small room, pausing at every sound that comes from the hallway. It's nearly noon and more people are showing up to Rebren. I can hear them passing by, their voices muffled by the door. After breakfast, I wasn't taken to a viewing room with the others, instead, I was brought back to the concrete room. I pick at the skin around my nails as I count my steps. I've already picked my nails to stubs earlier today.

The door handle rattles, pulling me from my pacing. I pause, slowly turning towards the door. The door flies open and two Handlers stand on either side of the opening.

"Is my *trainer* here?" I ask, spitting the word.

The Handlers don't respond. One of them pulls out a pair of handcuffs. "Don't be difficult, 732," Richard says.

I stare at him, my reflection staring back at me in his helmet. "He's here, then."

Richard offers me the handcuffs in response. I sigh and step closer to him, offering up my scarred wrists. The thin metal is cool around them. I keep my head down as we walk through the various hallways. We pass by the viewing rooms and I keep my eyes trained on my feet, not wanting to see the rest of the Workers.

The administration rooms are all the same. A table with two chairs on one side with a single chair on the other. The side with one chair has a hook where the Workers are cuffed to. The walls are a simple gray, with a bright light above the table. Richard gestures to the chair and I slowly sit down, resting my cuffed hands on the table.

"Don't be snarky to this man, 732," Richard advises as he locks me to the table.

I meet his eyes. "You've never given me advice before. Why start now?"

He sighs. "Figured you need all the help you can get, considering your situation," he explains and then walks out, shutting the door hard. The sound echoes in the near empty room.

The empty chairs glare at me as they wait for their occupants. Across from me, the buyer and a Rebren Employee will sit as they sign paperwork and go over the rules. I pick at my nails, chipping them against the handcuffs. How long will they make me wait here this time? Will it be hours or just a few minutes?

The door opens again and I sit up. The Boss walks in, followed by a man with white hair dressed in a suit. A Handler follows behind them. The man looks at me and raises an eyebrow. I meet his piercing gaze and keep eye contact. His blue eyes seem to pin me to the chair, and a flash of recognition crosses his face.

The Boss and the man sit down across from where I am chained.

"732," The Boss starts, pulling my attention from the newcomer. "This is Mr. Robert Caulder, your new owner."

I lean back in my chair, making a show of examining the man. "Have you signed paperwork yet?" I ask. Richard' warning flashes through my mind. *It's too late now.*

The Boss sighs, shaking his head. I can feel the Handler tensing behind me, his leather gloves creaking as he tightens his grip on the strange prod. Mr. Caulder holds up a hand, stopping the Handler.

"No, 732, I have not," he says, leaning forward.

I smirk. "Then, technically and legally speaking, you're not my owner yet," I say. The cuffs make a *clicking* sound as I shrug.

Mr. Caulder stares at me, maintaining our prolonged eye contact. He leans back, motioning to the Handler.

I feel a jolt go through my body and I fall forwards, barely catching myself on the table. My breath comes in short pants as I steady myself against the metal table. My hands shake and my grip falters, causing my head to slam onto the edge. The Handler behind me grabs the back of my neck and pulls me back against the chair. I wince as pain shoots through my head.

"I will not tolerate that kind of speech or behavior, do you understand 732?" Mr. Caulder asks, his voice icy.

I glare at him, blinking away my hazy vision and still struggling to catch my breath. "Or what?" I ask, gasping.

Mr. Caulder tilts his head to the side thoughtfully. "732, I am asking if you understand the rules. This is not a time for negotiations."

I sit up fully, calming my breathing. "I'm not negotiating," I start. "I'm simply asking for further clarification on what happens if I do act out of line."

"It is not your place to ask questions. It is your place to obediently follow," he says. "I will ask one more time: Do you understand?"

I feel rage build in my chest. Out of all the people I've worked for, none have been more infuriating than this man. I glare at him. "I understand," I say through gritted teeth.

Mr. Caulder nods and turns back towards the Boss. "May we continue?" he asks him.

The Boss nods. "We discussed most of the details over the phone. Our current contract states that 732 needs training and you will train him until he is workable or deemed untrainable," the Boss explains, setting a pile of paperwork in front of him.

"That is the plan. There hasn't been a Worker yet that I can't train," Mr. Caulder says, shooting me a pointed look. I curl my hands into fists, trying to control the swirling magic under my skin as it reacts to my growing anger.

The Boss slides the pile of paper over to him. Mr. Caulder produces a pen from inside his jacket pocket and signs the stack of papers. I watch, my stomach dropping with every signature he adds. With every flick of his pen, more and more of my life gets passed to his hands until all the papers are signed. My life, my choices, my fate. All in the hands of the man in front of me. I clench my jaw, take a deep breath, and close my eyes. I'll find a way to get out of this. I always do.

Mr. Caulder finishes signing the paperwork and passes it back to the Boss. "Is that all?" he asks.

The Boss nods, gathering up the papers and sticking them in a manila folder. "That is it. 732 is yours," he says.

Mr. Caulder smiles and turns to face me. "732, you will address me as 'Sir' from here on out. Do you understand?"

I look up from the papers and meet his gaze. All I hear is the sound of my own breathing. My choices, my freedom, my fate. The power hungry look in his eyes makes me bite back a comment. Slowly, I look back down at the table. "Yes, sir," I whisper.

Mr. Caulder nods and stands up, pushing the metal chair backwards. He says his goodbyes to the Boss and motions for me to follow.

The Handler unlocks the cuffs from the table and grabs my shirt, pulling me up. Mr. Caulder walks out of the cramped room and the Handler pushes me after him. I am led to the side of the building where Workers and new owners leave. Mr. Caulder gestures to a sleek sedan in the parking lot. The Handler pushes me into the back of it and secures me to the seat with a chain and hook drilled into the floor. I lean back, resting my hands in my lap and letting my head fall against the headrest. I close my eyes. *One last shot.* I think. *If I can not cause a problem for long enough, I can figure out a way out of here.*

The driver's door opens and Mr. Caulder climbs into the sedan. He doesn't say anything as he pulls away from Rebren. There is a tinted window separating the front from the back, similar to what I've seen of police cars. I can't see through the front windshield, and I can't hear the music I know is playing from the radio, as much as I long to. The windows in the back are also tinted, cutting off any view of the outside world. The drive isn't the longest I've been on, but it does take a few hours to get to our destination. I feel the sedan slow to a stop. My door opens and a Handler unhooks my chains and pulls me out of the car. I blink against the sun assaulting my eyes as I stumble out of the car. When the spots clear from my vision, I see a large house with an ornate fountain out front. Stone bowls stacked three tiers high with water spilling over the gold plated rims. The driveway is patterned after cobblestone and the fountain sits in the middle of the circular driveway. There is a stone walkway leading up to the wooden front door. A brick path leads around the house to what I can guess is the backyard.

"732, welcome to your new home," Mr. Caulder says, walking over to us from around the car.

I watch him, tensing as he approaches. I clench my hands, grabbing the loose chain that hangs between the cuffs, and grip it tightly.

"There are a few things we need to do before you can get settled in," he says and leads us into the garage. Light streams in from large windows that sit high on the wall. The space is tidy and clean, much different from my parent's garage back in Normal, Illinois. Sitting in the middle of the empty space where a car might go is a single folding chair and a small table with clippers on it. I pause in the doorway, causing the Handler to bump into me.

"What is this?" I ask, heart pounding

Mr. Caulder turns around and raises his eyebrow.

"Sir," I say through gritted teeth.

He nods in approval. "732, you are in need of a haircut. You'll thank me later," he says and motions to the folding chair.

I don't move. "Why?"

Mr. Caulder raises an eyebrow, ignoring my question. "Sit in the chair, 732."

The Handler shoves me forward and I stumble towards the metal chair. Reluctantly, I sit. The seat is cool beneath me and I fight to stay still as shivers rack my body. Mr. Caulder picks up a pair of scissors and starts hacking away at my near shoulder length hair, dropping large clumps to the ground around his feet. Once it's short enough, he takes the clippers and shaves the rest of it off, making long passes over my head. The air feels cold as it hits my newly exposed skin. As soon as he's done, the Handler grabs my shoulder and pulls me up. I glare at him and Mr. Caulder, avoiding looking at my hair on the ground. My head feels cold and too light, as if there is no resistance to my movements.

"Before you are shown to the shed, there is one more item of business," Mr. Caulder says, pulling something out of his pocket and breaking me from my thoughts. "All Workers at my house are required to wear one." Mr. Caulder shows me what looks like a thick silver necklace before reaching for me and locking it around my neck. It is tight and I can feel it move everytime I swallow. The faint swirling I normally feel under my skin quiets immediately.

"What is that?" I ask, reaching up to touch it. My hands start to shake as my magic seems to be forced into a corner.

Mr. Caulder smiles. His blue eyes are icy as he watches me. "It blocks magic."

My eyes snap to his. "What?" I ask, feeling my heart pound. The silver chain feels like it's tightening, cutting off my air flow. My breathing speeds up and I cover the chain with my whole hand.

"I heard what you did back at Rebren," is all the explanation he gives me. "Welcome to your new home, 732," he says and walks off.

The Handler pulls me out of the garage by my arm and towards the brick path that leads around the house. There is a large, nicely kept backyard with two giant buildings almost the size of a small house near the back fence. The Handler unlocks my shackles, opens the door to the closest Workers Shed, and shoves me inside. I glare at the Handler as the door closes, the lock clicking firmly into place.

I turn around slowly and see a large group of men, all in the standard Rebren clothing with silver chains around their necks. I rub my wrists to stop my hands from shaking as I look around. One of the men approaches me, coming from the side. He has a soft smile and bright green eyes. His brown hair has grown out to just above his ears. He looks familiar and I wrack my brain as he walks towards me. My heart drops as I remember who he is, and where I know him from.

"Welcome to…" he starts to say before his eyebrows furrow and his smile drops as he gets closer. "Adam?" he asks softly.

Jake.

# CHAPTER NINE

## 54

My heart drops and my blood is cold as I meet the green eyes in front of me. Adam stares at me, eyes wide and mouth halfway open. Caulder shaved his brown hair off, leaving a perfect view of his Mark sitting high on his neck and the white bandages sticking out from underneath his shirt. My little brother has grown nearly as tall as me, but looks sickly and pale with a large bruise covering the right side of his face.

"54?" 06 asks. "Everything okay?"

I blink a few times and take a breath. "Yeah," I call over my shoulder. "Everything is fine!"

I put a hand firmly on Adam's shoulder, steering him away from the front door. He flinches and shoves my hand off, stepping away from me.

"What are you doing here?" I hiss at him, grabbing his shirt instead to keep him moving. Adam glares at me with haunted eyes, pushing away from my grasp a second time. His shirt is rumpled and he brushes the wrinkles out.

"I could ask you the same thing!" He whispers, almost spitting the words. The noise from the washing machines nearly drown out his words. Adam seems torn between anger and disbelief. He briefly touches my shoulder before pulling his hand back as if I was on fire, curling his fingers into a fist at his side.

I sigh at his question, running a hand through my hair and looking to the side. "I'm here for a reason, Adam," I start.

At the sound of his name, my brother freezes and I hear him breathe in. "I had hoped that you'd never get involved with Rebren, much less end up here. Please tell me this is by *chance* that you're here, and not for a very specific reason." My eyes flick to the bandages poking out underneath his shirt.

Adam catches the movement and quickly adjusts his shirt, pulling the shoulders up to cover the white tape. "It doesn't matter," he says quietly, looking down at his feet. "I'm here now."

"What is it?" I ask softly, putting a hand gently on his shoulder. Adam stiffens beneath my touch and steps back, eyes snapping up to meet mine.

He shakes his head and looks away. *Why can't he look at me?* "Where have you been?" he finally asks, his voice hoarse.

My breath catches in my throat at the question. "What do you mean?"

Adam finally looks at me for more than a brief glance. The tears in his eyes stand out against the hard lines of his face as he glares at me. "You didn't come back with mom and dad. Was the program always like this?" He takes a step towards me, fists curling at his sides.

I nod, holding my hands up in front of me. "From the beginning. They took me away from Mom and Dad, tattooed this-" I motion to my Mark "-onto me, and locked me in the back of a cop car. They've advanced in their processes since the start, but it's been the same idea."

I watch the muscles in Adam's jaw clench as he looks to the side. He opens his mouth to say something but doesn't get the words out before a tall man slings a tattooed arm across Adam's shoulders. Adam tenses and straightens up.

"Hey there," 06 says and sticks out his hand to my brother. "I'm 06, it's nice to meet you."

Adam eyes his hand before glaring at him. "732," he says curtly.

06 smiles and pats Adam's shoulder. "54, how are you doing? You had a bit of a rough time earlier today."

I blink a few times. Adam meets my eyes, one eyebrow raised. "I'm fine," I brush off. "You know how Caulder is."

06 nods, his blue eyes growing sympathetic. "That bastard."

That teases a smile from me.

732," 06 starts, turning his attention back to my brother, "I'm sure you've had quite the day. Let's get you cleaned up and settled in. 54, is it okay if he takes the bed next to yours?"

"Uh, yeah. That's fine," I stammer out.

06 winks at me. "Perfect." With his arm still around Adam, he starts walking towards the beds. "How about a shower to wash the stink of Rebren off you, hmm?"

Adam shoots me a helpless look as he's unwillingly dragged away. I shrug and smile at him. 06 will treat him well enough.

"I see the resemblance," 12's cajun accent sounds next to me.

I turn to see him standing with his arms crossed. "How long have you been standing there?" I ask.

"Not long." He pauses. "So what are you going to do about it?"

I rub my eyes and let out a sigh. "I'm not sure yet. I didn't expect him to show up, or even be in the program at all."

12 is silent, watching 06 get Adam settled in. The poor kid looks so uncomfortable and stiff. The taller man hasn't dropped his arm, and keeps introducing him to the rest of the men.

"He has to come with us, 12. He has to," I mutter. "I can't leave him behind."

I can feel the older man tense beside me. “He better not get in the way then,” he says tersely. “He looks sick and weak, and was probably sent here to die.”

I turn towards him, crossing my arms. “You get those thoughts out of your head right now, 12. He is not weak, and he will not die here,” I promise. “He’s coming with us, or I’m out.”

12 raises an eyebrow, a bored expression on his face. “You’d choose to stay here for him over being free?”

I glance back over at Adam, who lets out a strained laugh. “Do you have any family, 12?” I ask.

“Why do you think I want to escape so badly?”

I meet his dark eyes. “Just give me a week, and I’ll have this figured out.”

12 nods. “One week. Then we make our move.” He starts to walk away, work gloves tucked in his back pocket.

“He’ll work with us, I’m sure of it,” I call to him as he walks away. I glance one more time at Adam as 06 finally shows him the bathroom, a bundle of clothes and soap in his arms. Adam looks relieved as he steps through the doorway, and can’t seem to get the door closed fast enough.

I make my way to my bed, kicking off my shoes and setting them on top of my trunk. I settle against the wall, kicking my feet up. Adam is here, which complicates things. Our plan was to take tonight and leave, sneaking out through the hole in the bathroom that leads to the waste pile. It wouldn't be pretty or comfortable, but we'd get out. I rub my eyes, sighing.

The bed next to me creaks and I drop my hand. Adam is spreading the rough sheets over the bed with half of a scowl on his face. The bandages wrapping around his shoulders have disappeared and I can faintly see the tail end of what looks like a whip mark. My magic flares against my palms.

"How was your shower?" I ask him softly.

His green eyes flick to mine briefly before tossing the single pillow on the bed. "Fine."

I sit up and swing my legs over the side of the bed. "Talk to me, Adam," I whisper. "Why are you so angry?"

"What makes you think I'm angry?" he spits, snapping his sheets over the bed.

"The glares? The short answers?"

Adam sighs and meets my gaze. "I'm tired, Jake. It's been a long day. I've been beaten, bought and sold, taken across the state, or further, and had a chain locked around my neck like a *dog*. All I want to do is go to sleep to get some semblance of escape from the hell my life has become."

I stand up and walk around the bed, slowly approaching my brother. He scrubs a hand over his face, stopping to rub his eyes. I gently pull him close. His body tenses at my touch, and he stumbles into my arms. He smells of the cheap soap Caulder supplies us with. Slowly, Adam relaxes and wraps his arms around me. I lightly rub small circles on his back, like our mom used to do. Adam bunches my shirt in his fists as he holds me tighter. He's buried his face in my shoulder and I can hear him sniffle every few seconds.

Adam eventually pulls away, ducking his face and turning to face the wall, messing with his pillow.

"We'll get out of this, I promise," I say softly.

Adam nods, wiping at his eyes.

Hesitantly, I put a hand on his shoulder. "Are you hurting?" I ask.

He shakes his head 'no'.

My eyes flick to the gashes peeking out underneath his shirt. "How old are these?"

That gets him to turn, staring at me with red rimmed, wide eyes. "It's fine," he states. "They don't bother me."

"How old are they? They look newer."

The scowl returns to my brother's face, green eyes darkening. "A week, maybe more. I lost track," he mutters.

I can feel my magic swirling in my palms. "Get some rest. Caulder is… unique in his methods."

Adam scratches at the tattoo on his neck and turns back to the bed. “It’s better than what we get at Rebren,” he says, a smile teasing its way onto his face.

I laugh. “Not by much.”

He meets my eyes, the scowl is gone. “Anything beats Rebren commodities. The springs are nearly poking through the mattress!”

I chuckle. “They were pretty uncomfortable to sleep on,” I admit. “This is more like sleeping on a wooden slab.”

“I’ll take it over the springs. It’s uncomfortable, especially when the springs dig into fresh wounds,” he says softly, trailing off. Adam’s hand strays up to scratch at his Mark again.

I rub his shoulder once more before sitting back down on my bed. “I’ll see you in the morning. Get some sleep,” I say, lying down and kicking up my blankets.

Adam does the same, awkwardly settling into the bed. “Jake,” he whispers softly.

“Yeah?”

“I’m glad you’re here,” he says, voice barely audible. “I’m glad you’re with me.”

“Me too,” I lie. I’m going to get him out, even if it means I stay.

# CHAPTER TEN

# 732

"Stop smiling like that," I say after hours of work, tossing another armful of sticks into the bag my older brother holds. Sweat drips down my back and along the sides of my face. We've been working outside all morning hauling logs and cleaning up sticks left behind from the tree's that have been cut down.

"Like what?" Jake says.

"Like life is good and you're not working for a man who literally bought you to haul logs all day." I bend down and grab another armful of sticks, grateful for the long sleeve uniform.

Jake laughs, eyeing the Handler nearby. "Oh, is that why you're grouchy?"

I look up at him as I scoop up another armful of sticks. The physical work hasn't seemed to affect Jake at all. Unlike the rest of us breathing hard and looking like we're nearing collapse, Jake seems to thrive off the physical work. He almost looks like he's gotten off an easy run. "Grouchy?" I feign shock as I push the sticks down into the black trash bag in Jake's hands. "I have a naturally pleasant demeanor."

He opens the bag a little wider for me. "Mom definitely thought so."

"Yeah?"

"Oh yeah," he says softly. "You were her little sunshine."

I shake my head, bending down to grab more sticks. "Yet you're the one with the goofy grin," I say, turning the conversation away from Mom or anything to do with home. "How can you be cheerful, considering the circumstances?" I ask.

He looks down as the Handler passes us. When he's far enough away, he starts talking again. "It's not bad out here. Fresh air, sunlight, hard work. It's when we go inside that I dread." His eyes get a distant look in them as he stares at the bag in his hands.

I stand up, popping my back before grabbing some more sticks. "In the shed?" I ask. "Isn't that off limits to Handlers? The one safe space?"

He shakes his head, blinking, and makes room in the bag for more twigs. "Not the shed. You'll see," he whispers.

"Why won't you tell me?" I ask. "What has got you so rattled that you won't tell me what you're afraid of?"

Jake is smiling when he looks at me, but there is a pain in his eyes that I can't find the words to describe. "What makes you think I'm hiding anything?" He says, tying the bag closed and tossing it onto the trailer.

I clench my jaw and follow him to the trailer to grab another bag.

*  *  *

Lunch is held in the large lodge at the edge of the worksite. We file into the industrial kitchen where there are women dressed in the brown Rebren clothing cooking with silver chains around their necks, serving us food. As usual, the Handlers stand at every doorway and hallway with guns in their hands.

I follow Jake to a table and sit on the wooden bench across from him. A tall dark skinned man and 06 join us, setting their plates down. 06 gives me a tired smile before he starts eating.

Jake keeps glancing to the side. "Top of the line stuff here, eh?" He whispers with a tight smile. That earns him a glance from the new man, who taps a quick rhythm on the tabletop. Jake taps a similar rhythm back.

I take a bite of the plain sandwich and shrug, watching the two men's hands. "Are you okay?" I ask.

Jake nods and continues eating. A Handler passes by, eyeing us. We eat the rest of our meal in silence.

I'm about to finish off my food when a Handler walks up behind me. "732," he says.

Jake looks up at me, his jaw clenched. I take a deep breath and turn around. “Yes?” I ask, looking the Handler in the eye.

“Come with me,” he says.

I glance back at Jake, but he slightly shakes his head and looks down at his food. I glance at 06, but he doesn’t show any sign of hearing the conversation. Swallowing, I stand. The Handler leads me away from the table, away from Jake and the others. I follow him upstairs. We stop at a door and the Handler knocks twice. My heart is pounding, blood pulsing against the metal around my neck. I reach up and rub my Mark, my fingers straying to the chain. I pick at it, my nails flaking against it.

“Enter,” Mr. Caulder’s voice says from behind the door.

The Handler opens the door and pushes me inside. Mr. Caulder sits behind a large, wooden desk. There is a pile of papers in front of him that he’s reading over. The room is laid out like an office with a bookshelf against one wall and a filing on the wall closest to the desk. A map of the worksite hangs on the wall above the filing cabinet. The Handler closes the door and stands in front of it.

“Sit, please,” Mr. Caulder says without looking up, gesturing to the chairs in front of me.

Slowly, I slide into the chair across the desk. *This is very new.*

Mr. Caulder picks up some papers from the side of the desk.

"What is this about?" I ask. "I was enjoying a very plain sandwich."

Mr. Caulder stops and raises an eyebrow, looking up at me over the bridge of his nose. His hawk eyes pin me to the chair. That look makes me freeze. Usually, people ignore me or lash out and try to quiet me. But that look… It sends shivers down my spine.

"732, you are nineteen, am I correct?" He asks, bringing the papers to the middle of the desk. He folds his hands over top of them and straightens in his chair, staring at me.

"Yes," I say.

He looks at me again.

"...Sir?" I say hesitantly.

He nods and looks back down. "Good, you haven't forgotten that rule," he says.

I fiddle with a loose string on the hem of my shirt under the table. *Just figure out what this is and then you can figure out how to proceed from there.*

"You, 732, have given many people much grief over the past three years," he starts. "You started with simply running away, then escalated to hacking, thievery, and ending with property damage. I'm surprised that they don't send you straight to the Lab or get rid of you all together."

The Lab. Images of my brief time there with Sam flash through my mind. The mention of it sends a chill through my body.

"Tell me why they haven't sent you straight to the Lab, 732. You've been there, I know. And they want you back, or so I hear. So why do they keep you available for sale at Rebren?" he leans back in his chair, clasping his hands in his lap.

I swallow. "If I fail here, they'll send me there," I say bluntly.

He doesn't say anything, just sits there, staring at me. He raises an eyebrow and tilts his head down just barely, as if he's waiting for something.

I press my lips together and breathe deeply. "Sir," I say as I breathe out. *I'm going to get very tired of that word.*

He nods. "You didn't answer my question. Why are they trying to train you and haven't sent you to the Lab already? Why keep you after all these attempts?"

"Because I'm young and a hard Worker, I just need more training. At least that's what they tell me, sir," I explain, nearly spitting the title.

He nods. "And they're patient enough to wait for you to be trained," he says, thinking. After a moment, he leans forward. "I hear their patience is running thin."

I don't respond, opting to glare at him instead.

"If I hadn't volunteered to train you, you'd be in the Lab already," he says. "I saved you, 732. The very least you can do is cooperate."

"Saved me, huh?" I ask quietly, looking to the side.

"Speak up if you're going to speak out of turn," Mr. Caulder says.

"You saved me?" I repeat louder. "Which is better? The Lab or here? I'm not free either way. So, what exactly did you save me from?" I ask.

Mr. Caulder is silent, unphased by my outburst. "Freedom is no longer in your vocabulary any more, 732. You are insignificant and nothing more than cheap labor. You are not free, nor will you ever be. This is your life now. You better get used to it."

I've stopped fiddling with the string and I've started rubbing my finger nail. My heart is pounding. *Insignificant. Cheap labor.* "Why should I?" I snarl.

Mr. Caulder leans forward. "What is that on your neck? The tattoo?" He points out.

My hand goes to it, covering it.

"That right there tells me who you are, where you came from, and any other information I would want to or need to know about you. Nothing about you is private. You cannot escape what runs through your veins. That is what got you here. *You* are the reason you are not free. *You* are the reason you are here. Why are you angry at me when you really should be angry at yourself?" he asks coldly.

"I didn't choose this! Do you think I'd want this? Being treated as if I'm property and the endless beatings? The whippings for something I can't control? I didn't choose it, nor would I in a thousand years! You cannot pin this on me when I did *nothing* to choose this," I say, leaning forward. I feel my magic swirling under my skin.

Mr. Caulder stares at me.

"I am here because people like *you* are afraid of people like *me*. And you can't stand to lose your position of power. So you take people like me and lock us up, pretending to teach us control, because you're scared of what is inside of us. You treat us like property because you feel threatened," I spit.

Mr. Caulder is speechless. Slowly, he stands and walks around the desk. He pulls my chair away from the desk and pulls me up by my shirt. "You could not be more wrong," he whispers.

I glare up at him. "Am I?" I whisper back.

He ignores me and walks away, letting go of my shirt. He walks back to his chair behind the desk. He's silent for a long time before speaking again. When he does speak, his voice is back to its icy calm. "You caused quite the ruckus two days ago in Rebren," he says.

I clench my fists in my lap, my heart still pounding. "I did," I respond.

"Tell me what went on."

"I escaped. Got caught. Not much more to it," I say through gritted teeth.

Mr. Caulder scribbles something down on the paper he was reading. "How did you escape, 732. Tell me exactly what happened."

I breathe deeply, willing the magic inside me to calm. "I used magic to blow up the lock, then I ran down the hallway. A Handler saw me and I got caught."

He nods. "Did they punish you?"

"No, sir. They said they'd leave that up to you."

Mr. Caulder nods. "You know the punishment for use of magic, obviously," he states. "As for the running, that is another story." He pauses. "Why did you run, exactly?"

I glance at the Handler behind me before turning back to Mr. Caulder. He didn't stop me when I shouted earlier, most likely at Mr. Caulder's words. "I don't like it here," I say flatly. "Simple as that, sir."

Mr. Caulder nods and stands up, walking to the window, and turns his back to me. "Was this your first time trying to run from Rebren?"

Why is he asking all this when he is given a copy of my history? He's clearly proven that he knows my past. He just wants me to admit what I've done. "Yes, sir," I answer.

He is silent for a while. "I think a week of weighted shackles will do you some good," he says eventually.

"What?" I blurt out, leaning forward.

Mr. Caulder turns around and smirks. "Yes, I think that will be good. Running is not tolerated and you need to learn not to." He nods to the Handler. "You are dismissed, 732." He looks up at the Handler and nods once.

Mr. Caulder sits back down and picks up a different paper, adjusting the glasses sitting on his nose.

The Handler grabs my arm and pulls me out of the chair, dragging me out of the office. Blood pounds in my ears as he drags me down the hall to a different room. This room has a hook hanging from the ceiling and a plastic tarp covering on the floor. The smell of blood is strong. I stumble over my feet on my way in and Daniels shoves me to the middle of the tarp.

"Stay," he growls and walks over to a plastic bin. Metal rattles as he digs around. I glare at him as he approaches me with large shackles, blood crusted to the outside of them.

I clench my jaw as Daniels roughly grabs my arms and locks them onto my wrists, pulling the hook down and looping the long chain over it. The hook rattles as Daniels raises it with a button on the wall, stretching my arms above me until my feet are barely on the floor. The Handler cuts the back of my shirt open, exposing the half healed wounds from my last escape attempt and magic use. I close my eyes when I hear the whip uncurl, the leather hitting the floor. I grab onto the chain and brace myself for the sting of the whip. I clench my jaw shut when the first strike falls.

*One.*

# CHAPTER ELEVEN

## 54

A thump comes from upstairs. I pause, lowering the small section of my sandwich. 06 meets my eyes briefly before looking away as a Handler passes by.

*Has anyone else gone upstairs?* I tap on the table.

*No. Just 732.*

I curl my hand into a loose fist and tap my knuckles on the wood, breathing deeply. A faint *crack* comes from upstairs and I glance at the stairs.

A kick hits my ankles. 06 is staring at me. He shakes his head 'no.'

*Can you hear that?* I ask 12 as another crack sounds from upstairs.

The older man pauses and then shakes his head in response. *You have unnatural hearing, remember?*

I let out a small sigh and picked my sandwich back up. *Right.* I tap. Crack after crack sounds in rhythmic succession. I don't touch the remainder of my food as I sit and listen, hoping that sound isn't what I think it is.

A door creaks open and a strong metallic scent fills the room. I freeze.

*What?*

I don't respond to 12's taps, listening to the sound of tripping feet and dragging chains.

*54, what is it?*

Slowly, I turn in my seat to see Adam struggling down the stairs, bleeding and with a chain linking his ankles together, with his head held high. Each step is slow, and his nose twitches with the movement, the only sign of pain he's willing to show.

"Clean yourself up," the Handler growls, shoving him towards the small bathroom.

Adam glares at the man as he walks back to his post before making his way towards the bathroom, stumbling over the chain that drags between his feet. Without thinking, I push away from the table and grab the handle before he can. Adam stares at me in confusion before I open the door and usher him in. Hesitantly, he walks into the dingy bathroom and I close the door behind me.

Adam is silent as the door closes. I motion to the toilet while I rummage in the cabinet for the medical supplies I know are stashed under there. When I look back at Adam, his eyes are closed and he's hunched over, hands covering his eyes.

"Adam," I say softly.

He sits up and looks away, wiping his eyes with the back of his hands. "It's nothing I haven't gone through before," he whispers, clearing his throat with a cough.

Medical supplies in hand, I make my way over to him. "Tell me what happened," I ask softly.

Adam just shakes his head and shrugs, wincing at the movement, exhaling sharply as he lowers his shoulders.

I sit down on the edge of the bathtub and gently start peeling what remains of his shirt from his back. The Handler took time to slice his shirt instead of simply tearing it in half like they normally do. Adam tenses as the action pulls at his wounds. "Scale of one to ten," I say, peeking at his face from over his shoulder.

He doesn't respond right away, staring at the wall. "Eight," he finally whispers.

My fingers twitch and I clench my fists, magic pulsing at my fingertips. *It won't work anyways. Not with the chain still around my neck.* I think. Tossing the scrapped shirt into the tub, I examine his back. Twenty stripes are bleeding and raw. Underneath the fresh wounds are countless criss-crossing lines, all in various stages of healing. Some of them are faint and fully scarred over. Some have new, raw skin that is pink and soft. *What have you been through?* Taking a deep breath, I turn around and start filling the bowl under the sink with water and peroxide, grabbing a rag from the cabinet on the wall. "Why'd they whip you?" I ask, trying to keep the tremble out of my voice.

"I used magic. Why else?" He says.

I nod to myself. *Stupid. Why else?* "Right. So what is the chain around your ankles for?" I ask.

Adam pulls his feet closer to him as if he's trying to hide them from my view. "I ran," he says, still staring ahead at the wall. He's started fiddling with the small metal pendant that almost matches the one around my neck.

"Cold cloth," I say before gently pressing the wet rag to his back. He hisses and drops his head to his chin, his shoulder tensing. "You ran recently?"

"Two days ago. In Rebren," he says through gritted teeth.

"Ah," I say, dipping the rag into the bowl of water and ringing it out. The water turns pink as blood swirls to the edge of the bowl.

"Why are you doing this?" He asks quietly.

"Why wouldn't I do this?" I retort.

"You're going to get in trouble. This is supposed to be a punishment."

I laugh as I wash his back. "This is simply preventing infection." *Although I would be able to do more if this wretched chain wasn't around my neck.*

"You're sure you won't get in trouble?" He looks over his shoulder.

I flash him a smile before returning my attention to his back. "Caulder doesn't care what I do as long as I don't use magic."

Adam furrows his eyebrows. "What about the Handlers?"

"They don't do anything unless on Caulder's orders." I finish washing his wounds and start to bandage his back, pressing clean gauze to his back and sealing it with medical tape. I cover the whole area with a white adhesive bandage before adding one more layer of gauze and a second bandage. I stand and dig out a fresh shirt from the upper shelf of the cabinet. I toss it to Adam. "Wear that," I say, grabbing the bowl and the rag.

He slowly shrugs on the new shirt. It's a few sizes too big but it will do for now until he gets back to the Shed. Adam stands and shuffles over to the sink, the chain dragging along the wood floor. "Thanks," he says quietly.

I nod. "Any time," I say. Seeing him like this… I look away. I can feel my magic pulsing at my fingertips in time with my heartbeat, the heartbeat that hasn't veered from its perfect rhythm in years. I sigh as I ring the rag out in the sink. "I wish I could do more," I whisper.

Adam glances up at me, confused, before looking back down at his feet. "What do you mean?" he asks. "It's not like you can heal me or anything like that."

I pause, trying to come up with something. I let out a tense laugh. “Nothing crazy like that,” I lie.

There is a pounding at the door. Adam and I lock eyes before I walk over and open it. There is a Handler on the opposite side of the door.

“Finished yet?” he asks.

I smile. “Just finished cleaning up.”

“Time to get back to work,” he says, grabbing my shoulder and pulling me out of the washroom. He grabs Adam next, ignoring his grimace of pain as his fingers dig into the fresh wound. I bite the inside of my cheek. Adam and I walk through the now empty dining area and back out into the worksite. I grab a black trash bag from the trailer and hand it to Adam.

“My turn,” I say and tug on a pair of gloves.

# CHAPTER TWELVE

## 54

With a sigh, I roll out of bed when the five o'clock alarm goes off. I push my shaggy hair out of my face and lean over to check on Adam. He is lying on his side, back towards me. His shirt is lying on the floor and his bandages are tinged red. *Those need to be changed.* I press my lips together and place a hand gently on his shoulder. He tenses slightly at the touch but then takes a deep breath in.

"I'm up," he whispers.

"How are you feeling?" I ask.

He doesn't respond.

A few of the other men have gotten up and are walking around, getting ready and gathering their things. A few of them glance at us. 06 raises his eyebrow. I give him a quick smile and nod.

Adam finally sits up, facing me. "What were you doing at the table yesterday?" he asks, staring at me.

I furrow my eyebrows. "What do you mean?" I ask.

"You were tapping on the table a lot? What was that about?" He pushes himself to the edge of his bed and grabs his shirt off the ground.

"Oh, that?" I laugh. "12 taught me morse code when I first got here. We use it to talk to each other when we can't speak openly. The Handlers haven't figured it out yet," I explain. Adam's face lights up with a mischievous look I've never seen from him.

"They don't know?" He asks, leaning forward. There's a spark in him that I haven't seen since he's arrived here.

I smile. "Not one clue."

He smiles. "Teach me. Please, teach me."

I nod to 12 who currently sits on his bed, massaging his calf. "You'll have to convince 12 to teach you. Good luck, though. He doesn't like making friends."

"Bet," he says, going to stand. He takes one step and the chain around his ankles pulls taunt. He throws out a hand and collapses back onto his bed. I smell the metallic scent of blood again, the wounds on his back tearing through their fragile scabs. I reach out and steady him.

"What happened?" I ask.

He shakes his head. "I…" He pauses. "I don't know. I guess I'm not used to this thing."

My fingertips pulse with my heartbeat, my magic wanting to escape. Wanting to heal. I pull my hand back. There is something wrong with this, wrong with Adam. His wounds bled so much yesterday, and they barely clotted and scabbed over if they were bleeding this morning. Chewing on the inside of my cheek, I stand up.

"You need to get ready," I say. "I'll be here when you're finished."

He nods, making his way to his trunk, slowly this time. I watch him struggle with the chain and be cautious not to aggravate his wounds any more. I glance at 12 and see him blinking.

*He's not going to make it.*

I glare at him, setting my jaw. *He will.* I blink back, turning away from him and straightening my blankets.

* * *

A Handler grabs my shoulder as I step out of the truck and pulls me to the side. Adam takes one step towards me but stops at my glare. "What is this?" I ask calmly.

The Handler doesn't respond, instead steering me towards the lodge where Caulder is standing on the porch. My gut twists as we draw closer.

"54," he says. "Did you rest well?"

His question makes my blood run cold. "Yes, sir," I say softly.

"Good. You'll need your strength today," he says and walks into the lodge.

The Handler doesn't have to propel me to follow. My feet feel heavy as the wood creaks under my steps. Instead of going upstairs to his office, Caulder walks underneath the stairs and down the hallway, leading me to the small living room. He sits down on the couch and motions to a stiff wooden chair for me to sit.

"I had a check up yesterday," he starts as the Handler stands in the doorway.

I stay quiet, unsure of how to proceed.

"My Doctor is telling me to have it removed and to follow up with chemotherapy," he explains as he rolls up his sleeve. "I want you to take a look and see what you can do." Caulder holds his bare arm out to me. The Handler walks behind my chair and unhooks the silver chain from around my neck. I swallow as he walks back to his post.

Getting off the chair, I kneel in front of Caulder, supporting his arm in my left hand while I place my right hand on his forearm just below the elbow. I close my eyes and feel my magic rejoice at the newfound freedom.

I breathe in.

Caulder blood flows through his veins. It's rich and strong. He takes in a breath and I can feel the oxygen fill his body, his heart pumping it through in a steady rhythm. His lungs expand fully, and I turn my attention to the cluster of deadly cells sitting in his chest. They are dark and twitching, trying to grab any nutrients they can from the healthy cells nearby.

I breathe in.

"It's grown," I whisper, eyes still closed. "And it's going to continue to grow at a fast rate."

"Do what you can."

I feel my magic gathering at my fingertips, pulsing warmly against Caulder's skin. The pendant grows warm against my chest as I will my magic into Caulder's body. Breathing deeply, I direct the white mass towards the mutated cells. The mass envelops the tumor, destroying all the growing cells and trying to work its way towards the center of the tumor.

Sweat drips down my temples as I send more and more magic towards the tumor. I feel my strength leaving me as I push all I can towards it.

I can't see the mutated cells through the white mass attacking it. Slowly, it dissipates, unable to survive long outside of my body. When my magic fully disappears, the tumor looks almost unaffected. There is a new growth of healthy cells around the tumor, but I can't get rid of the mutation.

I open my eyes and lean back on my heels, removing my hands from Caulder's arm. Sweat drips down my neck and my hands shake when I reach up to wipe it away.

"Well?" Caulder asks as he unrolls his sleeve.

“I was able to promote new growth around the tumor, sir,” I start. “But I can’t affect the growth itself. I’m not that strong. If I was able to practice-”

Caulder holds up a hand. “I hope you’re not asking to use your magic on anyone else, 54,” he says calmly.

“No, sir,” I apologize, settling back into the wooden chair.

“Good.” Caulder leans back against the couch. “You can’t get rid of it? I’d like to avoid surgery.”

I shake my head. “I’m not strong enough. I’m not sure I ever will be, sir.”

Caulder looks out the window, the one that faces away from the worksite, and looks out into the beautiful forest around us. “You are dismissed,” he whispers.

The Handler locks the chain back around my neck and pulls me out of the chair. I blink against the sunlight as I stumble across the porch. I am led to a small group of Workers and handed a bag. I quickly scan the crowd for Adam but can’t see him. 1048 walks up with a bundle of sticks in his arms. He hesitantly dumps the sticks in and quickly walks away.

* * *

Adam finds me after the day is done. He looks like he’s in rough shape; pale and sweating. I can see some smears of red along his neck and bleeding into his shirt. He stumbles through the doorway of the Shed and immediately turns around and glares at me, the chain around his ankles wrapping itself around his feet.

"What was that about?" he hisses.

I put my hands on his shoulders and steer him away from the doorway. I catch the Handler turning towards us, but doing nothing to stop us. "It was nothing," I respond, trying to sound casual.

Adam shrugs off my hands. "Sure. You getting brought to Caulder at the beginning of the day is casual. Was it something to do with you helping me during lunch yesterday?"

I shake my head. "No, it wasn't." I motion for Adam to remove his shirt and I start removing the old bandages.

"Then what was it?" He glances at me over his shoulder.

I gently wipe the dried blood off his back and place new bandages on top of the wounds. "Training, that's all."

Adam turns around again. "For what?"

I raise my eyebrow at him.

He shakes his head. "He's not training your *magic*, is he?" Adam whispers.

Taking in a deep breath, I nod. Adam stares at me with wide eyes. “It’s all about control, that’s why I’m here. I can’t control it.”

“None of us can,” he mutters, walking away. He grabs the bandages and stuffs them in the small trash can as he passes it. He tosses his bloody shirt into the washer and starts collecting dirty shirts from the men wandering around. They’ll toss the rest of the clothing in the washer as they exit the shower. None of us want to walk around naked. I rub a hand over my eyes and walk towards 1048.

“How arc you doing?” I ask him.

The young boy looks up at me. “Fine,” he says.

“How are your wounds?” I motion to his back.

He looks to the side. “Fine.”

“Want me to take a look?” I ask.

1048 rolls his eyes and goes back to making his bed, having washed his sheets last night. “I said they are fine. Go bother someone else.”

I nod and walk away, pressing my lips together. I remove my shirt and drop it into the washer.

# CHAPTER THIRTEEN

## 732

I exit the bathroom, folding my towel over my arms as I make my way towards the thin bed. The shackles chaff against my skin, the moisture from the shower doing nothing to alleviate the pain. Jake is taking the rest of the dirty clothes from most of the men and dropping them into the washer. I watch him, my eye catching on his unmarked back. There's not a mark on him. I furrow my eyebrows. If he's here because of magic use, why doesn't he have any scars anywhere?

I shake my head and continue to my bed. I pass a tall man with dark hair.

"732," he says in a heavy accent that I can't place. "We haven't officially met." He sticks out his hand.

I stare at his hand. Scars criss cross along the back of his hand, trailing up his wrist and stop along his mid forearm. Hesitantly, I take his hand, shaking it. His strong grip nearly crushes my hand.

"And you are?" I ask.

"12." He studies with me with dark eyes. "How do you know 54?"

I glance at Jake. "Does it matter?" I cross my arms over my chest, holding his gaze.

12 tilts his head to the side, almost amused. "Just curious, is all. You seem to know him well."

I feel my heart start to pound and my magic swirls. "It wouldn't be any of your business if I did, either way," I snap as I glare. "What do you want?"

12 flashes me a quick smile. "54 seems to think that you'll escape. Is he right?"

I don't answer him.

He steps closer to me, forcing me to step back. "Are you strong enough, 732?"

"Intimidation doesn't work on me," I hiss, stepping forward, the chain rubbing against my skin.

"There you are, 732!" 06 says as he walks up to us. "I wanted to check in, see how you're doing."

12 takes a step back, straightening up. 06 puts a hand on his arm. "Everything alright here?"

"We're fine," I say, turning towards my bed.

I feel a hand on my shoulder and I spin around, fist clenched. I stop when I see it's 06. "How was today?" he asks softly.

"It was fine. Sucked, but fine," I turn back around.

06 walks to the other side of the bed. "Can I ask what happened yesterday?" He leans against the wall, resting a hand on the bedpost.

I toss my towel into my trunk and close it, setting my shoes on top of the lid. "You can ask," I respond shortly.

I see him smile. "But will you answer?"

I meet his eyes and the corner of my lip twitches up.

"Obviously the lashings are from magic use," 06 explains, eyes flicking to the bandages wrapping around my shoulders. The Handler didn't care where he hit, just that he hit me. "It couldn't have happened here, since yesterday was your first day. So it had to have been from an earlier encounter with Caulder? What I can't figure out is the chain."

I drop whatever smile I have and pull the sheets back from my bed. "You figured all that out by, what, looking at me?"

"Simple observation," he says calmly.

Nodding, I settle against the wall, resting my weight on my heels. "I tried to run from Rebren," I explain softly.

06 lets out a soft whistle. “Rebel,” he says quietly. When I look at him, he’s smiling.

I sigh. “Didn’t do me much good though,” I start, picking at my fingernails. “I’m still stuck in the same cycle as I was before.”

“But you have more experience than you did before,” he says softly.

“What is that supposed to mean?”

06 sighs and glances around before speaking. He finds Jake still by the washer and dryer. “I want to get out of here,” he whispers. “I need to get home.” He runs his fingers over the large tattoo on his left bicep, the one of a whale jumping over a boat.

“You want my help?”

06 chuckles and looks down. “Ridiculous, I know. We’re in the same spot, and you might be worse off than me.”

I chew on my lip, watching Jake as he starts walking towards us. “You’ve been thinking about this for a while, obviously.”

“Years.”

“Escape?” A young voice asks.

I jump and nearly hit the dark haired kid next to me. “How long have you been here?” I hiss.

"Long enough," he says. "I can be helpful in an escape."

"How so?" 06 asks, leaning forward.

The boy shuffles his feet. "I can get around without being seen."

"Obviously," I point out. "Even Handlers? Caulder?"

He nods. "I can help."

06 and I exchange glances. He shrugs in approval. I turn back to the boy. "We can use all the help we can get."

The boy beams. "I'm sure with the three of us, we can get out!"

I can't help but smile at his enthusiasm. Innocent, innocent boy. Too innocent. "We'll talk tomorrow."

He almost hops back to his bunk.

"Get some sleep, 732," 06 says and slaps me on the shoulder. I flinch at the contact, but with him well as he leaves.

Jake tosses his stuff into his trunk and flops onto his bed. "You had quite the crowd over here," he states.

I climb under my sheets. "Yeah. 06 wanted to discuss some things."

"1048 was over here, too."

I turn to face him. “Who?”

Jake nods to the young boy settling into his bunk. “The black haired kid. He’s 1048.”

“How old is he?”

“Sixteen.”

I shake my head and lay back against my pillow. “That seems way too young for Caulder.”

Jake shrugs, hands behind his head. The light flips off, drowning us all in darkness. “Do you feel your magic inside of you, Adam?” He asks after a while.

I shift against the lumpy pillow. “Always. Why?”

“What does it feel like?” His voice is soft.

I let out a long sigh. “Do you remember those videos mom would put on for us as young kids?”

“Those baby videos right?”

“Yeah, the exact ones. Do you remember when they would put colors in water, and it would swirl around and shimmer?”

Jake’s chuckle is quiet, but lightens the stiff darkness. “You were always mesmerized.”

I smile and rub the pendant in my pocket. “That’s what it feels like. Shifting and swirling under my skin.”

"That's an impressive description. You should be a writer," he jokes.

I swat a hand through the air. "Nah. I never liked to read." I pause. "What about yours? Your magic?"

Jake is silent for a while before answering. "It feels like a bright, LED light sitting in the middle of my chest."

"What color is it?"

"White. And it only grows…"

I turn to face him, although I can't see him. Only a vague outline of his shape. "What? Do you use your magic?"

Jake's answer is soft. "I've had plenty of time to use it."

"And they let you?" I ask, propping myself up on my elbow.

"There's a reason I'm here, Adam," he says softly.

*What's that supposed to mean?* "You mean to tell me that my *older brother* has been *breaking* the rules?"

"I'm here because I can't control when my magic acts up." He pauses and I can hear him getting his breathing under control. "It was in my first house, two weeks in, when I found out how hard it actually is to control my magic. I accidentally sliced my thumb open while cutting carrots, trying to prep for dinner. Everyone, including me, was shocked to see no wound when the blood was wiped away."

His voice gets softer. He doesn't continue for a while. I nearly ask what happened next when he continues. "They spent the afternoon trying to make me control it. House after house was the same. I'd get hurt, my magic would act up, they'd send me back after a punishment that resulted in more magic use. The house before this one-" he pauses again and I hear cloth rustling as he grips the sheets."It doesn't matter. What matters is that I'm here in this shithole because I can't control the very thing that ripped me away from mom and dad and you."

I don't have a good response. His magic is acting the same as mine. Uncontrollable and angry.

"There are much better places to be than here," he says.

"It doesn't change the fact that we are here as a source of cheap labor for the people that do buy us," I retort. "Even the places that are less brunt work, it's all the same. It doesn't change the fact that they ripped us from our homes, our families, to live this life, if you can even call it living."

"If I can't even control my magic that is relatively harmless, what about those with dangerous magics? You can't control yours and it's one of the more dangerous, I've heard," Jake says. "How would you feel if mom and dad got hurt because of your lack of control? Would you rather that over this?"

I feel my blood boil and my magic stir. "If they taught us to control it rather than beating us any time it showed, I'd have a lot better control than I do now. And then nobody would get hurt," I snap. "Are you really defending *them*?"

"I'm not defending anyone," he grumbles.

"It sure sounded like you were," I say, rolling over. Jake doesn't respond and eventually, I hear soft snores from his bed.

# CHAPTER FOURTEEN

## 732

"732, welcome back," Mr. Caulder says, motioning me to sit in the chair across the desk.

I shuffle over and sit down, the chains scraping against the ground.

"How was your first week?"

"It's too hot for fall, sir," I say dully. Jake and I were put in the group that sorted the logs. We've spent the morning sorting, lifting, and moving logs of all different sizes to their respective places.

Mr. Caulder nods. "And how are you settling in with the other Workers?" He asks.

My heart skips a beat. "Fine," I say. "They've been fine."

Mr. Caulder smiles a knowing smile. He stands. "I'm sure it has been. 54 has been showing you around, then?"

I swallow, fiddling with my fingers under the desk. "Yes, he has," is all I dare say.

He walks to the window and clasps his hands behind his back. "I've noticed you two have been getting close. You two have been nearly inseparable since you got here." He pauses, sending a look over his shoulder. "Which makes me wonder if there's been any previous history between you?" He returns his gaze to the window.

I can feel my pulse pounding against the silver chain on my neck. "What makes you wonder that?" I ask.

"Oh, nothing major." I can hear the smile in his voice. "The simple fact that he hasn't left your side since you arrived here." A pause. "There is also the matter of similarities in your features."

"What are you implying, sir?" I ask, leaning forward.

Mr. Caulder turns around to face me. "I am *implying* that you two knew each other before Rebren. I would go so far as to say that you are related somehow," he says.

I feel my blood run cold. I force my features to remain neutral as I stare into Mr. Caulders gray eyes. I don't respond to him.

Mr. Caulder smiles. "Ah, that's it, isn't it? You two are related."

"You're assuming that we are related because of a few physical similarities?" I ask. Blood pounds in my head. I can't think straight. Jake can't be brought into this. Things could go south in an instant. I need his attention off of him and onto me. This man… he holds not only my life in his hands, but Jake's too. "I would suggest not lying to me, 732. I have both yours and 54's files here which state your background," he says, placing a hand on a stack of papers. "I wanted to see if you'd cover up for him or not."

I shake my head, leaning back in the chair. "You knew? Then why let us stick together like we have?" I ask. A part of me doesn't want to know the answer. A different part of me is scared that he'll separate us. All of me is scared of what he'll do to Jake to keep me in line. What lengths is Mr. Caulder willing to go to in order to keep me in line?

Mr. Caulder sits down and leans forward. "To see what you'd do. How would you react to him being here? I am curious to see how rebellious you're willing to get with him on the line." He smiles when he sees my expression. "You've already thought of that, haven't you?"

I grit my teeth. "Keep him out of this," I say. It comes out as almost a growl.

Mr. Caulder raises an eyebrow, sitting up straighter.

"My problems are not his fault," I continue. "He is left out of whatever goes on between the two of us."

"That's not how it works, 732," he says. "See, I own you. I own him. I can do whatever I please to the both of you. If I want to bring him into this, I will. It's up to you to decide if you're going to force my hand on the matter." He leans back in his chair.

I grit my teeth as I feel my magic swirl beneath my skin. "I'm the problem, not him."

"Which is why it would be a shame for him to be punished for your mistakes." Mr. Caulder smiles. "It has been a week. I'm going to trust that, if I take those shackles off your ankles, you aren't going to run. After all, you have a lot at risk here. Do you understand, 732?"

I take a deep breath and nod. "I understand, sir," I say, glaring at him. "However, taking off those shackles would only make it easier for me to escape."

"Mr. Caulder raises an eyebrow. "Have you already forgotten what I can do if you step one *toe* out of line?"

I cross my arms over my chest. "You'll have to catch me first."

"Is that a threat, 732?" Mr. Caulder's voice is cold.

"Are you taking it as a threat?" I lean forward. "You thought training me would be easy, but I think you've underestimated me. I'm willing to do *whatever it takes* to get out. Think on that, *Sir*, before you think I'm going to be *easy*." A smile works its way onto my face as I stare at Mr. Caulder.

He meets my glare with one of his own. "I think we'll leave those on for now, then," he says coldly. "I'll see you in a week to re-evaluate the situation. I do hope that your mindset changes, for your sake as well as 54's." He turns to the Handler behind me. "Watch him, Handler Daniels."

“Yes, sir,” the man behind me says. Daniels grabs my shirt and pulls me out of the chair. Mr. Caulder watches as I am shoved out of the room, stumbling over my feet. I can feel his icy gaze following me into the hallway.

* * *

“What happened today? I thought you were supposed to get the chain off today?” Jake asks back at the Shed.

I shrug him off, feeling oddly optimistic. “I did exactly what I’m good at: I caused trouble.”

Jake rubs his eyes and sighs. “Why, Adam?”

“Because I need to. You need to trust me on this,” I say as I walk towards my bed to where 06 and 1048 are talking. Jake trails behind me.

“So?” 1048 asks, eyes wide and hopeful.

I flash him a smile. “They should be focused on me for the next week.”

06 breaks out into a smile and 1048’s face brightens up. “Move forward with stage two tomorrow?” the young kid asks.

“What’s stage two?” Jake asks behind me.

06 and 1048 jump as if seeing him for the first time. I turn around. “We’re going to get out of here. All of us.”

Jake takes a quick glance around the room. "*Everyone*?" He whispers.

I nod. "1048 can sneak around without being seen. People listen to 06, and I'm good at providing distractions…" I trail off as I remember Mr. Caulder's words.

Jake grabs my shoulders and pulls me closer to him. "Why put yourself at risk?" His eyes are full of worry.

I pat his arm. "I'm used to it, and the Handlers are already on edge around me. I can use that to our advantage. Nobody will be looking at 1048 when he makes his move."

Jake shakes his head.

"54, it's a good plan. It will work," 06 says, placing a hand on his shoulder.

"Can you be sure of that?" Jake asks him.

"I can only hope. That's all we have left." 06's eyes are sincere. Something in his gaze makes Jake back down.

"Can I do anything to help?" He asks. I turn to face 06 and 1048. The young boy hasn't said a word since Jake arrived.

"What could you do to help?" 1048 asks.

Jake's face falls. "I'm… not sure," he whispers.

“Then don’t help.” His excitement has faded away and his features have turned hard.

Jake doesn’t respond and he looks at his feet.

“There is something 54 and I can help with,” 12 says behind me.

“And what is that?” I ask, crossing my arms and facing him.

12 smirks. “A way to communicate.”

I turn towards Jake. “The tapping you do at lunch?” He smiles sheepishly at me.

“Morse Code,” he says and turns to 12. “What’s in it for you?”

“I get home.”

I meet 06’s eyes. He shrugs. “We could use that. Can you teach us tonight?”

This earns us a smile from 12 and it sends shivers down my spine. “We only have all night.”

# CHAPTER FIFTEEN

## 54

The September sun beats down on me as I dump a bundle of sticks in a large black bag. The rough wood scrapes at my arms as the sticks fall out of my grasp. The small scratches disappear in an instant as my magic rushes towards the tiny wounds.

Rhythmic tapping sounds from across the field. *732, now*. 12 has been watching the Handlers, looking for a chance for Adam to cause a scene, letting 1048 slip past unseen. I find my brother in the field as I trudge back to the pile of sticks. Adam straightens up and then bolts across the field, chain flying behind him.

The Handlers shout and three of them run after him.

*1048, go.*

I don't see the young boy, and I don't try to look for him. I put my head down and continue about my work like I'm supposed to. Shouting still comes from the direction Adam ran, getting closer and I realize that Adam is shouting at the Handlers as he's dragged back. The Handlers hold both his arms, and one has a hand on the back of his neck. I watch as Adam is dragged up to the Lodge, and my heart starts to pound. 1048 isn't back yet.

“Are you going to get moving or just stand there and gawk?” 1048’s voice says quietly behind me.

I spin on my heel and face him, eyes wide. “You… did you…?” I trail off, staring at him.

1048 smirks a little before grabbing some sticks. “Get back to work, 54,” he says as he walks towards the bag.

I look towards the Lodge where Adam is being shoved through the door. His shouts are quieted by the barrier of wood between us. My stomach twists knowing what my brother is being dragged towards. I grab a bundle of sticks and walk the same path back towards the bag.

* * *

Adam finally stumbles through the Shed door after the workday is over. He keeps his head ducked down as he slowly makes his way to his bed. I catch his shoulder and he shoves me off.

“Adam,” I start.

“I’m fine,” he mumbles. “Did 1048 get them?”

I lean against the wall and cross my arms over my chest. “Go ask him yourself. He won’t tell any of us until he tells you first.”

He faces the wall and sighs deeply. “I can’t,” he whispers.

I furrow my eyebrows. “Why not?” I put a hand on his shoulder again and I feel him stiffen under my touch. “What happened today, Adam?”

Finally, he slowly turns towards me. “I knew what I was getting myself into when I ran,” he says. “But it hurts more than I thought it would.” He flashes me a sorry excuse for a smile as he looks up at me through a black eye, split lip, and a purple bruise forming on his cheek. I can only guess what he’s hiding underneath his clothes.

I pull him into a hug, holding him gently as if he might break. I feel him hesitantly wrap his arms around me and breathe deeply. Eventually, he pushes away and steps back. “I’m fine,” he whispers. “Where’s 1048?”

I nod towards where the black haired boy and 06 stand in a corner. Adam makes his way over to them, favoring his left leg, and I follow behind.

“Ouch,” 06 comments on Adam’s appearance.

Adam shrugs. “Did you get them?” He asks 1048.

The boy smiles and reaches behind his back. He pulls out a pair of baby blue office scissors. A small, mischievous smile tugs at Adam's lips.

“Where are these from?” He asks, gently taking them from 1048’s hand.

“The desk, of course.”

Adam smiles and turns around, facing the growing group of men in the shed. He straightens his posture and I see him tense with pain. "Who wants a haircut?" he shouts, voice strong.

The sullen men turn around and stare at him, all small mutterings quiet. Adam holds up the scissors with pride and a smile. From behind him, I see 06 grinning like a maniac. He stands up and walks towards Adam.

"May I?" He gently asks the man closest to us, gesturing to the trunk.

The man's eyes go wide and he nods, stepping back.

06 pulls the trunk over and sits on it, back towards Adam. "Go ahead," he chokes out. 1048 walks over and stands with his back facing the wall with his arms crossed over his chest. For the first time in the months since he arrived at Caulder's, 1048 smiles.

Adam glances at me over his shoulder and flashes me a wide smile before turning to 06's wavy, blonde hair. "Any specific length?" he asks with a hand on 06's shoulder..

He pauses, thinking. "Short."

Adam hesitantly pulls 06's hair out of his normal bun at the base of his neck. His blonde hair falls past his shoulders. Adam slowly takes a section of 06's hair and snips it off with the blue desk scissors, close to his scalp. Immediately, the rest of the men stand up and quietly talk, walking towards the corner where the four of us are. A line starts to form. I smile at them. Adam finishes cutting 06's hair, a pile of it forming behind the trunk.

"Can I…" A middle aged man with glasses asks, gesturing to the scissors.

Adam nods and hands them to him, stepping back. The man gestures to 1048 by the wall. He looks stunned. "Me?" 1048 asks, pointing to his chest.

The man nods and 1048 hesitantly sits down on the trunk. The older man starts snipping away at 1048's black hair. The boy has tears in his eyes. He rubs his hand over his freshly cut hair and wipes a hand over his eyes. 1048 cuts the older man's hair, takes the blue scissors from him, and then trades off to the next man in line. Soon, a large pile of hair has formed and 06 sweeps it away. The men who have had their hair cut have already started showering.

The last man hands the scissors back to Adam. "Thank you," he whispers, tears pooling in his eyes.

Adam smiles and nods, patting him on the shoulder as he walks away.

"You've connected a lot with these men, Adam," I say, resting a hand on his shoulder. This time, he doesn't tense. He shakes his head and faces me, a genuine smile tugging at his lips. His split lip has cracked and there is a small smear of blood on his chin.

1048 and 06 walk back up to us. “Are you two going to partake in the fun?” 06 asks with a smile, running his fingers through his choppy hair.

Adam turns and hands me the scissors, tugging off his shirt. “Whatever you can, cut it,” he says.

I walk up behind him and run a hand through his brown hair. It’s grown out a few inches in the past couple weeks, just barely brushing his ears. I ruffle his dirty brown hair, getting a small chuckle out of him before taking a small section and making a cut close to his scalp. I watch Adam flex his fingers as I silently as the scissors quietly *snip snip snip* away the strands. I’m brought back to when mom would cut our hair when we were little boys. She’d take us out to the back patio with a kitchen chair and a towel draped around our shoulders. Mom would tuck her comb between her pinky and ring finger and make small cuts, making sure that the style would match evenly across our heads.

I pat Adam’s shoulder and step back. “I didn’t do as well as Mom, but it works.”

He runs his hands over the choppy cuts and smiles. “Your turn,” he says, taking the scissors from my hands.

I smile and sit on the trunk. Adam combs his fingers through my hair. It reaches nearly to my chin now. I feel him pull back sections and start cutting. I feel tears prick my eyes. For the first time in years, *I* control what is done to me. I have a say in this action, it’s my choice to let Adam cut my hair. I sniffle and quickly wipe my eyes. When Adam’s done, he ruffles my short hair and steps back. “Ta-da,” he says. When I turn around, he's got his arms crossed and a goofy grin on his face.

"What did you do?" I ask.

He shakes his head. "My best," he laughs.

We quickly make our way to the bathroom, gently shoving each other to the side, and peer into the dirty mirror. My hair is extremely choppy and sticking up in places. Adam's hair is too short to look too bad.

"Never, and I repeat never, go into hair styling as a career," I joke, combing through my hair, trying to make it lay flat.

He throws his head back and laughs. A genuine laugh that I haven't heard since leaving home. I smile as I make my way out of the bathroom.

"Take a shower," I call over my shoulder.

I hear Adam chuckle, and the door closes.

# CHAPTER SIXTEEN

# 732

"Who is responsible for this?" Mr. Caulder's voice shouts. Jake and I are standing near the middle of the group with 06, 12, and 1048. Jake is watching the other men, all whose heads are down. The usually noisy field is silent and it seems that even the birds are holding their breath.

"I'm not going to ask again. Who is responsible for this act of rebellion?" His eyes scan the crowd. They land on me and he raises an eyebrow.

My heart pounds. *The plan.* I open my mouth, but am cut off by Jake.

"I am," he says, his voice strong. Mr. Caulders gaze falls on him with a shocked expression. Jake stands tall, back straight and head held high. The men around us all turn to look at him, their eyes wide. My stomach drops and I turn to face him. Jake won't look at me, instead holding Caulder's terrifying gaze.

"54? You did this?" He asks. I swear there is confusion and disappointment in his voice.

Jake nods. "I did."

Mr. Caulder looks at me, then back at Jake, then nods to himself. "Very well," he says. "54, please come with me."

The men step aside, making a path to Mr. Caulder. Jake slowly walks towards him.

I watch him walk away, the Handlers following behind him. He's taking the blame and why am I not saying anything? Why have I not spoken up and stuck to the plan? Why am I standing here frozen? Why am I so scared?

"Get back to work," Mr. Caulder says and turns away, leading Jake into the Lodge.

I can't breathe. Why did Jake speak up? Why did he take the blame? I'm supposed to take it so that the Handlers attention would still be focused on me. The rest of the Workers silently separate into their groups, grabbing materials from the trailer nearby. I can't move, staring at the door Jake and Mr. Caulder disappeared through.

"Get to work," Daniels says, shoving a rake into my hands. I blink and look at the tool I hold.

"C'monn, 732," 06 whispers to me, nodding to Daniels. The Handler is staring at me, expecting me to join the others. I grit my teeth and drop the rake. Daniels shouts after me as I run towards the Lodge.

I fling the door open, startling the women who work in the kitchen. Their eyes follow me as I sprint up the stairs, the chain nearly catching on each step, and Daniels right behind me.

"Hey!" He shouts behind me. "You want to run straight towards the beating this time?"

I ignore him. Gasping, I burst into Mr. Caulders study. Both Mr. Caulder and Jake look at me with wide eyes. Jake is standing with his hands behind his back, facing Mr. Caulder seated behind his desk. Daniels appears a moment later, grabbing my arm.

"I'm incredibly sorry, sir," he says, trying to pull me out of the room. "I'll deal with him."

I jerk out of his grip. "It was my idea," I say.

Jake presses his lips into a line, staring at me.

"732, you were behind the stolen scissors and unapproved hair cuts?" Mr. Caulder asks.

I square my shoulders and nod. "I was in here all day, wasn't I? When would 54 have the chance to steal them, *Sir*?"

Mr. Caulder looks back at Jake. "And what do you have to say about this, 54?" he asks.

I look at Jake, standing there so calm and collected, as if he has the situation under control. His breathing is even and he stands perfectly still, despite the flaming gaze Mr. Caulder has him fixed under. "732 did not act alone, sir," he says slowly.

"Quit lying, 54," I spit. Jake stares at me. I meet Mr. Caulders gaze with a stone cold expression. "I stole the scissors. Is that more believable to you, *sir*?"

Mr. Caulder smiles and nods, leaning back in his chair. "That, I do believe more," he says. He turns back to Jake. "Why were you lying for him?" he asks.

Jake grits his teeth, slowly turning back to Mr. Caulder. "I…I felt…" Jake trails off before looking at the ground.

"Finish your sentences, 54," Mr. Caulder snaps.

Jake stiffens. "I felt the need to protect him, sir."

*Jake…*

Mr. Caulder nods. "Perhaps due to a familial bond?"

Jake stares at him, eyes wide. "How did…?"

Mr. Caulder smirks and my stomach drops. "I know more than you think, 54." He turns towards me. "732, I will not tolerate this rebellion any longer. You will receive fifty lashings. As for you, 54," he turns back towards Jake, "Lying is not tolerated here. I thought you learned this when I whipped that boy. But obviously not. You will watch 732 receive his punishment, and then you will watch as I punish him for your lying."

Jake steps forward. "Sir, please-"

"Do not argue with me, 54!" Mr. Caulder shouts.

Jake freezes.

"You were doing so well, but apparently our lessons haven't stuck. You will sit and watch 732 take beating after beating until you understand your place here. Do you understand?" Mr. Caulder is standing now and is staring down at Jake.

Jake is trembling. "Yes, sir," he whispers.

"Good," he says. "Daniels, Lowe, take care of them." I feel Daniels grab my arm again. My stomach sinks as Jake and I are dragged out of the room. The two Handlers shove us towards the back room. Daniels forces me in first, locking my wrists into the thick shackles attached to the chain hanging from the ceiling. Lowe shoves Jake to his knees and chains his hands behind his back to a hook on the wall.

"I'm so sorry," he whispers.

I don't respond to him, staring at the wooden wall in front of me. One of the Handlers presses the button and the chain raises, pulling my arms up. The other Handler cuts open the back of my shirt and slowly peels the bandages off. I wince as the scabs are torn off the recent wounds. I grip the chain that connects my wrists together and close my eyes.

"There isn't any more skin for us to whip, Daniels. Just scars and scars. Probably doesn't even have nerves there anymore," Lowe says.

"Robert gave the order. Fifty lashings," Daniels responds. A whip uncurls and hits the tarp covered floor.

"Will it even do anything?" Lowe asks.

"It'll slow him down, stop him from doing anything stupid for at least a few days."

The whip cracks and my back lights on fire. I squeeze my eyes shut and count to silently count to ten. The next hit lands on count seven.

I can hear Jake crying from his place on the wall. Why is he the one crying when I'm being whipped? He got himself into this situation. If he would have just stuck to the plan, he wouldn't be here.

Seven. Crack.

I feel tears stream down my face as the pain gets more intense with each hit. I've lost count of how many strikes have fallen.

"Alright, let him down," Daniels says. I hear the whirring of a motor and I am dropped to the ground, hitting knees first.

"Adam? Adam, please get up," Jake whispers.

"What was that, 54?" Lowe demands, stomping over to him. I watch through blurry vision as the taller Handler grabs my brother's shirt and pulls him forwards. "More rules broken?"

Jake looks at Lowe with tears in his eyes. "Please just beat me, for once! Let me take my punishment! Stop hurting others for things *I've* done," he pleads.

Daniels drags me up and chains my hands to a hook above my head. At least I'm sitting.

"What good would it do, 54? I've seen what happens when we try. It doesn't stick. So why would we start now?" Lowe growls.

"Please. I'm begging you."

Daniels approaches me, a thick wooden pole in his hands. Lowe lets go of Jake and steps back. Daniels glances at him before preparing to swing. "This is for lying, 54." I close my eyes as the first blow falls.

* * *

Jake practically carries me down the creaky stairs and to the small bathroom. He sets me on the toilet and starts grabbing things from the cabinet.

"Jake," I whisper, leaning against the counter. "I can get myself cleaned up."

He looks at me over his shoulder. "You can barely stand."

"I can do it," I whisper, pushing myself into a straighter position. "I used to do it myself all the time in Rebren."

"Adam," he says sternly. "It's my fault you're like this so stop being stubborn and let me help you."

I glance at his shaking hands holding the bowl of supplies and slowly nod. Jake starts working slowly on my back. I wince against the pain, holding back flinches everytime he presses the cloth to my ruined back.

"Why?" Jake whispers as he starts taping the bandages on.

"I couldn't let you do that," I say over my shoulder. I can barely see him through my blurry, tear filled vision. "Why didn't you stick to the plan?"

He presses another layer of bandages on. "I can deal with the injuries."

I turn around, ignoring his glare and the shooting pain, and face him. "The plan was I would take the blame so that the Handlers would be distracted dealing with me, leaving 1048 to do his part," I hiss. "And I would have been brought up there anyways. You don't get punished, just watch others take a beating meant for you."

Jake looks hurt. "What I told Caulder about protecting you is true," he starts. "I couldn't watch you get dragged off to be beaten again."

"I was willing to make a sacrifice so that we could go *home*, Jake. I was thinking of the end goal when we made the plan. I want to go *home*," I whisper. "Don't you?"

He doesn't respond, standing up and putting the dirty bowl and rags in the sink. I stand up, supporting my weight on the counter, and start rinsing out the rags as he washes out the bowl.

"I can't control it," he finally whispers. "Mom and Dad… they'll think I've learned nothing."

"You're not going to learn control here, Jake," I say softly. "Insecure people are scared of what we can do, and that's why you're here."

"I just need more time—"

"Don't give me that spiel about control," I cut him off. "We both know that Rebren isn't teaching you control." I pause. "And besides, Mom and Dad won't care about that. They'll be happy to see you."

Jake dries his hands and sets the bowl under the sink. He tosses me a shirt.. He opens his mouth to answer, but is cut off by pounding at the door.

"Get out, both of you, and get back to work!" A Handler shouts.

We glance at each other before Jake opens the door. The Handler steps aside and follows us back outside.

They never came for the scissors.

# CHAPTER SEVENTEEN

## 732

I wake up to tapping on my pillow and my body screaming in pain.

*Dot-dash. Dash-dot-dot. Dot-dash. Dash-dash.*

I blink and rub my eyes with the back of my hand. The action exposing just how sore I am.

*Dot-Dash. A. Dash-dot-dot. D. Dot-dash. A. Dash-Dash. M.*

Adam.

The same pattern repeats again.

I slowly roll over, nearly crushing Jake's hand. He's smiling. "Hey, good morning," he says softly.

I groan and look towards the ceiling. "Already?" I ask. After the beating I took yesterday, and then working the rest of the day, I'm not sure I'd be able to crawl out of bed today.

I see Jake nod out of the corner of my eye. "Unfortunately." He stands and offers me a hand. I grab it and I wince as he pulls me up into a sitting position. My back screams in pain and my body protests, but I ignore it, running a hand through my short hair.

"Let me take a look," Jake says, motioning to my back.

I look down, but slowly remove my shirt and turn my back towards him. Jake silently changes my bandages, patting me on the shoulder when he's done. "Come on, we've got to get going," he whispers.

I sigh and stand as well, changing my clothes as quickly as I can and making my bed before standing near the door with the other Workers. 06 puts a hand on my shoulder and gives it a reassuring squeeze. "Nearly there, 732. We're almost out."

"I knew what I signed up for," I whisper with a smile. "I can rest when we're out."

"We might have to adapt today," Jake says. "I have a feeling Caulder is going to take both 732 and me into his office for a *chat*."

06 tilts his head to the side in confusion. "Because of your comments yesterday?"

Jake nods, looking down at his feet.

"I'll signal when the Handlers are distracted. Just listen for it, okay?" I tell 1048 who stands off to the side with his arms crossed.

"Caulder beat you for his punishment, didn't he?" the boy asks.

"It was a group effort punishment. We both did some stupid things up there," I explain, finally understanding why 1048 dislikes Jake so much. The stripes on his back have scabbed over and are starting to close up, but it's still a fresh wound to him.

"What makes him so special?" he asks.

I meet Jake's eyes. "Mr. Caulder has his own agenda. Once we're out, it won't matter."

That seems to calm the fire in 1048's eyes. The Shed door opens and we are ushered out one by one and led to the transport truck.

* * *

"Sit, 54," Mr. Caulder says curtly as we enter his study, led by Daniels and Lowe. Jake slowly sits in the chair across the desk. Daniels pulls me over to a large tarp and a hook dangling from the ceiling.

"Do you remember how this goes or do you need a reminder?" Mr. Caulder asks Jake.

"I remember, Sir," Jake says quietly.

Daniels cuffs my hands together and attaches the cuff to the chain swinging from the ceiling.

“Good. Let’s get started,” Mr. Caulder says, picking up a few papers. “Yesterday you lied to and argued with me, as well as tried to bargain your punishments and called 732 by an unapproved name. Is this all true, 54?”

Daniels stands nearby with the same wooden pole in his hand. My stomach twists at the situation, but the attention on Jake gives me the opportunity to figure out how to signal 1048.

“Yes, sir. It’s all true,” Jake says. His hands are clasped tightly in his lap and I catch him rubbing his thumb over his knuckles. A nervous habit he picked up from Dad.

“Four hits, Daniels,” Mr. Caulder says as he scribbles something down.

I grip the chains and close my eyes, bracing myself. Four quick hits come directly to my midsection and I gasp for breath. I stumble backwards, swinging away from Daniels and his wooden pole, my feet scraping against the tarp.

That’s it!

“How often have you been calling 732 unapproved names?”

Jake is silent, thinking. He starts scratching at the back of his hand.

“Don’t lie, 54. The punishment will only be worse if you do.”

Jake swallows and slowly answers. "Nearly every day."

Caulder's office should be right above the downstairs bathroom, near the table where we all eat lunch. 12 should recognize the patterns and let 1048 know.

"Ten hits, Daniels."

They come quickly, leaving me gasping with tears in my eyes. As I stumble away, I stomp with my heel the message: *12, go.*

Jake glances at me before looking back at Mr. Caulder.

"What else have you lied about, 54?" Mr. Caulder asks, staring Jake down.

"Nothing, sir," Jake says.

Mr. Caulder raises an eyebrow. "How can I trust you? You've lied to me before."

"I simply wanted to protect 732. Yesterday was the only day," Jake explains.

I shuffle my feet, tapping out a rhythm. *12. 1048. Now.*

"732 stop moving about," Mr. Caulder snaps.

I still. Daniels adjusts his grip on the pole. I have to hope they got the message.

"Every time a punishment is given, you try to bargain with me. Do you understand how this is detrimental to your future, 54?" Mr. Caulder leans forward, clasping his hands on the desk.

"Sir," Jake starts. "You aren't planning on selling me back to Rebren. What other future are you implying?"

Mr. Caulder raises an eyebrow. He raises a hand to Daniels in preparation. "The future where you are not punished and do not have outbreaks like this, 54. You are correct, I do plan on keeping you, but I do not like this behavior."

Jake nods. "I wanted to clarify, sir."

Mr. Caulder lowers his hand.

He's not planning on selling Jake? Why keep him around if he's causing so many problems? What about Jake makes him stand out to Mr. Caulder?

"I need your word that you won't try and bargain your punishments any more, nor argue with me again."

"I promise, sir," Jake says.

"Good." Mr. Caulder waves a hand and Daniels unhooks me from the chain. "You are dismissed, 54."

Jake looks at me before standing up. Lowe leads him out the door and shuts it quietly.

"732. Sit," Mr. Caulder says.

I shuffle over to the chair Jake just vacated and sit down, awkwardly maneuvering around the chains.

"Ever since you arrived here, you have been nothing but a bad influence on those around you," he starts. "I'm starting to think you can't be trained, and that your purpose is best served in the Lab. What do you say to that?"

My skin crawls at the mention of the Lab. "I say my purpose is best served outside of Rebren, sir," I say.

Mr. Caulder raises an eyebrow. "What are you suggesting, 732?"

"That you let me go. Me and all the other Workers here." I lean back in my chair, letting my hands settle in my lap.

Mr. Caulder scoffs. "Even if that were possible, you are too unpredictable to have roaming around the streets."

I smirk. "Let's test it, shall we? You let me free and I'll show you how well behaved I can be."

Mr. Caulder laughs, shaking his head. "No, I don't think so. I'll be watching you closely, 732. Any move you make to cause more problems, I'll send you straight back to Rebren. Am I understood?"

I smirk. "Understood, sir."

Mr. Caulder nods. "Dismissed."

1048 is nowhere to be found. I stand with 06 and Jake in the corner where we cut each other's hair, anxiously looking towards the door.

"When did you last see him?" I ask, tapping my foot quickly.

"He was with me in the field, then disappeared when we got on the truck," 06 says. He rubs the large tattoo on his arm and looks towards the door.

The lights will shut off at any minute, and 1048 is not here.

"Could Caulder have caught him?" Jake asks.

*"Nothing but a bad influence on the others."* Mr. Caulder's words float in my mind. Does he know morse code? Has he understood everything we've said?

The lights shut off, plunging us in darkness.

*Are you three going to bed or are you going to stand there all night?* 12 asks from his bed.

*1048 is missing* Jake quickly taps out.

*You sent him to get us all out. What do you think he's doing?*

There is shuffling of feet around me.

*You think this is purposeful?* 06's slow taps sound.

*What else could it be? 732 has done his job wonderfully.* 12 says. *Now sit down or be quiet.*

I hear 06 slide down the wall and settle on the ground. Eyes adjusted to the dark, I can make out his figure slumped against the wall. I use the wall for support as I sit down next to him.

*He'll be okay,* I tap softly.

06 pats my arm. Jake sits on the wall opposite us. He taps my foot with his and I can feel his smile through the darkness. I breathe in, bruised sides protesting, and tap his foot twice in response.

* * *

The lock rattles and I shoot up, all sleep leaving my body. I struggle to my feet and look towards the door.

"Guys?" 1048 whispers.

06 and Jake scramble to their feet and I see 12 make his way over.

"1048! Where have you been?" 06 asks, embracing the young boy.

Keys jingle. "The plan, remember?" 1048 says as he pulls away from 06. A key ring jingles in his hand and he offers it to me.

I move closer to him and take the keys. They are heavy in my hands. I flip through them, not believing my eyes. The door is open and there are no Handlers around. "How'd you do it?" I ask as I bend down and fiddle with the chain around my ankles.

1048 smiles proudly, his face illuminated by the moon. "Magic." And then he disappears, vanishing right there.

"1048?" I whisper. Jake, 12, and 06 look around as well.

The boy appears slightly to my left. "With this on" he gestures to the chain around his neck "I can only hide objects I'm touching. Which made grabbing the keys easy."

I return his smile and finally unlock the shackles. With a sigh, I stand up. "Genius, 1048. Let's get out of here." I start walking across the grass field towards the house, following the stone steps to the garage.

"What are we doing now?" 06 asks.

"Well, we need a car, don't we?" I say, smirking at him. "I just happen to know how to hotwire a car."

I feel Jake stiffen next to me. "How did you learn that?"

I rub the back of my neck. "There's a reason I was sent to Mr. Caulder for bad behavior."

1048 jumps up, pumping his fist in the air. "We can go home!"

I fiddle with the keys in the garage door lock for a minute before finding the right key and slowly ease the door open. I can feel my magic swirling excitedly under my skin at the rebellion. It pulses at the edge of the chain, wanting to be free. *Just a little longer* I think to myself as I approach one of the cars. It's a sleek, black car with tinted windows and a pointed front. I try the handle and it opens.

A light clicks on and I blink, putting a hand to shield my eyes. "What do you think you're doing?" A woman asks.

I glance up from the car and see a woman in her mid-fifties dressed in a blue t-shirt and dark jeans standing in the doorway to the house. I duck into the car, reaching underneath the steering wheel to remove the panel before I am dragged out of the car.

"Let me go!" I shout, trying to pry away the hands that are wrapped around my midsection.

"We need to run," Jake says in my ear. "She ran back inside for a Handler. We need to run now."

I turn and stare at him "A car would be so much faster!"

"They can track the car!" Jake finally lets me go, gesturing to where 06 and 1048 stand. 12 is nowhere to be seen. He must have slipped out when he saw the woman. 1048 looks terrified, 06's hands protectively on his shoulders. "Come on, 732," 06 whispers.

I nod, closing the car door and sneaking up to the doorway. The night air blows through the open door, irritating the open wounds on my back. My magic flares and I reach a hand up to the chain around my neck.

"Is the key to these things on this ring?" I ask 1048.

"How am I supposed to know that!" He shrieks.

I let out a grunt, magic slamming against the barrier, and search through the keys. I find a small key, barely big enough to fit through a pinhole. I gesture for 1048 to turn around. Grabbing the silver chain, I stick the key into the small lock. The key doesn't go all the way in. I try again, almost shoving it in.

"That's used to get a SIM card out of a phone, 732," Mr. Caulder says.

I spin around, shoving 1048 behind me, and glare at the man at the top of the stairs. My heart pounds and my magic flares.

"I knew you had something up your sleeve, but this is not what I imagined. I'm impressed," he says, stepping down a few steps.

My hands flex behind me and the flares get stronger. The pendant in my pocket grows warm. *Not now, not now, no no nononono.*

Footsteps echo behind the four of us, and I know Handlers have entered the garage.

"I'll make a deal with you, though," Mr. Caulder starts, reaching the bottom of the stairs. "If you go nicely into the basement and wait there until Rebren arrives, I won't hurt you or your accomplices."

"What's the other option?" I ask, clenching my free hand into a fist, keeping on hand on 1048's arm. Maybe, just maybe, I can make these flare ups work. If I play my cards right.

Mr. Caulder has reached the front of the car. "You've seen what the Handlers are capable of. I'm sure they have some anger at being woken up to deal with you. I'll let them express that anger all night."

"And if I choose neither option?" I ask, straining to control my magic. *Come on, get closer.*

"732, you are not in the position to argue with me." Mr. Caulder's voice is cold.

A Handler grabs my shoulder. My magic flares up and I shout as it exits my body. Lights flicker and I hear others scream as I fall to the ground. The smell of burnt rubber and rotten meat fill the garage. Dark shoes enter my field of vision and I lay on the ground, gasping for air.

"You made a mess, 732," Mr. Caulder says.

I lift my head to glare at him. He's standing with his hands clasped behind his back. His posture is a picture perfect image of control.

“I can’t imagine what the Handlers will do to you tonight.” Mr. Caulder starts to walk away, back towards the house.

I feel hands grabbing me again. I try to rip free of their grasp, but I can’t seem to gain full control over my body. The Handlers pull me to my feet and I see the first Handler lying on the ground, smoke rising from his body. Looking around, I see 1048 in the same state and 06 with angry red burns covering the right side of his body. Jake is slowly pushing himself to his feet, looking unscathed.

“Adam?” He asks, voice raspy. He pushes off the ground, but is immediately grabbed by two Handlers. “Adam, wait!”

I blink through my blurry vision. “Jake?” My voice seems weak to my own ears. The magic has left me cold.

I lose sight of him as I am dragged through a side door that leads to a cold stone hallway. The sound of metal grating on stone pierces through my head. I wince as I am shoved through the squeaky door. Cold chains are locked around my wrists and ankles and I start shivering. Blood drips down my back, the bandages having been torn open during my outburst. I can hear Jake shouting, his voice echoing through the hallway. The Handlers leave, locking the door and plunging me into darkness.

# CHAPTER EIGHTEEN

## 732

I can feel a bruise forming around my right eye. The Handlers' footsteps fade the further they get from my cell.

"Adam?" Jake asks, his voice strained.

"I'm fine," I groan. "You?"

"I'm okay," he responds.

I lean up against the wall, breathing deeply. Exhaustion weighs heavy in my bones.

"You're not hurt too badly?" Jake says.

"Nothing new," I lie. I prod at my ribs. At least one is broken and a couple fractures.

"I heard them hitting you, stop lying," he says. "They didn't… they didn't whip you, did they?"

I find a tender spot and suck in a breath. "Nope," I strain. "Nope just beat me. I think they broke a rib."

Jake is silent.

"Did they… hurt you?" I ask slowly.

"No." His voice is soft. "No, they left after locking me in here."

"Good." I lean back, letting my hands fall into my lap and my head rest against the stone wall.

"Caulder's going to sell you back to Rebren," Jake says.

"Not you?" I ask, eyes still closed. The alarm should be going off soon to wake the rest of the Workers.

"Caulder likes my magic too much. He won't sell me," he says softly.

"What magic do you have, Jake?"

He doesn't respond to that.

"Jake?"

He sighs. "I can heal."

"What do you mean? Heal yourself?" Each breath in feels like fire as my lungs expand, pushing against my throbbing ribs.

"Yes. And others," Jake says quietly.

"You can heal other people?" I pause, holding my breath. "Is that why you keep wanting to bandage others up?"

"Yes." His answer is almost inaudible.

"So Mr. Caulder is going to keep you to be his own personal doctor?" I ask.

"Something like that."

The stone digs into my skull and I shift, causing white hot pain to streak through my body. "How can he trust you, though, after you tried to escape with me?"

Jake doesn't answer, and I think he might have fallen asleep. "I don't know," he finally whispers.

I don't respond to him. I give up on trying to find all the new injuries, letting my eyes close and focus on breathing.

Footsteps echo down the long hallway. I sit up and hear Jake's chains rattling as well. My door opens and three Handlers stand there with thick chains in their hands. The first one holds one of the silver chains that goes around my neck. Glaring, I push myself up until I'm standing. The Handlers roughly switch out the chains and lock the new silver chain on. My weak magic flinches away from the chain. The Handlers pull me out of the room and I catch a different group doing the same for Jake. He follows after me as we are led down the hall and back out into the garage. The lights are still off, but the bodies have been cleared out. The black car's tires have melted to the concrete. My stomach twists at the site. Where did they take 06?

Sunlight blinds me and I blink away the momentary blindness. All the Workers, men and women, are gathered around Mr. Caulder's porch. I see some of the men glance at

Jake and I. Mr. Caulder is standing in the middle of the porch. The Handlers bring Jake towards him, holding me off to the side.

"Last night, these Workers," Mr. Caulder shouts, pointing to Jake and me, "snuck into my house to steal my car and escape."

My heart pounds as I watch Mr. Caulder and Jake. "Let this be settled now. There will be no more rebellion or talk of escape," he says, pulling out a small handgun.

"No!" I shout, tugging at the Handlers who hold me. "Stop it!"

Jake's eyes are trained on Mr. Caulder as he levels the gun at him, his breathing even.

"Don't! Please don't!" I cry. I can feel tears fill my eyes. "Please!"

"Let this be an example to you all of what happens when you forget your role," Mr. Caulder seethes and pulls the trigger.

My scream rips from my throat as I pull against the Handlers' grips. I feel my magic stir inside me, but the pendant stays cold in my pocket. Jake crumples instantly, collapsing onto the grey concrete porch. Mr. Caulder stands over the Workers, staring at Jake. He waves his hand and the Handlers grab him by the arms and drag him away, leaving a trail of blood behind him. His head falls back and I see his eyes. The eyes that once held so much life are now dull.

Blood pours from his chest, a wound that will not heal despite how much he's already survived.

I hear myself crying, screaming, but can't seem to do anything but watch as the Handlers drag his body past me and around the side of the house. The Workers are corralled towards the transport truck to be brought to the worksite, leaving me alone on the porch with a monster. The Handlers beside me don't loosen their iron grips.

I see someone walk up. They snap a few times in front of my face. I blink and raise my head to look at them. Mr. Caulder smiles. "There you are. I have a job for you," he says.

I glare at him and I feel my body start shaking. "You monster," I rasp.

Mr. Caulder blinks and tilts his head. "I'm only doing my job," he says. "I did warn you what would happen if you stepped out of line."

I try to lunge at him, but the Handlers hold me back. I snarl at him as they force me to my knees. "You needed him," I gasp, feeling a void open in the middle of my chest, threatening to swallow me whole.

"What makes you think that?"

"His magic. You needed his magic," my voice breaks.

“I can find another,” Mr. Caulder brushes off the topic. “Despite that, there is a mess on the porch. I need you to clean it up,” he says.

I glance at the blood on the porch. The *mess* on the porch. It’s not Jake’s blood, just *a mess*. The void gets bigger, threatening to swallow me whole.

“Rebren is already on their way. You’ll be leaving with them once you’re done. I do believe this is goodbye, 732. Enjoy your time in the Lab.” Mr. Caulder turns and walks into the house, stepping over the pool of Jake's blood.

The Handlers drag me towards the blood splatter and toss rags and sponges towards me. A large bucket with soapy water is placed next to me. I feel a shove on my back and I stumble forward, hand splashing in the puddle. I freeze, unable to move. Red covers my hand and spots dot my arm.

“Get to work,” Daniels growls.

I can’t breathe. Can’t do anything more than stare at the puddle of red. My body shakes more violently and I feel myself hyperventilating.

The transport truck pulls away from the house. Black smoke puffs from the exhaust pipe as it bumps down the driveway.

“Get working, 732. Rebren will be here soon,” Mr. Caulder says, walking out from the garage.

Slowly, I remove my hand from the puddle of blood and grab the rag. The soapy water turns pink with each rinse.

# CHAPTER NINETEEN

## 732

I barely notice when the Handlers walk me to the Rebren van and push me onto the metal bench. They switch out the shackles on my wrists and ankles, and lock a chain around my waist. They leave the silver chain around my neck. The van rocks as they climb out. I don't move, don't fight it, staring ahcad at nothing instead. Jake's blood is still on my hands and my clothes, sticking to my knees.

The dim yellow light flickers on and we start moving. I lose track of time, staring at the wall in front of me. They are taking me back to Rebren, back to the Lab. Back to Sam and his magic sucking machine. I lean against the wall, letting the movement of the van numb the thoughts that threaten to swirl around. Let the vibration of the tires on the pavement drown out the sound of the gunshot echoing in my ears. I squeeze my eyes shut.

Jake is dead.

He was shot right in front of me. My own scream echoes in my ears, meshing with the gunshot.

*He wouldn't even look at me.*

I feel tears pool around my eyelashes. I squeeze my eyes shut, causing some of them to drip down my cheeks.

Why didn't he look? Why didn't he try and fight?

Why didn't I try to stop Mr. Caulder?

A sob bubbles up from my chest. I lean forward, resting my elbows on my knees. I clench my hands together, causing the dried blood on my hands to flake off.

Jake's blood.

I flinch backwards, opening my eyes. I wipe my hands on my blood soaked pants, smearing it everywhere. Tears flow freely, sobs wracking my body as I desperately try to wipe his blood off my hands.

I lean back up against the wall, pressing the back of my stained hands to my forehead, and sob. Jake is gone and there's nothing I can do to bring him back. They beat me and he listened all night, then they shot him as an example, dragging his body to be dumped into an unmarked grave to be forgotten about. He's never going home. Because *I* messed up. He's never going to see Mom and Dad again because he was following *me*.

Who will tell Mom and Dad?

I cry harder. Who will tell our parents that their son is dead? That he was shot for helping me? How long will they wait until they tell my parents? Will they ever tell them?

My fingers tingle and I clench my hands closed. The pendant in my pocket grows warm. The tingling spreads up my arms and to my chest. I hold my breath and try to will the tingling to go away.

The van stops moving and the back doors open, letting the sun flood in. I feel hands wrenching mine down, unchaining me from the ceiling of the van. More hands go to the shackles around my ankles and to the chain around my waist.

I open my eyes when the hands leave me. There are two Handlers who stand in front of me. I blink at them and look away. The Handler closest to me grabs my arm and pulls me up, shoving me towards the door. The metal is cold under my thin shoes. Two more Handlers are waiting on the pavement. They grab my arm and yank me out of the van, tears still streaming down my face. At least I'm not sobbing.

The building we walk towards is different from the one they normally bring me to. This one simply says *Rebren Program for Magic Control Laboratory: Illinois Campus* over the door.

I am shoved towards a desk.

"2157732," one of the Handlers states. He sounds like Daniels.

My head is shoved to the side and a scanner beeps. I stare at my feet, tears running silently down my cheeks and dripping off my chin.

"Returned due to bad behavior. Harold wants him checked into the Lab."

"Any damages?" A different male voice asks.

"Damaged garage and electrical. Totaled car. Two deaths. One severely injured," Daniels rattles off.

A chair creeks as the man behind the desk looks at me. "Him?"

"Hence why he's unsuitable for work."

I look up at the man, feeling my magic swirl violently.

The man shrugs and types at his computer. "Processing room 8 is open."

Hands dig into my neck and force me forward. The Handlers lead me to a processing room and push me onto the bench. They unlock the shackles, switching them out for the ones attached to the bench, and the silver chain. The tingling in my hands gets stronger and the pendant nearly burns my skin through my clothes. I cry out as my magic leaves me in a rush, exploding in no specific direction. Pipes burst and guns go off. Water sprays out from the shower in the corner. I fall to the side, nearly sliding off the bench, as I hear different footsteps rushing around me. Eventually, the tingling stops. My vision is blurry and black near the edges. I hear people shouting as my head hits the ground.

* * *

Blinding lights wake me up. I try to sit up, but I can't move further than a few inches. Looking down, I see my hands chained to the railing of what looks like a hospital bed and a strap around my midsection. I'm lying in a bed. Someone changed my clothes and cleaned the blood off my hands. There is a beeping noise coming from above me. I look up to see a monitor above my head with wires and cables coming out of it. The wires and cables lead to something underneath my loose gown. There is a needle stuck into my elbow, similar to when they would draw my blood. It's attached to a bag next to the monitor.

The door opens and a man in black scrubs walks in. "732, you're awake," he says and grabs a clipboard. "How are you feeling?"

I look around the room. "Where, where am I?" I ask, my voice hoarse.

The man glances at me. "You're in Rebren's Laboratory, medical wing," he says.

I watch him as he checks the monitors..

He writes something on his clipboard. "What do you remember?" He asks, pulling over a chair and sitting down.

"I..." I trail off, looking around. *Medical wing? Was I in that bad of shape?* "Jake, he..." I swallow. "Jake is dead. He was shot," I whisper. "The porch... they made me clean up his blood." I pause, looking at my hands. They look clean, but I can still feel the blood coating my hands, underneath my nails.

The man glances up at me before continuing writing.

“I don’t know how I got here,” I say finally.

The man nods. “You passed out after we removed the magic blocker,” he says. “Things started exploding and you were unconscious, lying on the ground.”

I look up at him. “I used magic?” I ask softly.

The man nods. “As soon as you’re well, you’ll be sent to the testing floor,” he says, standing.

I feel a chill run through me. “Testing… floor?” I ask.

“Your magic is strange and we want to know why,” is all he says before walking out. The door closes with a soft *click* behind him, leaving me alone with the numbness that waits to overcome me.

# PART TWO

# CHAPTER TWENTY

# ABBY

My footsteps echo against the tile as I make my way to the meeting room, manila folders in my arms. I fumble for my badge as I come to a stop by the door. It takes three swipes against the keypad before the light flashes green and the door unlocks.

"Good mornin', Ms. Sommerfeld," Jackson Gravett, my second on this project, says in his southern drawl as I walk into the room. I set the folders in my arms on the table and smile at him, pushing my glasses up.

"Good morning, Mr. Gravett," I respond. "How's the Subject doing today?"

Jackson gestures to the monitors mounted on the wall. "He's recovering well since his outburst. Although he still has some open wounds on his back, but those will heal in time," he relays to me. "His ribs are another story in general. We've wrapped them, but they will take more than a few days to heal fully."

I examine the information displayed on the screens. Vital signs look good; below average when compared to other Workers, but average for his history. He's shown no signs of rebellion or even struggle since being returned, excluding his outburst that first day. What happened at Robert Caulder's place to cause this big of a change in him?

I skim through the report written by Caulder before turning back to Jackson. "He's been relocated to his room?" I ask.

Jackson nods, looking up from the folders on the table. "Yes, ma'am. He gave no fight whatsoever, which I found strange, given his history."

I nod. "What are his hormone and dopamine levels?" I ask, clicking through different screens.

"Low," Jackson states.

I scour the information and wonder why they are so low? I nod. "Thank you," I pause. "What is the plan today?"

"We plan on getting a magic reading, if possible," Jackson states, leaning back against the table.

"And if you can't?"

"We'll use the new prototype to draw it out and capture it, using it for study," he pauses. "We haven't had many chances to use it in the field yet, Ms. Sommerfeld. It'll be interesting to see how it reacts to the Subject's particular magic."

I hide my shaking hands behind my back as I nod. "I understand, Mr. Gravett," I say. "I think it would be beneficial to use it in this case, due to his magic's history. Safer."

Jackson nods.

“I’ll be observing today,” I say. “I thought it would make the Subject feel more comfortable.”

Jackson nods again, looking at his feet. “I’ll record my findings,” he says, looking up with a smile.

“Thank you, Mr. Gravett,” I say, returning his smile.

I grab the folders off the table. Jackson holds the door open for me and we both walk out, heading towards the testing room.

“Bring 732 to testing room 1, please,” Jackson says into a handheld radio. The radio clicks and a garbled voice responds. *“Yes, sir.”* Jackson heads to the testing room to wait for a Handler to bring 732.

I head to the observation room that’s positioned on the other side of the large one way mirror. I set my folders on the small table and sit in the cushioned chair. The login screen blinks at me as I jostle the mouse. The only sound in the room is my tapping on the keyboard. 732’s profile pulls up and I click through the different reports.

*Bad influence on those around him. Completely untrainable. Suggested isolation from other Workers.*

*Magic outbursts. Out of control. Rebellious. Disrespectful.*

*Hard worker, yet sneaky hands. Will grab anything and use it against you.*

I rub my eyes and sigh, closing the reports. From the beginning, 732 has been a handful and caused nothing but trouble.

A beeping noise sounds from the other room and Jackson watches the door. A Handler brings a scrawny young man covered in bruises in. 732 doesn't seem to register anything as he's brought to the center of a large black mat.

"Good morning, 732," Jackson says, grabbing the sensors. "My name is Jackson Gravett and we'll be working together."

"Great," 732 mumbles, his voice rough and low. "Can't wait." He stares at the one way mirror with a blank expression as Jackson attaches wires and sensors to his temples and chest.

"I've just got to stick these on you and then we can get going," Jackson explains.

There is no response from 732. He simply kept staring at me. Familiar green eyes pin me to my chair. It's been almost four years and this is the first time I've seen him. I lean forward. There seems to be nothing left of the boy I knew. The boy who would climb trees and sneak in through windows. The boy who always had a mischievous smile plastered to his face. His once bright eyes are sunken and empty, surrounded by black and blue. His hair is thin and sticking up in places. Beneath the bruises, I can tell he's paler than he used to be. There is a small strip of even paler skin around his neck from where the magic blocking chain sat.

"I'll be back here, monitoring everything. I just need you to focus on the one item, 732."

I stand up and exit the small room, heart pounding. I nearly run to the bathroom and collapse against the wall, pressing the heels of my hands to my forehead. When did he get so thin? "Oh, Adam…" I whisper, leaning my head back against the cool wall.

"Ms. Sommerfeld?" Someone asks.

I lower my hands and stand up. A young intern stands there, her red hair spilling around her shoulders. She's looking at me with wide eyes.

"Are you okay?" She asks.

I smile at her. "I'm fine. Just needed a minute to breathe, that's all." I dust off my blazer and walk calmly out of the bathroom. It takes me two swipes of my keycard to get the door unlocked and I settle into the cushioned seat again.

"What a mess, Adam. What mess have you gotten yourself into this time?" I whisper, watching as Adam tries and fails to use his magic.

# CHAPTER TWENTY ONE

## 732

The gray door in front of me has a small window looking into it and a deadbolt lock above the handle. I stare blankly at the plaque on the door that reads *Room 6* on it as the Handler fiddles with the keys behind me. He finally gets the right key out and unlocks the deadbolt. The door swings open and I am unceremoniously shoved into the room. I stumble over my feet, putting a hand out to steady myself against the wall. The door shuts with a loud clang, leaving me in the bare room alone. Standing just inside the doorway, I examine the cold room. My breathing is the only sound I hear. Even my steps are silent. The bed is a simple mattress on a flimsy frame with a small trunk sitting at the end. A toilet and sink sit in the corner, with an old shower head hanging from the ceiling. The rickety plumbing pipes are secured to the wall, yet look like they'll fall apart with a single use. I slowly make my way to the bed and lie down. It creaks with my weight. I stare at the flickering yellow light on the ceiling, feeling numb.

Hours must have passed before the door opens again, letting in a flood of light. I blink and sit up, the bed creaking. Two Handlers stand in the doorway, staring at me. My bare feet hit the concrete floor, and I made my way towards them.

One grabs my arm and drags me along hallways that look the same until we come to a plain white door with the words *testing room 1* on it. The door opens to reveal a room exactly like the one where I used my magic in before.

*Maybe Sam is still here.*

The Handler drags me over to the black mat and tells me to stay there. I do and wait for anything to happen. A man in blue jeans and a button down shirt walks out from around the corner.

"Good morning, 732," he says in a heavy southern accent as he grabs some items off the table. "My name is Jackson Gravett and we'll be working together."

I watch him, unmoving from my spot on the mat. "Great," I whisper. "I can't wait."

Jackson smiles warmly and walks up to me, wires draped in his hands. "I've just got to stick these on you and then we can get going," he says.

I nod and follow his instructions. The pads are attached to my temples and a few on my chest under my shirt. I look away, my eyes falling on the mirror on the other end of the room. My reflection stares back at me blankly with empty eyes surrounded by rings of bruises.

"Just focus on the one item, 732," Jackson says from behind the computer. When did he get there? "No punishments, just like last time, okay?"

I blink and slowly turn away from the mirror and face the pile of wood on the table. Why does everything feel so numb? I can barely feel my magic underneath my skin. I reach for it, but it refuses to come. I reach again, but it almost feels like it's dodging my grasp. Closing my eyes, I try to feel it inside me. The large golden mass that used to swirl lazily under my skin now seems like it's curled into itself, making itself as small as it possibly can. Almost as if it's trying to hide.

I open my eyes and face the computer station. "I can't," I whisper to Jackson. My voice sounds weak and hollow, barely echoing in the room.

Jackson has his arms crossed as he studies me. "What do you mean 'you can't'?" He asks.

"It's hiding from me," I say.

Jackson shrugs and raises the protective wall. "We'll have to try a different method then," he says, leading me towards a padded table. My heart starts to pound, shaking me from the growing numbness. "You're not going to use the needle thing again, are you?" I ask.

Jackson shakes his head 'no.' "Since your magic won't respond to you, we're going to give it a nudge," he says. "It's different from the needle. Less invasive. Sit up here, please."

I take a step back instinctively, my instincts telling me to run. "How?"

Jackson grabs a small metal prod that has a clear container on the end of it. It has three long fingers with pads on each end. "With this."

I feel blood rush from my face. "What is that?" I whisper, backing up a few steps more, running into the chest of the Handler.

"It's going to draw your magic out of you," he says. "Come sit up here."

I shake my head and feel my legs start to shake. "I am not getting anywhere near that thing," I say quietly. Even my voice shakes.

Jackson sighs and lowers the prod. "Are you ready to try again then?" He asks, nodding towards the black mat and the pile of wood.

I nod quickly. "I, I can try again," I stutter. "Just don't use *that*."

Jackson puts the prod on the table and motions for me to get back onto the mat. The protective wall lowers again. I focus on the wood pile. My magic does not respond, retreating deeper inside itself. Hiding. I groan and close my eyes. *Why won't you work?*

"732?" Jackson asks, his voice muffled.

I don't respond, still trying to grab my magic. *Come on, you pile of mass. You're always so quick to rush out, but now you hide? What has gotten into you?* My magic retreats further. The pendant in my pocket stays cool.

"732," Jackson says more sternly.

I snap my eyes open and see smoke rising from my skin. Jackson stands on the other side of the plexiglass wall, eyes wide. He presses a button and the wall raises.

"Let's call it a day," he says.

"You're not going to try that prod thing?" I ask.

He shakes his head walking towards me. "Not today," he says, removing the sensors. "Maybe another day, if we still aren't seeing success this way."

"I don't understand," I whisper.

Jackson doesn't respond right away. "Whatever it is, it's something we can figure out."

I nod. The Handler leads me out of the testing room and back to my concrete room. The deadbolt locks into place and I fall onto the bed. I feel the numbness creep in again, pulling me into a dark abyss with nothing around me.

# CHAPTER TWENTY TWO

# 54

I wake up gasping, sore, and hungry. The whole left side of my body is stiff. My stomach growls loudly, as if sensing my return to consciousness. Groaning, I push myself into a seated position. Caulder dumped me back in the room he locked me in after the escape attempt, except this time without locking the chains on my wrists and ankles. He even removed the silver chain. My pendant still sits around my neck, although it is cool to the touch. My magic must have healed me long ago, waiting for me to wake up. I prod at my shoulder where the bullet hit. Despite being sore, there is no evidence that I was even injured. Gritting my teeth, I stumble to my feet and make my way to the door. I rest my forehead on the bars as I check for Handlers.

My stomach growls again.

I press a hand to my stomach as if the action will quiet it and place my other hand on the handle. It turns and the door swings open, nearly causing me to collapse. Slowly, I take a step outside of the room.

There are no Handlers nearby. I see the door to the garage and I slowly make my way towards it. My heart pounds and I keep checking over my shoulder despite the wall at the other end of the short hallway. The only way in or out of here is through the garage. I press my ear to the door, resting a hand on the doorknob. No sound comes from the other side. Carefully, I ease the door open and peek into the garage. The door is open and a red truck sits in the driveway. Caulders ruined car has been removed. I hear voices coming in through the open door to the house.

"It's all fixed up. The electrical should work with no issues," an unfamiliar voice says.

"I appreciate the work you do," Caulder responds. "I'll let you know if I have any other issues."

The truck has to belong to the electricians. Gritting my teeth, I quickly make my way across the open garage to the truck.

"How much do I owe you?" Caulder asks.

"Five hundred," the stranger says.

I struggle into the bed of the red truck, slamming my shoulder against the raised edge. I bite back a groan and curl up the corner.

"Did you hear that?" The stranger asks.

"The thud?" A different stranger asks. Their voices get closer and I hold my breath.

"Sounded like it was coming from the truck," the first stranger says. Dirty hands grip the edge of the truck. The man's tan face appears over the edge and stares at me. He blinks a few times and glances at my clothes. "Mitchell, did I leave a tarp in the garage?" He shouts, looking over his shoulder.

My heart pounds in my chest and I can feel my body shaking.

"The big one hasn't been packed up yet. Ready for it?" The other stranger, Mitchell, responds.

"Yeah, bring it over," the man above me looks back at me. He offers me a quick smile before turning towards Mitchell. The second man appears with a tarp in his hands. He glances at me and freezes.

"Brad, what-"

The first man, Brad, cuts him off. "Thanks," he says and grabs the tarp. He reaches into the bed and lays the tarp over me. "Grab hold of that. Make sure it doesn't fly away," he whispers. I grab the tarp in both hands and pull it closer over me.

"What's going on?" Mitchell asks.

"Tell you in the truck," Brad says, his voice getting softer.

The doors shut and the truck rumbles to life. I grip the tarp tighter as the truck starts moving. Finally, I let myself breathe normally. I'm leaving Caulder's place. My breathing turns shaky and tears prick my eyes. I'm leaving. I'm finally leaving, after years and years…

Adam isn't with me.

*"NO!" He screams. "Stop it!"*

*I can't even look at him as Caulder approaches me with the gun leveled directly at my chest. I do my best to keep my breathing level as I keep eye contact with Caulder. His eyes are filled with wrath. His lips raise into a small smirk, one that only I can see. One that says* I'll see you soon.

*"Don't! Please don't! Please!"*

*His screams tear through me in a way my magic cannot heal.*

*"Let this be an example to you all," Caulder says and pulls the trigger.*

I squeeze my eyes closed, stopping the tears that spill over. I'll get him out once I know where these men are taking me.

*  *  *

The truck rumbles to a stop and I feel it shake as someone gets out. The men have left the truck running. Hands tug at the tarp and I reluctantly let it go. Brad and Mitchell are staring at me. Brad smiles hesitantly.

"Hey, kid," Brad says.

I blink, unsure of what to do. "Can I ask what you're doing in my truck?"

I swallow. "Escaping," I say quietly.

Brad nods, glancing at Mitchell. "My name is Brad Harrison. This is Mitchell Stoores. What is your name?"

"54," I mumble.

Brad furrows his eyebrows. "Do you want to be called 54?"

I pause. "You want my *name*?" I ask.

Brad nods, offering an encouraging smile.

"Jake," I say.

"Okay, Jake. It's very nice to meet you." He reaches a hand towards me. "Can I help you out?"

I hesitantly take his hand, letting him pull me up and help me climb out of the truck bed. We've stopped in the middle of nowhere. There are no houses in sight and the sun is setting behind the treeline. Will they dump me here?

Brad shrugs off his jacket. "There you go. Are you hurt?"

I shake my head 'no'.

Brad smiles and holds out his jacket in one hand. "It's a chilly night, and you've been in the back of a truck for about an hour. Do you want a jacket?"

"I'll get it dirty," I state. *Oh stupid. Stupid. Stupid. Why did you say that?*

Brad shrugs. "It's washable." He offers me his jacket again.

*Just take the dang thing.* I reach out and take the jacket. It's warm when I put it on.

"Where are you trying to get to, Jake?" Brad asks.

I pause, staring at him. Where am I going? We didn't get that far in our planning, and now Adam and 06 are gone with 1048 dead…"Away," I say finally.

Brad nods and looks at Mitchell. "I figured, or you wouldn't have climbed into our truck. Did you have any place in mind?"

I shake my head again, glancing around.

"Can we give you a lift?"

I step back. "Do you want to take me back?" I ask.

"No!" Brad says, holding out his hands. "No, Jake, I…" he trails off. "When I saw you in the truck, I knew you were taking the one shot you had to escape. I want to help you."

"Why?" I ask, wrapping my arms around myself.

Brad seems at a loss for words.

"Nobody else wants to help people like me," I say. "So why do you?"

Brad sighs, rubbing the back of his neck. "You looked so scared, and I couldn't let you stay there. You need help that I can give. Why wouldn't I want to help you?" He says, looking concerned.

I stare at him, examining his eyes, his body language. He seems genuine, as if he really does care. Finally, I looked down. "I can't go back to Caulder. And I can't go back to Rebren. They'll tell him I escaped and then…" I trail off. "I just need to get away." Brad is silent for a while. "Will you come with us, Jake?" He asks softly.

I look up. He has his hand on the door of the truck. "Where?" I ask.

"A small town in Kansas."

I nod. A small town far, far away from here. Perfect.

Brad opens the truck door and I climb in.

# CHAPTER TWENTY THREE

## 54

I wake up to the truck shutting off. My cheek sticks to the leather seats as I slowly sit up. My left side is still sore, but the rest of my body is starting to feel somewhat normal. Large wounds take a while to heal, apparently. Something falls onto the floor. A thick, blue blanket sits in a pile on the ground. I pick it up and set it on the seat next to me.

Brad turns around and smiles. “Hey there,” he says softly with a smile. “Did you sleep well?”

I nod slowly. “Yes, sir,” I say.

He smiles again. “Great! We’ve made it home,” he says and climbs out of the truck. He opens my door and steps back. I slowly climb out of the truck.

The night air seems to sink into my bones. I pull Brad’s jacket tighter around me, glancing up at the sky. Stars are littered across the midnight blue backdrop. How long has it been since I’ve seen the stars? I look back down and see Brad smiling. “Come on inside. It’s warmer in there,” he says quietly.

I nod and follow him up the walkway. The yard is neatly trimmed and there are flowers growing in the planter boxes. Children's chalk drawings litter the concrete pathway.

"Looks like Maisley and Gavin got into the chalk again," Mitchell says.

Brad laughs softly. "They sure did. Their drawings are getting better," he says.

I'm careful not to step on the drawings on my way up, lest I ruin them. There is a butterfly next to the welcome mat. I go to remove my shoes, but Brad stops me.

"You can leave those on if you'd like," he says with a smile. He opens the door and motions for me to walk in.

Hesitantly, I do. The carpet feels soft under my feet. I pause, wiggling my toes in my shoes and rock back on my heels. Brad sneaks around me.

"You don't have to stand in the doorway," he says. "Please, have a seat." He motions to the living room.

I glance at him, raising an eyebrow. He smiles. "It's okay. You don't have to be afraid here."

I walk to the opening of the living room and glance at him again. He gives me an encouraging nod. I slowly make my way to the couch. It's a brown, leather couch with pillows and blankets on it. When I sit, I feel like I'm sinking into the cushions. *How long has it been since I've sat on a couch?* The only other furniture I've sat on in the past years has been the wooden benches in the Lodge at Caulders.

Brad and Mitchell walk into the kitchen, leaving me alone amongst the couches. I look around. It's a nice house. A brick fireplace sits on the wall across from me. A love seat sits diagonal from it. There is a TV above the fireplace. A piano rests on the wall closest to the door. I can hardly see anything through the windows. I go to stand when Mitchell walks past the opening and back outside. I freeze, waiting for him to come back. When he doesn't, I stand fully and walk over to a window. It looks over the backyard. There is a swing tied to a tree, a trampoline, and a sandbox out there. There is a fence surrounding the whole yard. I don't see a Workers shed. Odd.

"Checking the place out?" Brad asks.

I back up from the window and turn towards him. He's leaning against the door frame.

"Yes, sir," I say. *Let this be an example to you all.* "I, I'm sorry, I'll sit back down."

Brad looks confused. "You're fine, Jake. If you want to walk around, I get it. You did just spend 8 hours in the truck," he says. He scratches the back of his neck. "If I may, where are you from?"

I hesitate. "Illinois," I say. "I can't go back there."

"I don't intend to send you back there," he says.

I nod. “They’ll ask my parents. I can’t put them in danger.”

Brad is silent for a while. The door opens. “Wait here. I’ll be back,” he says, then leaves the room.

I sigh and run my hands through my choppy hair. I just messed up *again*. Now he’s going to realize what he got himself into and take me back. Or call Rebren to come get me. I sit back on the couch and rest my head in my hands.

Brad walks back in. “Jake,” he says softly.

I sit up.

“There is someone I want you to meet,” he says.

I stand and follow him into the kitchen. There stands Mitchell and an older woman. She smiles when I walk in.

“Jake, this is my mother, Maria,” Brad says.

The woman, Maria, stands and walks over to me. She extends her hand to me. “Jake, it’s good to meet you!”

I take her hand and shake it. “You as well, ma’am,” I say.

“Are you hungry?” She asks.

My stomach growls at the question. “I’m okay, ma’am,” I say. I’ll be okay until morning, if she decides to feed me tomorrow

She gives me a soft look. “I figured you’d say that. I have something waiting at the house for you.”

“Jake, she’s going to take care of you,” Brad says.

I nod, not fully understanding.

“Well, you look like you’ve had a long journey. Let’s get home and you can get some rest,” Maria says.

“I’m alright, ma’am. I’m just here to work,” I say.

She waves a hand. “Oh, nonsense.” She grabs my arm. “We’ll be on our way,” she says as she starts walking towards thc door.

I look over my shoulder, catching Brad’s eye. He smiles. Maria opens the door and leads me to a white car with a beautiful interior. She opens the passenger door.

“In you go,” she says, motioning me to sit in the car.

I slowly get in, sitting in the clean, white leather seat. Maria closes the door and walks to the driver's side.

*No chains? No van?* I am in the passenger seat of a car. I sit back, trying to process what is happening.

The drive is short and quiet. I don’t do much but stare at the empty road. Maria has soft music playing. After a few minutes, we pull up to a small farmhouse.

“Welcome home,” Maria says, getting out of the car.

I do the same, slowly unbuckling and climbing out of the car. I feel like I'm leaving smudges of dirt everywhere I touch. There are purple flowers lining the walkway to the house. The interior of the house is well kept and clean. Cream colored carpet, a light gray paint on the walls. I can't seem to see a speck of dirt anywhere.

"You can leave your shoes by the door. I'll show you your room and we'll get you cleaned up!" Maria says.

I slip off my dirty, threadbare brown Rebren shoes and tuck them neatly by the wall. Maria leads me to a room upstairs with a queen bed, a large dresser, a window overlooking the yard, and a floor to ceiling bookcase. My jaw drops as I take in how large it is.

"I have some of Brad's old clothing here. It'll have to do until we go shopping." She holds out a pair of gray sweats and a white printed t-shirt. "Will these fit for tonight?'

"Will Brad be okay if I wear them?" I ask, stepping closer to her.

"Of course!" She hands me the clothing. "Let me take the jacket so I can hang it up."

I look down to see I'm still wearing Brad's jacket. I shrug it off.

"There. Here's the bathroom. Take your time. Holler if you need anything. When you're done, come downstairs. I have some food for you," she says and closes the door.

I stare at the bathroom, confused. Turning, I finally see what everyone sees: a boy with dirty, matted hair who's too skinny for his clothes. He has sunken cheeks and hollow eyes. No wonder they decided to take me away. I look pathetic. I rub my neck and the Mark. At least they took off the chain.

The shower is refreshing. Unlimited hot water, soft soaps, and soft clothing afterwards. I start to wonder if the bullet did kill me and this is heaven. But why would someone cursed with magic end up in heaven?

I spend what seems like too much time in the bathroom. The water is soft and smells so good. The rag isn't itchy and doesn't rub my skin raw. The sweats and t-shirt feel like the softest things I've worn. Honestly, I could curl up on the rug and fall asleep right here. I find a brush and comb through my choppy hair. I smile at the thought of our haircuts, combing my fingers through my hair. My hair feels so soft and fluffy with these soaps.

I take a deep breath and rest my hand on the doorknob. Thoughts race through my mind. Maria seems nice enough, it shouldn't be too bad. House work, maybe a little yard work. I'd do anything to work in the house. I rest my head against the door.

*A loud band sounds in the garage, throwing me to the side. My magic acts up, healing the bruises and the ringing in my ears.*

*"You made a mess," Caulder says to Adam.*

*I groan and push myself up. Adam is lying amid three bodies. 1048's and the Handlers' are smoking and 06 is badly burned. His chest rises and falls rapidly. If he doesn't get to a hospital soon, he could die.* Or I could heal him.

*"I can only imagine what the Handlers will do to you tonight." Caulder walks away, back into the house.*

*Handlers start to drag Adam away. I push myself up further. "Adam? Adam, wait!" I shout. Handlers grab me and pull me up.*

*"Jake?" Adam says weakly.*

*The Handlers drag us to a side door that leads to a small hallway and lock Adam and I in separate rooms, locking us away where we can't cause any more problems.*

My eyes snap open and I shake my head. *Focus, Jake.* I count to three in my head and open the door. I slowly walk down the stairs. Maira is setting a few plates full of food on the table. She smiles when she sees me.

"How was your shower?" She asks.

I nod, looking down. "It was good. Thank you," I say.

"I'm glad," she says. "It's not much, but it'll hold you over until breakfast." She motions to the food laid across the table. A good sized steak sits on one plate and a plate of vegetables sits next to it. My stomach growls at the sight. Maria sits in one chair at the table, gesturing for me to sit in the one closest to me. Hesitantly, I slide into the wooden seat.

"Please, eat," she says.

"Are you sure? This is all so…nice."

Maria waves her hand. "Nonsense. Now eat."

I gently spoon some vegetables onto the empty plate. Maria pushes the plate of steak closer to me.

"All for you. I had some earlier."

Mouth watering, I cut a small bite and eat it. The flavor alone is nearly enough to make me cry. Hunger gets the better of me and I eat everything as fast as I can. My stomach feels bloated when I'm finished.

"Was that enough for you?" Maria asks.

I nod. "More than enough, ma'am," I respond.

She smiles. "Come with me. I've got your bed set up." She leads me back up to the room. "This is your room. All to yourself," she says and grabs some things out of the closet. "Will it be enough?"

I look around in awe. "Y, yes ma'am," I stutter out. *All mine?*

Maria pats my arm. "Here are extra blankets if you get cold." She hands me the blankets in her arms. "Will you be okay for tonight?"

I nod. “Yes, ma’am.”

She nods and smiles again. “Wonderful. I’ll be downstairs if you need anything.” Maria walks out and gently shuts the door. I let out a breath and turn and face the room. I walk to the bed and crawl into it. I nearly sink into the mattress. It feels like I’m lying on feathers. I pull the blankets up and quickly fall asleep.

# CHAPTER TWENTY FOUR

## 732

Numbness greets me when I wake up. I blink the sleep out of my eyes, only to roll over on the creaky bed and stare at the wall, letting the growing dark void envelope me. Eventually, I find my way into a fitful sleep that leaves me tangled in the thin sheets. There is a smell coming from the other side of the room, most likely a meal. I roll back over and stare at the ceiling, not moving from the bed. My door opens and light streams in. I blink against it and roll over, facing the wall again.

“732, you can’t stay in bed all day,” Jackson’s southern accent sounds from the doorway.

I roll over so I’m facing the wall, tugging the blanket further up my body.

He sighs before I hear a scraping sound and footsteps that follow. There is creaking at the end of my bed as Jackson sits down. “You can’t starve yourself, either,” he says softly.

The smells are stronger as he brings the food closer to me. “I don’t care anymore,” I mumble into the sheets I’ve pulled up to my chin.

Jackson puts a gentle hand on my shoulder, turning me to face him. "You're not going to just give up," he says.

*Why do you care?* I think, but I don't have the energy to say the words. I just blink and turn back to the wall.

"Want to know how I know? Because you're a fighter. You always have been. You may not care right now, but I care that you aren't keeping up your strength. Eventually, you'll find the will to start fighting again," he continues. "But right now, I need you to be strong for the tests we are going to be running, okay? So work with me on this."

"Why kill him instead of me?" I whisper. "Why not test and study his magic, his useful magic, instead of trying to study my destructive power?"

Jackson is silent.

"He could heal, he told me. Imagine the people you could have helped, the good you could have done. But you killed him and his magic. Yet you let mine, which has caused you so many problems, live," I go on, finally speaking the words that have been circling my head the past week.

"Who are you talking about, 732?" Jackson asks.

"54, my…54," I stutter out, squeezing my eyes shut to stop the tears.

"Robert Caulder killed him, 732," Jackson says quietly. "We didn't have a choice in the matter."

"Bullcrap," I say, finally sitting up. I reach for my magic tentatively, but it still strays away from me. "You all function the same, work together. He had orders not to kill me, but what about him?"

Jackson rubs his eyes and holds my gaze. "That was not my decision to make."

"What. About. Him?" I ask again. "I know you keep notes on us."

He puts the plate of food down in the middle of the bed. "I don't even know who you're talking about, 732. 54 was probably there for the same reasons you were," Jackson says. "If you to him there, that's fine. Is that why you're acting like this? All mopey and pathetic? Because Robert Caulder shot a friend you made last week?"

I glare at him, which seems to sap all my energy. "He was my brother," I whisper.

Jackson's face falls slightly. He doesn't respond for a while. Instead, he pushes the plate closer to me. "Eat," he says softly. "You're going to want it today."

I grit my teeth, no longer caring to hide the tears in my eyes, before grabbing the plate and shoving the now cold food into my mouth. Soon after I take the first bite, the numbness takes hold again, driving out all residue of anger. All that's left is the void. I finish the food and silently follow Jackson out of my room and back to the large testing area with the mirror on the wall. He quietly leads me back to the black pad with the wood lying on it. Jackson grabs the sensors that stick to my skin and walks towards me. He puts them on my chest and my temples; the same places as last time. When he steps back, the safety wall is lowered in place.

"732," Jackson says. "We're going to do the same thing we've been working on the past few days."

I nod and close my eyes, searching for my magic. Like this morning, and the days before, it hides. My magic withdraws so deep that I can hardly find it. I search, trying to envision the wood in front of me catching fire.

Nothing.

Nothing but the numbing darkness that surrounds me.

"I can't," I whisper, the two words quickly becoming the most used words in my vocabulary. "I can't find it." I don't have to open my eyes to know that Jackson is shaking his head and already has the wall rising.

"732, I need you to work with me," he says, closer to me.

I turn towards him, finally opening my eyes. "I'm trying. My magic… It's hiding."

Jackson sighs and rubs the back of his neck, looking towards the mirror.

*It's not a mirror,* I think. *It's two way glass. We're being watched.* Something about that breaks through the dark shroud. Someone is watching, recording, and analyzing everything that is happening. Every time I fail, someone is watching, as if I'm no more than a laboratory rat for them to mess with.

But, that's why I'm here, isn't it?

Jackson looks back to me. "We need to make some progress here, 732," he says. His voice is strained as if he is holding back some emotion. "And this obviously isn't working."

I just stare at him. *Lab rat.*

Jackson nods his head towards the padded table. "Please?" He asks. "I don't want to resort to manhandling you."

"I don't have a choice in this, do I?" I ask. My skin crawls at the realization. I never had a choice. It was always going to come to this. "Even if I say no, it's going to happen, isn't it?"

Jackson looks down for a moment. "Yes," he says, meeting my gaze. "It will."

I take in a deep breath and walk over to the table and sit. There are straps hooked to it. I swing my legs over and lie down. *Lab rat.* That's all I am anymore, a nameless number with a magic to study. A puzzle to figure out. I've become 2157732.

Jackson quietly fastens the straps around my ankles and my wrists, securing one over my head. By the time he's done, I can barely move. He disappears from my field of vision, only to return with that same small prod with the clear container on the back of it.

Illinois. State. 21.

"This may hurt," he says, flipping it on. A blue light shines from the side that's pointed towards me.

Normal. City. 57.

Jackson starts lowering the prod. My pulse quickens inside my chest and my magic swirls inside of me, being pulled by the blue light.

Adam Carlson. Name. 732.

The prod hits my chest and I scream as my magic is pulled out of me, ripping and tearing its way through me. The darkness that quickly pulls me under is a welcome relief that I gladly fall victim to.

# CHAPTER TWENTY FIVE

## ABBY

I sit with my back to the one way mirror, not wanting to see Adam passed out on the table, and face Jackson who is pacing the small room.

"What are you thinking about?" I ask. "Is it how he reacted to the prod?"

Jackson shakes his head. "I had a talk with 732 this morning," he starts. "I think I know why his magic is acting the way it is."

I cross my arms. "Why?"

"Does 732 have a brother registered at Rebren?" He asks, finally stopping his pacing and leaning up against the wall.

I tilt my head. "We try to keep family members separated," I state. "You know this."

Jackson looks to the side, tapping his fingers on his arm. "What if we made a mistake?"

"Our systems are too good," I say, shaking my head.

Jackson stares at Adam through the glass. He hasn't moved since passing out. Jackson left the Handler in there to monitor him.

"Can we check on a 54 who was registered to Robert Caulder?" Jackson asks.

I raise an eyebrow. "What is this about?"

"2157054. Please, just check."

"Jackson, that's Normal, Illinois." That's home.

"Abigail, please." His eyes lock on mine, pleading. "If I'm right, I know how to help get his magic to cooperate."

I hold his gaze, not wanting to believe him. If he's right… "Fine," I sigh. I cross the room and open my computer, facing Adam. Two clicks bring me to Rebrens registry. "What's the number again?"

Jackson puts a hand on the table, leaning over me. "2157054."

I type in the number, glancing up at Adam's form. The prod sits next to him with hardly any of his magic in the clear container. His magic is golden and swirls lazily in the jar.

The search loads and 54's profile pulls up. Jake Carlson stares at me with large, fearful eyes. The skin on his neck is red from the recent tattoo. My stomach drops and Jackson taps his fingers anxiously on the table. Scrolling down, I see his registry history. Jake was returned multiple times due to magic use. His final registry is to Robert Caulder. I glance up at Jackson.

"What did 732 tell you?" I ask slowly.

Jackson slides into a chair. "He said that Robert shot 54."

I lean back, wrapping my arms around myself. "Shot him?" I ask softly, glancing at Adam.

"Am I right? It's his brother?"

I nod. "That makes a lot of sense about his behavior."

Jake's dead.

"What do we do about it? How do we get his magic to react?" I ask Jackson.

He's sitting with his hand tucked gently under his chin, staring off into space. "We give him a reason to react. Pull him out of his spiral."

"You think he's in a spiral?" I ask. "He could just be depressed."

Jackson shakes his head, eyes focusing again. "He's spiraling, Ms. Sommerfeld. He asked me why Robert killed 54 and his 'useful magic and left his destructive one live'. That is the beginnings of a spiral."

I stare at Adam. He's starting to stir and the Handler stands up, motioning to the mirror. "How do we pull him out? We don't want to antagonize him and cause bigger problems for ourselves."

"I'll think of something. Give me the day."

I nod, closing out of Jakes profile. "You better get back to the Subject, Mr. Gravett. He's waking up."

Jackson slowly stands up. He taps his knuckles on the table a few times, staring into space again. "What would help you, Ms. Sommerfeld, if you watched your sister get shot?"

I shake my head. "I couldn't tell you. I honestly think I would need time."

Jackson nods. "Maybe that's what we give him. Time."

"Since when did we start caring about the Subjects mental health, Mr. Gravett?" I ask.

"Since the Subjects mental health started interfering with our tests, Ms. Sommerfeld." Jackson gaze is hard.

I sit forward in my chair. "Then you better fix this, Jackson. He's our best Subject. His magic is the strongest we've encountered. We *need* these results."

Adam groans and Jackson's eyes fly to him. "I will, Abigail," he says and walks out.

I sigh, resting my head in my hands. Jake is dead and Adam is grieving. His magic is unresponsive due to his emotional state.

"Welcome back to the land of the living," Jackson says as Adam sits up.

"You mean that thing didn't kill me?" he rasps.

Jackson chuckles. "And rid us of your sunny personality?"

Adam seems to recoil at the comment. "What's next?" He mutters.

"We try again."

His shoulders slump forward and he nods.

I tug on my hair, brushing it backwards. For all we know, this could kill him. We don't know enough about the prototype to fully understand its effects on the Subject's body. All we know is that the Subject has to be awake in order for it to draw out magic. And Adam is in no condition for us to be using it. His body is still too weak. Bruises still litter his face and I can tell the scabs on his back are fragile. Blood dots the back of his shirt. I sigh and reach for the speaker.

"Mr. Gravett, that's enough for today," I say.

Jackson glances at the mirror and nods. Adam, thankfully, doesn't recognize my voice. He simply slides off the table and walks to the door, waiting for the Handler to lead him back to his rooms.

"Make sure that 732 gets plenty of rest and food. He needs to keep up his strength," I say.

"Yes, Ma'am," Jackson says, placing a hand on Adam's shoulder. The Handler unlocks the door and Adam follows him out. Jackson cleans up before joining me again.

"Since when do we care about the Subject's mental health, Ms. Sommerfeld?" Jackson asks, mocking me.

I sigh, rubbing my temples. "That prototype could very well kill him, Jackson," I groan. "What are we doing?"

Jackson sits down. "Maybe we let him rest. Give him some chores to do while he recovers from his many injuries and let us figure out how to pull him out of the spiral."

I nod. "Maybe you're right. Maybe we should care about the Subject's mental health," I whisper.

Jackson is silent.

"Maybe we screw it for now. Have him work for us and when he acts up, send him back here for a week until he shapes up again," I ramble.

"If we need to, that might work," Jackson says.

"Don't tell me you're considering that."

He shakes his head. "Not seriously. Not yet. Let's see where he's at tomorrow, then assess."

I nod, gathering my things up. My phone started to ring. "Let me know if you have any other ideas."

"Of course."

I walk out, raising the phone to my ear as I quietly shut the door. "Mayor Greenbrough, thank you for calling. I have a proposal for you…"

# CHAPTER TWENTY SIX

## JAKE

"Good morning, Mrs. Harrison," a tall man covered in ink says as we walk up to the brick building. "I never thought I'd see the day when you'd make an appointment."

Maria smiles and pats the man's arm. "It's not for me, Henry. It's for my new friend, Jake." She turns around and motions me forward.

With my hands stuffed in my pockets, I step up next to her. I stand a few inches taller than her. Henry offers his hand to me. "Nice to meet you. I'm Henry Rholan, the *finest* tattoo artist in town."

I shake his hand. "Jake Harrison. Nice to meet you," I say, using Maria's last name just as she told me to this morning.

"Come on in, you two! What can I do for you?"

Maria walks into the building. "Jake needs a tattoo. A very *special* tattoo."

Henry raises an eyebrow. "Special?" He turns to me. "What do you have in mind?"

"Can we talk in a more private area, Henry?" Maria asks, eyeing the other customers.

Henry smiles. "Of course. I've got a private room back here." He leads us past three different people getting various tattoos. One woman is getting a large image on the back of her calf. Another man is getting something done on his shoulder. A third woman is getting what looks like a paragraph tattooed on her forearm. She smiles at me as I pass. I feel my face get hot and I look at my feet.

"Alright, what can I do for you, Jake?" Henry asks as he shuts the door.

I glance at Maria. She nods encouragingly. I unzip the jacket and pull down the collar, exposing my Mark. Henry blinks a few times, nodding.

"A very special tattoo indeed," he whispers. "Maria, I've always trusted you, and I'm sure this is your way of returning that trust, but what you're asking me to do is criminal. I hope you realize this."

"I understand. And I know you feel the same way about this that I do," Maria says.

Henry sighs loudly before grabbing a binder off a table. "Sit here in this chair, Jake," he says, patting the large black chair.

I slowly make my way over and slide into the chair. Henry sets the binder in my lap and flips over to a few pictures in sheet protectors. "Do you have any specific design you want?" he asks me.

"No, sir," I say quietly.

Henry rolls over to me in his own chair. He flips a couple of pages before tapping a picture. "What about this one?"

The image is of a large dragon clawing its way up the side of someone's leg. I quickly shake my head 'no.'

Henry smiles. "I didn't think so. You don't look like the figurative type. How about this one?" he flips a few more pages and taps at a few different skull designs.

I raise one eyebrow and look at him. "Not the figurative type, but the edgy type?" I ask.

This earns a laugh. "I'm just offering! You could be the type for a skull and I'd never know!" He flips a few more pages and lands on a few images of different flowers. "How about these?"

I look closer at the images and nod. "Can you do a mix of them?"

"Sure can. Which ones do you like?"

I point to a few of the designs. Henry makes note of them and moves the binder back to the table. "How big, or do I get liberty in that?"

"Big enough to not look suspicious," I say, feeling giddy.

"You got it, boss."

* * *

I examine the large floral picture on my neck in the bathroom. Henry started low on my arm, pulling the picture up my shoulder and onto my neck. He covered my Mark with a large leaf attached to a tulip. He covered the whole tattoo in a lotion and put plastic wrap over it. My magic swirls happily, finally being used without being locked up. The skin around the tattoo should be red and angry, but is instead a healthy color as if the tattoo has been there for years.

"Jake, honey," Maria calls from the bottom of the stairs.

"Yes, ma'am?" I call back.

"Brad and Kate invited us for dinner!"

I tear my eyes away from my neck and peek out the door. "Tonight?" I ask.

"Yes! In about thirty minutes."

My heart pounds. Thirty minutes…? We just got back from the parlor. I can't prepare something that fast. "Oh, okay, um…I can make a… something," I stutter out, running downstairs. "A salad or a…salad."

Maria stops me with a hand on my shoulder. “You don’t need to prepare anything. They invited us. And told us specifically not to bring anything,” she says with a smile.

“Oh,” I say. *What?*

“Go get your shoes and we’ll get going,” she says, gathering her white purse and her shoes.

I grab my new black shoes—Maria threw everything from Rebren out that first night—from the front door closet and find Maria waiting by the garage door. I follow her to the car and slowly climb into the passenger seat. Even after getting into this car multiple times over the past couple of days, it still feels strange to sit normally in a car. In a normal seat with a regular seatbelt. No chains and benches.

We travel to Brad’s house along the same road we took when I first got here. Past all the houses and the little shops. It’s not a long drive and Maria always puts on soft music.

Brad's house looks different in the daytime than it does in the dark. The yard looks full of life and there is commotion going on inside the house. There are new sidewalk chalk drawings this time. We pass one of a dragon and one of a star on our way to the door. I’m careful not to step on them as I pass.

When the door opens, smells drift out immediately. Spices and the smell of homemade dessert. Hesitantly, I follow Maria into the house.

“We’re here!” Maria calls as she puts her shoes in the closet.

“Grandma Mia!” A young boy with dark curls shouts. I hear little feet on wood as the boy runs to Maria.

“Hello, little Gavin!” Maria says and picks him up.

I quietly close the door and remove my shoes, setting them in the same closet as Maria’s.

Brad comes around the corner and smiles. “Mom! Thanks for coming!” he says and gives her a hug.

“I wouldn’t miss it, honey,” she says.

Brad waves her in. “Don’t be a stranger. Kate’s in the kitchen,” he says. He looks at me. “Jake! Good to see you again! How are you doing?” He asks. He sticks out his hand for me to shake. “I like the new addition.”

I smile and take his hand. “Thank you. I’m doing well, sir,” I say.

His smile widens. “That’s great to hear. How are you adjusting?”

I shrug. “I think I’m doing alright,” I say. “It’s strange to wake up in my own room, that’s for sure.” I feel my smile soften slightly at the words.

Brad doesn’t seem to know how to respond. After a moment, he says “I’m sure it’s quieter?” he asks.

I chuckle. “In a way,” I say quietly. I take a deep breath. “What is for dinner?” I ask, moving away from Rebren and Caulders.

Brad blinks and leads me to the dining room where I first met Maria. “We are having true southern fried chicken dinner tonight. You are in for a treat!” he says.

The dining room has a large wooden table in the middle of it, right under the beautiful chandelier. Maria is already sitting there with Gavin and a little girl with wispy blonde hair squeezed on either side of her. A woman with dark hair in a blue shirt sets a pot of potatoes on the table. She smiles when we enter.

“Welcome! You must be Jake,” she says.

I nod. “I am, ma’am,” I say, extending my hand. She shakes it.

“It’s wonderful to meet you,” she says. “I’m Kate, Brad’s wife.”

“It’s nice to meet you, Kate,” I say.

Brad walks around and puts an arm around Kate’s shoulder. “Please, have a seat,” he says. He pulls out a chair for Kate and she sits down with a smile. I slide into one of the chairs across from Maria. Brad sits across from Kate. The little girl runs over and sits next to me.

“Hi,” the little girl says in a breathy voice.

I smile at her. “Hi,” I say back. “What’s your name?”

"Maisley," she says sweetly.

"It's very nice to meet you, Maisley," I say. "I saw your chalk drawings outside. They are very nice."

She smiles and hides her face in her hands.

The smells wafting up from the table are heavenly. There is chicken on one side of the table and a pot of potatoes sits on the other. Gravy and mixed vegetables are scattered around the table. My mouth waters at the sight and smell.

Brad leans forward. "Welcome to dinner, everyone," he says. "Let's dig in!"

Kate puts some cut up chicken onto Maisleys plate and a smaller piece of chicken onto Gavin's. I slowly grab a chicken and spoon some potatoes onto my plate. I almost don't know what to do with it all, there is so much food. All home cooked. Not the steamed and nearly inedible food we were fed in Rebren. I almost cried at the first bite. The chicken melts in my mouth and the potatoes and gravy have so much flavor, it's nearly enough to overwhelm me. So much better than the sandwich I had at lunch, which I thought was the best thing I had eaten, Maria and I got for lunch while we were shopping. I press the back of my hand to my eyes. When I pull it away, it's wet.

"Jake, are you alright?" Maria asks softly.

"It's really good," I choke out.

Maisley hands me a napkin, setting it on my arm. I smile and take it, quickly wiping away the tears. The rest of my food is quickly eaten and I go back for seconds.

# CHAPTER TWENTY SEVEN

## 732

I stand in the middle of the testing room a week after the disaster with the magic-sucking-prod. Jackson is typing furiously on his computer and the Handler is lounging in his regular chair by the door with his arms crossed and legs extended.

"Are we going to do anything today, Jackson?" I ask softly.

"In a moment," he says, staring at his computer.

I sighed and walked over to the table. Will I be back here or on the mat today? I run my fingers along the edge of the padding and look at the one way glass. My bruises have faded and are hardly visible anymore and my hair is growing out. I walk closer to the glass. "Are you watching me?" I whisper.

There is no response from the woman on the speaker.

"I know you're watching me. What do you want from me?"

"732, who are you talking to?" Jackson asks.

I turn away from the glass. “I know there’s someone watching me behind the glass.”

Jackson finally looks up from his screen.

“What is so important about my magic that you need to study it?” I ask.

He leans against the desk. “We want to understand how it works. What makes you think your magic is the only type of magic we study?”

I cross my arms. “Before I was sold to Caulders, I was told that my magic is different than most you’ve seen.”

Jackson nods and pushes away from his computer. “You’ve got a point,” he says. “Yours is different and we haven’t seen anything like it. However, we have seen something close to it.” He pushes open the door. “Handler Ian, please bring in 1113.”

I step forward. “1113? Another Worker?”

Jackson steps aside to let in the Handler and a young boy in dull Rebren clothing. The skin on his neck is red and irritated around his Mark. His blonde hair is disheveled and sticking up in places. He’s shaking as he steps into the room.

“What are you doing, Jackson?” I ask, feeling glued in place.

He shrugs. “We want to understand what makes your magic so different. Young 1113 here had an incident similar to yours when his magic manifested.”

I shake my head 'no'.

"We're going to figure it out, 732, with your magic or his."

The dark void cracks open and I march forward, putting myself between 1113 and Jackson.

"Don't touch him," I growl. "You want my magic? Fine. Take it."

A smirk plays at Jackson's lips. "Get on the mat, then."

"What are you going to do with 1113?" I ask.

"He'll stay here. If this doesn't work, he's our next best option."

"It'll work." I turn and walk onto the mat. The same woodpile is there, taunting me. I feel my magic finally start to stir under my skin. *There you are.*

Jackson attaches the sensors to my temples and chest. "You're sure you can do it this time?"

"Are you going to keep asking me the same questions or are you going to shut up and lower the glass?" I ask.

He raises an eyebrow. "I know Robert Caulder didn't allow you to speak to him like that," he says.

"Robert Caulder didn't allow a lot of things, yet I did them anyway," I snap.

With a shocked expression, he walks away, lowering the protective glass. Back in a cage. I see 1113 staring at me. He must have just come from being tested for magic. He stands against the wall behind Jackson. His Handler, Ian, sits in the chair next to my Handler.

"Whenever you're ready, 732," Jackson says.

I flex my fingers and face the wood pile. My magic swirls faster under my skin. *Finally.* I close my eyes and focus on the swirling. My pendant gets warm. My fingers twitch and I can feel my magic gathering and seeping out. Opening my eyes, flick my fingers towards the wood. It starts smoking. I try again, breathing deeply. The logs shift. I try one final time, thrusting a large chunk of magic at the pile. It erupts with a crack and I jump back.

I hear slow clapping and I turn. Jackson is applauding me with a smile on his face. The glass starts to rise. "I knew you had it in you," he says.

"Did you get what you needed?" I ask, out of breath.

"Mostly. There's a few different tests I want to run, but this is a start," he says.

I furrow my eyebrows. "What other tests?"

Jackson waves me forward. "Have you ever had a check up where the doctor will put force on a limb and ask you to try and not let them press down?"

"Once, yeah. When I dislocated my shoulder at fourteen."

"It's like that, but with magic. Hold out your wrists."

I do and Jackson locks thick shackles onto them. 1113 eyes go wide and he seems like he's trying to melt into the wall. I don't know what to say to reassure him, so I simply stay quiet.

"Go back on the mat and try to push your magic out."

"Out," I repeat. "Out where?"

Jackson shrugs. "You figure that out. Just get it past the cuffs."

My magic swirls angrily under my skin. "Y'know, it doesn't like being locked up," I call to Jackson as I make my way back to the middle of the mat.

"What doesn't?"

"My magic."

He gives me a strange look as the glass is lowered again. "Whenever you're ready, 732."

I breathe deeply, and close my eyes. *Look, I hate it too. So let's get these things off.* My magic almost seems to respond to my thoughts. It swirls more furiously and I try to push it past the cuffs. The cuffs are a stronger version of the silver chain. I made it past that, I can make it past this. I push harder. My pendant grows warmer. I grit my teeth as my magic slams against the cuffs over and over again. The cuffs start to grow warm. I let out a shout as my magic explodes out of me. A loud crack sounds and the cuffs fall from my wrists. I collapse to my knees, gasping for air.

"That's enough for today," the woman's voice says over the speakers again.

I look up at Jackson. He nods and raises the glass.

"Well done, 732. That was impressive," he says, crouching down next to me. He removes the sensors and then helps me to my feet. "Handler Daniels will take you to your new room. From now on, you'll be sharing with 1113."

"Don't you think that's a bad idea?" I ask.

Jackson frowns. "Why do you say that?"

"Because I'm a bad influence on others. He's going to learn rebellion before he learns any of Rebren's rules."

Jackson chuckles. "732, we aren't worried about rebellion here. We use it to our advantage. The more riled up you are, the easier it is to test your magic."

My stomach drops and I push away from him. "You tricked me into using my magic?" I ask.

Jackson sticks his hands in his pockets. "It worked, didn't it?"

"You *manipulated* me and *traumatized* him! Look at him!" I gesture to 1113, trembling by the wall. "He can barely stand because he's so scared! How can you think this is even close to ethical?"

Jackson glances at the blonde boy pressed up against the wall. "It keeps you in line," is all he says.

"Keeps us in line?" I laugh. "You're sick, you know that? Twisted and sick." I stomp past Jackson and towards 1113.

"P, please don't, don't hurt m, me," he whispers, tears springing to his eyes.

"I'm not going to hurt you," I promise. "Let's get out of here, yeah?"

The boy nods.

I put an arm around his shoulders and gently guide him to the door. Daniels pushes the door open and leads us to a new room on the other end of the building. This room has two rickety beds and is slightly bigger than my old one. 1113 walks in first and I follow. Daniels locks the deadbolt behind us.

I turn towards 1113. "We're going to get out of here. I promise," I tell him. "Where are you from?"

"B, Bardstown, Kentucky," he whispers.

"I'm from Normal, Illinois." I pause. "Did they bring you straight here?"

The boy nods.

"How many days of travel?"

"Just one, I th, think. We drove for a long time." His shoulders are hunched and he's glancing around the room, noting each piece of furniture and the lack of windows.

I sigh and run a hand over my face, sinking into one of the beds. It creaks. "They brought you here specifically to push me," I whisper. "I'm so sorry."

"Why are they calling us numbers?" He whispers.

I look up at him. His tears have left trails on his dirty face, making his blue eyes stand out. "To make us think like them. To make us feel less than human," I sigh.

"What do I call you, then?"

"732," I say softly. "Sit down, 1113. The bed won't eat you. We're safe here."

The bed creaks as he sits down, perched on the edge. "They don't come in here?"

I shake my head 'no'. "Some kind of unspoken rule. They don't come into our rooms or the Shed. Our sleeping quarters are ours."

"What's the Shed?" he asks.

I lean up against the wall, pulling my feet onto the bed. "When you're sold to work in a house, they keep us in what's called a Shed. It sounds like exactly what it is: A large, insulated shed with plumbing and a bed. It keeps us out of the way when we're not working."

"I thought this place was supposed to teach us about controlling our magic?" 1113 asks.

I shake my head and close my eyes, resting my head against the concrete wall. "Nope. They're a bunch of liars."

1113 is silent.

"They'll bring us dinner soon," I say after a long stretch of silence. "I think they forget about us sometimes, so it takes a while."

The bed creaks as 1113 shifts. "How long have you been here?"

I run a hand through my choppy hair. "I've been at Rebren for around four years. The Lab…" I trail off. Most of my time here is foggy and meshes together. "Too long."

"How long will I be here?"

I don't answer, feeling that pit in my stomach open up again.

"732?" he asks tentatively.

I crack an eye open. He's staring at me, completely frozen in place.

"How long will I be here?" His voice is shaky and tears wait to fall.

"I don't know," I whisper.

The first tears fall and he takes a shaky breath in. "Why don't you know?"

I chew on the inside of my lip. "The Lab is where they send Workers like me: stubborn, trouble makers who refuse to listen to anybody. They usually don't send newbies here."

He takes a deep breath. "I want to go home," he whispers.

"Me too, 1113. Me too."

1113 stays silent, and I hear his bed creak. A minute later, quiet sniffles come from his side of the room. There's nothing I can say or do to make him feel any better or any less scared than he already is, so I stay silent. My magic swirls uncomfortably under my skin, wanting to escape. 1113 will eventually become one more casualty in my growing list. I lay down and let the numbness crawl over me until it occupies every spare crevice it can fill, dragging me back down into the void.

At least until dinner comes.

# CHAPTER TWENTY EIGHT

# ABBY

I pace back and forth in the small observing room. "I think it went well, all things considered," Jackson says from his seat at the table.

I nod. "Bringing in 1113 did provoke a reaction, and his magic woke up."

"Why are you pacing, Abigail?"

I shake my head. "1113 is brand new. We could easily sell him. Why'd you choose him instead of someone we can spare? He's also *young*. He could get hurt. We still don't know how unpredictable 732's magic is going to be now that he's using it daily."

Jackson leans forward in his chair. "I chose him for two reasons. One is that if 732 didn't shape up, we can use his magic for testing until 732 snaps out of it. The second is that 732 needs someone to protect. If I brought in someone his own age or older it wouldn't have the same effect. He'd withdraw more. 732 has a sense of protection. I read what Richard put in his notes last time he was returned. Did you see that?"

I shake my head. “Richard is a Handler, not a buyer.”

Jackson leans back. “He spent the most time with 732 and saw something worth reporting. Read it.”

With a sigh, I pull up Adam’s chart again and scroll down to the notes. True to Jackson’s word, there is a note from Nate Richard.

*Stubborn and can’t seem to keep his mouth shut. Thinks he can do what he wants when he wants. Protective and will do anything to fight what he deems as unjust. Needs a firm hold and a thick chain. Will probably get himself killed for doing something stupid one day, or by pissing off the right person.*

I shake my head. “So you chose a sixteen year old we tested yesterday?”

Jackson nods. “Again, it worked.”

“So what do we do with 1113 now? Just leave him in his room when 732 is being tested?”

Jackson shakes his head. “No, that’s counterproductive. The Subject needs to see 1113. The boy being there means 732 will be feeling something other than depression, which will keep him from spiraling.”

I nod, finally understanding.

Jackson leans back in the chair. “And, if he stops cooperating, we use 1113 for our tests. That’s bound to pull him out of a spiral.”

I stare at him, eyes wide. "Human leverage?"

Jackson meets my eyes. "Isn't that what we've already done today?" he asks softly.

"You didn't touch the boy, though, Jackson. That's the difference."

"We're drawing lines in our morals even though we've gone far past already by working at this institution?" Jackson leans forward.

I run a hand through my hair. "We're *not* touching that boy."

"But touching 732 is okay?"

"732 has brought this upon himself!" I shout, feeling my heart pound within my chest. "He has had *years* to shape up, but has chosen not to. 1113 turned sixteen yesterday. He has done *nothing* to be here." Tears prick my eyes and I sink down into a chair, putting a hand to my eyes.

"Abigail," Jackson starts softly. "I know you don't believe a word of what you just said about 732."

I shake my head. "I have to," I whisper.

"Why?"

Despite my best efforts, tears started to run down my cheeks. "Because it would make my job *so much* easier if I did."

Jackson is silent. "I see how you get nervous every morning in debrief, and how you've asked about him more than the others we've worked on. I hear it in your voice when you tell me to stop for the day. Abigail, it's not hard to recognize that you know him."

I drop my hand and look at him. "He's my Subject," I state. "He has to stay my Subject."

Jackson shakes his head. "But he's not *just* your Subject, is he? He's your friend."

A small sob escapes my chest. "One of my best friends," I choke out.

Jackson stares at me, waiting.

I shake my head and wipe my eyes. "We will discuss this further tomorrow," I say, shoving the emotion back inside its box. At least until I get home. "Until then, 1113 is not to be touched."

Jackson nods. "Understood, Ms. Sommerfeld. Have a good night."

I gather my things. "You as well, Mr. Gravett." Nobody talks to me on my way back to my car. The drive home isn't long. Fifteen minutes through the city. It's after the evening rush and the streets are generally quiet. However, I'm not going to my apartment just yet. At the grocery store, I turn left towards the college and park in the visitor parking of Colton's complex. Months ago, I used to drive this route every day. This is my first time in three months coming to see him. Leaving my files in the car, I grab my purse and head into the mens housing. As always, there was a strange smell in the lobby. I pass a couple making out on the couch on my way to the stairs. Colton lives on the third floor. Taking the elevator would be longer, and would undoubtedly have more than a few drunk students in it.

"Abby?" Colton asks as he answers the door. I hesitantly smile.

"Hey, Colt. Have some time to talk?"

Colton glances into his apartment, exposing the new scar that runs from his ear to his collar bone to me. "Zach is here, hope you don't mind," he says.

"Is that a girl?" Zach asks.

"Not what you think, Z," Colton responds, rolling his eyes.

"She pretty?"

"Gross," Colton mutters, rolling his eyes. "Give me a minute." He shuts the door, leaving me outside. A minute later the door opens again and Colton steps out, shoes and jacket on.

I smile at him. "I know I didn't text before. I just got off."

Colton shrugs, shoving his hands in his jacket pockets. He walks with a slight limp to the stairs.

"We can take the elevator," I say.

Colton raises his eyebrows. "What about the 'stinky college boys'?"

I smile. "I took it on my way up," I lie. "There wasn't anyone in it."

Colton shrugs again and presses the down button. "So why stop by?"

I sigh. "It's work," I start. This earns me one of Colton's signature 'looks'. For this look, he's got one eyebrow raised and a nearly blank stare with just enough judgment behind it to make you rethink everything you're about to say.

"Work that is relevant to both of us?" he asks.

I nod. "I was assigned a new project a couple of weeks ago and… I don't know if I can do this one, Colt," I say as we step into the surprisingly empty elevator.

Colton presses floor 1. "You don't know if you can keep experimenting on people, you mean."

"You should understand the reason why I do it, Colton. I took the job because, maybe there would be something that could've helped…" I stop at the second look of the night. Colton's jaw is clenched and his eyes are hard. "This project is different," I say instead.

"How?"

"Because it's Adam, this time."

Colton simply stares at the door, unmoving, which tells me enough. The door sliding open shakes him from his expressionless state as he coldly makes his way to the front of the building. He almost doesn't seem to see the couple on the couch as he shoves the front door open.

"Colton," I say softly, catching up to him. "Say something."

He turns on his good heel, facing me. "You're experimenting on my best friend, Abby. What do you want me to say?"

"Are you forgetting that we were close, too?"

"Then quit." He turns around and keeps walking down the sidewalk.

"And leave him there in the hands of someone else?" I jog after him. "What would you do?"

Colton simply keeps walking.

"I need your help," I say, my voice breaking.

He turns and I see his signature stern expression. "With what, Abby? An experiment on him?"

I shake my head. "I want to get him out." Colton pauses. "I've got a place he can stay with someone who will take care of him. But I can't get him out alone."

He stares at me with a similar look he had in the elevator. “Break him out?”

Tears spring to my eyes. “I can’t do it anymore, Colt,” I whisper.

Sighing, Colton limps over to me. He pulls me into a tight hug, almost like the ones he gave me before his accident. I melt into his embrace, letting the tears fall onto his brown jacket.

“What do you need me to do?”

# CHAPTER TWENTY NINE

## JAKE

"What can I get started for you today, sir?" the young woman in a red uniform across the counter asks, startling me. Brad gently nudges me forward. I had told him I wanted to try this on my own. I stumble towards the counter, feeling my heart pound in my chest.

"What, what's good to get here?" I ask, glancing up at the menu above her head.

She nearly laughs, looking down at her computer. "At Wendy's?" I can hear the judgment in her voice.

My cheeks burn and I scratch the back of my neck. "I don't usually come here," I mumble.

"Our burgers are most popular," she says, composing herself.

I glance at the menu again. *Why are there so many options?* "Um…"

"Do you like bacon?" A young woman with blonde hair asks next to me.

My mouth moves open and closed like a fish gasping for air. "Yes, yes," I stutter out, blinking and trying to get a grip on reality.

The young woman nods to the menu, her blue eyes scanning back and forth. "Their number one is good."

I smile and nod my thanks, repeating that to the woman behind the counter. She taps a few things on her screen before asking, "and for your drink?" This time, she taps the machine next to her. There are stickers of different soda brands on the top.

"Uh…"

The blonde woman leans over. "Do you like caffeine?" she whispers.

I shake my head 'no'.

She smiles softly. "Their lemonade isn't bad. Give that a shot," she says and continues ordering her meal.

I order a lemonade and get out the credit card Brad gave me.

"Any sauces?" the woman behind the counter asks.

*Why are you still asking me questions? I just want to pay and leave.* "Ketchup please," I mumble.

"$11.86 is your total."

I tap the card against the machine in front of me. It doesn't do anything.

"You have to swipe it," the woman says, setting my drink next to the machine with the sauces next to it.

My cheeks burn hotter and I swipe the card. The machine beeps and I almost sigh in relief when the woman hands me a receipt and says "have a nice day."

I grab the small paper and walk to the side, meeting Brad by the utensils.

"You did great," he says.

I rub the back of my neck again, looking at my feet. "I forgot how to order food," I mumble. "It's a simple task; how could I forget that?"

Brad puts a hand on my shoulder. "How long have you been gone?"

"Six years," I admit.

"And you went through a lot. It's okay that you've got to relearn a few things. No big deal. We'll work through it." He looks around, leading us to a table. "Who was that blonde woman you were talking to?"

I look around, spotting her sitting with a couple of other young women, laughing. "I'm not sure. She was kind, though."

Brad nudges me as we sit down. “You should talk to her. Ask her out. It’ll help you practice talking to people and get a date!”

I chuckle, shaking my head. “I don’t know if she’ll want to go out with me…” I glance down at my hands. “I’m not what she is probably expecting.”

Brad places a hand on my arm. “She could surprise you.”

“Order 54?”

I tense up, looking around. Brad furrows his eyebrows and glances around as well. “Jake, are you okay?”

“Order number 55?”

Brad looks at his receipt, and then at mine. “Your order number is 55. Your food is ready,” he says, explaining.

I take a deep breath and nod. “Right. I knew that. I’ll be back.” I stand up and walk to the counter, looking at my feet.

“What number?” A young man asks on the other side of the counter.

“54, uh, no 55,” I stutter, looking at my receipt again. “55.”

The young man slides a tray of food forward and I grab it. I turned and immediately ran into someone. We both drop our trays, scattering fries and burgers across the floor.

"Oh my goodness! I'm so sorry!" the young blonde woman says, bending down to pick up the scattered food.

I bend down as well, scooping fries and the wrapped burgers onto the trays. "I'm sorry," I say. "I didn't see you. I'm sorry."

She laughs, standing up and brushing a strand of hair behind her ear. "You're okay. It was an accident. We both caused it."

"Can I get you a replacement meal?" I ask, looking down at our trays of ruined food.

She smiles. "Do you think they'll replace it for us?" She glances at the people working at the grill. The young woman walks up to the counter and gets the attention of the young man. "Excuse me, can you help us?"

"Of course," the young man says. "What can I do for you?"

She gestures to the trays. "We had an accident. Is there any way we can get replacements for our meals?"

The young man nods. "What were your order numbers?"

The young woman looks at me first with a smile. I look at the receipt still clutched in my hand. "55," I whisper.

"54," she says. The number doesn't sound harsh coming from her. It doesn't carry the weight of the past six years. It sounds soft and gentle.

The young man hands us our replacement food and we discard our old trays. "We were supposed to meet today, apparently," the woman says.

I chuckle. "Apparently."

She extends a hand, balancing the tray on her arm. "Sara Newman."

I shake her hand, holding my tray close to my body. "Jake Harrison." I pause. "Can I buy you lunch one day? Saturday?"

Sara pauses, smiling brightly. "I'd like that. Here," she pulls a pen from her purse, setting the tray on the utensils counter and grabs a napkin. She quickly scrawls a short string of numbers on it and hands it to me. "Does around 11 work?"

I nod. "It does."

Sara smiles again. "Great. I'll see you soon, Jake Harrison," she says as she walks away, grabbing her tray of food and rejoins her friends.

# CHAPTER THIRTY

## 732

"732, really?" Jackson asks as I lean against the wall with my arms crossed. "We have work we need to get done today."

"Correction," I start. "*You* have work you need to get done today. *I* don't have to do anything besides stay alive." 1113 sits on the floor on the other end of the room, watching us with wide eyes. The past couple of days, he's taken to finding a corner where he can watch but stay mostly out of sight.

Jackson rubs his eyes. "My work cannot be done without you," he grumbles.

"You said it yourself, the more riled up I am, the easier I am to test. Here's your wish, Jackson."

"This isn't riled up. This is being stubborn. There's a difference," he says, walking towards his computer. "I need you to cooperate, 732. We're making great progress on your magic. We can't stop now!"

"Tell me why you're so interested in it, and then I'll decide if I want to continue," I say, propping my foot up on the wall.

"That is not information you are entitled to." He starts walking towards the table and my heart starts to pound.

"Because I'm just your supplier?" I ask, my voice shaking.

"Because you're barely human!" Jackson barks, turning around to face me.

I clench my jaw. *Lab rat. Only a number*. "Look me in the eyes when you say it, coward," I hiss, glowering.

Jackson slowly steps closer. "2157732. Laboratory rat of the year. Hardly a thing, not enough to call human." He takes another step. "Explosive and dangerous, can't be trusted around civilians." Another step. "Rabid like a *dog*, needs to be kept under lock and key at all times." Another step. He's almost on top of me. "An object."

I glower at him, anger rising like a bubbling pot of magma inside my chest, replacing the fear.

Jackson sees the conflicting emotions and nods. "Get on the table, 732. We have work to do."

My whole body shakes. "Why?" I whisper. "Why not the mat today?"

"I need a sample of your magic. That's the only way to get one."

I glance at the table and the horrifying three-fingered prod lying on top of it.

"I could always ask 1113 for his help," Jackson says, glancing at the boy in the corner.

I shake my head. "Leave him out of this. I'll get on the table and give you your sample."

Jackson steps back, letting me shakily make my way towards the table. 1113 sits up straighter.

"732?" he asks softly.

"I'm fine, 1113. Whatever happens, stay there, okay?" I say, sitting on the table.

The boy nods.

I smile at him as I remove my shirt, exposing the remaining bruises and scars. I lay back and let Jackson secure straps around my wrists and ankles. The one on my head pulls at my hair and I wince.

"Want a countdown?" Jackson asks, grabbing the prod.

"Just collect your sample," I say, clenching my hands into fists to hide the shaking.

An electric hum fills the air as the prod is turned on. I close my eyes and focus on my breathing. In, hold. Out, hold. In, hold. Out-

Everything burns. My magic swirls in a crazed frenzy, trying to escape the pull of the prod. My eyes snap open and my body convulses. I gasp. My scream sounds muffled by the pounding in my head. Everything feels like it's being lit on fire. Black swims at the edge of my vision.

"Stay with me a little longer, 732," Jackson says. His voice somehow cuts through the pounding in my head.

I cry out, feeling my magic being torn out of me.

Finally, the hum leaves the air. Jackson removes the prod and releases the strap on my head. I close my eyes and focus on breathing.

"You did great," he says gently.

"For a lab rat?" I rasp as I catch my breath.

Jackson pats my shoulder. "I needed you awake for this, and there was one way to make sure you stay awake."

I crack my eyes open. "What do you mean?"

Jackson smiles kindly at me. "Trust me, I don't believe those things I said, 732."

"Jerk," I say.

He chuckles and releases my wrists and ankles. "Luckily, that's all I need today."

I sigh and relax, letting my head roll to the side.

"Rest here, then we'll get you back to your room," he says.

I nod, breathing deeply. My magic swirls angrily, pulsing under my skin, causing it to burn.

"Are you okay?" 1113's hesitant voice asks.

Groaning, I push myself up.

"Whoa," Jackson says, immediately running to catch me as I stumble off the table. He steadies me with a hand on my back and chest.

"I'm fine," I whisper. "Just need to get moving, then I'll be okay."

1113 grabs my arm and puts it ovcr his shoulder. "I can get him there," the boy says to Jackson.

"Daniels, help him. He looks like he's going to collapse carrying 732."

My Handler stands up and walks towards where 1113 and I stand. I lean on 1113 and straighten up. "We're fine," I say.

The Handler stares at us. He looks at Jackson who shrugs. "Just make sure they get there," he says, unscrewing the jar from the prod.

1113 and I slowly start to make our way towards the door, one shuffling step after the other. Daniels walks closely behind us all the way to our shared room. Daniels opens the door and waits for us to get into the room before closing it, throwing the deadbolt.

1113 helps me sit down on my creaky bed.

"What was that, 732?" he asks me as he sits on his bed.

I lean against the wall, letting out a long breath. "Another test," I whisper.

"This was different than the other tests, though," he states.

I shake my head. "Still a test. Jackson wanted a sample of my magic. They've gathered one before, but it was a different method. They both suck."

"Will they do that to me?" 1113's voice is soft, barely audible.

A pit forms in my stomach. 1113 is here *because* of his magic, whatever it is. Because it's similar to mine. "I won't let that happen," I say and push myself up. My limbs protest and my magic flares.

"How?" He has tears in his eyes and he's shaking again.

I pace from the back wall to the door, trying to get my limbs to move normally. "We're going to get out of here. Tonight."

I'm still pacing when midnight rolls around. 1113 lays on his bed with his arm over his eyes, breathing deeply. I press my ear to the door again, listening for any footsteps.

"1113," I whisper, jostling his leg.

He kicks at me and groans, turning to the side.

I shake him again. "1113, we're getting out of here," I hiss. "Wake up."

"Now? Can't we wait a few more hours?"

*Teenagers*. "Nope. Gotta go now."

With a sigh, he sits up and swings his legs over the edge of the bed. "Do you have a plan?"

I press my hands to the door, right above where the deadbolt should be. "Kind of." My magic swirls angrily under my skin. I grunt and push it into the lock. *Gently, come on.* The deadbolt pops. I flash 1113 a smile over my shoulder. "Let's get out of here."

I crack the door and glance out. Nobody is in the hall. 1113 and I slowly make our way down the hall.

"Do you remember what way you came in?" I whisper.

He nods, pointing to the left. He stays behind me as we round the corner and run straight into a woman in a white coat and a Handler. She gasps and the Handler steps forward.

"Hey-" I start before he bashes the butt of his gun into my head.

# CHAPTER THIRTY ONE

# COLTON

"Colton! You can't do that! He's fragile!" Abby hisses at me as she rushes over to Adam now unconscious in the blonde boy's arms. The boy is staring at us with fear filled blue eyes. Adam's limp figure rests in his arms. I'm shocked at how different he looks, I almost didn't recognize him. He's so thin and covered in bruises. A large tattoo sits on his neck and I can see the tips of some old wounds and scars wrapping around his neck, brushing his collarbone.

"Did you want him to recognize us?" I ask. My voice sounds weird, contained in the helmet. This whole uniform seems over the top. The only purpose I can see it serving is to be intimidating.

"You're helping me carry him," Abby says, reaching for one of Adam's arms. The boy takes a step back and tightens his grip on Adam.

"Don't touch him," he whispers, voice wavering.

I blink, stunned, at the boy's bravery. From what I know of Rebren, those here don't often take any stance of defiance. "I'm not going to hurt him," she whispers, holding her hands up.

“Liar.” He clenches his jaw, holding my gaze. His fingers dig into Adam’s shirt and my friend's head rests on his shoulder, mouth slightly open and his short, shaggy hair falling back.

“I did just hit him with a gun, Abby,” I point out, slipping the weapon into the holser at my hip.

She looks at me over her shoulder, green eyes blazing. “Another reason why you shouldn’t have hit him.” Abby turns back to the boy. “1113, I promise I’m trying to help him. My friend and I,” she motions back towards me, “came to get him out.”

The boy glances towards me with a doubtful expression. “He looks like the people who brought me here,” he whispers.

I reach up and remove my helmet and give the boy a smile. “Hey, I’m Colton,” I say.

He glances at the gun at my hip, then back to Abby.

“Will you come with us? I’m sure Ad-732 would appreciate seeing a friendly face,” she says, taking another step forward.

*732? 1113? What’s with all the numbers?*

The boy takes another step back, dragging Adam’s feet on the ground. “You’re behind the testing, aren’t you? You and Jackson?”

Abby tenses but eventually nods. “I am.”

"How can I trust you?" the boy asks. His voice has gotten even quieter and I see his hands shaking. He can't be more than sixteen, and he's terrified. What happens here to turn people into fearing everyone?

"Hey, kid," I start. The boy turns his eyes towards me. "I don't work here. I just snuck in here with Abby. I go to school here in Chicago doing Pre-Med and I pour my milk before I pour my cereal. Can you tell me your name?"

Abby and the boy are staring at me like I'm crazy. The boy blinks. "You pour your milk before your cereal?" he asks.

I nod. "Controversial, I know."

"What are you doing?" Abby whispers.

I wave a hand at her. "What's your name, kid?"

He chews on his lip. "My *name* name?"

I nod.

"Connor," he says quietly.

"Nice to meet you, Connor," I say. "We're not strangers. I trust Abby and yes, I know what she does for work. I'm not happy about that either, but I trust her and so can you. What do you say?"

"Why?" he whispers.

"That guy in your arms is my best friend. His name is Adam and I want nothing more than to get him home. Come with us, Connor," I say.

He glances down at Adam, who groans. "You'll get us out of here?" He asks, tears forming in his blue eyes.

I nod, holding out my hand to him. "Can I help you carry him?"

Connor nods and loosens his grip on Adam. I limp over and grab Adam. My hip protests at the amount of walking I've done today and all the stairs. I slept weird on it last night and it's been off all day.

"Let's get you both out of here," I say as I drape Adam's arm around my shoulder. I grip his hand and hold him as Connor gets his other arm situated.

"Colton, I can carry him. Your leg…" She trails off as I give her a stern look. She nods and steps back. "It looks like we'll be taking the elevator down, seeing as we have…" She motions to Adam's limp form. His head hangs down and I spot scabbed over stripes running down his back, disappearing underneath his shirt.

Connor and I follow Abby to the elevator. At midnight, the Handlers stop patrolling in the Lab. At least, that's what Abby tells me. That doesn't stop me from holding my breath as the doors slide open, revealing an empty hallway. Connor and I hobble out of Rebren and to where Abby has parked her black sedan. She quickly opens the back door for us.

“Alright, help me lift him in,” I say to Connor.

“Colton, let me help, please,” Abby says softly.

I shake my head. “I can do this. He’s not too heavy,” I lie. I turn back to Connor. “You ready?”

The boy nods and starts helping me get Adam situated in the backseat, shifting his torso until he’s sitting up against the seat. Connor quickly gets him buckled in. Adam’s head leans against the headrest, his mouth slightly agape. The tattoo on his neck is fully visible. My eyes flick to the nearly identical one on Connor’s neck and I shake my head.

“Hop in on the other side, kid,” I tell him as I limp to the other side of the car. Abby is watching me from the open driver's side door.

Connor quickly runs to the other side and climbs in. A click tells me he’s already bucked before I can slide into my seat. Abby starts the car and I let out a breath.

“Okay, Abby. Where are we going?” I ask as she pulls out of the parking lot.

She smiles. “Bowling Green, Ohio.”

# CHAPTER THIRTY TWO

## 732

I wake up to light streaming across my eyes. "Five more minutes," I rasp. Blinking, I roll over and raise a hand to my eyes, rubbing them and pulling my blanket up.

That's not my blanket.

My eyes fly open and I sit up. The thickest comforter I've seen falls from my chest. I'm no longer in the dull Rebren clothes. Instead, I'm dressed in a simple blue t-shirt and gray sweatpants. The pendant weighs heavy in my pocket. The bed I'm lying on is not the creaky bed in Rebren's Lab. Looking around, I see that I'm not in mine and 1113's room in the Lab. This room has one bed, a full size dresser on one wall, with a full size mirror on the other wall. The bed I'm lying on is large and I seem to sink into the mattress and it doesn't creak when I move. The light is streaming in from a large window with blue curtains hanging on either side of it. *Where is 1113? Where am I?* With my heart racing, I pull the covers back further and swing my legs over and my feet hit carpeted floor.

I freeze.

Carpet. This room has *carpeting*. Soft, fluffy carpet cushions my tender feet. I fully stand up and walk to the door. It has a golden handle that I hover over. I take a deep breath, reach for my magic, and turn it, expecting it to stop.

It doesn't.

The handle turns all the way and the wooden door cracks open. Slowly, I walk down the hallway. The house is extravagant, the nicest I've been in.

*Will whoever brought me here have me and 1113 clean it?*

There are two more doors on this hallway. Hesitantly, I open the one closest to me. It looks like another bedroom, but there is nobody in it. A pair of shoes sits by the wooden desk, and a blue jacket hangs off the back of the chair. The second door leads to a closet full of sheets and towels. Shaking my head, I make my way down the lacquered wooden stairs and onto the hardwood floor. At the bottom of the stairs, I pause. There are paintings decorating the walls and a marble statue sits in the space between two curved staircases. There are two hallways on either side of the front door. The one on the left looks like it leads to more rooms. The one on the right looks like it leads deeper into the house. All the doors on the left hallway lead to offices, a library, and a game room. I linger at the library, wanting to stay and relax. Shaking my head, I exit the room and turn down the second hallway. Lining the walls of the second hallway is more artwork and large windows on the opposite side. The pictures are of different locations; one is of what I think is New York, and the other is London. There looks to be a city in Spain and one in Mexico.

Voices drift towards me. I slow down, looking down the hallway. I quietly walk towards the sound. There is a light coming from an open door at the end of the hallway. I peek around the doorway to see a clean, stainless steel kitchen. There are five people standing in various spots in the kitchen. A man with caramel colored hair and a trimmed beard leans against the counter by the fridge. He has round glasses that sit high up on his nose. He's smiling, laughing at something that was said. A young woman with blonde hair and bright green eyes sits on the counter near him. Her socked feet dangle and swing as she listens.

"He said that?" She asks, leaning forward.

Someone laughs a deep laugh. "He did!"

I lean in a little more to see the speaker. The man is… young. He has dark blonde hair and nearly gray eyes. He stands with his hands in his pockets and leaning against the counter. A large scar runs from just below his ear and disappears under his shirt. I furrow my eyebrows. I know him from somewhere. He laughs again and I blink. I step fully into the doorway.

"Colton?" I ask.

Everyone stops, turning towards me. Colton stares at me with wide eyes.

"You're awake!" He shouts, walking towards me. I take a step back instinctively, and I see a hint of something, anger maybe, flash across his eyes.

"Adam!" A familiar voice shouts. 1113 jumps off the table and jogs over to me. I smile and wrap an arm around him. He's dressed in a red button up and blue jeans, not in the brown Rebren clothes I last saw him in.

My name echoes in my ears. Adam. Not 732. Not a number. Just Adam. Like Jake had called me.

"Hey there," I say. "Are you hurt?"

He shakes his head 'no'. "How do you feel?"

"Fine." I furrow my eyebrows. "You know my name?"

1113 nods, smiling again. "They said you were their friend." He nods towards Colton and a woman with black, curly hair.

"Adam, I'm glad you're up," she says, her voice familiar. "You're looking better."

Her black, curly hair is pulled back into a tail and her green eyes stare me down. "Abby?" I ask.

She nods with a smile.

"It's good to see you up, Adam. We were worried that you wouldn't wake up," the man behind me says.

I turn around, pushing 1113 behind me, and face the older man. "Who are you?" I ask.

The man offers me a smile. "I'm Oliver Greenbrough. This is my daughter, Hailey." He extends his hand. I look at it, then back at him.

"How'd you convince The Boss to sell us?" I ask, staring at him.

Mr. Greenbrough lowers his hand. "I didn't," he says. He nods to Colton and Abby behind me. "They got you both out. There's nothing to be afraid of here, Adam. Young Connor can tell you that."

"Connor?" I turn around. 1113 smiles and waves.

"That's my name," he says. "And it's true. Abby and Colton got us both out."

I turn to my friends. Both of them stand there, Colton with his hands in his pockets and Abby with her arms gently crossed in front of her. "You don't just *get* people out of Rebren," I say.

Abby smiles and shrugs. "We do."

I step back, shaking my head. Keeping one hand on 1113, Connor's shoulder, I raise my other hand to scratch at my Mark. "How did you do it?" I ask.

"We snuck in. Colton blocked the cameras, and we worked together to get you out. You, uh, hit your head and Connor helped us carry you out," Abby explains.

I nod, looking around the kitchen, avoiding all of their gazes. “And what are we here to do?” I ask quietly, feeling that sinking feeling rise up again, threatening to swallow me whole once more.

Colton shakes his head. “We didn’t bring you here to do anything, Adam,” he says.

Mr. Greenbrough cleared his throat and stepped forward. “They brought you two here to stay with me until you’re ready to join the others,” he says.

My eyes snap up to his. “Others? What others?”

“I take in people like you and Connor in, helping them escape from Rebren,” he says. “I have a friend who owns a large plot of land that is more secluded than here. He watches over them there. Your friends,” he nods to Colton and Abby, “asked me to help you.”

I nod absentmindedly, thinking. There are others who have gotten out. Others like me, with magic, who have gotten out and are *living* life, not merely surviving till the next day.

“Adam,” Mr. Greenbrough says, “Will you walk with me outside?”

I glance at Connor, who smiles and gives me an encouraging nod. I nod and follow him through tiled hallways and through a large sliding glass door that leads to the backyard.

The yard is massive. A small pond lies in the back corner of the yard. There is a stone walkway that cuts through the grass that leads to the pond. A garden lines the back fence and trees shade half of the yard. A small Workers Shed sits in the opposite far back corner of the yard. Birds chirp and a butterfly flies past us.

"I will understand if you and Connor don't want to stay here, Adam," Mr. Greenbrough starts out, clasping his hands behind his back. "My friend and I have found that it's less unsettling for those we rescue if we give them a little personal space to figure things out before introducing them to the others. The people we get out tend to be a little…"

"Skittish?" I finish for him.

He smiles. "Yes, skittish." He pauses. "If you two feel ready, however, to join the others, I can have Hailey drive you down there tonight. You both seem to feel more comfortable around people than most of the others."

I let out a snort. "I'm not, trust me," I whisper. "I just know how to hide it better. Connor is probably more comfortable. He's barely sixteen."

Mr. Greenbrough doesn't respond. He just listens.

"For the past four years, everyone I've been around has tried to make me into a mindless nobody. I've seen what it's done to those around me, and I didn't want that to happen to me." I finish softly and look at my feet. The wind blows softly, pushing my choppy hair back.

“How can I help you feel comfortable, Adam?” Mr. Greenbrough asks softly.

“What?” I ask, not sure I heard him correctly.

He smiles softly at me. It’s unnerving how many people are smiling. “What is one thing you can think of that you want right now?”

I look away, closing my eyes and breathing in deeply. *My brother to be alive.* “Pizza,” I whisper finally.

“Then I’ll order a pizza. Any specific kind?”

I stare at him, blinking. “You’rc… ordering a pizza? Because I *want* one?” I ask finally.

He lets out a soft, innocent sounding laugh and nods. “Yes, I am. What kind would you like?”

“What about Connor? Colton and Abby?”

“I’ll get a few different types. What type would you like?” He assures me.

“Uh, pepperoni, please?” I answer. *I’m dead. That has to be the answer to how bizarre this is. I’m dead.*

“I’ll get right on that,” he says. “Is there anything else I can do to help you right now?”

“I don’t know,” I answer softly.

He nods and opens the door to the house. "Just let me know," he says. "You and Connor both have free roam of the house and the yard. Feel free to explore anything. I'll leave you be for now." Mr. Greenbrough walks inside the house and quietly closes the door.

I turn around and face the backyard again. The sunlight feels great and I sit on the edge of the porch, letting my bare feet rest on the grass. For the first time in years, I'm outside without anybody around me. Nobody to fear and nobody to watch me. The wind continues to blow softly and carries the scent of summer on it, reminding me of days before the Rebren Program when Jake, Colton and I would play games and run around the neighborhood. Times when I didn't have a Mark on my neck and magic in my veins. I lean back on my hands and close my eyes. Happy times. For the first time in weeks, the numbness doesn't try and claw its way up. For the first time in months, I am completely alone. For the first time in years, I feel relaxed.

* * *

Colton opens the sliding glass door. "Hey, Adam," he says. "How are you doing?"

I give him a thumbs up from my place in the grass. A while ago, I had moved from sitting on the porch to laying in the grass, letting the sun cover me and the grass caress my skin. My eyes are closed, but I hear him walking up to where I lay, his footfalls uneven.

"Are you enjoying yourself?" He asks.

“It’s nice,” I say quietly.

I feel him sit down next to me. “It is,” he agrees.

I take in a deep breath and my eyes fly open. Something smells *delicious*. I look over at Colton, who is smiling and holding a thin box in his hand. “What is that?” I ask, pushing myself into a sitting position.

Colton hands me the box. It’s warm and the cardboard feels oddly greasy. “Your pizza.”

My jaw falls open and I can’t get the top off fast enough. Inside sits a large pizza with multiple pepperoni’s strewn on top. Steam rises from the pizza, hitting me in the face. I close my eyes and breathe in deeply. “That smells heavenly,” I groan and go to grab a piece before stopping myself. I glance at my hands. The memory of Jake’s blood coating my skin crawls its way to the front of my mind. His blood is gone, it has been gone for weeks. All that I see is clean, pale skin, yet I still feel the sticky blood under my fingernails. Colton watches me, his brows knitting together in confusion.

“What’s wrong?” He asks.

I shake my head and grab a large slice of the cheesy pizza. “Nothing,” I say. I hand him a piece before taking a bite of my slice. More flavor than I thought I could taste explodes in my mouth. Grease coats my mouth as I eat. It seems to warm me up from the inside and I quickly finish my slice and move onto my second one. The food seems to drive all the pain from the past four years back. Colton eats his food slowly, a grin plastered on his face as he watches me. Before I know it, the pizza is half gone and I feel more full than I have in years. I wipe my hands on a napkin Colton had brought and lay back down.

"That was delicious," I say, laying my hands on my chest. My stomach feels bloated, as if I could pop if I ate one more bite. Colton lies down with me.

"I agree," he says. "I'd go so far to say it was better than the pizza place back home."

I turn my head to look at him. "I can't remember how it tasted, but I *do* remember that it was the best thing I had eaten. Don't disrespect my pizza like that," I say. This gets a full laugh out of Colton, teasing a laugh of my own out of my chest.

"Alright, alright," he says. "I won't disrespect our pizza back home."

"Good," I say.

Colton and I lay there in silence for a while. "It's good to have you back," he says quietly.

"I guess I'm glad to be here," I whisper. "I'm glad I'm not *there* anymore."

"With any luck, you won't go back," he says. He's quiet for a while before saying, "You don't have to answer but what happened, Adam?"

I let out a low chuckle. "What part are you referring to?" I ask. The numbness hovers, just as it always has, at the edge of my mind. Refusing to go away but waiting to swallow me whole again.

He glances at me before continuing. "Abby mentioned that you were covered in blood when you went to the Lab."

I press my lips into a thin line and nod once. *How did Abby find out?* "Are you asking why I was covered in blood or why I was taken to the Lab?"

"Was it your blood?" He asks slowly.

I shake my head. "No," I finally say. "It wasn't mine." *It was Jake's. That I can still feel on my hands no matter how many times I wash them.* I don't offer any more explanation than the answer I've given, and Colton doesn't press. He simply nods. Thankfully, the numbness seems to be staying at bay. Colton doesn't ask any more questions and I don't say anything more, content to just lay in the silence with him, basking in the sun.

# CHAPTER THIRTY THREE

## 732

Yawning, I enter the kitchen. The clock on the stove reads 6:45. Connor's still fast asleep in his large room down the hall from mine. Despite the plush bed and the extra blankets, I've found it harder to sleep these past weeks. I lean against the counter as I wait for the water to boil, hanging my head and closing my eyes. I could fall back asleep right here if my body would let me. The cool marble helps shock my system awake.

"Good morning, Adam," someone says.

I spin on my heel and face the speaker. Mr. Greenbrough enters the kitchen, wearing a gray t-shirt and plaid pants. His thin framed glasses are the only thing on him that looks slightly put together.

"Good morning, sir," I say, standing up straighter, resting my hands on the counter beside me.

Mr. Greenbrough waves a hand and makes his way to the fridge. "Call me Oliver," he says. "Sir is too formal."

I don't respond, watching him as he opens the fridge. The light reflects off his glasses. "Are you hungry?"

"I can make myself something," I respond softly.

Oliver glances sideways at me. "What were you going to make?" He asks.

I chew on the inside of my cheek, fiddling with the hem of my shirt. "Hot chocolate?"

Oliver smiles softly and shakes his head. "Let's get something to eat. Do you like bacon?"

Bacon? When was the last time I had bacon? "I don't know, sir," I say slowly.

Oliver nodded and pulled out a pack, setting it on the counter next to the stove. "Bacon it is then." We stay in silence for a few minutes before he speaks. "Is Connor still sleeping?" he asks as he lays the thickly cut meat on the pan.

I nod. "He hasn't experienced the joy of Rebren's alarm."

"Is that sarcasm I hear?" Oliver asks.

I freeze, straightening my back. "Is that a problem?" I snap.

Oliver glances at me as he flips the bacon. "No, no. I was…" he says quickly. "How's the hot chocolate coming along?" He nods his head towards the kettle on the boiling pad.

With a flush rising in my cheeks, I grab the kettle and set it on a hot pad beside the roll of paper towels. "Do you want some?" I ask quietly.

"I'd love some. Thank you," he says.

The sizzling of the bacon gets louder as he finishes flipping each piece. As I grab two mugs from the cabinet, I close my eyes and shake my head. *Stupid. He was only trying to joke with you.* With a sigh, I start mixing the hot chocolate.

"How long have you been up?" Oliver asks, breaking the tense silence.

"Not long. I got up around six," I say, offering him a mug.

"Early riser. Must be Rebren's *fantastic* alarm system," he says with a smirk, slowly sipping his drink.

I cup mine in my hands and smile at his peace offering. "Sarcasm, Mr. Greenbrough?" I ask.

Oliver chuckles and sets the mug on the counter. He starts pulling the bacon off, setting them on a paper towel covered plate. "My friend, Jason, asked if he could stop by today," he says. "What do you say?"

I raise one eyebrow. "Why are you asking me?"

"I'm asking to know how open you are to meeting new people," Oliver says, handing me a plate of bacon.

I gratefully accept the plate. “Jason is the guy who helps you with the Workers?” I ask, picking up a piece of meat. It’s perfectly cooked and the flavor explodes in my mouth.

Oliver nods, leaning against the counter and nibbling at his own bacon.

“Sure,” I say.

Oliver opens his mouth to say something.

“Did someone cook bacon?” Connor asks groggily.

Mr. Greenbrough grabs the last plate on the counter and hands it to Connor with a smile. “Just for you. Did you sleep well?”

Connor nods, rubbing his eyes, and grabs the plate. “Adam? I thought you’d still be asleep.”

“Can’t sleep past six,” I state.

He furrows his eyebrows as he bites into the bacon.

“Connor, I have a friend wanting to stop by today. Are you up to meeting someone new?” Oliver asks, leaning back against the counter.

Connor nods. “Is it your friend who rescues Workers?”

Oliver smiles. “The very same.”

"I'd like to meet him," the young boy says. Connor washes his plate and sets it on the drying rack. "When is he coming by?"

Oliver glances at me, a question in his eyes. I nod in response, lowering my gaze to my plate. One last piece sits on the white porcelain.

"He'll be in town around noon," Oliver says. The water turns on again and the pan scrapes against the counter as he brings it over to the sink. "I'll let him know that you want to meet him."

I nibble on my last piece of bacon. A churning pit opens up in my stomach, different from the numbness that sits at the edge of my mind. Connor and Oliver chat excitedly as they do the dishes and I can't help the smile that works its way onto my face. Connor doesn't recognize the danger, if there even is any, of trusting this new person. He doesn't understand that this could be a plot to simply get us back to Rebren. I shake my head and quietly wash my plate, leaving them to their conversation as I make my way to my room.

* * *

Connor and I are playing chess when Jason arrives. The knock at the door startles me and my knee hits the table, rattling the pieces. I glance up from the game board, looking towards the door. "Are you okay, Adam?" Connor asks.

I nod, watching Oliver appear from around the corner and walk to the front door.

I lean back in my chair to look around the wall. A large man with a long, curly beard stands in the doorway. Oliver reaches out to grasp the man's hand in his own. The man's hand completely covers Olivers. I can feel my heart racing as I watch them. *He could grab each of us in one hand and without any struggle from us.*

"Jason, I'm glad you made it safely," Oliver says warmly.

The large man, Jason, smiles and chuckles, sounding more like a deep rasp than an innocent laugh. "I'm grateful you invited me today, friend," Jason says, his voice is deep, yet still has a light sound to it.

"Please, come in." Oliver opens the door wider and the large man steps inside. Jason removes his dirt covered boots and sets them off to the side.

"New painting?" He asks, gesturing to the picture that hangs above a small table in the lobby. It's of what looks to be Greece, overlooking the bright blue ocean with white round roofs on a cliff face.

"Yes, we traveled to Greece a few months ago as a family," Oliver says.

Jason smiles. "I'm sure Hailey had the time of her life."

Oliver rubs the back of his neck. "Too much fun, I believe. She met a man there, some sailor I think."

Jason's eyebrows rise. "And have you met this young man?"

"A few times. He seems like a solid person, but only time will tell."

"I have a few friends I'd like you to meet," Oliver says, steering the conversation.

I quickly turn back to the game. Connor is watching with one eyebrow raised.

"Are you sure you're ready for this?" Connor whispers.

I nod again, moving one of my pawns forward.

"The two you told me about over the phone?" Jason asks.

"Adam and Connor. They got here a few weeks ago," Oliver explains. Their voices are getting closer as they walk towards the living room. Footsteps stop in the doorway. Oliver looks at us and gives me a soft smile. "Are you two ready?" he whispers.

Nodding, I take a deep breath.

Jason comes into view. I stand when he enters, with Connor quickly following after. The man seems to tower over me, even though he's only a few inches taller than me.

"Adam, Connor, I'd like you to meet my friend, Jason," Oliver says, appearing next to the large man. Connor walks up and stands close to me, his shoulder brushing mine.

Jason smiles and gives me a nod. "It's nice to meet you, Adam. Connor," he says. The smile Jason gives us reaches his eyes, forming smile lines that frame his hazel eyes.

I extend my hand to him. Jason glances at it and his smile deepens. I can feel the callous on his palms when he shakes my hand. "It's nice to meet you too, sir," I say.

Mr. Greenbrough gestures to the couches. "Shall we?" he says.

"So, Adam, where are you from?" Jason asks as he sits down in one of the chairs.

"Normal, Illinois," I answer, settling onto one side of the couch.

He nods. "I've driven through it. It's nice," he says.

I nod. *It's home*, I think.

"And you, Connor? Where are you from?"

"Bardstown, Kentucky," Connor answers, sitting down on the other side of the couch. He tucks his feet underneath him.

Jason nods, leaning back. “I’ve never seen that town specifically, but Kentucky is beautiful.” He pauses. “How old are you, Connor?”

“Sixteen,” the boy next to me answers.

“And what about you, Adam?” Jason asks, turning towards me.

I clench my jaw. “I, uh, don’t know,” I mumble.

The man's smile drops. “We can figure it out, I’m sure,” he says.

I don’t respond, instead leaning back against the couch.

“How are you both adjusting?” Jason asks after a stretch of silence.

Connor glances at me. “Pretty well,” he starts. “I wasn’t in Rebren that long, but I like it better here than I do there.”

Jason nods. “And you, Adam?”

I shrug. “Fine.”

Neither Oliver or Jason speaks. They simply watch me. Connor picks at the hem of his shirt, glancing up at me.

I shift in my seat, uncomfortable underneath their gazes.

"How have you been sleeping?" Oliver asks.

I turn to Oliver, furrowing my eyebrows. "Is this an interrogation?" I ask, straightening my back and lowering my voice.

Jason and Oliver look at each other and shake their heads. "I simply want to understand where you are at before introducing you to the rest of the group, Adam. I don't want to overwhelm you," Jason explains.

"Overwhelm me?" I repeat softly. "Why would you worry about that? What is it that you need me to do?" I lean forward, resting my elbows on my knees.

Connor shifts, watching me. "Adam, I don't think they have bad intentions," he whispers.

I hold Jason's gaze. My magic swirls under my skin.

"Why would they bring us here just to send us back?" Connor continues.

"Profit," I answer.

"And go through the trouble of breaking us out just to make some money? That seems like a lot of work."

I finally break eye contact with Jason and turn toward Connor. "You trust them?" I ask. "You trust *him* after just meeting him?"

Connor nods. "They don't treat us like the people at Rebren did. They are kind and care about us. Adam, think," he turns fully towards me, crossing his legs on the cushion. “They gave us new clothes that aren’t itchy, actual beds that won’t fall apart, free range of the house and yard, a room with *windows*. I know I wasn’t there for a long time, but there are differences in the way Oliver has treated us over the way Rebren treated us. Our doors lock from the inside and there are no tests you have to do.”

I hold his blue-eyed stare for a while. My heart pounds as I consider the possibility that I can trust Jason and Oliver. “What if you’re wrong?” I whisper and my hands start to shake. “What if this was all another test?”

Connor smiles. “There’s no Handlers,” he states.

“That we know of.”

Connor glances at Oliver and Jason. “It has to be one of those two, and I doubt it’s either of them. Handlers are cold, terrible people. Oliver made us bacon this morning, and Jason is calling us by our names.”

I look at my hands.

“I have a daughter with magic,” Jason says and I meet his eyes. He’s smiling softly. “She’s able to weave beautiful illusions with only her mind. When I learned what Rebren was doing, I did all I could to get her out. It took me a few months, but I was able to find her. She’s now living with the rest of them, safely hidden away from Rebrens prying eyes.”

I glance between Oliver and Jason, finally staring at the floor. The churning pit grows bigger and bigger inside my chest. "Do you promise you won't send us back?" I ask shakily.

"I promise, Adam. I will not send you back," Jason responds.

I nod, sitting up straighter. "I want to meet the others," I say. Connor grins and nods his agreement.

Jason's smile gets bigger. "How does tomorrow sound?"

"Tomorrow sounds great."

# CHAPTER THIRTY FOUR

## 732

A large blue suitcase sits open on my bed. Sunlight warms my bare arms as I stand in front of the window. My shirt sits draped over the edge of the suitcase, leaving me in just my pants and socks. A dog barks, and soon after a couple walking their dog pass by the house. I lean against the window sill, my nose nearly touching the glass.

"Adam?" Connor asks softly.

I turned quickly. He's standing in the doorway, his face a mix of confusion and pity. I grab my blue shirt and toss it on, covering the scars and marks, tucking the pendant under my shirt. My first day here, I found some string and wrapped it around the metal, just as I had seen Jake do.

"Are you," he clears his throat, "Are you packed?"

"Almost," I say quietly.

He's quiet as I quickly stack my few clothes and small back of toiletries into one side of the suitcase. I nearly laugh at the large suitcase, seeing how little space my belongings take up. They barely fill one side.

"What happened to your back?" Connor asks softly.

I sigh, straightening up. My magic swirls under my skin. "Rebren doesn't like it when you use magic," is all the explanation I offer.

"But they let you use magic in the Lab?" Connor walks into the room further and sits on the desk.

"The Lab is different," I state as I close the suitcase with a *zip*. The numbing pit opens wider, threatening to consume me again.

Connor shifts in the chair.

"Are you packed?" I ask.

"Yup. There wasn't much to pack..." He pauses again. "What's the pendant that never goes away?"

I turn and face him, leaning against the bed. Connor has his metal pendant in his hand and is rubbing his thumb along the edge. I pull mine out from under my shirt. "It's supposed to tell us what kind of magic we have and was created at our first use of magic." I fiddle with mine. "It also helps you gauge how your magic is doing, I think."

Connor looks up from his pendant. "How so?"

"It's always gotten warm for me when I'm close to using magic," I explain. The pendant hasn't been warm since I left Rebren. No matter how long it sits next to my skin, it's still cool to touch.

Connor's eyebrows furrow. "Really? So it's a warning like the beeping when you back up a car?"

"Pretty much."

"Did you need to control it much in the Lab?"

I clench my jaw together. "Umm," I start. "Not really. I still don't really know what I'm doing with it yet."

Connor nods.

A knock sounds against the doorframe. "Hey boys," Oliver says and steps inside the frame. "Jason is here. Do you need help with your bags?"

I shake my head 'no'. Connor bounces up and grabs his suitcase from the room down the hall.

Oliver leans against the doorframe and watches as I pull the suitcase from off the bed. It's neatly made with any sign that I had been here stripped from the room. I slip into the black shoes I'd set at the foot of the bed and fix the chair against the desk.

"How are you feeling?" Oliver asks.

"You all keep asking me that," I point out. "I'm fine." I hesitate with my hand on the string to close the blinds, staring outside. I can see a dark blue truck in the driveway. It's got a few pieces of wood in the back with sandbags tucked along the sides.

"I simply want to check in," Oliver says.

"Nobody has ever cared before," I say as I close the blinds with small *clunk clunk clunk* sounds as the blinds drift back and forth against the wall. "I'm doing as fine as ever."

Oliver simply watches me. "You don't have to be alone in this. Jason and I, as well as your friends, are here to help." He straightens up. "Ready to go?"

I grab the suitcase and nod, following him down the stairs. Connor is chatting with Jason in the entryway. Jason smiles as we approach. He's changed into a blue plaid jacket and a plain grey t-shirt. The heavy, dirt stained boots are still on his feet.

"Adam! How was your evening?" He asks.

"It was fine," I respond.

Jason's smile grows. "Let's get your bag in the truck and we'll be on our way. Does that sound good to both of you?"

Connor nods, smiling.

Jason leads Connor and me to his truck. He gestures to the suitcase in my hand. "May I?" He asks and I nod, holding it out for him. He gently takes it and loads my bag into the trunk of his large truck and steps aside, holding the back door open. "After you both," he says with a smile.

"Do you want to sit in the front, Adam?" Connor asks, partially in the back. He's hanging out of the door with his hand on the roof.

I rub my thumb along the side of my finger and slowly walk towards the truck. My heart pounds. Something in the back of my mind keeps yelling that this is a trap, that he's going to take us back to Rebren. "Sure," I say, climbing into the passenger side of the truck.

The inside of the truck is clean. The seats are a soft fabric and the seats are comfortable to sit in. As I look around, I don't see any chains or locks. There is a click coming from the backseat. I watch Jason walk around the front of the truck and climb into the driver's seat. The truck shakes as the door shuts and the large man settles into his seat.

"Are you ready for this, Adam?" He asks softly, his hand on the ignition.

"Why wouldn't I be?" I ask, leaning back into the seat.

Jason's eyes flick from the seatbelt to the buckle. "When was the last time you rode properly in a car?" He asks.

I freeze, suddenly feeling very self-conscious. "I was sixteen," I mumble.

"It's okay to not remember, Adam," Jason says softly. "I don't expect you to be perfectly normal right now. I don't expect you to have it all together either. You've been through a lot and it's alright not to remember that you have the freedom to buckle yourself in and out of a car."

I stare at him, feeling something break through the growing numbness. Relief? Freedom? I feel tears sting my eyes and I turn away from him, quickly wiping them away. Against my best efforts, more tears begin to fall. Silently, I take the belt and buckle it in. I stare ahead at the driveway and set my hands in my lap, silent tears still streaming down my face.

Jason, thankfully, doesn't say anything as he turns the key, bringing the truck to life. I feel the familiar feeling of the vehicle moving, but seeing the landscape pass by at the same time is new. I forgot how green the world is and how bright the sun can be when it's reflected off the hood. I lean forward, mouth falling open.

"Adam, you're acting like you haven't been in a car," Connor says.

"Not like this," I whisper. "Not in a while."

"How'd you get around in Rebren?" He asks, leaning forward. I catch Jason glancing at me before looking back at the road.

"Transport vans," I answer, watching a bird land on a telephone pole.

"Those big vans where they lock you in the back?" Connor asks, appalled.

"The very same."

I hear him lean back. "Do you ever see the sun? Get to go outside?"

"Quite often, actually. Just not at Rebren," I state. "At my last house, I was working outside all day."

"But not for enjoyment? Do the Sheds have windows?"

I shake my head. "No, we weren't allowed to be outside unless we were working. And there are no windows in the Shed. Can't have your Worker escaping through an unguarded window."

"That's terrible."

I nod in response.

"Would you mind if I put on some music?" Jason asks after a stretch of silence. Cars pass by us as we enter onto the highway. I see people of all different experiences in the cars. Some have their trunks filled with things, others are laughing. Some people are alone in their cars. I see children in the backseats and parents taking care of them.

"Sure," Connor says.

"Any requests?"

"The Killers?"

I furrow my eyebrows at the name. *That sounds familiar.*

Jason nods and hands his phone to Connor. "Pick your favorite," he says.

Connor eagerly takes the phone. Jason reaches over and presses a button on the panel in the middle. A minute later, music starts playing softly. Guitar and drums sound over the speaker. Connor starts quietly singing along, and the lyrics come back to me. I start to nod my head to the beat, feeling a smile work its way onto my face. Music, actual music. Not some random song that plays on repeat in my head.

"Where did Oliver get you from?" Jason asks casually.

I glance over at him before looking back outside. Air blows in from the vent seated in front of me and I lean into it. "The Lab."

Jason raises an eyebrow. "The Lab?" He smiles. "I bet you caused some trouble?" He glances over at me and smirks.

I can't help but share his smirk. "Yeah," I agree. "I caused some trouble."

He nods. "I respect that. You both came from the Lab?"

I nod. "They brought Connor in because of me," I say slowly.

Jason shakes his head. "Connor seems quite happy. He wasn't hurt, was he?"

"No. He was there purely for… motivation." That's all I offer.

Jason nods knowingly, drumming his fingers on the wheel.

"How many people are at this place?" I ask, breaking silence.

Jason shrugs. "A fair amount. Around thirty I want to say," he says.

I raise my eyebrows. "How have you guys gotten away with this?" I ask, leaning back, rubbing the seam on my jeans.

"Oliver puts himself at risk, buying Workers and taking them in. We've risked a lot on Rebren not checking on purchased Workers. Turns out we were right and those who aren't returned tend to slip through the cracks. Of course, all it takes is one person to check the records to know that Oliver has way too many Workers for his needs or to fit in the shed even. Once the Worker is used to being around Oliver, and somewhat used to being free, he calls me." He glances over at me again. "Generally, I visit three to four times before offering to take you with me. You two are a special case, it seems."

I raise my eyebrows at him in confusion. "How?" I ask bluntly.

"You don't seem as scared as the others," he says. "Must be part of the trouble you caused Rebren."

I smile. "Must be," I say. "I never quite learned how to be the most obedient Worker."

"Ah," he says, "That makes sense."

We fall silent, listening to the music that is playing softly. Connor switches the music a few times, jumping between different artists. I take in the world as we pass it. We drive for about an hour and a half before Jason turns onto a dirt road that takes us to a large house. I feel my jaw tighten as I stare at it. Large windows draw my attention up the three, maybe four, floors of the house. A wrap around porch that disappears catches my eye and brings my gaze back down. I examine the large, tended yard with all its trees and flowers. Windows to clean, a porch to sweep, a yard to tend. Inside, I can only guess at the hallways and rooms that need attention. There must be an industrial size kitchen in there. Who better to bring in than Workers who think they are free?

Only a number.

The opening of my door jars me from my thoughts. When did we stop moving? When did Jason get out of the car? I blink and turn to face Jason. He is leaning against the door and smiling. "Ready to meet everyone?" He asks. Connor appears next to him, smiling.

I blink a few more times and look back at the house. I can faintly hear people shouting and laughing nearby. I catch a glimpse of someone running by one of the windows, brown hair blending into the wooden frame. I nod and unbuckle my seatbelt, sliding out of the car and standing next to Connor. Jason leads the two of us across the grass yard that separates the house from where the truck is parked. The porch creaks when I step on it and I pause, watching Jason walk through the door. My heart pounds, everything in me is screaming to turn around, grab Connor, and run. When have I followed someone into a house? When have I willingly been so obedient? When have I ever been this quiet without a gag?

Jason turns around and his smile falters. "Adam?" He asks.

I glance around at the porch and the yard again, shifting my weight on the wooden board. "Why did you bring us here, Jason?" I ask, feeling something rise up within me.

Jason slowly walks out of the house and softly closes the door. "I brought you here so you can feel normal," he says.

"Normal," I whisper to myself. "How?"

Jason's green eyes are soft when I look into them. "It was too soon, wasn't it?" he asks. "Bringing you here?"

"How did you really get me out of Rebren?" I ask, stepping up one step. The wood groans underneath me.

“Abby and Colton snuck in and got you out,” he explains. “They took you to Oliver Greenbroughs house where you two have been for the past two weeks.”

I grit my teeth. “Why?” I ask.

“I was told you specifically needed to get out.”

Only a number.

I glance around, catching someone looking at Jason and I through the front window. My heart races. “What is really in that house?” I ask, glancing at the door.

“People just like you. We helped them escape,” he says.

I take a step down. Everything seems like it’s spinning. I can feel my heartbeat inside my chest, trying to burst through. My magic swirls underneath my skin, trying to escape.

“Adam, it’s normal to feel scared. To feel anxious,” Jason says. His gaze is soft when he looks at me. “We don’t have to go inside quite yet if you don’t want to.”

Why does my chest feel tight? Am I breathing? I take another step down, backing away from the house and bumping into Connor. “What is happening?” I rasp, finally meeting Jason's gaze.

Jason studies me and takes a step forward. I take another step back and he stops. “I can’t help you if you won’t let me get close,” he says slowly, holding up his hands. He glances at Connor behind me. "Connor, why don't you head inside?"

The boy shuffles his feet behind me. "Adam, are you okay?" he whispers.

My pendant grows warm against my chest and my hands start to shake. 1048's body, smoking on the ground, unmoving. A Handler lies next to him. 06 with half his body burned. "Step away from me, Connor," I rasp.

"Adam-"

"Please!" Connor backs away until he's standing a few feet from me. I meet Jason's eyes. "Where am I?" I ask. I can feel my magic pulse at my fingertips as my hands hang at my side. "What state?"

"Ohio. Near the Kentucky border," he answers.

I raise a hand to my head. Ohio? By Kentucky? Why bring me here? What's so special about Ohio? Jason goes to take another step forward and I throw my hands out.

My magic pulses, rushing out of me and I fall to the ground, gasping. The pendant scorches my skin. Jason dives to the side. When I look back up at the house, there is a large, smoldering hole in the porch near where Jason was standing. He pushes himself up, coughing. Ash and wooden splinters fall off of his back. He looks at the hole, then at me. I hang my head, staying on my hands and knees, shaking. I hear Jason's footsteps get closer. He crouches next to me.

“Adam,” he says softly. “Are you okay?” he asks.

I look up at him. Slowly, I nod. He gives me a faint smile and holds out his hand. I look past him to the porch that now has a large, smoldering hole in the middle of it. My stomach sinks.

“Are you feeling well enough to walk?” He asks.

I nod again. My magic retreats back to its regular spot, swirling inside.

“Would you like to come inside? There are some people waiting for you and Connor,” he says softly.

I glance back at the hole in the porch before looking back at Jason. Feeling the pit in my stomach grow, I stand up. Jason smiles and leads us inside, stepping around the smoldering wood and opening the door.

People scatter instantly. I see teenagers peeking at us from around the corner. Jason leads Connor and me to a large sitting area behind the stairs.

“Adam!” Abby says and rushes up to me, tackling me in a hug. “Are you okay? We heard a boom and the house shook.” She pulls back and examines me.

I stand there with my arms pinned to my side. “Abby?” I ask slowly. “What are you doing here?”

“We came to see you,” Colton says, walking up behind Abby. His gait seems more even today. She nods in agreement.

I look between both of them. “But I just…” I motion over my shoulder and look towards Jason. He smiles and shakes his head.

“An accident,” he says. “I’ll get it patched up in no time.”

“That was you?” Colton asks, drawing my attention back to him. “The loud boom?”

I nod, feeling my back itch with phantom pain.

Colton walks around Abby and puts a hand on my shoulder. “Come on,” he says. “I’ll show you and Connor to your room.” He starts walking down the hallway we just came down and up the stairs. I hear people walking around upstairs, their footsteps echoing through the floors.

“There are a lot of shared rooms here,” he says as we walk up the stairs.

The wooden banister is worn with years of hands running up and down it. I brush my fingers over it, feeling the dents and divots in it.

“We figured you and Connor would want to room together. Jason said there would be no issue there,” he continues.

I nod as we round the corner. Colton pushes open the door to reveal a room larger than the one at Oliver’s. My jaw dropped as I saw the large windows on two walls of the room. Two beds sit on opposite sides of the room, along with large dressers, and two desks. The walls are a nice shade of red with gold trim around the windows and doors. The carpet is soft and fluffy, I can feel it through my shoes. Colton lounges on one of the beds, watching me with a smile.

“Do you like it?” He asks.

“I…” I trail off, turning in a circle. “It’s massive.”

“So much bigger than what we were given at Rebren,” Connor whispers, walking towards one of the beds.

“Fit for two comfortably,” Colton says. “Will you both be alright here?”

I finally look at him and nod.

Colton smiles. “Great. Are you hungry? Dinner should be cooking.”

# CHAPTER THIRTY FIVE

## COLTON

I find Adam sitting on the porch with his legs dangling over the side, watching the sun set. He's still dressed in the same blue t-shirt and jeans he arrived in. A white mug sits next to him. I lean against the door, debating on whether or not I should bother him. He seemed tense at dinner—shoulders tense and his fake smile tight. As soon as he could, he disappeared from the kitchen. Only Connor was in their room, unpacking.

A slight breeze blows through the trees, making its way to the porch. With a sigh, I push off the doorframe and walk towards Adam.

"May I join you?" I ask.

Adam glances over his shoulder before nodding, still looking out towards the yard. The wood groans beneath my weight as I settle down beside him.

"I figured you'd be inside," I start, unsure of what to say. "It's getting chilly."

He shrugs, leaning back on his hands. "I didn't notice."

I glance down at the empty mug beside him. “What’s going on?” I prod. “You were tense at dinner.”

With a deep breath, Adam leans forwards, resting his elbows on his knees. “It’s just strange,” he offers. “Being around so many people. I guess I don’t know what to do with myself,” he whispers.

“You’re free. You can do whatever you want to.”

He shakes his head and closes his eyes. His voice is soft when he speaks. “Four years, Colton. It’s been four years of people pushing me around and telling me what to do all the time. I wasn’t allowed to do whatever I wanted.” He pauses, swallowing. “I don’t remember what to do with free time.”

I am silent, letting his words sink in. I’ve known that Rebren wasn’t all it said it was when Abby started working there. I only thought that it was the testing and experimenting that was different. Apparently, the corruption runs deeper than the Lab. “Do you want to talk about it?”

He slowly shakes his head. “I can’t,” he whispers.

I wait, hoping he’ll say more. “Why not?” I ask when he doesn’t continue.

Adam breathes in deeply and slowly releases the air. “There’s too much,” he says. “Too much time, too many things went wrong, too much pain…”

I furrow my eyebrows. “They hurt you outside the Lab?”

Adam shoots me a sideways glance. “You really don’t know what goes on in there?” He asks.

I shake my head ‘no’.

He chuckles, looking back towards the setting sun. It has nearly disappeared behind the trees. “It’s not a program for magic control,” he explains. “It’s a market for rich people to get cheap labor. We’re bought and sold like tools for people to use at their leisure. We can’t use our magic, and are punished if we do. We’re conditioned to do what we’re told, be quiet, and not to think.” He shakes his head, looking at his hands. “They treat us like objects, like the numbers they tattoo on our skin.”

I listen, sick to my stomach. Parents are willingly giving their children to this program? Finally, I speak. “Do you want to help us break more people out of Rebren?”

He furrows his eyebrows and looks towards me. “What?”

I nod. “I think it would be good for you. You can help people escape that terrible place.”

He stares at me, blinking. “Colton, I can’t. I’m…” he trails off.

“Who said you can’t, Adam?” I ask.

Adam gestures to nothing in particular, his hand straying up to scratch at the tattoo on his neck. "I'm… I can't," he mumbles. "People get hurt when I try to help."

I lean forward. "That was before. We have so many more resources available to help better," I say softly.

Adam stares at me, his green eyes haunted and hurt. He blinks a few times while looking back down at his hands, rubbing his fingers together.

"Just come to the meetings and then you can decide," I encourage softly. "Please."

Adam meets my gaze again. There is less pain in his eyes this time. Slowly, he nods.

The meeting consists of Jason, Oliver, Abby, Adam, Hailey, and I. Adam sits quietly at one end of the table, picking at his fingers and fiddling with the strange necklace.. I lean back in my chair, arms folded. Abby at Oliver spread a large blueprint of Rebren's main building on the table. Jason stands with his hands on the back of his chair. Hailey sits next to her father, arms crossed and fingers tapping lightly on her arm.

"Welcome everyone," Oliver says, clasping his hands together. Adam looks up from the papers on the table and locks his gaze on Oliver. He looks like a caged animal caught by a predator, clenching his jaw and tensing his shoulders.

"I'm sure you've heard that we're attempting a new method of getting Workers out of Rebren."

"How did you do it before?" I ask, leaning forward.

Oliver looks at me, then down at the table. "I would go in and buy one Worker every few months. It's worked thus far, but you and Abby have shown us another way to get people out."

Abby leans forward, resting her elbows on the table. "That was a one time thing, Oliver. I pulled a few strings and was able to get us in. And that was only the Lab. I'm not sure we could do it again," she says, glancing towards me.

"Do you have a plan, Oliver?" I ask.

The Mayor glances at Jason. The larger man nods. "We use the Handler uniform you have. That'll get us access anywhere in the building, am I correct?" He looks at Abby who nods.

"You'll need a key card, though," she says. "I can get one."

Oliver nods. "Do you know where the Workers are kept in Rebren's main building?"

Abby shakes her head. "I only know the Lab layout."

Oliver sighs, running a hand through his salt and pepper hair.

Adam leans forward. “Is that Rebren’s main building?” he asks, nodding to the blueprints on the table.

Jason nods. “We were able to retrieve them last week, thanks to Hailey.”

“I know the layout,” he offers. “I can help there.” Adam glances at me before looking back at the papers. His green eyes roam over the paper before gesturing to a section of rooms. “These are the processing rooms. After a Worker is returned, or brought from a testing center, they enter through these doors-” he points to a side door, “and then are brought there to shower, receive medical attention if they need it, and wait for an available room.” He motions to a section of rooms that connect to Rebren’s main lobby. “These are the viewing rooms. During Rebren’s operating hours, five to seven Workers are kept in each room. There is a large window looking into the room.” Finally, he points to rows of rooms that are separate from the main lobby. “These are the private rooms where the Workers are kept after hours, or after they’ve just been returned. They are kept in windowless, small rooms with a bed, a small shower and a toilet. That’ll be your best bet to break someone out. There are cameras in the other rooms, but not the private rooms. I’m not sure why that is, but it makes it really easy to cause problems when you’re not being watched.” Adam leans back, scratching at the tattoo on his neck. There are silvery lines that wrap around his wrists.

Oliver leans back, staring at the blueprints. “So how do we get in?” he asks.

“We go in at night, after Rebren closes,” Abby says. “They rely on cameras at night and there are less people to get around.”

“That’s not true,” Adam says softly. “In the Lab, they rely on cameras. They don’t expect Workers to be strong enough to break out. In the main center they patrol every thirty minutes at night. There is one Handler assigned to each hallway.”

“So we have someone on the inside patrolling the hallway we are aiming for,” I say.

“That would require someone to go in for a shift,” Abby says, looking at me with one eyebrow raised. She glances down at my leg. “Are you volunteering?”

I swallow, leaning back. “We don’t have to go in for the full shift, that’s the thing,” I explain. “We distract the Handler for an hour, sneak in dressed in uniform, get our Worker, and get out of there. Handler goes back to duty and we’re long gone.”

Abby leans back, chewing on her bottom lip like she does whenever she’s thinking. “That just might work. I can provide a distraction,” she says finally.

“I can knock out camera’s for a few minutes, making it look like a system glitch,” Hailey states.

“I can be our driver,” I offer. “That leaves one person to get in dressed as a Handler, get the Worker out, and get out of Rebren.”

"I can do that," Adam says. All eyes turn to him. Oliver's eyes go wide.

"Are you sure you're ready for that, Adam?" He asks.

He nods. "They'll be wary, afraid, especially if a Handler bursts into their room late at night. I can ease that fear a little. I'm one of them."

I shake my head. "You're not one of them," I say.

Adam chuckles softly. "I am, though," he says. "They marked me just the same. The magic swirling under my skin sets me apart from you. Sets *them* apart from you. They won't believe you're there to help them. They can't trust you."

I look down, nodding. It took a lot of convincing for Connor to come with us, and then it was only because we knew Adam. Finally, I nod. "Okay. If you feel ready for it, let's go for it."

Adam nods and I see a hint of a smile across his face. "Let's do it."

# CHAPTER THIRTY SIX

## 732

The sun momentarily blinds me as I walk outside, a cup of hot chocolate in my hands. Blinking to clear my vision, I sit down on the edge of the wooden porch, letting my legs hang over the side. Teenagers and young adults chase each other in the yard, some of them playing basketball in the driveway. A few of the older people sit on the other end of the porch and talk softly. Their laughter floats on the wind, washing over me. I let out a deep breath, thinking about the upcoming events of the day.

"You must be new here," a girl says, startling me. She sits in the dirt by the steps, pulling weeds out of the flowerbed. She smiles up at me with bright blue eyes.

"I got here a few days ago," I say, taking a sip of the hot chocolate.

The girl nods to herself. "Welcome, then," she says. "I'm Allivane." The girl extends her gloved hand to me.

"Adam," I say, taking her hand. Her dark hair is partially covered by a pastel pink handkerchief and pulled back into a messy bun, exposing her neck. There is no

Rebren Tattoo there. "I'm sorry if I'm prying, but do you have magic?"

Allivane smiles sadly, still brushing her hand back and forth over the dirt. She removes her glove and cups a drooping flower in her palm. Instantly, the purple flower petals perk up and it stands upright, facing the sun. "When I turned sixteen, it was very clear that I still had magic. I sneezed in the kitchen and every plant in the house grew ten feet. My parents saw that the people who went into Rebren weren't coming out. My parents didn't want me to end up stuck in Rebren." She meets my eyes, leaning back against the stairs. "I had a few friends who were 'studying abroad'-" she makes air quotations around the words, "-that picked me up and took me to their hideout. We stayed in hiding for two years before an unlucky shopping experience got us caught. Missy caused a distraction that allowed us to escape the store. Pipes burst and water was everywhere. But Rebren was waiting in the streets. By the time I got out, Missy and Jensen were already unconscious and in handcuffs. I ran back inside, escaping out the side door. Along the side of the building there was a small patch of grass. I buried myself in the earth and tunneled my way out. Jason found me a few days later and took me here."

I scratch at my Mark. "How long ago was that?" I whisper.

"Four months and eleven days," she states, pulling up a weed and tossing it onto the deck. It lands next to the steps, small dirt clods coming off the roots.

“Your friends, were they taken to Rebren?” I ask

Allivane nods. “I keep hoping that they’ll show up here, that Jason and Oliver will get them out, but maybe they are too heavily guarded. Or already at a house, although I doubt they would go willingly.” She smiles sadly as she continues pulling weeds. “Missy and Jensen, they are fighters. The minute Jensen found out what was going on, he fought his way out of the testing center. He burned three vans down as he left. Missy refused to go in and ran instead, damaging major Rebren machinery in the process. I know they’ll survive.”

I look to the side, watching the group playing basketball. “Rebren is prepared for anything,” I say softly and take a sip of my drink.

“Did anyone ever try to escape?”

I nod, setting the cup off to the side. “I did, multiple times.” I see her look up at me from the corner of my eye, her gaze trained on me. “I earned every one of my scars with each new attempt.”

“How far did you get?”

I run a hand through my hair. It’s grown out since Jake cut it. It falls unevenly around my face now, brushing the middle of my ear. “At Rebren, I made it down the hallway before a Handler caught me. He gave me a nasty bruise for that. In a house, a group of us nearly succeeded.” I clear my throat. “We weren’t successful and Caulder made an example of us. He…he shot Jake and sold me back to Rebren." *Let this be an example to you all.*

Allivanes face drops. "They kill people for trying to escape?" She whispers. The plants near her knees start to droop.

"Caulder does. He did it to scare other Workers. Most of Rebren doesn't kill people. But, like I said, Rebren is prepared for anything." I scratch at my Mark again.

She is silent, probably thinking about her friends.

"Why do you garden the long way when you can control plants?" I ask.

"I like feeling the ground and the connection to the plants. It relaxes me," she says, turning her attention to the drooping plants. "Reminds me of days on the run. We used to hide in caves I'd create from the Earth. Hiding in big cities is dangerous for people like us. I was able to tunnel underground, cause the bushes and trees to bend and grow. Gardening with my hands reminds me of those days." She smiles.

"I understand the sentiment," I whisper.

"What magic do you have?"

I meet her curious eyes. "Explosive." It swirls under my skin at the mention of it.

Allivane nods to the porch. "Was that you?"

I look behind me at the fresh spot of wood. It stands out against the rest of the old and weathered wood. I smile. "Yes, that was. On accident."

* * *

She laughs. "Most things are on accident around here. Nobody means to damage anything. Ben over there," she nods to a young man playing basketball, "accidently set the kitchen on fire while attempting a flambe using his own flame. Heather caused a power outage while exploring the depths of her magic." She turns back to me. "When I was sixteen, I accidently sent a house plant growing into the chimney and through the windows. I'm sure the porch isn't your only accident."

I shake my head, chuckling. The scars on my back itch. "No, it's not."

She smiles. "There you have it. Accidents happen." She stands up and takes off her gloves. "It was nice talking with you, Adam. I'll see you around."

"You too," I say as she walks back into the house, the door gently squeaking closed behind her.

I sit in the back of the truck, my arms resting on the helmet in my lap. My heart pounds and I tap my fingers to no particular rhythm on the helmet. Colton is sitting behind the wheel, gently turning into the parking lot. Hailey has her computer pulled up and is furiously clicking and typing on it. Unlike my first time in Jason's truck, it's silent as we slowly roll to a stop. We pull into a stall behind a patch of trees.

"Hey," Abby says quietly from next to me. "It's going to be alright."

I nod, glancing at her before looking out the front window, staring at the grey building. "How do you know you'll be able to distract the Handler?" I ask.

Abby shrugs. "I'll think of something to say," she says. "Or fake a problem that I can't fix."

"And you're sure he'll follow you?"

Abby nods. "The Handlers love to show off their strength. He wouldn't turn down an opportunity to show up the others."

I nod again, still tapping at the helmet. Abby puts her hand on my arm. I still, tensing up at her touch.

"Hey," she says again. "It'll work. And you're not going to get caught. Keep that helmet on and you're unrecognizable."

I hold her gaze. Her eyes are soft and warm, making me feel calm. I slowly nod again.

Colton turns and gives Abby and I a nod paired with a confident smile. "Remember the number?" He asks me.

"Room 13," I respond, moving the helmet off my lap.

"Remember, walk in confidently. Say hello to the lady at the front desk as you pass. After that, walk towards the hallway and Abby will already have taken care of the Handler. From there, take the side door out. Do you remember where that is?" Colton asks.

"Behind the wall separating the lobby from the private rooms," I say.

Colton nods. "Abby will exit through the front door, escorted by the Handler. We will wait here for both of you to make your way back here."

"I have the camera's playing a loop of the current feed for the next thirty minutes. Will that be enough time?" Hailey asks, turning in her seat.

We both nod. "See you soon," Abby says, then slides out of the truck, quietly shutting the door behind her. I watch her go, count to thirty, and then slide the helmet over my head. My heart pounds as I climb out of the truck, my black boots crushing the rocks underneath me.

"Good luck," Colton says, giving me a smile.

I nod and close the door. Walking in these boots feels like I have the weighted chain back around my ankles, except I can take as long of strides as I want. These boots are heavy and bulky, much different from the thin tennis shoes they give us for working. I flex my fingers, feeling the gloves hugging my fingers. My palms are already getting sweaty and the fabric starts to feel constricting.

*Just make it past the front desk and to room 13.* I think. *Grab the Worker and get out of Rebren. Then make it to the truck where I can take this blazed thing off.*

The doors to Rebren loom over me. The words engraved above them seem to see right through me. *Rebren Program for Magic control: Illinois Campus. Teaching your children since 2016.* With shaky hands, I take a breath and push open the door. The woman sitting behind the desk has her curly red hair loose around her shoulders today. Her thick framed glasses frame her green eyes. She looks up at me.

I nod to her, heart pounding. "Good evening," I say, trying to keep the tremor out of my voice.

"Welcome," she says warmly, returning back to her computer.

I continue walking past the desk, turning down the viewing room hallway and make my way towards the private rooms. There are multiple hallways that are organized by tens. Ten rooms in each hallway, with ten or so hallways on each floor. I enter the second hallway, finding room 13. Looking around, the Handler assigned to this section is nowhere to be seen. A clipboard hangs next to the door. I glance at it briefly as I pull out the key card Abby acquired. The black box on the door beeps and flashes green. I slowly pull the door open and slip in. A man with choppy blonde hair and angry red burns pushes himself into a seated position. The blanket falls down from around his shoulders and I see the large tattoo that covers most of his left arm. "What's going on?" 06 asks, voice thick with sleep.

I remove my helmet and tuck it underneath my arm.. "06?" I ask.

The man tosses his legs over the edge of the bed and stumbles up to me. "732?" He asks.

I nod, any words getting stuck in my throat.

He shakes his head, looking me up and down. "How did you… What are you doing?"

I clear my throat. "Getting you out," I answer." I shift the helmet under my arm. "I have a few friends who are waiting in a truck. We don't have much time."

06 nods and tugs on his shoes.

I push open the door and tug the helmet back on. 06 follows me as I walk down the hallway. As we turn the corner, I freeze. The Handler Abby is supposed to be distracting stops in front of us.

"Evening?" he says slowly.

"Evening," I respond, grabbing 06's arm. *Shoot shoot shoot shoot.*

"Is everything alright?" he asks, nodding to 06 next to me.

“The Boss wants to talk with him,” I say, remembering Handler Greets from months ago. Whatever the Boss says, goes.

The Handler in front of me adjusts his belt. “He didn’t tell me anything,” he says. “Are you sure?”

“The Boss told me, because you already have a duty. Do you have an issue with that?” I ask. “We can go together if you’d like to take it up with him.” My palms start to feel sweaty inside the gloves and I am grateful for the helmet to cover the panic in my eyes. I can feel my pulse in my ears.

The Handler steps forward. “The Boss isn’t supposed to be in tonight? Can I see your ID?”

I will my hands to stop shaking as I fish out the fake ID and hand it to him. It has my picture on it, but with a fake name underneath.

He takes it and glances at it. “Remove your helmet, please, Mr. Ray.”

I let go of 06’s arm and remove my helmet. The uniform collar covers my Mark. The Handler glances between the ID and my face.

“You’re sure he said tonight?” The Handler asks skeptically.

“I’m positive. I can show you the message,” I say, reaching for a phone that I don’t have.

“I’d like-” he cuts off his words and straightens up, handing my ID back. “No, I don’t need to,” he says. “I’m sorry for delaying you.”

I take the ID back, confused. The Handler turns around and starts walking down the hallway.

Turning towards, 06, I nod down the hallway. “We need to get going,” I whisper, tugging my helmet back on my head. 06 follows me as I start walking again. I check my watch and my heart pounds. The door comes into view and I almost run towards it. “My friends are waiting in a red truck,” I explain as I press my ID against the black box.

“How did you do all this?” 06 whispers as we walk outside.

“I’ll explain in the truck.” The night air makes its way past the uniform and cuts through my skin. “The truck just past those trees.”

06 stares at the trees. “Is this real, 732?” he asks.

I nod. “This is real, I promise.”

He nods and starts walking towards the trees where the truck is parked. I quickly open the side door and nod for him to get in. Abby lets out a sigh of relief.

“You’re cutting it close, Adam. The loop *just* ended,” Hailey says, turning around in her seat.

I climb into the truck and close the door, tossing my helmet to the ground. “We ran into an issue that… solved itself.” I pause.

“What issue?” Abby asks as Colton pulls away.

06 glances between everyone, almost pressing himself into the seat.

“The Handler came back early,” I state, staring at her. “How long was your distraction?”

“It was as long as I could keep him there,” she explains. “How’d you get out of it?”

I shake my head. “I actually don’t know…” I trail off, looking to 06. “Do you know what happened?”

He swallows. “I knew you didn’t have a phone on you. I simply persuaded him to let the matter drop.”

I furrow my eyebrows. “How?”

“Magic.”

I smile. “Is that how you got everyone to like you at Caulders?”

06 shrugs. “More or less. At Caulders, I had to be touching someone for it to work.”

“Like how 1048 had to be touching something to make it disappear.”

He nods. "Do you know how 12 and 54 are? I was told about 1048's fate, and that you were sold to the Lab. What about those two?"

"12 disappeared after the explosion and 54…" I clear my throat. "He, uh…"

06 places a hand on my shoulder. "I know, 732. I'm sorry."

I meet his eyes. "How?"

He taps his temple. "Magic. It also wasn't hard to see similarities when you stood right next to each other."

I nod, looking down at my hands in my lap. Inside the gloves, I can feel Jake's blood coating my hands.

"We've got a few hours until we're back at Jason's. Get comfy," Colton says.

"Do you need me to drive, Colt?" Abby asks.

"I'm fine, Abby. Driving isn't an issue."

The truck falls silent as we roll through the sleeping city.

The safehouse is quiet when we return. Ben, one of the older men at the house, is waiting in the living room. I walk next to 06 as we climb the wooden steps. The sun is starting to rise behind us. My jacket is completely unzipped, exposing the black t-shirt underneath. I left the helmet and gloves in the truck. Jason greets us as we enter the living room.

"How did it go?" He asks.

"Fine. We made it with seconds to spare." Hailey says, setting her bag on the couch.

Ben stands. "But you weren't followed?"

Colton shakes his head. "Nobody realized there was something wrong."

06 and I entered the living room.

Jason smiles and extends his hand to 06. "Welcome. I'm Jason," he says.

06 shakes his hand in a firm grip and smiles. "Nice to meet you. I'm… Brandon," he says.

Ben walks up. "I'm Ben. We'll be rooming together," he says, extending his hand.

06, Brandon, shakes his hand. "I look forward to it."

I watch as Ben and Brandon disappear upstairs. Colton, Abby, and Haliey make their way towards the kitchen. With a sigh, I start making my way up the worn stairs.

"Adam, where are you going?" Colton asks, turning around and looking through the banister at me.

I stop, looking around. "To my room…"

Colton smiles softly. "Are you hungry?" he asks.

I blink again. It's not time for breakfast yet, but he's eating? I look back up the stairs. "Connor will want food," I state.

"He's asleep, Adam," he says. "And there is plenty of food when he gets up. Come get something to eat."

I scratch at my Mark, my fingers catching the string around my neck. I have access to the kitchen *whenever*.

"Adam?" Colton asks.

I blink a few times. "Yeah, yeah I'm coming down," I say, climbing down the stairs and following him into the kitchen with a smile plastered on my face.

I can get used to this.

# PART THREE

# *TWO YEARS LATER*

# CHAPTER THIRTY SEVEN

## ADAM

I wake up to a pillow being slammed into my face. With a groan, I push myself up and glare at the unfortunate person. I turn to see Colton behind the couch, one of the pillows clutched in his hands. He's grinning. "Meeting in ten," he says.

"Did you have to hit me with the pillow?" I ask groggily, throwing my legs over the edge and standing up.

Colton shrugs. "Did you have to fall asleep in the living room instead of your room? Connor is starting to get worried about you."

I roll my eyes. *The couch was the closest thing and I knew I couldn't make it up the stairs.* "Why's that?" I ask.

Colton places his hands on the back of the couch, leaning forward. I glance at his hip and then his hands. He catches my gaze and straightens. "You've been passing out on the couch more and more. Almost like you're sick." He raises an eyebrow.

I wave a hand. "I'm fine." I start making my way towards the kitchen. I'll be right there. Just have to grab something to eat."

Colton shakes his head and limps up the stairs.

There are a few people chatting around the long table. Some of the older people we've gotten out. I nod to them as I rummage through the fridge.

"Adam, how was your nap?" Ben asks. Beside him, Brandon plays cards with Heather.

I chuckle, looking inside the large fridge. "It was relaxing," I say, grabbing a Dr. Pepper and closing the fridge door. Ben is smiling as he sips his drink.

"It looked relaxing," he jokes.

"You should try it sometime," I say, giving him a nod and walking out of the kitchen, taking my Dr. Pepper with me. Over the past couple of months, my magic has been flaring up. Jason built an unmeltable room in the barn after I nearly burnt down the woods. However, after a flare up, I'm so tired that I can barely make it to the couch somedays.

The stairs creak as I slowly make my way up to the office. Most everybody is outside, as they tend to be when we hold our meetings. A few people are wandering around and in their rooms. I catch a glimpse of Connor gardening with Allivane out of the second story window. I smile. Over the past two years, he and Allivane have become nearly inseparable. The office door is cracked open and I can hear hushed whispers from my place at the window. I turn, slowly walking towards the office.

"I still don't think it's a good idea," Colton says, his voice strong and unwavering.

"Do you have another one you'd like to present?" Abby snaps.

"This will have to do until we can figure out something else," Oliver says softly. "Can we agree on that?"

"As soon as we figure something else out, we get him out," Colton says.

"Agreed."

I furrow my eyebrows and my heart starts to pound. What isn't a good idea? Is this something that will come up in the meeting? I take a breath and knock, pushing the door fully open.

"Hey," I say, plastering a smile on my face. I twist the top of my drink open and set it on the table.

"Finally," Colton says as I settle into my chair. "Fall asleep again?"

I roll my eyes at him. "You're jealous of my couch nap and you know it," I say, taking a sip. The sweetness of the soda chases away the burnt taste that's become ever present in my mouth. “What’s on the agenda today?” I ask as I sink into the swivel chair.

Oliver leaned forward, clasping his hands on the table in front of him. “I’ve been in contact with some of my colleagues, and they are willing to help us put Rebren out of business for good.” His eyes flick to Abby and Colton. “However, they are requiring proof of the injustices done to Workers.”

I set my Dr. Pepper back on the table. “The thousands of people torn from their families isn’t proof enough?” I ask. “Aren’t parents worried that their kids aren’t coming home?”

Oliver meets my eyes. “They agree with us. There is plenty of proof if you know where to look. But you have to understand who it is we are working with now. This is the government. If there is no hard evidence, there won’t be any headway,” he explains. “Luckily, Abby has a solution to that.”

“There is a file filled with all the data from the Lab. Anything done there, it’s in that file,” she explains. “That should be enough to convince them.”

“How’d you find out about this?” I ask, leaning forward.

“I have some friends in Rebren,” she offers in explanation. Abby tosses her hair over her shoulder as she looks at Colton. He meets her gaze with a sympathetic expression.

I grab my drink again, untwisting the top and look between the two of them. "The same friends who helped you get a fake badge and Handlers uniform?"

She nods. "The same."

I nod and take a swig of my drink. "Alright. So the question boils down to," I say after I swallow. "How do we get this file?"

"That's the issue," Oliver starts. "It's on a secure floor in the Lab, and the room is locked with a passcode. Once you're in, it's easy from there. It's getting there; that's the issue."

I lean forward, resting my elbows on my knees. "I've got a uniform," I say. "And I have no problem talking my way around Handlers and staff, as we've discovered."

Abby looks at Colton and then Oliver. "You'll have to go in during the day," Abby finally says. "During Market hours. They'll know something is wrong if that specific computer is accessed after hours."

I lean back, tapping my fingers on the cap. "That's the hard part," I finally acknowledge. Rebren is crawling with people during the day. Workers being transported, Handlers moving from post to post, and potential buyers wandering around the viewing rooms. There would be no room for error.

Colton nods. "You'll have to make it past everyone, get the Worker out, and grab the footage. All without being spotted."

"Would we need to get a Worker out this time?" Abby asks.

"Yes," I say immediately. My Dr. Pepper sloshes in the bottle as I roughly set it down on the table. "We aren't going in and not getting someone out. I can do it."

Colton leans back in his chair, crossing his arms. "That's a lot of sneaking around. Can you really do it?"

I raise an eyebrow. "Colton, other than Brandon, I'm the most capable one here to do this."

Oliver shifts in his chair. "Are you completely positive, Adam?"

I breathe in deeply. "I can pass the Worker off to Abby, who will take them to Colton and Hailey, who wait in the truck. While Abby gets the Worker out, I will work on getting the footage off the computer and meet them at the truck after," I explain. "That also helps Hailey with the footage, leaving her to focus on one area at a time."

Abby leans back, crossing her arms over her chest. "That could work," she says softly. "If we time it right, it could work."

I lean forward, clapping my hands on my knees. "Great. When do we leave?"

# CHAPTER THIRTY EIGHT

## JAKE

My alarm goes off. Blinking, I groggily reach over and silence it. Next to me, Sara stirs and drapes an arm across my waist. I give her arm a gentle squeeze as I climb out of bed. Her blonde hair is sprawled across the pillows and I can't help but smile at her. Books from her classes sit on her nightstand. Her computer is shut on top of the stack and her reading glasses are neatly folded and set to the side.

The cold air hits my bare chest and I quickly pull on a shirt and make my way towards the closet. My work clothes are hung up together in a corner of the small closet. I grab one of the black polos and a pair of pants from the dresser. The clothes are softer than the ones I had worn for years at Rebren. These clothes are soft and professional. They are comfortable and the shoes are meant for standing for long hours.

"Jake?" Sara asks groggily. I peek out of the closet to see her sitting up, messy hair falling on her face.

"Good morning, darling," I say softly and make my way towards her. I sit next to her and she cuddles closer to me, wrapping her arms gently around me.

"Good morning," she whispers, leaning her head on my chest.

I brush back her hair. "I didn't wake you, did I?"

She shakes her head 'no' against my chest.

I smile. "You can go back to bed, Sara," I whisper. "It's a Wednesday. You don't have class."

"I have my group meeting," she mumbles. "In two hours."

I rub her back. "Ah. Are you feeling up to going?"

She nods. "I'm only barely out of the first trimester, Jake." She sits up and stares at me. "I can still function reasonably well."

"I never doubted you."

She raises a finger. "And the morning sickness has passed."

I kiss her singular finger. "I'm glad."

Sara smiles and taps me on the nose. "You'll be late if we stay here much longer," she says, climbing out of the bed.

I stand as well. "Duty calls," I state.

She flashes me a smile over her shoulder as she heads towards the bathroom. “Unfortunately. I’ll see you after work.”

I slip my wedding ring on my finger, pocket my wallet and keys, and grab my phone off its charger. “I love you, Sara,” I say, catching her wrist and pulling her in for a kiss.

“I love you too, Jake,” she says when we part. “Now get going, you giant dork.”

*   *   *

“Good morning, David,” I say as I walk in through the large double glass doors. As always, the warehouse smells of rubber, metal, and cardboard.

“Morning, Mr. Harrison,” David responds with a nod of his head. He barely glances up from the computer in front of him.

“Ordering truck today?” I ask, grabbing my badge from its hook behind the desk.

“Nah. Going through the orders processed overnight. Do you want to know how many people decide to order parts at 3 am?” He asks, clicking something.

“Do I want to know?” I ask with a chuckle.

“Around fifty. Who is thinking of this stuff? Are they high?” David rants.

“Good luck,” I say.

He waves a hand in the air. “You gotta put it together. I pity you, Harrison.”

Shaking my head, I make my way to the back of the warehouse, nodding to people as I pass. Large shelves full of auto parts and other auto related products make long hallways. Boxes of all sizes meant for shipping sit in neat piles at the front of each shelved hallway. I grab my clipboard from the wall to start inventory for the day.

“Jake!” A loud voice shouts.

I turn, pen halfway to the paper. “Jan! I didn’t realize you were coming in today,” I say, capping the pen and walking over to my boss. He gives me a hug and pats my shoulder. “How was the vacation?”

“Much needed!” he says. “It’s a wonder what some time away from work can do to a man.”

I nod in agreement. “A wonder in deed,” I say. “You look like you got some sun in Hawaii.”

Jan chuckles and motions to his sunburnt nose. “Apparently, applying sunblock once doesn’t get you through a whole day of snorkeling.”

“It’s been a while! You’re looking stronger,” he says as he changes the subject, gripping my shoulders.

I let out a nervous laugh. “All that time you’ve got me back here lifting cases and packing parts builds up the muscle fast," I say, trying to deflect from the topic. My magic helps a lot, too. As I've been working out, my magic quickens the recovery process, leading to faster muscle growth.

"Apparently. I should be back here more," he jokes. "Did you add onto your tattoo as well?" He asks, gesturing to my arm.

I glance down to see the floral picture stretching down nearly to my elbow. I had it lengthened after someone at the store commented saying it was strange that I started where it did. "Yeah. Thought it needed a bit more," I say with a shrug.

Jan smiles. "I like it. It suits you," he says, patting me on the shoulder. "I'll be around later. Keep working hard!"

"I always do," I say softly. I tap the pen against the clipboard in my hands, staring at the shelves in front of me. Two years later and it almost feels wrong to be working a simple job with little to no supervision, much less to get paid for it. I get to arrive and leave unsupervised, eat delicious food on my break, talk to my coworkers whenever I want, and there are even some company parties I attend. I shake my head. It almost feels unfair after the years I spent in Rebren.

I finish up inventory and start stacking cases from the truck to load onto the shelves. David hasn't sent back the orders yet, so I have some time to kill. The forklift sits across from the large bay door where the cases and pallets are stacked. The truck came this morning around 4 am, leaving those on morning shift to organize and put away the parts. The rumble of the forklift engine soothes my thoughts and makes my magic hum. I take a deep breath and start moving the pallets, raising them up to the height of the shelves. I go to push the pallets onto the metal shelves, but the machine doesn't move. It clicks and whirs in protest. I try putting it in reverse and it makes the same noise.

"What game are you playing?" I whisper, leaning out of the cab and looking at the pallets. There is a string tangled around the pallets and prongs. I sigh and shake my head. "Always causing problems, aren't you?"

I turn the key and the engine quits rumbling. With the forklift turned off, I carefully climb over the cab and onto the prongs. They tremble with my added weight and I unconsciously hold my breath as I shuffle my way to the tangled pallets. My foot slips off the thin metal and I start to fall. Reaching out, I grab the plastic wrapping on the pallet and kick my feet towards the shelves, trying to get any sort of footing. The plastic wrapping starts to tear and I look up to see the pallet sliding forward, the prongs tipping down ever so slightly. With a grunt, I swing myself towards the shelves and let go of the plastic. The pallets fall and my fingers skim the shelves. I hit the ground with a thud, my vision going black.

* * *

"Jake? Jake, can you hear me?" Jan's muffled voice calls as if I'm hearing him through water.

I blink away my fuzzy vision and shake my head. My magic hums and swirls, rushing towards the broken and battered parts of my body. Warmth floods my body as it works and I struggle to sit up. Firm hands grab me and help me sit up. I glance down at my clothes to see blood splattered across my shirt and onto my pants. I raise a hand to my head and feel warm blood there, but no cut. My head pounds and I gently massage it, trying to cover the lack of cut from Jan.

"Jake?"

"I'm fine," I croak as I stand up. Jan is there in an instant, helping me out of the rubble. His hands hold me steady as I take a wobbly step forwards.

"Are you sure? Should I call an ambulance?" He asks, leaning in to take a look at my head.

I clasp a hand over the spot where I should have a cut. "Just a headache. It looks worse than it actually is," I reassure him. I turn and look at the broken pallet and ruined merchandise. "I'll… I can clean it up."

Jan shakes his head. "No. You are sitting down and we will call Sara to come get you," he says. "You do not need to be cleaning this up. Are you sure you don't want to get checked out at least? You might have a concussion."

I blink a few times to clear my head. The headache is fading and my magic retreats back to its usual spot. "I'm fine. I can get the mess, really," I say. "I broke it after all."

Jan walks me to the break room and sits me down, settling into a chair next to me. “You hit your head. I’m calling Sara and you’re going home to rest,” he says.

Deciding it’s best if I don’t push, I lean back in the chair and wait for Sara to get here, hand still clamped on my head.

# CHAPTER THIRTY NINE

# ADAM

I sit in the back of the truck, my heart pounding. People stream in and out of the front doors, some with Workers in tow, some without. Handlers roam about as they transport Workers or head in for their shifts. My throat seems to close up. After years of sneaking in after hours, this is the first time since I was brought to the Lab that I've been back during the day.

"Adam?" Colton asks from the driver's seat. "You alright?"

I nod, slipping the helmet on. "Fine," I croak out.

Colton taps his fingers on the back of the seat. "Are you sure? There is still time if you want to switch out."

I raise an eyebrow. "How's your leg today?" I ask.

Colton's face darkens at the mention of his injury.

"That's what I thought," I sigh. "Just old memories is all. I'll be fine." My back starts to itch, as if the bandages are still there. They haven't been for over two years. There hasn't been anyone around to whip me for using my magic. I tighten the glove straps around my wrists and open the door. "Be back soon." My boots crunch on the pavement and I have to close my eyes momentarily. For a moment, I'm back at Rebren with chains around my wrists and hands clamped onto my arms. Taking a deep breath, I start moving towards the large building, blending with the crowd.

Using the employee entrance, I pass by the desk and continue on. *"Identification and reason for return?"* A woman's voice repeats in my mind. Adam Carlson here to steal vital Rebren information.

The lobby is alive with activity, making it easy for me to move around people unnoticed. Many Handlers walk around, helping me seem inconspicuous. The uniform seems to cave in on me as I make my way around the crowd. How do the Handlers stand this uniform with all these people? It's too constricting and heavy, the helmet alone causing my breathing to speed up.

Other Handlers nod at me as I pass. I nod back purely out of keeping my cover, my heart feeling like it'll burst out of my chest. Hopefully, this is the last time I'll have to do this and Rebren will be taken down in the near future.

"Just make it a little longer. Then you can panic," I mutter to myself. I pass by a Handler holding onto a young boy's arm, dragging him towards the administration rooms. The boy looks up at me with tear filled eyes. My magic starts pulsing as he gets closer.

"Please," he whispers. "Please help me."

His Handler jerks on the boy's arm. “Quiet,” he snaps.

The boy whimpers but falls silent. I am frozen in place by his tears filled blue eyes. They turn a corner and disappear from view. I take a deep breath and force my feet to move. Ghosts of chains and grips tighter than manacles press down on me.

*“Why did you stop?”* Colton asks in my ear.

“Momentary distraction,” I whisper. “Almost there.”

The viewing rooms are full of run down Workers. I find number 50 and swipe my ID across the black box. It blinks green and the lock pulls back. I open the door and stand in the doorway. Seven sets of hollow eyes turn and stare at me. I hold my breath, feeling my heart race inside of my chest.

“212015,” I call out, willing my voice to be steady.

A tall, thin man stands. He’s older with thinning brown hair. My stomach dropped. “There is a buyer, sir?” He asks slowly.

I nod once. 15, my friend, walks towards me with his back straight but eyes cast down. I grab his arm and pull him out of the room, locking the door behind me. The walk to the administration room where Abby waits is not long, but the silence is overwhelming. The man next to me is quiet, unlike how he was at lunchtime.

The black box on the door to the administration room blinks green as I swipe my ID. Abby waits there, pacing. She's chewing on her nails when I open the door, pulling 15 inside as well.

"Adam! You made it!" she says, throwing her arms around me. I hug her back.

I remove my helmet when we part, setting it on the table. "No issues yet. I assume Hailey has the camera's in this room?" I ask.

She nods. "For the next ten minutes."

"Perfect." I turn towards 15 and smile. "Long time, no see."

The man smiles and nods once. "How did you get out?" he asks.

I gesture to Abby. "She and a few friends helped me a couple of years ago. I'm here to return the favor."

15 looks skeptically at Abby standing behind me.

I smile again. "You can trust her."

He nods and steps forward. "Fredrick Laybell, nice to meet you." He extends his hand towards Abby.

She smiles and takes it. "Abigail Sommerfeld. Nice to meet you, Fredrick. Want to get out of here?"

"Yes, ma'am." Fredrick turns towards me. "Will I see you again?"

I nod. "As soon as I finish with today's shenanigans."

He shakes his head at that. "Rebellious teenager," he mutters under his breath. "Stay safe."

I pat him on the shoulder and grab my helmet. "I will." I put my helmet back on and slip out the door, heading for the stairs. There aren't any Handlers in the stairwell. I flex my hands in my gloves, feeling Jake's blood underneath my nails and coating my skin.

*"One more floor, Adam,"* Colton says over the com system. *"You're almost there."*

"Got it. Door is next to the supply closet. Passcode 5721," I repeat back to him. The further up the stairs I go, the more my back itches. *Just keep going.*

I make it to the third floor without running into anyone.

"Hailey, cameras?" I ask, pausing in the stairwell.

*"Cameras are out. You have one minute to get into the room,"* she says.

I crack open the door and slip out of the stairwell. The Lab storage computer is kept here specifically to stop exactly what we're doing: stealing vital information. Once we get these files, we are one step closer to ending Rebren forever. Once I get this information, I'll be one step closer to going home.

The computer sits alone on a single desk on the far wall of the room. I ignore the light switch on the wall and enter the room. Slowly, I make my way to the computer and pull the chair close. I remove my helmet and gloves, setting them on the ground beside me. The flash drive is hidden inside my coat pocket. Unzipping it, I grab the tiny black stick and plug it in. The computer beeps and the screen turns on, asking for a passcode. I enter it and a singular file folder pops up.

"Okay, Abby, what file is it?" I ask.

*"It should be titled today's date in the experiments folder. We need everything,"* she says, slightly out of breath. She and Fredrick must have just gotten to the truck.

Nodding, I click through folder after folder. A title catches my attention. '2157732'. I click into it and dozens of files pop up, all titled differently. Some are titled records, some are titled with questions. Hypotheses, I realize, from my time in the Lab. "Abby, there's a folder here with my name on it," I say.

*"Focus, Adam. You've spent time in the Lab. There's going to be a file on you,"* she directs.

I check the dates, unable to help the budding curiosity. Most of the files are dated from years ago. Except the one titled 'revived'. That one is from a few days ago.

"This one is from Monday," I whisper. My hands start to shake.

*"Please focus,"* Abby says. *"Just get the files we need and get out of there."*

I chew the inside of my lip, debating. With a sigh, I exit out and find the folder titled with today's date. My leg starts to bounce as I open it.

It's empty.

What? "Abby, the folder is empty," I whisper. How is it empty? "Do I have the wrong one? Is there another folder?"

There is no response from Abby or Colton or Hailey.

I take a deep breath, searching the other folders, nearly going into the one on me. "Abby, walk me through this. Where else could the footage be?" My hands shake again. Why aren't they responding?

The door handle rattles. Feeling sweat drip down my back, I turn around. The door opens and light floods the tiny room. I blink at the contrast, shielding my face from the light. When my eyes adjust, I see the Boss and two Handlers standing in the doorway.

I smile sheepishly. "Hey, I was just doing some maintenance on this computer."

The Boss raises an eyebrow. "Really, 732?"

I shrug. "You can forget you saw me, right? And just let me leave?"

He shakes his head and smiles, looking down at his feet. "You know I can't do that. Why don't you stand up and let the Handlers check you in?"

"You can't sell me. I'm too rebellious."

The Boss looks me in the eye. "Who told you that?"

"You did. When you sold me to Caulder. That he was my last chance." I stare him down, straightening my spine. "So why not let me go? I'll cost you more money and resources than I can offer."

The Boss shakes his head. "You'll see. Play nice and you won't get hurt." He walks out, motioning to the Handlers.

"Easy or the hard way?" the one on the right asks. Daniel. *My* Handler from Mr. Caulder's house.

"Fine," I say softly, looking to the side. "I'll come with you." The line in my ear is still silent. Why had they abandoned me?

The Handlers bring me to the second building, the Lab, using a sky bridge that connects both buildings. They lock me in a processing room, taking extra precautions with how tight they lock the manacles around my wrists and ankles. They snap one of the silver chains around my neck. My magic flares but cannot make it past the chain. At least not without great effort. The Handlers leave me without a word, not even bothering to take my stolen uniform.

After what seems like hours of waiting, the door opens. A Handler holds the door while my visitor walks in.

My visitor is Abby.

She walks in with her hands in her back pockets. Her long dark hair is loose and flows down her back, differing from the bun she had it in this morning. She's wearing her glasses and a pair of converse shoes. Different clothes than she was wearing earlier. Abby flashes me a sheepish smile as the door closes.

I smile back at her, standing. "Abby, you have no idea how happy I am to see you."

She looks down, kicking her feet. "It's good to see you unharmed," she says.

I shrug. "They had me before I said anything. No use fighting." I pause. "The files weren't there."

Abby nods, still looking down. "I know."

I freeze, picking at my fingers. "You know? Then why did you have me come here? Why didn't we all leave when we could?" I pause. "Why was there a file on me dated this week?"

Abby looks up at me with tears in her eyes. "Because we…" her voice cracks. "Because we need those files, Adam. Without them-"

"I know, without them, we can't fully take down Rebren. I was in that meeting too, Abby." I take a deep breath, my magic swirling uncomfortably under my skin. "You said you knew where the files were."

"I know where they will be," she says softly. "They don't exist yet."

"What?" I whisper. "Please tell me you don't have something to do with that folder, Abby. Please, get me out of here," I plead. The shackles all of a sudden feel very constricting. I can feel my pulse against the chain around my neck. The chain seems to close in, cutting off my air. My heart rate accelerates, blood pounding in my head.

Abby looks heartbroken. A few tears fall when she blinks. "Please trust me, Adam. We need that information. It needs to exist. I need you to trust me on this."

"Stop being cryptic, Abby. What do you mean?" I say, taking a step towards her. The chains pull taunt, stopping me. The shackles tug at my wrists, pulling them back. I clench my hands to stop them from shaking.

She shakes her head and looks down, knocking on the door. Tears drip down her cheeks. "Just please trust me, Adam," she says softly, then turns and walks out.

"Wait!" I shout. "Abby! Don't leave me here! Please!" I strain against the shackles again, feeling them tear at my skin. "Abby! Please! Don't abandon me! Please!"

The door shuts and the sound echoes through the metal room like laughter. I collapse against the bench, feeling truly alone.

# CHAPTER FORTY

## JAKE

"Jake, what happened?" Sara asks as she helps me climb into the car.

I hold the ice pack against my head and lean back against the faux leather seat. "Just a work accident," I say. "I'm really okay."

Sara gives me a sideways glance before shutting my door. I watch her with clear vision as she walks around the car and slides into her seat. She's silent as she turns out of the parking lot. Cars fly past us on the highway as Sara speeds up. "What kind of accident?"

"Fell off a forklift," I mumble. "I'm fine. Just a small scrape." I brush a finger over a blood splatter on my shirt.

"The blood says differently," she says, placing a hand on her head. "I should be taking you to the hospital, not home."

I give her a reassuring smile. "Head wounds bleed a lot," I state. My head has long stopped bleeding, although my head still throbs slightly. "I will be okay. I promise."

"Do you need a hospital or just rest?" Sara finally asks.

"Rest," I say.

With a sigh, she shakes her head. "Alright. You must have one exceptionally hard head."

I shrug and offer her a shy smile. "Runs in the family, I guess."

Sara raises an eyebrow. "You were adopted."

"All the more reason to guess." I pause. "How was your meeting this morning?"

Sara shrugs, drumming her fingers on the steering wheel. "It was fine. One person did all the talking and the rest of us nodded and let her run the show."

I grab her hand and rub small circles with my thumb on the back of her hand. "Are you annoyed at that?"

She pursed her lips. "I'm more annoyed that we had the meeting. It was generally useless and took up more time than was necessary."

"We'll go out tonight. Have a nice evening and relax."

This earns a small laugh from her. "You fell off a forklift today. I don't think we should be going out."

We pull into our parking stall and I gently turn her face towards me. "Sara, darling, I'm fine. We can go out tonight. I'll shower and get cleaned up and we'll go."

Her blue eyes flick to my head. "Are you sure?"

I nod and reassure her with a smile.

She smiles. "Okay, then. We'll go. But I'm driving."

Sara holds my hand the whole way up the stairs that lead up to our apartment, her hand nearly crushing mine. My magic swirls around my hand, soothing away any semblance of pain.

Once we are inside with the door closed, I pull her against my chest and wrap my arms around her. I feel her smile against my chest. She pats her hand on my arm. "Go shower, you're covered in blood," she says with a smile, finally pulling away.

I give her a kiss atop her head before making my way to the bathroom. The light flickers on and hums. My reflection stares at me in the mirror. Blood has completely covered my front and dried on the side of my neck, covering my tattoo. Some splatters have made it onto my pants and my hair sticks to my skin. The last time I was covered in blood, I was escaping Caulder and had been brought to Maria and Brad. I shake my head and strip off my shirt, starting the shower.

* * *

"Wear this," Sara says as I walk into the room, a towel wrapped around my waist. A pair of pants and a shirt hit me in the chest and I barely catch them.

"What is this?" I ask, examining the blue button up and dark jeans.

"An outfit for dinner tonight," she says, smirking. She's already dressed in a patterned blue dress that hugs her curves. Her small bump where our baby is growing is accentuated. She's doing her hair in front of the mirror on her vanity. Sara's always preferred to do her hair standing up, bending over to get her long hair curled.

I quickly pull on the clothes she threw at me. I turn towards her as I button the long sleeved shirt. I put a bandage over the spot on my head where there should be a cut. "You're looking sexy," I say, sauntering over to her.

She smiles and continues curling her hair, twisting the strands over her fingers and letting it fall.

"How's our baby doing?" I whisper, sneaking behind her and rubbing my hand on her baby bump.

"*He* is doing fine," Sara says, raising her eyebrow in challenge at me in the mirror.

I smirk and rest my chin on her shoulder. "Our *daughter* is growing well?"

Sara puts the curling iron down and turns around, lacing her fingers together behind my neck. "Our *son* is very hungry." She smirks and starts swaying side to side.

I brush a curled strand away from her face. Her blue eyes are framed by the black liner and mascara she's applied. "Then let's get both you girls some food," whisper.

Sara pulls my head down and kisses me before releasing her hold. "Get your shoes on, love."

I tug on some socks and my nice brown shoes. I pocket my wallet, phone, and keys, and follow Sara out to the car. "Which restaurant are we going to?" I ask.

She smiles. "You'll find out."

I lean back and enjoy the drive. Sara is by far a better driver than I am and knows this area better than I do. She takes us to a nice seafood place. "A nice relaxing dinner, right?" She asks.

I smile. "The perfect choice."

Sara gives me her signature smug look before exiting the car. I follow her lead. She links her arm through mine as we walk through the doors. Immediately, smells and spices waft through the opening.

"Table for two, please," I ask the hostess.

The dark haired woman nods and leads us to a table. I pull out Sara's chair and push it in for her.

"Why, thank you," she says with a smile.

I slide into my own chair. "Of course, my darling."

Our waiter gives us our menus and walks away, giving us a few minutes to look over them.

Sara flashes me a smile and glances down at her menu. "I'm thinking a little bit of sushi and a little bit of salad on the side?"

I nod, flashing her a smile. "I think that's great," I say.

People pass us on their way towards their tables. A man in a dark blue suit with close cropped brown hair pauses. "I'm sorry to interrupt," he says, walking over to our table.

I look up and I'm met with a familiar gaze. The man's eyes flick to my neck. I lean back and cross my arms. "Yes?" I ask, feeling my heart start to pound.

Lowe, the Handler from Caulder's house. "Do I know you from somewhere?"

I frown, picking at my shirt with the hand that's covered. "No, I don't believe so."

He straightens up. "I was sure," he whispered. "Where are you from, sir?" His eyes again flick to my neck, to where a simple tattoo should be.

"St. George, Kansas," I state. "If you don't mind, I'm trying to have a nice dinner with my lovely wife." I raise my eyebrows at him. *Please leave me alone. Please don't recognize me. Please don't take me back there, to him.*

Lowe nods and steps back. "Of course. Enjoy your meal, sir," he says, turning on his heel and continuing down the aisle.

"What was that about?" Sara asks, reaching across the table.

I am still staring at him as he sits down. *How did you find me? What are you doing all the way down here?* As if in a daze, I grab her hand and give it a squeeze. "I'm not sure," I whisper.

The waiter returns. She gives us a smile and asks what we would like to order. Sara smiles and tells her what she wants to eat.

"And you, sir?"

I blink and turn my attention to the waiter. I give her my order and hand her my menu as well. The woman walks away, leaving us alone again.

"Jake, are you sure you're alright?" Sara asks quietly. "Is your head bothering you?"

I shake my head. "Not at all."

Sara looks over her shoulder at the man sitting a few feet away from us. "Are you sure you don't know that man? You've gone pale."

I smile to reassure her. "He looked like someone I met years ago. But it's not him," I lie.

Sara smiles and squeezes my hand. “Let’s forget about it and enjoy our night, okay?”

“Alright.”

# CHAPTER FORTY ONE

## ADAM

They leave me in the processing room for hours. I stare at the blinking red light on the camera, daring them to come into the room. Daring them to put me back into the Lab, to make me into their perfect lab rat.

The lock clicks and I turn my attention to the door. I don't stand this time, choosing instead to glare up at my next visitor from the metal bench, tracing my thumb along the edge of the shackles. My magic swirls angrily at being locked away again. The Boss walks in, followed by two Handlers who stand in the doorway.

"You're not going to explode on us if we touch you, are you?" The Boss asks calmly.

My magic pulses under my skin, but not nearly enough to be dangerous. The pendant around my neck stays cold. "Not unless you want me to," I say.

The Boss raises an eyebrow. "I understand why you're upset. I'm asking if you can stay in control."

I smirk. "I'm always in control."

The Boss's expression doesn't change. "Good. The Handlers here are going to unchain you and take you to your room. You are going to cooperate with them, understand?" he says.

I glare at him specifically. "And what if I run?" I ask, leaning back and tilting my chin up.

One of the Handlers advances and jabs me with the strange prod he carries. A volt shoots through my whole body, feeling too much like the prod in the Lab years ago. I double over, wrapping my arms around my midsection. It takes me a moment to recover my breath. I gasp for air as the Boss answers.

"The Handlers have been given permission to use whatever means necessary to get you back should you run," he says. "You've just experienced one of them. Do you want to find out about the others?"

I glare up at him again. "No, sir," I spit.

"Good. Behave and everything goes smoothly. Disobey and things get nasty," he states then nods to the Handlers. They push me into a sitting position and unlock the cuffs on my wrists and ankles, uncovering the red lines that are left from my previous struggle. My insides are screaming at me and my magic is flaring, unable to escape.

The two men pull me to my feet and push me out of the room. Tugging my arms from their grasps, I turn and glare at them. "I'm not going to run away," I growl. "You don't have to hold onto me everywhere we go."

The Handlers let go of me but still stay close by my side, nearly brushing my shoulders. We walk down multiple identical hallways and up a flight of stairs until we stop at a simple metal door. This looks exactly the same, yet so different from my previous time in the Lab. We must be on a different floor. There is a black box on the side next to it. The Handler takes out his key card and swipes it against the box, unlocking the door. The Handler on my left gives me a shove and I walk into the room. I don't turn around as I hear the door close and the lock slide into place, trapping me again. Different location, same situation.

I take a deep breath and examine the room. It's one of the nicest rooms I've seen in Rebren's Program. There is a window with normal, simple blinds on the wall opposite the door. Sunlight streams in through the half closed blinds. I linger on the window. *They've never given me a window before. Workers are too dangerous to have a potential to escape.* Blinking, I turn my attention to the rest of the room. There is an actual bed that looks somewhat comfortable underneath the window with a small wooden dresser on the right wall. No trunk sits at the foot of the bed. There is an open door on the left wall leading to a separate bathroom that includes a shower and a bathtub, with a sink and cabinet. A chair sits in one corner of the room. Inside the dresser are five different pairs of gray sweat pants and gray t-shirts. There is another drawer holding three pairs of thicker sweatpants and sweatshirts and some thick socks. The bottom drawer holds socks and underwear. Inside the bathroom is a small closet that holds towels, soaps, and a basic emergency kit.

"Still a prison," I mutter, turning away from the closet.

I shrug off the Handler uniform and pile it on the chair. They didn't give me any shoes, so I put the heavy boots next to the dresser. Abby told me to trust her, but then abandoned me to Rebren? I sit on the bed, staring at the dresser. If the footage doesn't exist, but it will, why didn't we wait until afterwards to steal it? Why is there a folder with my number created on Monday? Why am I really here? I rub my eyes and stand up. Grabbing a pair of thick sweats, I make my way to the bathroom. I might as well take a shower while I wait for whatever is going to happen next.

* * *

Hot steam fogs up the mirror, obscuring my reflection. I towel dry my shaggy hair and quickly get dressed in the sweats. I walk back into my room to see Jackson leaning up against the wall, reading. He's dressed casually, with a brown leather jacket over a gray t-shirt. He looks more like he belongs on a farm than he does in the Lab. I freeze in the bathroom doorway. Jackson closes his book and smiles.

"732, wonderful to see you again," Jackson says in a deep, southern drawl. He extends his hand towards me warmly.

I don't shake his hand. Back to the number. "What am I doing here, Jackson?" I ask.

Jackson nods and lowers his hand, tucking his book under his arm. “Your magic is… unique,” he says. “We want to study it.”

“I’m here to be a lab rat again,” I say. Just a number, nothing more.

Jackson shrugs. “In a sense,” he says, walking to the door and hovering his id over the black box. “Want to get out of this room?”

I grit my teeth and slowly nod. It’s better than being trapped inside this room.

He smiles. “Great.” The black box beeps as he swipes his card. The lock clicks and the door groans open. Jackson grabs the handle and pulls the door open. “After you,” he says.

I slowly walk out of the room, my bare feet against the cool tile. The silver chain rubs against my skin, still wet from my shower. The chain traps water between it and my skin since I can’t get a towel in between to dry off. I can feel the chain every time I swallow. Jackson walks slightly in front of me, hands in his pockets and book tucked up against his side.

“What were you reading?” I ask, trying to break the tense silence.

“Hmm?” he asks, slowing down until he’s directly next to me.

I nod to his book. “In my room.”

“Some self-help book on raising kids,” he turns it over in his hands before tucking it back under his arm. “Figured it could help me a bit.”

I raise an eyebrow. “You have kids?”

He smirks at me. “You sound shocked.”

I shrug. “I guess I don’t see Rebren Employees as family focused.” When Jackson doesn’t respond, I continue. “You tear families apart by stealing us away and keeping us here, buying and selling us as if we’re tools. Kinda hard to think that you have families of your own when you treat us like this.”

Jackson lets out a long whistle. “You’ve got a point,” he says.

It’s quiet before I ask “How many kids do you have?”

Jackson smiles. “Two little girls. Addie and Tyla.”

“Cute.”

We stop at a simple door. Jackson taps his id card against the black box and opens the door, revealing a doctor's office. “Another visit to the doctor?” I ask with a raised eyebrow.

Jackson glances at me out of the corner of his eye. “You say that as if you’ve been here before.”

"Not here specifically, but I've seen a lot of doctors here," I say and walk in before him.

"Probably for a good reason then," Jackson says softly, following behind me.

There is a dark haired woman who leads me to a chair. "Please, sit," she says.

I do, rolling up my sleeves and holding out my arm to her. She smiles as she sits in the rolling chair next to me. The woman isn't phased as she tugs on a pair of pink gloves. "How are you today, 732?" she asks.

"I've been better," I state, leaning back in the chair.

"I can understand that," she responds. "I just need a few vials today."

I nod and watch her as she inserts the needle and hooks up the tubes. I barely feel the needle go in. I watch my blood flow through the thin tube and into the vial, red and rich.

"I'm dying, aren't I?" I ask after a long stretch of silence.

Jackson tenses from his spot on the wall and the woman pauses in her work before continuing, grabbing another vial and fitting it to the tube. "What makes you think that?" he asks.

I shrug my right shoulder, careful not to disturb the needle sticking out of my left arm. "All the signs are there,"

I start. "It started with all the testing before I was sent to Caulder's place. My magic has been flaring up and I taste burning in my mouth all the time. I pass out after using it and I can barely make it to my room. Now, you're doing more tests. It all adds up." My insides are still burning from the prod earlier and my magic swirls uncomfortably in my chest.

Jackson takes in a breath and nods. "I guess we weren't too discrete, were we?"

"No, you weren't," I smirk. "So what am I really here for? Does it have something to do with the new folder created this week?"

"They told me you were found in the computer room," he mutters. Jackson flicks some invisible lint off his jacket. "I didn't lie to you in telling you that we want to study your magic, however, it's for a different reason than you're probably thinking."

"And what reason is that?" The nurse removed the needle and places a bandaid over top of the site. She rolls her chair and vials to the other side of the room where the long counter sits.

"To help you live," he says simply.

I nod and stand up, shaking out my arm. "Let's get to it then."

# CHAPTER FORTY TWO

## ABBY

The truck is silent as we pull up to the large house. Colton hasn't spoken a word since we left Rebren. Frederick sits in the back with Hailey and hasn't stopped looking out the window. He's an older man with greying hair.

Colton parks the truck and turns it off. He clenches his jaw and stares straight ahead.

"Colton?" I whisper.

"What's done is done," he mutters and climbs out of the car.

I turn around and smile at Fredrick, who's watching the few people run out of the red painted front door. "Are you ready?" I ask.

He gives me a hesitant smile. "I don't know what to expect," he says quietly.

Hailey grabs her bag and stomps away, following Colton into the house.

“There’s going to be a lot of new people, but people just like you,” I explain. “Jason owns this house and takes care of everybody. You’ll like him.”

“Will 732… Adam be okay?” His eyebrows furrow in concern.

I nod. “He will. We’ll figure out a way to get him out.”

Frederick nods, unbuckling quietly. I walk with him around the truck, meeting the small group of people.

Connor runs up to me, Allivane right behind him. “Where’s Adam?” His blue eyes look from the truck to Fredrick and then back to me.

“He got caught.”

*“Abby! Please! Don’t leave me here!”*

“We did everything to get him back, but we weren’t able to.”

*“Please, just trust me.”*

Connor’s face falls. “He’s back in the Lab?” he whispers, horrified. Behind him, Allivane furrows her eyebrows. I forget she never was involved with Rebren.

I put a hand on his shoulder. “He’s strong. He’ll be okay.”

Connor meets my eyes. “Are you sure?”

I nod and offer him an encouraging smile. "I'd like you to meet someone, though." His eyes move to Fredrick standing slightly behind me. Connor extends his hand.

"Nice to meet you. I'm Connor," he says.

Fredrick takes his hand, the taller man smiles warmly at Connor's thin frame. "It's nice to meet you, Connor. I'm Fredrick." The older man adjusts his glasses as Connor smiles at him.

Jason approaches us, putting a large hand on Connors shoulder. "A newcomer?" He smiles.

Frederick nods and shakes his hand. "Nice to meet you, sir. I'm Fredrick."

"Jason Roames. Would you like a tour and some new clothes?"

The tall man looks so relieved and nods. "Yes, sir," he whispers.

Jason led the man up the wooden steps and into the house. I catch Colton watching me from the front window. He waves me into the house. I say goodbye to Connor and Allivane and walk into the house. Colton is waiting for me by the stairs.

"Oliver wants to talk, and Hailey has some questions," he says, his voice monotone.

I take in a breath. "I'd be surprised if she didn't have questions."

Colton looks back out the window. "Did we do the right thing, Abby?"

I sigh, brushing my hair back from my face. "I hope so." Adam's pleas echo in my head, haunting me. The look on his face…

Colton starts slowly walking up the stairs, using the banister to pull himself up. I hold out my arm to support him. He ignores me and continues hobbling up step by step.

"Why are you so stubborn?" I ask, matching his pace. "Why won't you accept my help, or anyone's help for that matter?"

The look he gives me this time is a mix between a glare and his one vulnerable look. "I don't need help. I'll have to manage on my own eventually, why not start now?"

We step up another step. "Strength isn't doing everything yourself."

He's turned his attention back to the steps.

I hold out my arm again. "Let me help you," I whisper.

He doesn't move, doesn't step up. Finally, he loops his arm through mine and pushes off the step, leaning his weight into me. I brace him as we step up together, feet moving in synchrony just as they did after the crash. Step after step, we move together until we reach the second floor. I lower my arm, but Colton doesn't let go. He laces his fingers through mine, sending butterflies fluttering in my stomach, as we walk into the meeting room.

Oliver is sitting in his usual spot at the head of the table, and Hailey is leaning against the wall with her arms crossed. I quietly close the door and Colton leans against a chair.

"Care to explain why I was to cut communication when Adam needed us most?" Hailey asks with a raised eyebrow.

I sigh and sink into a chair. "The best place for Adam right now is the Lab," I start explaining.

"How. How is the place that *tortured* him the best place for him?" She pushes off the wall and moves towards the table.

"He's sick, Hailey. They have the materials to help him," I state, leaning forward and placing my hand on the table.

"Sick how?"

I rub my eyes. "His magic is acting strangely, and I'm sure you've noticed how he's been acting."

Hailey simply glares at me with her arms still crossed. Her platinum blonde hair falls loose over her shoulders.

"I'm not happy about it either," Colton chimes in. "That place nearly killed him before, and now he's back there. But they agreed to help him instead of simply experimenting on him."

Hailey turns to her dad. "Did you know?" she asks. "Were you in on this?"

Oliver simply clasps his hands together and presses them against his chin. Hailey throws her hands in the air and turns around. "I can't believe this," she shouts and then leans against the table, pressing her palms into the wood. "Since when did we send people *back* to Rebren instead of only getting them out?"

"Since they started dying without their technology!" I shout, slamming my hand on the table.

"You would know! You were doing the experimenting only a few years ago!" Hailey shouts.

I clench my jaw and glare at her. "It's because of that job that allows us to get into places we never could have before. Do you want to go back to doing it the old fashioned way?"

Oliver leans forward. "As soon as there is a solution, they've agreed to let us come get him. Until then, this is the best way to save his life."

Hailey scowls at her dad before stomping towards the door. "Next time there is a change in plan, include me. And next time we send someone back, get someone else to run security and tech." She flings the door open and storms out of the meeting room.

# *4 MONTHS LATER*

# CHAPTER FORTY THREE

# ADAM

My footsteps echo as I pace my room, waiting for Jackson. Light from the rising sun streams in through the open blinds. Unfortunately, the window doesn't open to let in fresh air. After going back and forth a couple more times, I move the chair from its corner of the room. I place it near the bathroom door and start moving the dresser. It scrapes against the floor and I freeze, waiting for something to happen, still waiting for someone to burst in and stop me.

Nothing happens. Nobody walks in.

I continue to pull it towards the corner where the chair was. It thuds against the wall and I push in the drawers that had slightly come out of their slots and step back. With my hands on my hips, I turn and face my bed. It sits nicely in the middle of my room, underneath the window. I walk to the other side of the bed and push it towards the wall. It also thuds against the wall, echoing in the bathroom. Stepping back, I examine the room. It feels more open, but I don't like where the bed is. I grab the foot and start pulling it back to its position by the window.

My door opens and I look at it over my shoulder, still pulling the bed. Jackson stands in the doorway, watching me with an eyebrow raised. He blinks a few times while I stare at him, frozen in place. "Are you ready?" he asks.

I examine the distance between the bed and the window. "Give me a second," I say and jog to the other side of the bed and push it towards its place under the window. Breathing deeply, I stand up straight and face Jackson. "Now I am," I say.

Jackson moves out of the way so I can exit my room. "How are you feeling?" he asks, not mentioning the room.

"Fine." Two days ago I stopped being sore. I can feel my magic swirling lazily beneath my skin again, happy that I no longer am wearing the silver chain. After a week, the Handlers stopped putting it on, trusting me to behave.

"Good," he says and starts walking down the long hallways.

I follow him, walking silently down the hall. Another day of tests, another day of doctors, another day of that machine… The large machine is similar to the prod they used years ago to suck out my magic, but on a much grander scale. Instead of filling one jar at a time and taking only a little magic, they attach multiple jars to what looks like a massive tube that I lay in all day and suck all my magic out in one go. The machine itself looks like a massive centipede, with the wires and cables sticking out of it looking like its legs.

"Jackson," I start, breaking the silence. "Remind me again why you have to take my magic."

Jackson breathes deeply, staring ahead. "Because you've been the healthiest ever since we started taking it out of you, and it's a great way for us to study it. Two birds with one stone."

"Hm," is the only response I give. "So, you take my magic and I no longer die?"

"Not quite," he starts. "Your magic is slowly drawing your body's natural resources, leaving you sickly and tired. The truth is that it will take you a while to die by your magic because it needs you to survive, so it can't kill you. But the weaker you are, the harder it is for you to survive against it. By taking your magic, we've given you a chance to recover."

I nod, thinking. I'll live here forever, destined to spend my life lying in a machine once a week that sucks a parasite out of me that will always come back. Week after week, month after month, year after year.

We near the room I call the leeching room and softly shake my head. I would rather let my magic slowly destroy me than spend the rest of my life here.

While Jackson is busy looking for his key card in his pockets, I turn and run the way we just came down.

"732?" Jackson calls.

I keep running, my bare feet slapping the tile. There has to be a stairway or an elevator around here somewhere. If I can get to the office, grab a pair of keys, get to a car, and finally get out of here.

"732, wait!"

I round a corner, grabbing the wall as I do. My heart pounds. Jackson's footsteps get louder and faster behind me. The elevator is right in front of me. I slide into it and frantically slam the down button.

"Come on, come on, come on," I mutter.

"732, stop!" Jackson shouts. He rounds the corner and his eyes go wide.

The elevator dings and I slip in as soon as the doors are open wide enough. I slam the close door button and hit the ground floor. The elevator lurches downward and I slump against the wall, heart pounding. *Easy part is done.* My thudding heart pounds faster the closer I get to the ground floor. The elevator dings again and the doors slowly slide open, revealing four Handlers and Jackson standing in front of them. Jackson has his arms crossed and is glaring at me. Hope leaves me as he shakes his head and walks into the elevator with me. The Handlers follow him and surround us. I back against the wall, staring at him. Jackson is silent as he presses floor 5 and steps back to stand next to me. When the elevator starts to move, he sighs.

"Why?" he asks, rubbing his eyes before looking at me.

"Can you honestly tell me that you would stay here in my position, even if it is the only way I can live?" I ask him.

Jackson is silent, chewing on the inside of his lip.

"I mean, all I do is go into that machine once a week, then I help in the kitchens twice a week because I'm too tired and sore to move the rest of the time. I see the doctor once a week, and that's it," I continue. "At this point, I'm just existing."

"You are still a Worker, 732. The magic you have is dangerous. What do you expect us to do?" he asks.

"You take mine once a week! I don't have *any* magic for most of the week!" I look away from him, feeling my anger rise and my magic swirl faster beneath my skin. "I'm bored, Jackson. I want to see the sun again, and not through a small window. Heck, I'll even settle for some stimulating reading material! If you were me, what would you do?"

Jackson stares at me, then nods, looking to the doors as they open. "I'll see what I can do," he says, then walks out.

A Handler behind me pushes me towards the open door. I glare at him over my shoulder before following after Jackson.

“For today,” Jackson continues as we make our way yet again to the leech room, “You are getting into that machine and we’ll discuss this later.”

I nod and follow him back to the leech room. The machine glares at me with all its tubes and jars as I walk in. I steer clear of it initially, removing my shirt and dropping it on the table that holds all the wires Jackson needs to attach to my body. Jackson eyes the dark stain on my chest that seems to get darker with each session. I stare at the wall, not focused on anything. The stain appeared after my first time in the machine and only continues to get darker. The doctors theorize that it is related to my magic being drawn out in large amounts, and that’s where it exits my body. They’ve found similar, smaller, silver markings spiraling up my arms. I trace the markings on my arms as I wait for Jackson to finish grabbing all the sticky pads. He doesn’t say anything as they are attached to my chest. He normally never does. This part of the prep is always quiet, neither one of us wanting to mention what Rebren has done to us. Once the pads are on, he leads me over to the machine.

“732,” Jackson starts.

“I’ll be fine,” I say and hop onto the table, lying down and letting him strap me in. One strap around each wrist, one around each ankle. One strap on my midsection and one over my head. Jackson attaches the wires to the table and their various spots on the machine. I close my eyes and focus on my breathing as the table lurches forward and starts moving towards the large opening. The doors slowly close above me, leaving me in darkness. I hear a faint clicking as the machine turns on. The blue glow appears and shines through my closed eyelids. My magic swirls at the pull, trying to resist it. The hum gets louder and I focus on my breathing.

*My name is Adam Carlson. I am from Normal, Illinois. I will survive.* I repeat over in my mind as the humming gets louder and the pull on my magic worsens. I groan. *My name is Adam Carlson. I am from Normal, Illinois. I will survive. I will survive.*

*I will survive.*

# CHAPTER FORTY FOUR

## JAKE

The list of available Workers glares at me. I scroll through, reading each number that comes up. 21481028, 27509847, 48627301. I tug at my hair as faces pass by. No sign of Adam, no sign of life. I click to a different campus, looking for him. 2134678, 2107463, 2157652.

Nothing.

I check another campus. Numbers flash by as I search for one in particular.

Nothing.

I've checked the seven campuses in Illinois, and the three in Ohio and there is no sign of Adam. Maybe Caulder decided to keep him, taking it as a challenge to train him. He did often brag that there wasn't a Worker he couldn't train. If that tumor hasn't killed him. I rub a hand over my eyes and sigh.

"Jake, are you alright?" Sara asks from the doorway.

I close the computer and turn towards her. "I'm fine," I whisper, slowly moving towards her. Her belly has grown and I gently place a hand on it. "How's our girl?"

She smiles. "Our boy is fine. He was kicking a few minutes ago." There is a light in her blue eyes that captivates me. She brushes a strand of hair back. "You've let your hair get long."

I nod, pulling her close. "Mid-life crisis, I guess," I mumble against her neck, closing my eyes and swaying back and forth.

"You're only twenty four. Hardly at mid-life," she whispers, wrapping her arms around my neck.

"Mm," I say, not wanting to tell her why I've grown it out. Lowe's confused expression keeps floating to the front of my mind. He recognized me. There's very few things that I can do that will make me unrecognizable to Rebren. One is the tattoo that covers half of my left side, and the other is changing my hair.

"I don't mind if you're growing it out," Sara whispers. "As long as you don't let it get too long."

I smile. "It won't get past my ears, I promise."

"Good."

A hard kick comes from Sara's belly and she gasps, grabbing my hand and placing it over top of the spot. "Did you feel that?"

I nod, watching with awe where my hand meets hers. Our baby kicks again, right over my hand. My magic swirls and I hold it back. The last thing I need right now is Sara finding out about my secret.

My watch beeps. “Time for work,” I whisper.

Sara gives me a kiss on the cheek before walking back into the kitchen where her school books are sprawled over the table. “I’ll see you soon. I love you.”

“I love you too.”

There are Rebren cars parked in the parking lot when I pull into work. Steadying my breath, I park the car and head inside. AC hits me as I walk through the automatic doors. David is sitting at his desk as usual.

“Morning, David,” I say with a small nod.

He nods as well. “Morning, Jake,” he says, taking a sip of his coffee.

I walk around the counter and grab my badge. “I saw Rebren vehicles in the parking lot,” I start. “What’s that about?”

David leans back in his chair and sighs. “Jan has some friends in Rebren. They stopped by for a visit or something. They wouldn’t tell me the details. Just asked for Jan and left with him,” he says. “They make me uncomfortable. Arrogant men who put themselves above others.”

I nod, tapping my fingers on the desk. Jan doesn’t suspect anything. I’m safe. “Thanks, David.”

He nods and leans forwards, going back to work. On my way to the employee locker room, I glance inside Jans office. Two Rebren employees are sitting across from him at his desk. I quickly slip on my yellow vest and head to the back. Hoping they won't stick around too long.

* * *

"Jake!" Jan calls from the hallway. I glance up from the clipboard, the pen hovering above the paper.

"Hey, Jan," I call back.

He waves me over to him. "How are you feeling? How's your head?"

I smile. "That was months ago. It's fine. Looked worse than it actually was."

He nods and pats me on the back. "I'm just checking. I want to make sure everything is still alright with you. Can I meet with you in my office? I've got some people I want you to meet," he says, steering me towards the door before I can agree. I can see the shadows of two men through the blinds. Rebren is still here.

"Can I ask why?" My heart starts to pound.

Jan smiles. "They've got some questions for a few of us around here," he says. He opens the door and motions me in. I walk in slowly, hovering near the wall. The two Rebren employees nod and smile as I enter.

"You must be Jake Harrison," the taller, red haired one says as he extends his hand. "My name is Landon Rudenburg."

I shake his hand and nod. "Nice to meet you," I lie. My skin crawls at his touch.

"Jerome Livenslide," the other one says, his voice low, and offers his hand.

I shake it.

Jan claps me on the shoulder and walks around his desk. "Glad we could all meet. Please, have a seat, Jake," he says and gestures to the open chair.

I sit, wary of the two employees.

"We've just got a few questions about the incident a few months ago," Landon says, settling back in his chair.

I tilt my head in confusion. "My incident, you mean," I say.

Landon nods. "Yes, your incident."

I lean back and cross my ankle over my knee. "I wasn't aware that Rebren was replacing HR," I state.

"Jake," Jan says.

Landon smiles. "No worries, Mr. Klarke," he turns back to me. "We don't normally investigate workplace issues; you're right. However, HR did not call us here. Mr. Klarke did. Can you help us understand why, Mr. Harrison?"

I look to Jan, who shrugs defensively, holding his hands out in front of him. My mouth goes dry. "Are you accusing me of something, Jan?" I ask.

He shakes his head and leans back. "Just trying to figure things out is all," he says.

I turn back to the Rebren employee's. "I fell and hit my head. I've got a hard head and I'm fine now."

Landon nods slowly, not fully believing me. "Incidents happen in the workplace, and we understand that," he says.

"And that's what it was. I filled out the proper report and took all the necessary steps. Can I go now?" I ask, setting both feet on the floor and leaning forwards.

"Do you have any other questions?" Jan asks the two men.

"Mr. Harrison," Jerome says, leaning forwards and clasping his hands together. "Have you had a history of magic running past the age of sixteen in your family?" He asks.

*Yes, but you don't need to know about Adam.* "No, sir," I say.

"And you were tested at sixteen?"

"Just like everybody else," I say. "I wouldn't be here if I had magic."

"Just one more question, Mr. Harrison," Landon says. "Do you remember where you were in March of 2021?"

I feel my heart start to pound. *They're* looking *for me. Caulder must have realized I escaped when I wasn't in the cell. He's* looking *for me.* "Home, I think?" I lean forward. "Why so specific and so far away? I wasn't working here, I can tell you that."

Landon nods and turns to his partner.

"That's all the questions we have for you. Thank you, Mr. Harrison," Jerome says.

I look at Jan with my eyebrows raised. "Am I free to leave?"

Jan nods. "I'll find you later. Thank you, Jake."

I nod and leave, closing the door on my way out. I find my way to the back of the warehouse and take a deep breath. Caulder, Rebren, is looking for me. They know I got away and now they're looking for me. Caulder must have figured out that I survived the bullet and now wants me back. He's alive, dang it. He's *alive.* I hoped that tumor would have killed him by now. I close my eyes and focus on my breathing. My heart is pounding in my chest. I can't let them get close, can't let them get to Sara. Maybe I could feign an illness for a couple of days. Use my vacation time and visit Brad and Maria.

Footsteps echo down the aisle and I turn, rearranging some things on the shelf.

"Jake," Jan says. "I don't mean to assume anything."

I turn around. "If you have questions, just ask," I say. "Why exactly did you call them?"

Jan sighs. "I have a friend who does business with Rebren. He asked me to be on the lookout for a young man in his mid twenties. He told me he might have tried to cover up his Mark with a tattoo. He also told me he would be in excellent health and would likely heal fast," he pauses. "I should never have assumed anything."

I shuffle my feet, unsure of what to do. "And you thought I was a candidate for this escaped Worker?" *Even though I am an escaped Worker.*

Jan rubs the back of his neck. "I was unsure."

I nod, turning back to the shelf. "I've got to finish up inventory, can we continue this later?" I ask.

Jan nods. "Of course. I'm sorry if you felt that I jumped to conclusions." He turns to walk down the aisle.

"Jan," I call after him. He turns. "What is your friend's name? Who is asking about the Worker?"

"Robert Caulder."

# CHAPTER FORTY FIVE

# ADAM

My door opens and I see a Handler standing in the doorway. He steps to the side as I approach. I make it just past the doorway of my room before he stops me, his helmet off. “You’re with me today,” he says with a smirk.

“Why?” I ask.

“You’ll see,” he says over his shoulder as he starts walking down the hallway, turning the opposite way than we usually take to get to the kitchens. It’s been two days since my time in the machine and I’m still slightly sore. Not sore enough to keep me in bed. I follow the Handler down the long, empty hallways. As we enter a section of the Lab I’ve never been to, I start seeing more Handlers. My skin crawls and I walk closer to my Handler.

We come to a stop at a pair of large, metal double doors that seem like they would belong in a warehouse. Double doors on the fifth floor of the Lab? “Where are you taking me?” I ask him.

He shoots a smirk over his shoulder and turns the handle. The door slowly swings inwards and I see the room beyond. It looks like a rec room. There are weights in one corner in front of a wall lined with mirrors, mats and pads in another. A few cardio and weight machines line one wall, and there is a large space in the middle for other things. A few people are in the room, all dressed in workout clothes. I stand frozen in the doorway, taking in the room. The Handler walks in, stripping off his outer jacket and tossing it onto the back of the chair. He tosses a few other things onto the chair: his weapons and wallet, keys and phone.

"You seem like you have steam to blow off," he says, turning to me fully.

I look back at him. "So you take me to the gym?" I ask. "I thought you didn't want Workers strong. Kinda defeats the purpose of keeping us locked up."

He smiles and tosses me a pair of fingerless, padded gloves and starts walking to the edge of the room where a raised and roped off section of mats sits. A sparring ring. The Handler climbs in and waves me over. I hesitantly walk over, clutching the gloves in my hands. I climb through the ropes and stand on the edge of the mat. The mat feels strange underneath my bare feet.

"Put on your gloves," the Handler says.

"Richard, what are you doing?" someone asks behind me.

The Handler, Richard, smiles and nods at the newcomer. "Helping the boy blow off some steam," he says.

I turn and see a woman standing there, her blonde hair pulled back into a tail. She's standing with her hands on her hips and her eyebrow is raised. Her black shirt is dark with sweat and I see her hair is slick with it. "A Worker?"

"This is 732," he says, motioning to me. "And, once he's learned a bit, you can get in here if you'd like. I'm sure he'd appreciate it."

"What?" I ask, turning back to Richard.

He smiles. "You've caused a lot of trouble around here. Most of us have wanted to hit you in one way or another," he states.

"The feeling is mutual," I say, finally figuring out what is going on. I strap on my gloves and flex my fingers. "So, how does this work?"

"This'll be good," the woman says, leaning up against the ropes to watch.

"What is going on here?" Jackson's voice cuts through the shouts and cheers that have filled the gym. A crowd has formed around the sparring ring where the blonde woman and I are standing. I'm holding a hand to my nose and she is smirking. We both look towards the door where Jackson is quickly making his way through the crowd. He pushes against the various Handlers in an attempt to get to the front of the crowd.

Richard walks up to him from where he was leaning on the ropes. "We were helping the boy blow off some steam," he says.

Jackson's gaze snaps to me. I shrug and smile, blinking back tears. I brush my hand under my nose, checking for blood. When my hand comes away clean, I lean against the ropes. "C'mon," I say. "They want to hit me, and I want to hit them. What better way?" I ask.

Jackson stares at me and I can't decide if he wants to rip me out of the ring or take the blonde woman's place.

"It's better than picking fights in the hallways," I point out.

Jackson lets out a long sigh and looks down. When he looks back up at me, he's smiling and shaking his head. "I want to see what you've got," he says.

I feel a grin work its way onto my face. I lock eyes with the woman standing at the edge of the ring and she raises her hands, smirking.

"Ready for more?" she asks.

"Let's get this show started," I respond.

We exchange blows, her hits landing more than mine. With luck, I land a hit on her jaw and she stumbles backwards. Her hand flies to her jaw. I freeze, fists still extended from my punch.

"Good punch," she says. She massages her jaw and nods to Richard. I pull my arm back and take a few steps back until I'm touching the ropes.

"Anybody else want a shot?" Richard asks.

Jackson grabs a pair of gloves from Richard and climbs into the ring. The blond woman nods once to me and climbs down. I nod back to her. I shuffle my feet as Jackson straps on the gloves and walks away from the ropes.

"So this was a good idea then?" he asks, raising his fists.

"I thought Richard thought of it," I state as I flex my fingers and raise my fists as well, matching his stance.

"Feet, 732," Richard says.

I glance down and adjust my stance.

Jackson shrugs. "I think I'm starting to agree with his choices. You seem less mopey today."

I raise an eyebrow. "I've been mopey?"

Jackson chuckles. "So mopey." He pauses. "Are you ready for this?"

I nod, flexing my fingers and curling them back into fists. "So ready."

"Good." He stalks towards me, taking a jab at my side. I dodge it.

“Do you often box with Workers?” I ask, taking a shot at his midsection.

He smirks. “Only ones that run to an elevator and try to get out of work,” he jokes.

I laugh. “So often then?”

He lets out a laugh at that, distracting me from his next couple of hits to my stomach. I grunt but swing wide, hitting his shoulder. He takes another swing at me, smiling.

“Jackson,” Richard says. “You’re getting a call.”

Jackson pauses and looks towards Richard, his fists still poised to strike. “What time is it?”

“12:15.”

Jackson straightens and removes his gloves, nodding to me. “Apologies, 732, I’m late for a meeting. We’ll do a rematch soon,” he says. He pats me on the shoulder on his way out of the ring. “You did well.” He grabs the phone from Richard and his jacket, nodding to the Handler on his way out.

# CHAPTER FORTY SIX

# ABBY

The Lab still smells the same. The same smells of bleach, burnt plastic, and chemicals. I pace the small meeting room, waiting for Jackson. Colton sits in a chair at the table, looking through the file I have pulled up.

"Why is it so long?" he asks as he scrolls to the first entry.

I lean against the wall. "He's been in Rebren since he was sixteen, Colt," I state. "Besides that, he did cause a lot of trouble when he was here."

Colton raises an eyebrow. "Adam?" He pauses, reading something. "There's a note here. 'Worker was caught trying to climb a fence, caused a nearby bush to start on fire. Punishment of twenty lashings were dealt. Worker returned due to rebellious behavior.' Abby, they *whipped* him?"

I nod, hand resting on my arm. "The punishment for using magic is twenty lashings."

Colton finally looks at me with a horrified expression. "You knew about this and you didn't do anything to stop it?"

I sigh. "I needed the job, Colt. And without it we wouldn't be where we are right now."

Colton shakes his head and runs a hand through his hair. "How long have you known about his magic doing this?" he asks.

"A few years. I wanted to see what would happen if we left it alone, but it just got worse."

Colton leans back in the chair right as the door opens. "My apologies, Ms. Sommerfeld," Jackson says and closes the door softly behind him. His generally neat appearance is rumpled and he's sweaty.

"What were you doing, Jackson?" I ask, sitting down in the chair next to Colton.

He smiles. "A short boxing match, blowing off some steam."

"A boxing match?" I raise an eyebrow.

"You let people box here?" Colton asks, leaning forward and pushing the computer towards the center of the table.

He nods and rolls his shoulders. "Our mutual friend packs quite a punch."

"You were boxing with Adam?" I ask, eyes going wide. "What trouble is he in now?"

Jackson shakes his head and chuckles. "He did try to escape yesterday, so today he is spending some time training with a trusted Handler," he explains.

I blink. "What?"

Jackson motions to my computer. "May I?" he asks.

I nod, and he pulls up camera footage from the Handlers gym on the third floor. Adam and a Handler are boxing in the ring, exchanging blows and dodging each other's fists. I've never seen a Handler so relaxed around a Worker, particularly not Adam. Many other Handlers surround the boxing ring, cheering for who, I'm not sure. Adam is grinning.

"That can't be Adam," Colton says, leaning forwards. "He looked half dead when we got him out of the Lab two years ago."

"Because he ran, his punishment is learning to fight?" I ask Jackson, leaning back, mesmerized by the footage in front of me. Adam *smiling* in Rebren? It nearly seems impossible.

"He ran because he's bored. I simply gave him something to do."

I watch Adam on the screen. There's a bounce in his step that wasn't there months ago, and he looks healthier despite his thin frame. He's been too thin since he came out of the Program. Maybe it doesn't have to be that way. "How have the tests been going and how is he taking them?"

Jackson clasps his hands together, leaning back in his chair. "The tests are successful, and we haven't had many problems. He seems to fear the machine, but he's brave."

"What tests?" Colton asks.

Jackson looks at me and leans back. "I'll let you do the explaining."

I turn towards Colton. "We've done a variety of tests on Adam, trying to force his magic to stop feeding on his body. Different drugs, exercise. What we've found works is pulling all of his magic out of him. It's a long process, often taking all day, but it's been working." I pause the footage and point to Adam. "He looks healthier than when he came here four months ago. Despite going into the machine, what pulls the magic out of him once a week, he's stronger."

Colton nods, staring at the image. "So what's the hold up? If you've figured it out, why is he still here?"

I look to Jackson for the answer. He sighs. "It's temporary. His magic will replenish after a week, and we'll need to draw it out again."

Colton leans back. "Is there a way to find a permanent solution? Or do you not want to lose your primary source of magic to study?"

Jackson holds Colton's gaze for a while, not denying his accusation.

"What else are you not telling me?" I ask, leaning forwards.

Jackson sighs, rubbing a hand over his eyes. "He wants to live his life, and I don't want him to feel trapped inside here. But I can't see a way where he can live outside of Rebren's Lab."

I grab my computer and pull up his medical chart, covering the footage of Adam's boxing. His most recent medical exam showed more normal levels of iron and oxygen and salt. His magic is feeding on his body and without magic, Adam is thriving. "Jackson, has he tried using his magic?" I ask.

He furrows his eyebrows, resting his elbows on the table. "No," he says. "His magic is angry and does not like being told what to do. The tests we run are difficult and dangerous. You know how out of control his magic is. How much damage it could cause."

I nod, tapping my finger against my arm. "I'm aware of his abilities. Try getting him to use his magic, see how it reacts. Get medical after. I want to try something. If we teach him to draw on the elements around him, it would stop the destruction in his body."

Jackson leans back. "That goes against every policy and law that Rebren has set in," he says softly. "He could never leave. He's already too dangerous and unpredictable.

You want him to learn how to use that power, one that is extremely destructive."

"What if he's only that dangerous because he doesn't know how to use it?" Colton asks. "What if Rebren is wrong about magic and those who have it?"

"I agree with Colton. What if his magic becomes more docile when it's used properly? Maybe we're going about this all wrong?"

Jackson rubs his fingers together, thinking. "I'll give it a shot," he says. "But no guarantees. You still don't want to see him?"

I shake my head 'no'. "That'll end badly for all of us," I say.

Jackson nods. "We'll start next week."

# CHAPTER FORTY SEVEN

## ADAM

I check both ends of the hallway before continuing down my route. After days spent in the boxing ring, the Handlers have ceased following me everywhere, leaving me to my own devices. With nothing else to occupy me, I started roaming the halls this morning. So far, I've found multiple empty rooms, a boiler room, a room full of glass jars, and many locked doors. There are multiple doors on this hallway, most all that I've tried are locked. I try the handle of the next one and it swings open. Hesitantly, I step into the lit room.

An open computer sits next to a cup half full of coffee and a notebook full of words scrawled in messy handwriting. I slowly sit down in the high backed office chair, touching the mousepad to wake up the computer. Files and videos pop up. The videos show a lab with jars full of what looks like golden glitter speckled with black. Turning my attention from the videos, I read the reports that are pulled up off to the side.

*Test 5. 732, batch 4.*

I lean forward, clicking through more of the files. Lengthy reviews on my magic, the tests, and me personally are written.

*Magic seems to be angry despite the Subject's semi-pleasant demeanor.*

*Subject seems to be healthy after weeks of the Machine test, proving our hypothesis of removal of magic. Magic seems to be keeping its host weak in order to grow stronger.*

I furrow my eyebrows and read further. The names of everyone involved in the different tests are listed at the end of the report. I read further, finding my way back years and years. The first report in the Lab is dated March 19, 2021. It is the first test they did with  Sam where they first drew out my magic.

*Subject gets aggravated when afraid, and doesn't like being told what to do. There is a general arrogance about the Subject and everything we try seems to make it worse.*

After the note, there is a detailed report on the tests they plan to do and the time they expect it to take. I smirk at the note, reading further and seeing *"Extremely stubborn and hostile towards employees"* written. I continue to scan the pages, seeing Jackson's name come across the screen. My blood chills at the name right next to his.

*Abigail Sommerfeld. Case manager.*

What? I shake my head, blinking. The screen in front of me doesn't change; Abby's name is still glaring at me. I stand up and stumble backwards, pushing the chair out of the way. Blood pounds in my ears, matching the beat in my chest.

I hear the door open. "732?" Jackon asks. "What are you doing here?"

I shake my head and push past him. Abby works for Rebren? Not only that, she was on my case? As a *manager*? And she never told me? Everything that was done to me, she gave the go ahead. Everything I went through, she could have stopped but didn't. Everything she had to give the green light to. The endless tests, the magic sucking prod… *Abby* was behind the one way glass. That day in the Lab, Jackson was looking to *her* for help. To *her* for guidance. *She* was the voice over the speaker, telling Jackson to stop when it got too far.

I don't know how I ended up in the gym, but Richard sets down his weights when I walk in. "732?" He asks.

I grab a pair of boxing gloves and turn to him. "Up for a match?" I ask.

He purses his lips and raises an eyebrow at me.

"Please," I ask, my voice cracking.

He lets go of whatever he was going to say and grabs his gloves, climbing into the ring. He sets his small towel on a nearby chair. I shimmy through the ropes and join him in the ring. He raises his fists, and I do the same, mimicking his stance. After boxing with him and him giving me pointers, I've become decent at the sport. Today was supposed to be my rest day, as Richard puts it. A day to let my body and muscles rest. Apparently, working out, mixed with the weekly draining of my magic, puts an extra toll on me and my body needs extra rest.

Richard blocks my blow, adjusting his stance. "What's got you so upset today?" he asks finally.

I raise my eyebrow and dodge his blow to my midsection. "Who said I was upset?" I ask.

"It's written all over your face and in your body language. You're extra aggressive with your blows today," he says.

I clench my jaw. "I'm here. Isn't that enough?" I say, going for his midsection, driving his point home with a second blow to his other side.

Richard blocks me, taking a shot at my exposed head. "I thought you'd resigned yourself to this life," he says. "This is a new type of aggression from you."

I duck and break away, pacing my side of the ring. "It doesn't matter if I'm here," I sigh, leaning up against the ropes.

Richard doesn't answer, but I feel him hovering nearby.

The doors swing open and Jackson storms in. "732, what were you doing on my computer?" He asks.

I glance up at him, his name right next to Abby's flashes in my mind. "Is she here?" I whisper, feeling my blood boil.

Jackson stops and understanding flashes across his face. "732-" he starts.

I stand up straight. "Is she here?" I ask, louder this time.

He shakes his head. "Not right now."

I look away, clenching my jaw.

"Come on down and we'll talk about this, 732," Jackson says. "I'll explain what I can."

I scowl at him before nodding. Jumping down from the ring, I remove my gloves and set them in the small cubby I pulled them from. Richard hovers around us, resuming his duties as a Handler. Back to treating me like a number. Just like everyone else in this building does.

"We're alright, Richard," Jackson says, noticing my agitation. "We're just going to have a chat."

"Sir?" Richard asks. His eyes flicker to where I pace.

"He doesn't have enough magic right now to be harmful. I'll be fine," Jackson explains. "Take a break."

Richard nods and leaves us be, closing the doors behind him.

"You saw your records," he states.

"Were you ever going to tell me?" I ask, feeling my heart pound in my chest. "I mean, it's been almost three years since I was brought here. Two years of *trusting* her and *working* with her. Were either of you going to tell me?" I ask. All those times we snuck into Rebren, Abby always got us in and out without much trouble. I should have questioned more…

Jackson shakes his head. "I figured out that you two knew each other a couple weeks into your time in the Lab," he says. "She asked me not to tell you when she brought you back. I guess she thought you wouldn't sneak into my office to use my personal computer." He raises his eyebrow at me.

"Should've made your office harder to break into," I dismiss. "How long has she been assigned to me?"

Jackson rubs the back of his neck. "Since you started having problems."

"How would she have known about that?" I ask. "How long has she been working for Rebren?"

"732, is this really important?" Jackson asks. "What's done is done. She's trying to save your life."

"She *lied* to me, Jackson!" my voice cracks. "For years! Her and Colton both. I want to know for how long."

The meeting… There is no footage needed. She wants more data on *me*. On my magic. That meeting was them discussing whether or not to send me back to Rebren. Colton, Jason, Oliver… All of them. They knew.

Jackson's mouth opens and closes. He stares at me for a while. "She started at eighteen. Abigail was hired on by the science department and has been working in our bio-science department ever since. She told me she took the job because she wanted to see if there was something here that would help Colton after the crash."

"The crash where he got the limp and the scar?"

Jackson nods.

I look away, pacing the space in front of the ring. Fog fills my head and my chest tightens up. "Why exactly am I here, Jackson?" I ask horsley.

"Your magic is killing you, 732. Or at least keeping you extremely weak. They thought the best way to keep you alive was to let *us* figure out how to keep you alive," he explains. "Abigail reached out to me and asked if I could put together a program specific to you and your magic. We were talking about it before she snuck you out years ago."

"Stop calling me that," I whisper. "Please." I lean against a chair, trying to collect my thoughts. "Why didn't she just tell me?" I sink further down into the chair, my head hanging low and my hands resting off my knees.

Jackson slowly steps closer to me. "She didn't want to hurt you," he whispers.

"This was her plan? To lie?" I close my eyes, feeling the emptiness where my magic should be swirling underneath my skin. *You're just too destructive for your own good, huh?* "How exactly is it killing me?"

Jackson sighs. "Come with me and I'll show you."

Jackson leads me to a part of the Lab I haven't been to yet. Large observation windows line the hallways, letting us see into the laboratory where they are testing magic. Multiple jars with black-flecked golden magic swirling inside them. *My* magic. Jackson and I stand in the hallway, watching the woman in a hazmat suit take a jar off the shelf and slowly open the lid. She takes a syringe and slides it in the small opening, removing some of the magic. The swirling gets faster and the golden color starts glowing brightly. I feel the small amount of magic I have start to swirl. The magic in the syringe pulses violently. The woman seals the jar and brings the small sample over to a rat. My gut twists as the woman inserts the syringe into the rat. The rat squeals and shrieks. Once the syringe is empty, the woman sets the rat down and watches it intently.

The rat is fine for a few minutes until it starts scratching at the injection site. Then it starts gnawing at its legs, its fur starting to smoke. It shrieks again and I see a small puff of fire dance along its jaw. The rat is burning from the inside out. It shrieks again before falling over, legs twitching and kicking uselessly. After another minute, it stops moving all together.

I hold my stomach, feeling sick. My magic swirls under my skin, almost as if it senses the rest of it on the other side of the glass.

The woman types something on the computer, leaving the dead rat on the table.

I put a hand on the wall, forcing air into my lungs. I look up at Jackson, who's watching with a strange look of concern on his face. "My magic does *that*?" I rasp.

Jackson solemnly nods. "That is what your magic does uncontrolled. We thought removing it from you would help, and it does. Only temporarily," he starts. "Abby has proposed a new test, if you are interested."

I look back to the dead rat. "What is her idea?" I ask, dragging my eyes from the sight.

# CHAPTER FORTY EIGHT

## ADAM

"Small pinch here," the nurse says as she inserts the needle into my arm.

I look at the wall, wincing as I feel it slide in. Jackson is leaning against the door frame. "I forget that you're afraid of needles," he says as he watches the nurse. "How? You've had hundreds stuck in you at this point."

"I've never been a fan. The fact that they happen frequently doesn't change that." The nurse removed the needle and places a band-aid over the spot.

"You're all good to go," she says. "I'll have the results when you come back."

Jackson nods a thank you to her and ushers me out of the office. A few doors down is the testing room where I was tested a few years before. Jackson opens the door and motions for me to walk in.

I'm again standing in the middle of the black pad with Jackson behind plexiglass. A different pile of wood sits on the ground, just like the last time I was here.

“Alright, 732. Ready to give this a shot?” Jackson asks, his voice muffled.

I nod, flexing my fingers. My magic swirls inside me, collecting at my fingertips. It’s been a few days since the rat died, and my magic is at full force. Now that I know what it’s doing, I can feel it slowly drawing upon my body, weakening me. “Let's try this,” I say.

“Fire at will,” he says. I glance over at him with a raised eyebrow and he’s smirking.

“You’re proud of that, aren’t you?” I ask.

Jackson simply shrugs and nods to the pile. “Are you going to do what you’re best at or just stand there?”

I shake my head in response and turn back to the pile of wood. I close my eyes and try to feel the wood just a few feet from me. Breathing deeply, I take a small portion of my magic and send it out to find the pile. With a start, I can sense it in front of me, a large mass of something to burn. The pendant resting against my chest gets comfortably warm. I use the same portion of magic and feel the oxygen around the pile. My magic swirls frantically, excitedly. I breathe in, letting the sensation fill me. My heart pounds in excitement and the rest of my magic swirls faster and faster. My magic swirls and rushes towards the wood. The pendant heats up, but not like the burning it used to be. I open my eyes in time to see a miniature mushroom cloud swirling in the air above the now on fire wood pile. The heat radiating off it is intense and I take a few steps back. Jackson knocks on the glass and waves me over. He presses a button and foam sprays over the fire, effectively putting it out. I walk over to Jackson on shaky legs.

"You lit the air on fire, which should not be possible without a catalyst," he says, running the footage back. I watch as the air catches fire, then the wood. Jackson gives me a sideways look.

"I don't know what happened, but that was fun," I say with a grin.

Jackson shakes his head, but I can see a smile tugging at the corners of his lips. "My guess is that it used your body to light the air but used the wood to light the pile." He straightens. "Blood draw timc, lct's go," he says.

I follow him out of the room and down the hall to the medical office. The same nurse who drew my blood this morning waits there.

"That was considerably less noisy than I expected," she says, tying her blonde hair back.

"He had some semblance of control this time," Jackson responds, settling back in a chair. "Unlike last time he had used magic here." He raises an eyebrow at me.

"I was not in control that time, and you know it," I retort. The large black chair waits for me in the center of the room. I climb into it and rest my arms on the armrests. The bandage on my left arm covers the previous needle site. "Besides, that was a while ago."

Jackson smiles and shakes his head. "And you didn't like us."

"Still don't, but I can make due," I point out. The nurse rolls over to my chair on her rolling chair, needle and tourniquet in hand.

"You seem to be in a better mood than usual," she points out, glancing up at me while she cleans a spot on my right arm.

"Are you trying to tell me that I'm not usually this cheery?" She matches my smile with her own.

"I'll take it over the usual grumpy 732 we get around here." She tugs on my skin, and I look away. "Small pinch." I wince at the poke but manage to stay still.

"What were his levels this morning, Hannah?" Jackson asks.

Hannah switches the full tube with an empty one. "Normal. His magic didn't have time to deplete anything terribly. What happened in the test?"

"He lit the air on fire before the wood pile."

A band aid replaces the needle. The tubes are placed in a machine and Hannah sits down, facing us. "The air? With nothing in it?"

Jackson nods.

"And how do you feel?" She asks me.

"Shaky," I say. "But really good. Like I've just gone for a good run."

Hannah tilts her head and bites the inside of her lip. She turns and rummages through a drawer, pulling out a magic testing device. "Hold out your arm for me," she says, coming closer.

I do, setting it on the armrest. The black box is strapped around my arm. It beeps once, twice, and then lights up green. My magic swirls lazily under my skin.

"Still full," she says, removing the box. "Your magic must give you energy if used properly. Giving instead of taking."

"Is this explicit permission to use my magic?" I lean forward, swinging my legs over the edges of the chair.

Jackson and Hannah make eye contact. "Until further notice, yes," Jackson says. "No punishments."

I sit up straight, processing his words. The scars on my back itch and I resist the urge to scratch them. It's almost as if they are laughing at me. "No punishment," I repeat.

He nods. "Don't abuse this," Jackson says, giving me a stern look.

I nod. "Of course not," I say with a smile.

# CHAPTER FORTY NINE

## JAKE

Sara and I walk out of the warehouse holding hands. Jan asked me to lock up after my shift and so I needed Sara to pick me up. The fresh night air hits me and I breathe it in. Sara gives my hand a squeeze. "The stars are bright tonight," she points out.

I look up, following her gaze. "They are."

"I'll get the car," she says quietly after a few minutes.

I nod and shut the door. "I'll finish locking up."

I pull her in for a quick kiss before she starts walking away. She gives me a smile as she leaves.

I close my eyes and tilt my head back, relishing in the cool breeze. Turning around, I pull out my keys and lock the door. When I turned back around, there was a group of three men waiting there. I pause and look at each one of them in turn. They are all dressed in black and have close cropped hair. The one in the middle has blonde hair and a large tattoo running from his hand up his arm.

"Hey, guys," I say. "We are closed, I'm sorry."

The blonde in the middle smirks. "We aren't here for the shop," he says. "We are here for you, 54."

Blood pounds in my ears. "I'm sorry?" I ask, tilting my head and straightening my spine.

The man walks towards me. "You heard me correctly," he says. "We've been looking for you for a very long time."

I take a step backwards. "I think you are mistaken," I say as evenly as I can, trying to keep the tremor from my voice. *Jan figured it out and told them where to find me.* "Who are you?"

The two other men rush me, grabbing my arms and pulling me backwards until my back hits the concrete wall next to the door. I struggle against them, trying to get my arms free. The man on the right simply shoves an elbow into my nose, knocking my head into the wall. I hear a crack and feel blood gush out. My magic instantly rushes towards the injury, stopping the blood flow.

*No...*

"Stop playing ignorant, 54," the blonde man says. "Robert Caulder has missed you. Thanks to your boss, you'll be back where you belong in no time."

"Jake?" Sara's voice asks.

The blonde man turns around and I see her standing near the corner, her face a mix of concern and confusion. Her hand goes to her belly, holding the baby protectively.

"Sara," I say calmly. "Listen to me. Get to the car and go home."

She shakes her head. "I don't understand."

"I am so sorry," I say as she backs away. "You need to forget about me." I can feel my heart breaking in my chest with each step away she takes. *I love you.* "Go."

Finally, she turns and runs, rounding the building and disappearing from my sight.

"A special someone?" The blonde man asks, turning back to me. "54, I'm surprised."

"Leave her out of this," I growl. I spit the blood in my mouth at him.

He dodges and laughs, pulling out one of the silver chains. I jerk in the men's grasp at the sight of it. I haven't seen one of those in years. The man twirls it on his fingers for a moment before stepping back, waving us forward. The men pull me away from the wall and tug my arms behind my back.

"If you put this on yourself, I'll leave her alone," the blonde man says, holding the chain out to me.

I stare at it before turning my gaze up to the man. "Do you promise?" I ask.

The man nods. "I give you the word of Rebren, we will leave her alone."

"How do I know you'll keep your word?"

The blonde man smirks. "Have we done anything that we didn't tell you about first?"

I pause, thinking. Rebren did warn us what would happen if we didn't listen and comply. They have kept their word in that aspect. I take a deep breath and slowly nod. "Fine," I whisper. "I'll do it."

The men release my arms and I take the chain. It's lighter than I thought it would be, for how heavy it feels around my neck. I undo the clasp and raise it to my neck. The cool silver seems to burn on my skin. My magic flutters in my chest, knowing it'll be contained.

Then I see the headlights. The small red car barrels forwards and thuds into all four of us. I drop the silver chain as my magic rushes to heal the broken and bruised parts of my body.

"Get. In," Sara commands.

I push myself to my feet and stumble to the passenger side door. Sara reaches over and unlocks it. I quickly climb in, pulling the door shut as she speeds backwards and away from the warehouse. I watch out of the rear windshield as the three men stumble to their feet, dazed and disoriented.

“What was that?” Sara shouts as we enter the highway.

I sink into my seat, turning around. “I’m so sorry, I should have told you,” I say and scrub my hands over my face. Dried blood flakes into my lap.

“Told me what?” Sara is still shouting. “Who were those guys and why were they beating you up?”

“They weren’t beating me up,” I whisper. My nose still throbs although my magic has healed it fully.

“The blood says otherwise!”

I brush a hand over my nose and mouth. More dried blood flakes off my face. “I’m fine,” I say. “That was Rebren.”

Sara glances over at me. “The Rebren Program for Magic Control?”

“Yes.” I sigh. “I should have told you. I’m so sorry.”

“Are you telling me that you have Magic?” Her hands grip the steering wheel so hard that her knuckles are white.

“Yes,I do.”

Sara runs a hand through her messy blonde hair, resting her elbow on the door. “Magic. You have magic,” she mumbles. “Of all things, it’s magic.” She falls silent.

"Sara," I start.

"Just, give me a minute," she cuts me off, flaring her fingers off the steering wheel as if to say stop with her hand.

I nod and we spend the rest of the drive in silence.

* * *

Pots and pans sound in the kitchen. I stand in the bedroom, a suitcase sitting at my feet. Sara's been in the kitchen since we got home. I quietly washed the blood from my face and grabbed the large suitcase from the hallway closet as the loud banging indicated how many dishes Sara had started baking. Rebren knows about me now, and the best thing I can do is get out of here. It's the safest option for Sara and our baby. For the family that took me in.

I start folding my clothes, gathering up all my socks and loose things and stuff them into the suitcase.

Sara knows now, and she knows I lied. My hands shake as I grab my shoes. What if those men had gone after her, too? I couldn't protect Adam; how can I protect her?

Sara walks in as I pile my shirts and pants into the suitcases. "What are you doing?" She asks softly, pulling me from my thoughts.

I pause and look up at her. She has flour smeared on her forehead and dusting her nose. "Packing," I state, looking down. "I figured you would…" I trail off. "You wouldn't want me around after tonight."

Sara lets out a sigh and sits on the bed. "I don't want that. I would never want that," she says quietly. "I love the man I met and married, and I don't want him to leave before we've even had a conversation. However, I do want answers. And truthful ones at that."

I look back at her and nod. "Of course."

"Are you and the man I fell in love with the same person?" she asks hesitantly, speaking slowly.

"Yes," I whisper. "I might have left a few things out, but I'm still me."

She nods. "Is Harrison even your real last name?"

I shake my head. "No, it's Carlson."

Sara leans back on her hands. "Alright, Jake Carlson, tell me your story," she says softly, saying the same thing she asked me when we went on our first date.

I put down the shirt I was stuffing into my suitcase. "I'm from Normal, Illinois," I start. "It was just my parents, my brother, and I." I wring my hands together in my lap. "I haven't seen my parents since I was sixteen. And I haven't seen Adam-" My voice cracks and I look away. "The last time I saw Adam was three years ago," I finish with a whisper. *When he watched me get shot.*

Sara stares at me from her spot on the bed. "How did you escape the Rebren Program?" She asks.

I smile sadly. “After an unfortunate incident that left me unsupervised for a time, I snuck out and climbed into the back of a truck bed.”

“What incident?”

I meet her eyes. “I got shot.”

“You got *shot*?”

I look away from Sara as horror spreads across her face. “I was shot as an example. Adam and I got a group together and started a rebellion. We got caught and I was used as an example.” I run a hand through my hair. “It was Brad and Mitchell’s truck that I snuck into. The Harrison’s took me in as their son and got me settled in.” Finally, I look back at her. She has tears in her eyes.

“How long ago?” She whispers.

I shrug. “Two and a half years ago now.”

Sara nods. “How did you survive the bullet?”

I smile. “I have healing magic. The bullet went straight through and my magic started healing the wound immediately. Although my body went into shock, my magic kept me alive. I woke up in a cell behind Caulder’s garage.”

Sara’s eyes are wide. “The blood tonight, when you said you were fine?”

I nod. “I really am fine. All healed up.”

"And your incident at work?"

"Healed before Jan got there."

Sara stands up and grabs a few of my shirts from the bed and stuffs them back into the dresser. She then holds her hand out to me and wiggles her fingers. I smile and grab her hand, standing. I step over the half filled suitcase and pull her close to me, cradling her head in my hands. She smiles at me sweetly. "Where were you shot?" She whispers, placing her hand on my chest.

My smile falters as I grab her hand and place it directly over the spot where a scar should be, but isn't. "Lucky for me, Caulder is a terrible shot, even at close range," I whisper. "He missed my heart by more than a few inches." *On purpose. To bring me back as his own personal physician.*

She is silent, pondering. Her face is soft and her eyes distant as she stares at where her hand rests. "How does your magic work, exactly?" she asks, looking back at me.

I gently trace circles on her arm with my thumb. "My magic heals me instantly," I whisper. "With any type of injury. I can also heal others, and monitor their health." I gently place my hand on her forearm. She watches my hand with an expression close to curiosity. She meets my eyes and nods ever so slightly, giving me permission to use my magic.

I reach for my magic and breathe in, taking a mental note of how much I have left.

I breathe out and will my magic into her. Her eyes go wide. I close my eyes and see her aching limbs and weary muscles. My magic instantly rushes to heal her and strengthen her. I see our child in her womb and see *his* growth. I feel a single tear escape my eyes at the sight of our son so perfect and small.

My magic rushes back to me and, when I open my eyes, I see Sara smiling with tears in her eyes. "He's beautiful," I whisper.

She lets out a small laugh and touches my face. "He?"

I nod, tears filling my eyes. "We have a son."

Sara starts crying, putting a hand over her mouth. "You are..." she trails off and kisses me. "Do not be ashamed of this."

I nod, feeling tears of my own slip from my eyes. "You're not afraid?"

She shakes her head no. "I'm not afraid of you, of your magic," she says.

I feel relief flood my chest. All those years of being afraid by my lack of control... all needless worries. "I won't let anything happen to you or our son," I whisper, pulling her close.

She rests her head on my chest. "I believe you, Jake Harrison."

# CHAPTER FIFTY

## ADAM

A knock on my door startles me from the book. "732," Jackson says, appearing in the doorway. I slowly put down the book and sit up.

"I thought you had already left for the day. What's up?" I ask.

Jackson sits in the chair in the corner. "I wanted to stop by and chat." He pauses before continuing. "The staff and I will be out of office tomorrow."

I tilt my head. "Why?"

Jackson sighs. "It's a holiday. Most everyone has the day off and the market section will be closed for the day. The only people here will be Handlers to guard the Workers and the cooks, although they'll be working part time."

I nod, leaning back against the headboard. "I see."

Jackson is silent and staring at his hands sadly.

"What holiday?"

He shakes his head. "Are you sure you want to know?" His eyes are soft when they meet mine.

"Please."

Jackson runs a hand over his hair. "The Fourth of July."

I look down. July. I've been here for five months. "Happy fourth," I whisper.

"Happy fourth," he responds. "You might be able to see the fireworks from your window."

I nod, forcing a smile to my face. "I'll be sure to be watching."

"I'll be sure to bring back some barbecue for you," he says, standing. "It's the best, if I do say so myself."

I smile. "I look forward to it."

* * *

The building is eerily quiet as I walk alone to the gym, a sandwich in my hands. I set it on a table and grab a pair of gloves. Fortunately, the Handlers have a punching bag I can use while there isn't anyone here to box with. I find a steady rhythm in the exercise, letting my breathing match my punches. The bag sways back and forth with the force of my fists, the chain creaking softly. I can feel the muscles in my back and shoulders tensing and relaxing with each punch. My magic rests comfortably, finally satisfied with being used properly. It swirls underneath my skin, flowing along my muscles and bones as I hit the bag, almost like an added strength. I feel sweat drip down my back and bead on my forehead as I focus on the bag.

The door swings open, banging against the wall and breaking my focus. I turn towards the door and see two Handlers enter. They are in full uniform with their hands hovering over their weapons, helmets on.

"Hi guys," I say hesitantly, stripping off my gloves and setting them beside my half-eaten sandwich.

"You're guard dogs aren't here, 732," the first one says.

I tense up, taking a step back. "What are you doing here, Greets?"

Greets backhands me. "You do not talk to me like that," he growls.

I stumble backwards, hand flying to my cheek. The second Handler walks up and grabs my arm, tugging me towards the door. Greets grabs the front of my sweat soaked shirt and pulls me towards him. "Do you feel untouchable, 732?" He asks. "Harold nor Jackson are here to save you."

I feel his breath on my face. Turning my face to the side, I try to shove away from him. "Let me go," I growl.

Greets chuckles and drags me out of the gym. "Not a chance," Greets says. "Now that I've got you alone, you're going to get what you deserve." The two Handlers drag me to the leech room with hands grasping my arms. I dig my heels into the ground, fighting in any way I can. Greets grabs a fistful of my hair and shoves me forwards through the doors. I stumble through them and turn to face them, fists raised. The two Handlers laugh and stalk towards me. Before I can get a punch in, Greets buries his fist in my stomach and bashes the other against my temple. Dazed, I trip backwards. Greets pushes me closer to the machine. I stumble, regaining my balance right as I hear the lock click shut. I turn to face the two Handlers again. Greets walks towards me as the second Handler heads to the Machine. They've both removed their helmets, setting them on the table.

"You can't do this," I say, backing up slowly.

Greets chuckles. "There's nobody here to stop me, is there, 732?" He grabs an empty prod off the table and swings it lazily. "It's just you and I here."

"And your buddy," I point out, risking a glance over at the black haired man. He managed to get the machine powered on, the blue light from inside the machine getting brighter and brighter. My magic stirs at the light. When I look back at Greets, he's nearly closed the gap between us. He adjusts the prod in his hands.

"He agrees with me," he says.

"On what?" I ask, holding out a hand as if that will stop him. My magic swirls down my arm, anticipating the danger in front of me.

A sick smile spreads across Greets's face. "That you are a nuisance and need some sense beaten into you." He swings the prod, hitting me in the side. I double over, gasping for air as I clutch my side. He hits me again, smacking me across the shoulders. I fall to my hands and knees. My magic swirls furiously, but the pendant stays cool.

"Greets, that's boring. Turn it on," the other man says.

I look up and watch as he turns the prod on. It hums to life. The pads on the three fingers open, close, then open again. I push myself back, reaching for my magic.. It gathers at my fingertips, ready. Greets steps forward, eyeing the glow coming from my hand.

"No, you don't," he says, taking another step, this time landing on my fingers. I cry out as I feel them pop underneath his weight. Greets smiles and adds more pressure. My magic roars. One after the other, they break. Tears spring to my eyes. Greets removes his foot, revealing my bent fingers.

"Don't worry, 732. They'll heal. Hopefully, by then, you'll have learned to behave properly," he says with mock concern. He lowers the prod and touches it to my chest. I scream as my magic tears through me and into the prod. When he removes the prod, I'm lying on my back, gasping for air.

"I've figured out the machine," the other man says.

Greets backs away, turning off the prod. "Are we going to do this the easy way or the hard way?" he asks me.

I push myself into a sitting position, my hand protesting, and glare at him. "You'll kill me if I go in there,"

I say, my voice shaking. "There are protocols and prepping that need to take place before-"

Greets backhands me, cutting off my words.

"You've survived worse," he says, pulling me up by my shirt. He drags me towards the machine.

I shove back against him, standing up. "This isn't something to be messed with," I continue. "This could kill me. You'd lose your job when-"

He backhands me again.

"Enough talking from you," Greets says. He undoes my belt and forces my jaw open, shoving it inside. I twist my head back and forth, failing in my attempts to free myself from his grasp. The belt is tightened and pinches my hair. "Now get in."

I reach up to undo the makeshift gag. Greets grabs my arms and throws me onto the table, locking my wrists into the cuffs. I thrash, shouting wordlessly at them. Maybe someone will hear my screams and come to investigate. The cooks are here, right? They'll be able to hear me.

Hope sputters out as the machine closes over me. My breathing comes in ragged pants as the light engulfs me. My magic is swirling furiously and I can feel the tug the Machine has on it. Tears leak out of my eyes and the pendant starts to burn against my skin.

*My name is Adam Carlson. I will survive. My name is Adam Carlson and I will survive. I will survive. I will survive...*

*I'm going to die.*

# CHAPTER FIFTY ONE

## JACKSON

I nod to Cynthia as I pass, a container of yesterday's barbecue tucked underneath my arm.

"Welcome back, Jackson," she says, tying her red hair back.

"Thank you. How was your holiday?" I ask.

"It was relaxing. And yours?"

"The same. Have a good shift," I say as I walk away.

There aren't many Handlers in the Lab. They aren't needed for most of the tasks we do, unlike the market section of Rebren. The only reason they find their way to the Lab outside of their shifts is for the gym, which Adam has tended to spend most of his free time in. I still don't know how the Handlers have agreed to let him use it. Most of them hate him and want to use him as a punching bag. All except Richard. The man has taken a liking to him, which isn't hard to do once you get to know Adam. Once he drops his rebellious act, he's quite enjoyable to be around.

I set my computer in my office, keeping the container and my coffee with me. The walk to Adam's room is short, probably why he chose to break into my office a few months ago. I shake my head. *That kid...*

I knock on his door and ease it open, cracking it just enough to peek my head in. “732,” I start before seeing that his bed is empty, still neatly made. His bathroom door is cracked open and the lights are turned off. I walk in, looking around. His blinds are open, letting in sunlight. Maybe he’s gotten up early to get in some exercise before our training today. Closing the door, I head to the gym. A few Handlers roam around as they get ready to start their workouts. A half eaten sandwich sits on a small table near the punching bag, as well as a pair of gloves. I furrow my eyebrows and leave. There is one other place I can look. He could possibly already be eating.

The only people in the kitchen are the cooks.

“Have you seen 732?” I ask Brenda, the head cook.

She shakes her head. “Not today,” she says, chopping up vegetables.

“Thanks,” I say and walk out. I pause in the hallway, thinking. He couldn’t have run, could he? It’s a possibility. Nobody was here to watch him.

“Are you looking for 732?” Richard asks.

“I haven’t seen him anywhere.” I pause. “He couldn’t have ran.”

"I saw the light on in the Machine room today," he offers. "He might be in there."

"The Machine room?"

He shrugs. "Not sure why, but it is."

"Thanks. I'll check," I say, heading off in that direction. The light is indeed on in the Machine room. I push open the doors. "732?" I call. The Machine is open and golden magic flecked with black swirls in the jars that are hooked up to it. Adam is curled up in a ball, his hands bound behind him, next to the Machine. I drop the container and coffee on the table and crouch next to him.

"732?" I ask, unlocking the cuffs. His skin is red and sweaty and the cuffs have made indents on his wrists. His fingers on his right hand are bent awkwardly and a belt has been used as a makeshift gag, cutting into his cheeks. I undo that as well, some of his hair coming with it as I pull it away. "Adam? Can you hear me?"

No answer. I turn Adam onto his back and see that the metal pendant around his neck is charred and smoking. I pull out my phone and dial Abigail's number. After 3 rings, she picks up.

"Jackson?" she asks.

"It's… It's Adam. Something happened and he's in bad shape," I say quickly.

"Adam… What do you mean?"

I look at Adam again. "I think he went through the machine unprepared. I don't know how, and I don't know why. I found him this morning. He's unresponsive."

She's silent.

"I need to get him out of here. Bring him back to you," I say. "He needs help."

More silence.

"Please, Abigail. He's dying."

"I'll send you the address."

* * *

"And why are you sneaking 732 out?" Richard asks as he helps me get Adam into my car. We prop him up and I lean his head against the seat.

"I can't help him here. And I can't let him die," I say, buckling him in. "I hope you understand."

Richard nods. "I don't want to know where you're taking him," he says. "Just help him. He's a good kid."

I nod, climbing into the driver's seat. I type in the address that Abigail sent me and start driving. I call Leah, letting her know that I won't be home tonight and why. Once I drop Adam off, I'll explain everything in detail.

The drive to the house is long, winding through backroads and forests. The directions take me into the mountains and down a rocky dirt road. The road soon opens up into a dirt packed driveway and a small clearing. A large, four story house sits at the end of the driveway. Abigail and another man with a long beard come running out. I quickly turn off the car and grab Adam out. He's hot to the touch and is sweating. I carry him up to them.

"Oh my gosh," Abigail says, a hand flying to her mouth.

The bearded man takes him from me. "I'll get him upstairs," he says and disappears into the house. I see Colton standing in the doorway, waiting for the man and Adam.

"Jackson, how can we help him? He looks…" She trails off.

I shake my head, thinking. "I don't know of any medicines we could try, however, Adam did say something about someone with healing magic. At Robert Caulder's place," I say. "I don't know if he's alive or not, but it's worth looking into."

She nods, chewing on her fingernails. "I'll look. Thank you." She turns to go into the house.

"Abigail," I call. She turns. "If he does wake up before then, he knows about your role." Her face falls. "He snuck into my office and saw the documents. By the time I got there, he had already seen everything. I'm sorry."

She nods, looking down. “He doesn’t seem to hate you,” she starts. “You might want to be here when he wakes up.”

I nod. “I’ll tell Leah and the girls to pack some things.”

# CHAPTER FIFTY TWO

## JAKE

Sara and I are sitting at the table, her banana bread from Monday sitting in the middle. We pick at it in silence. I hold onto her hand and smile. Her beautiful blue eyes meet mine and I can see her smile in them.

"I love you," I say softly.

"I love you too, Jake," she says back, grabbing a piece of bread and biting into it.

My phone starts to buzz.

I pat Sara's hand and check the number. Someone from Ohio. I stand and answer it, walking away from the kitchen.

"Hello?" I ask.

The voice on the other end of the phone is low and rough. "Hi, my name is Jason Roames. Is this Jake Harrison?" he asks.

"That depends, Mr. Roames. Why are you asking?" I pop my knuckles on the hand not holding the phone, flexing my fingers anxiously.

"I need his help, and I heard from a co-worker that he would be able to help me," Jason says.

"What kind of help are you needing, sir? Mr. Harrison is a busy man," I lie.

There's a pause from Jason. "A friend of mine is sick," he says slowly. "Fever, sweating, won't wake up. He had an… accident and we were told you could help him."

My heart starts to pound. *They've finally found me, and I've put Sara in danger this time.* "I'm sorry, I'm not a doctor. You were told wrong," I say, going to hang up the phone.

"His name is Adam."

I freeze, phone halfway from my ear. I see Sara walk into the living room, watching me with furrowed eyebrows.

"Adam?" I ask, touching the phone back to my ear. *Adam's alive?*

"Jake, he's not doing well and he needs what you can do," Jason says.

Sara grabs my hand, giving it a squeeze. "How did you know I can heal him?" I ask, my voice shaking.

"Adam mentioned it a few years ago to an acquaintance of mine. We thought to check if you were still alive. Can you help him?"

I look at Sara. She gives me an encouraging smile. “I can. Where is he?”

* * *

Sara and I are silent as we drive up the long driveway to the mansion of a house that Jason brought us to. We silently climb out of the car, Sara holding her belly, and walk up to the house. I knock on the wooden door and wait. The porch is nicely furnished, rivaling those in the south. Despite having a weathered look with paint peeling and chipped in places, there is a spot of brand new wood on the porch. I grip Sara’s hand as the door opens and a large man with a long beard smiles tensely.

“You made it just in time,” he says softly. He steps aside and ushers us inside. “I’m Jason. It’s good to meet you in person, however I wish it were under different circumstances.”

“Likewise. How is he?” I ask, my voice barely above a whisper.

Jason meets my eyes. “He’s barely holding on. I’ll take you to him.”

I nod, giving Sara’s hand a squeeze. “Stay down here. If anything happens, I don’t want you upstairs. Adam’s magic can be… unpredictable,” I say.

She nods. She gives me a kiss and pats my cheek. “Go save him.”

I smile and follow Jason up the stairs. The stairs creak slightly when I step on them, and the banister has multiple nicks in it with spots worn by many hands sliding up and down it. The door Jason brings me to is cracked open and I see someone pacing inside. Jason knocks and opens the door fully, exposing the room beyond it. It's large, but not overwhelming. There is a bed by the window and a figure lies on it. Two people stand by the bed, a young man with messy blonde hair and a young woman with long, curly black hair.

"Jason," the blonde man starts, walking towards us. "He's struggling. Please tell me that this is the guy."

Jason steps aside and lets me into the room. "This is Jake Harrison."

The man limps towards me. "Can you help him?"

I tilt my head, examining the young man in front of me. A large scar runs down his neck and he's holding a lot of weight on his right leg. "I can."

The young woman stares at me. "You're alive," she whispers.

I furrow my eyebrows. "I was never dead."

"What do you need?" The young man asks me, turning my attention back to Adam lying on the bed. "I need the room clear and the door closed," I instruct.

"But-" the blonde man starts to say.

I turn to him. “If something happens, I want it contained in this room,” I say sternly.

The man closes his mouth and nods, putting a hand on the young woman’s back and leading her from the room. She glances back at me before following the man down the stairs.

Jason nods to me and closes the door.

Hearing their steps quiet as they walk down the stairs, I take a deep breath and turn back to Adam lying in the bed. His skin is an angry red and he is sweating. His hair has grown out, but it’s thin and slick with sweat. His fingers on his right hand are broken. I pull a chair over, my hands shaking. *Oh Adam, what have you gotten yourself into?*

I gently pull his arm close to where I sit and place my hand on his forearm. I take another deep breath and close my eyes. Adam is barely breathing and his heart is fluttering at best. I instantly push my magic into him, not stopping to examine the rest of his body. Strangely, I don’t see any of his magic. Almost like it vanished, taking everything it could to kill Adam as it left. Nearly all the iron and sodium in his body has been eaten up and there is very little oxygen in his blood and lungs.

My arm starts to shake with the force of the magic rushing out of me. I don’t care. I’ll hold my hand on his arm for as long as it takes to heal him.

His heart beats stronger and faster. Adam breathes deeply, taking the first full breath I’ve seen him take since being here. I send my magic to the rest of his body, to the damaged and broken nerves, to his arteries and bones. Anything that has been destroyed by the golden mass that was inside of him, I heal. I form a pocket of magic that I order to stay there for extra healing, unsure if it'll even stay. When I open my eyes, Adam has stopped sweating and his skin is back to a healthy color. I lean back in the chair, breathing in and out deeply. My heart pounds and my hands shake. I wipe my forehead with the back of my hand and it comes away wet. I'm sweating.

I rest my hand on Adam's arm again, monitoring his vital signs. Everything is good and healthy. I don't dare let myself leave so soon. I sit there for hours, monitoring Adam, until there is a knock at the door.

I look up to see Jason walk in. "How is he doing?" he whispers.

I turn back to Adam. "He's doing fine now," I say. "I don't dare leave him. What if he…" My voice cracks. "What happened?"

Jason is quiet for a moment before he speaks again. "They were doing testing in the Lab. His magic reacted and soon, we got a call to come take him. He's not responding well anymore. That's when I found you."

*The Lab? What was he doing there if he's been at a safehouse this whole time?* I look at him. "His magic is doing this, Jason," I say. "His magic is drawing on his body's resources and causing miniature explosions inside of him. Iron, sodium, oxygen, and a source for combustion. That's what's happening." I shake my head. "Unless he draws from outside sources, he'll die in a week. His magic is only getting stronger and he's not doing anything to work on it."

Jason is thoughtful.

"He's actively avoiding using his magic, isn't he?" I ask.

Jason's eyes flicker from Adam to me. "I'm not sure what relationship with his magic he has. Jackson will have more of those answers for you. You might want to talk to him about how to help Adam."

I nod, looking back to Adam. His eyes flutter back and forth and he's started softly snoring.

Jason nods. "Go downstairs. I'll stay with him. Get some rest and be with your wife," he says.

I nod and walk out of the room. Jason takes my seat by the bed. I quietly close the door and walk downstairs. I find Sara in the kitchen talking with a man with brown hair and a woman with curled black hair. Sara smiles when I enter the kitchen. "How is he?"

"He's fine for now. We'll see what happens when he wakes up," I say, sliding into a seat next to her. I look at the man across from us. "Are you Jackson?"

"Pleasure to finally meet you, Jake," he says, extending his hand. "Adam yelled at me a lot about you."

I furrow my eyebrows and reach forward, shaking his hand. "Later, I want to know why. Right now, what can you tell me about Adam's magic?"

Jackson leans back, nodding. "Jason told me you might have some questions," he says. "There's a lot. Where would you like to start?"

"How did he end up like… that?" I ask. "Jason said something about the Lab?"

Jackson looks to the side. "I'm not exactly sure. I found him like that when I… I haven't watched the camera footage yet," he says.

"You found him like that?" I ask. "Before the accident, what was his magic like?"

"At first, it was doing what you are most likely expecting it to do. It drew on his body instead of outside sources. Once we started training and Adam started using it properly, that stopped. Adam told me he felt it rest. I'm not sure what that means," he explains.

I look back towards the stairs. "His magic is completely gone right now," I start. "And his body was a wreck. Do you have any idea what caused it?" I meet Jackson's eyes, pleading. Sara puts a hand on my arm.

Jackson looks at the woman next to him.

"He deserves to know, Jackson," she says. "They're family."

He sighs and looks back at me. "There's a machine that was developed in the Lab. We found that if we drew Adam's magic out of him, his magic couldn't kill him. It was working until we tried using his magic." He pauses. "There are protocols that need to be followed, prepping that needs to happen with the machine before Adam can go into it. My guess is that someone put him in without following those protocols or prep. Adam's magic reacted and… nearly killed him."

I lean back, processing his words. A machine. They put Adam in a machine that pulled his magic out of him? Adam couldn't have gone willingly into that thing. He fought so hard against Caulder and Rebren that I can't imagine him willingly doing anything they asked. Yet here is a man telling me that Adam *listened* to Rebren on this. "How do you know Adam?" I ask softly.

Jackson smiles sadly. "We met right after he was brought back from Robert Caulder's," he starts. "They took him to the Lab and assigned me to his case. We didn't make much progress before he disappeared from the Lab. Five months ago, he was brought back on terms of helping him survive his magic and nothing else. I was assigned to his case and I worked with him daily," he explains.

I sit up straighter. "You work for Rebren."

Jackson nods. "I won't tell your secret, Jake," he says. "I promise."

"How can I trust you?"

"Adam trusts me," he says simply.

I swallow. "How did you know who I am?"

"Adam," he says with a smile. "After Robert Caulder's place, he was completely different. The only thing that got any sort of reaction from him was a mention of you. Boy, did he yell and shout."

"Did Caulder hurt him?" I ask softly.

Jackson shakes his head. "No," he says.

I let out a breath. "Good," I whisper. "That's what was supposed to happen."

Sara's hand tightens on my arm. Jackson looks at me sadly. "Adam said that you died, Jake. Why did he think that?"

I meet his eyes. "Because, technically, I did." I tap a spot on my chest. "He shot me right here. His theory was that my magic would heal me faster than I could die. And, well, he was right. My heart stopped due to shock, only for a moment. Technically, I died and Adam saw that. He didn't know I survived the bullet."

Jackson's eyes are wide, although I can't tell if it's from shock or wonder. "Your magic…" his mouth opens and closes a few times. "That's amazing. And you can heal other people?"

"I'm severely undertrained and unpracticed, but I have healed others."

“Imagine the medical advancements we could make with your abilities,” he whispers. “One day, you’ll have to let me run some tests.”

I shift in my seat, swallowing nervously.

The woman next to Jackson pats his arm. “Honey, not everybody shares your same enthusiasm for work,” she whispers, noticing my discomfort.

Jackson gives me a smile. “Of course, only if you are okay with that.”

I let out a nervous laugh. “I’ll think about it.”

# CHAPTER FIFTY THREE

## ADAM

I wake up in a room that is swirling with colors. I blink a few times to make sure what I'm seeing is real. The walls are a shade of red, with gold trim around the windows and doors. The bed has a colorful, patchwork quilt on it. And the carpet is a fluffy looking tan. I sit up and see a brown dresser and desk, with a mirror on one wall and a wooden door that leads to a bathroom. Tree branches sway past the window that overlooks a field of dying grass and piles of fallen leaves from the trees all around. People run around outside, their shouts echoing up. I rub my eyes and shake my head. I have to be dreaming. I was in the Lab. Greets and the other Handler…

I shoot up, breathing hard.

"Welcome back to the land of the living," Jason says from the doorway. I turn to see him leaning up against the doorframe with his arms crossed. There is a smile on his face.

I look from him to my right hand and my perfectly straight fingers. "How long was I out?" I ask.

"Three days."

I look back at my hand, making a fist and then flexing my fingers. Healed, as if they were never broken. No scars and no residual pain. I shake my head. "That's impossible," I whisper. "How did I get here?" My hand strays to the pendant around my neck. There was a terrible burning feeling…

The pendant is black, almost as if it's been charred, although no residue rubs off onto my fingers.

Jason sighs and walks in, sitting on the chair that is positioned near my bed. "Jackson brought you. He called, saying that you weren't doing well. He drove you here. You looked sick; sweating and your skin was red. You weren't waking up. Abby said you were dying," he explains. He puts a hand on my arm. "We called someone to help you, Adam. He says you're fine now."

I shake off his arm and flex my fingers again. "That's impossible. The only person who could help me is dead."

"You don't know that," Jason says softly.

I toss my legs over the bed and walk to the door. "Yes, I do."

Voices float up from the kitchen as I make my way downstairs. The wooden railing is smooth underneath my shaking hand. Jamie and Heather rush past me, smiling. They don't seem to be on edge about the newcomer. When I enter the kitchen, I see a group of people sitting around the prep table in the center of the room. Abby and Colton sit next to Jackson and a black haired woman. They sit across from a man with brown hair that brushes the tips of his ears and a blonde woman who looks extremely pregnant. Abby looks up from the conversation when I enter the kitchen.

"Adam!" She says, rushing over to me. She stops a few feet away, placing her hands in her pockets. "You look better."

I press my lips together and nod. *Abigail Sommerfeld. Case manager.*

Colton pulls my attention away by clapping me on the back. "Good to see you alive," he says. I flinch backwards from his hand. I meet Colton's eyes, hearing his voice in my head discussing whether or not to give me up to the Lab. He lied, too.

"You invited Jackson to stay?" I ask, raising my eyebrow at him. Jackson gives me a small smile and a nod in return.

"Good to see you awake, Adam," he says.

I blink at my name. He's always called me 732, why start calling me 'Adam' now? "All thanks to you," I say.

"Adam," Abby starts. "There's someone here you should talk to." Her gaze falls on the man with shaggy brown hair. He stands and faces me. His bright green eyes meet mine and I stop breathing. The scar from the bike accident is still there, right above his left eye. A large floral tattoo replaces his Mark, and his smile…

"Hey, Adam," he says softly.

Jake.

I shake my head, hands trembling. "No," I choke out. "You're dead. You died."

"I know how it looked-" he starts.

The room starts to spin and I grab onto the banister to steady myself. "How it looked?" I step forward. "He shot you, Jake. You crumbled. You stopped breathing! They drug you away like a sack of grain! Your eyes were dead. You died, Jake! I saw it!"

"Caulder missed my heart. On purpose," he explains quietly, his hand resting on a spot right over his heart. "My magic healed me."

"On purpose?" I ask. "Why would he do that?"

Jake rubs the back of his neck. "To use me as his own personal healer."

"Why? He's a spry and crotchety old man, but healthy," I point out.

Jake shakes his head softly. "He has a tumor growing in his chest," he says. When I don't respond, he continues. "I was back in the cell he locked us in when I woke up. He didn't lock the door and I was able to get out and sneak into the back of Brad and Mitchell's truck.. Brad took me to his place and, well, I started a new life." He intertwines his fingers with the woman next to him.

My eyes flick from the woman with kind eyes to their intertwined hands, then to her swollen belly, and finally back to my brother. I take a deep breath, clutching the banister until my knuckles turn white. I feel the numbness try to creep in after all this time. "So you escaped. You got out." I watch his face for any hint of guilt. "Why didn't you come back for us?"

His face falls. "I thought about it almost every day right after I got out," he says slowly. "Then I got caught up in life."

"So you just left us there," I finish for him. "You left us to the mercy of Caulder and Rebren."

"He was supposed to leave you alone after I was gone," he says. "That was supposed to be the punishment, Adam. I was the example."

I shake my head and a small laugh escapes me. "No, he did not leave me alone," I start. "After you were so graciously dragged away, do you know what he made me do? The porch needed to be cleaned up, he said. He made me clean up your blood until there wasn't a speck left! Then he sold me to the Lab to become their lab rat." I feel tears trickle down my cheeks and sobs build in my chest. "I don't know what he did to 12, or 1048, or the rest of them. Luckily, we got 06 out. His name is Brandon, but you wouldn't have known that. You abandoned us, Jake. You abandoned *me*!"

There are tears in his eyes.

"You left me there alone," I choke out. "I thought this whole time, for nearly three years, that you were dead. That Caulder killed you." More tears fall. "But you were living life, happy and free, while the rest of us struggled to survive."

"Adam," he says, taking a step forward.

I move back, shaking my head. Abby steps closer to me. "Adam," she starts.

I shake my head and walk out of the kitchen, needing some space to think.

* * *

Jackson follows me out to the wooden swing set where I'm sitting, gently moving back and forth. He sits on the second swing.

"I brought you some leftover barbecue," he starts. "From the Fourth."

I look over at him. He's got a container of food in his hands and a smile on his face.

"Is it any good?" I ask.

He chuckles. "It's fine. It's only been a few days. It's just not as fresh as it would have been." He hands me the warm container and some silverware.

I take it from him. “Thanks,” I say. The pulled pork nearly melts in my mouth. The barbecue sauce is perfect for the seasoned meat. “This is really good, Jackson,” I say.

“I’m glad!” he chuckles. “I made it!”

I finish the pork quickly and lean against the chain of the swing, resting the empty container against my leg.

“How are you feeling, Adam?” He asks.

There it is again, my name. I look at my hand again. “I feel fine,” I whisper. “You… you called me by my name?”

It’s Jackson’s turn to sigh. “I found you lying on the ground of the Machine room…” he runs a hand along the backside of his neck. “You’re more than a number, Adam.”

I close my eyes and smile. “Do you know how many times I’ve told myself that over the past years?” I whisper.

“What happened, Adam? On the Fourth?” He asks.

I meet his eyes. “Greets and his buddy came in while there was nobody around,” I explain. “Pulled me out of the gym and to the machine room.” I flex my right hand again. “Greets broke my fingers when I tried to use magic and then he put me in the machine.”

“And the belt?”

My hand strays up to my cheek, where I felt the leather cut into my skin. No mark there either. “He said I was talking too much,” I whisper.

Jackson scrubs a hand over his face. "I'm so sorry, Adam," He whispers. "I shouldn't have left you there alone. I should have known… I should have taken you with me," he trails off.

"Jackson," I say. "You didn't know."

He gives me a look.

"I'm in one piece. I'm back at the safe house. And we figured out how to keep my magic from killing me," I explain. "Things worked out in the end."

He smiles. "And your brother isn't dead."

I clench my jaw and look away. "Yeah, and that," I mutter.

Jackson puts a hand on my shoulder. "Adam-"

"I don't want to discuss it right now," I say. The numbness tries to creep in. I don't want to deal with it right now.

"I understand," he says. "I'm guessing that you didn't see the fireworks?"

I shake my head. "No, but I heard them," I say with a smile. "I don't remember much, but I remember hearing them as I lay on the floor."

Jackson doesn't seem to know how to respond to that.

I tap the tupperware on my leg. “I can get this washed for you,” I say as I stand. “It was quite good.”

“I appreciate it, Adam,” he says with a smile.

# CHAPTER FIFTY FOUR

## ADAM

Jake and Sara sit across from me at the large table where dinner is being served. The food is strewn across the table where multiple people can grab what they want. I sit between Colton and Jackson. Colton and I still haven't spoken a lot since I woke up. Abby sits on the far side of the table, talking softly with Jason. Her eyes dart over to me every so often. Over the past couple of days, Jackson and I have worked on control with my magic as it slowly returns. I can feel it resting comfortably in my chest now. It still swirls and pulses, but we've seemed to reach an agreement where it doesn't kill me if I use it properly.

I can feel every time Jake looks at me, his eyes burning into me as I grab food from around the table. I glance up at him as I grab a roll from the bowl that is being passed around. His eyebrows are furrowed and his eyes are sad. I look away from him and pass the bowl to Colton.

*Dot-dash. Dash-dot-dot. Dot-dash. Dash-dash.*

My eyes snap back up to Jake, my heart pounding. He taps his fingers on the table next to his plate, looking at me with his sad eyes.

*Dot-dash. A. Dash-dot-dot. D. Dot-dash. A. Dash-dash. M.*

My blood starts to boil. I push my chair back from the table and storm out of the kitchen.

"Whoa, Adam? Are you okay?" I hear Colton call behind me.

"Fine," I say as I exit the kitchen. How dare he? He abandons us, abandons me, for years. Then he shows up, the savior who brought me back to life, and expects me to pretend like he wasn't gone for years? Like nothing ever happened and that nothing is wrong? He comes back with a *wife*, a new family, and a life that he's been living while he *left me* to Rebren. He *left me* to be tested on and beat and nearly die, all while he is living his best life and getting married.

I let out a frustrated yell, startling the birds around me. I pause. When did I get outside? The night air is chilly as I breathe it in, letting it sink into my bones and cool me from the inside out.

I hear footsteps behind me and I let out a sigh and turn around. "Jake, I swear-" I cut off my words when I see who's there. Frederick is slowly walking towards me, hands in his pockets. "Fredrick," I say.

He smiles. "Hey, Adam. I hope I'm not intruding on anything."

I shake my head. "No, not at all." I pause. "What has you out here?"

"I wanted to make sure you're alright," he explains. "I saw you storm out of dinner."

I run a hand through my hair and turn around. "Yeah," I say eventually. "I'm fine."

He walks up and stands next to me. "No, you're not. I know that look."

I glance at him. "Fred."

He shakes his head. "You can trust me, remember?" His gaze is soft and inviting.

"I trust you," I say softly, sighing.

"What's on your mind?" He asks.

I take a few breaths before explaining. "My brother, Jake, we had a plan to escape. We got caught and I saw him die. He shows up years later with a wife, a new life, and left me to Rebren. He had gotten out but didn't come back. I thought..." my voice breaks. "Why didn't he come back?" I feel tears build in the corner of my eyes. I blink them back and take a deep breath. "He just left me."

"Have you asked him why?" Frederick asks.

I glance at him. "No," I admit. "I'm so angry at him that I don't want to hear what he will say."

"Being angry is easier than letting go," he says. "It's not just him you're angry at, though, is it?"

I shake my head. *Abby, Colton, Jason... I can't tell him about them. He'd lose trust in them and our operation would fall apart.* "Did Abby and Colton tell you why I ended up back in Rebren?"

"They said that Handlers found you before you could get out. They took you to the Lab, or else they would have gotten you out sooner," he explains. "Abby said she couldn't get them to release you."

A good cover story. We haven't attempted breaking into the Lab yet. "They gave me up," I mutter. "My magic was killing me, so they gave me to the Lab to figure it out-" I cut myself off.

"They didn't tell you?" Fredrick asks.

Something moves in the bushes. I squint. "Get back to the house."

Frederick traces my gaze and nods. I follow him, both of us jogging. My heart pounds. How did they find us? How did they know we were here? Jason meets me in the doorway to the kitchen.

"Adam?" he asks. "What's going on?"

"There's someone outside the house," I explain. "I don't know how many."

Jason straightens. “Everyone, get to the basement,” he says.

The noise of the dining room quiets as the many people turn to face us.

Jason turns. “There are people outside. Everyone get to the basement.”

“I’ll figure out who they are and what they want,” I tell Jason as people stream past us. “And if they’re not friendly, I’ll get them to go away.”

He smiles at that. “I’ll make sure everyone is safe.”

“Thanks,” I say and head towards the living room. Colton is already there, watching out the window. Jake and Sara are talking in hushed tones in the corner.

Colton glances at me before turning back towards the window. “Are you going to blow them up?” He asks with a smirk, his eyes flickering to mine quickly.

A pang hits my chest. Familiarity. Joking with Colton used to come so easily. “Possibly. I’m definitely going to blow *something* up,” I say. “Who knows if it’ll be them or their tools.”

Colton smiles at that. “Good.”

We watch out the window in silence, the only sounds come from Jake and Sara’s hushed conversation. Taking a deep breath, I walk over to them.

"Jake," I say. "I want you in the basement."

He shakes his head. "No," he says.

*Stubborn jerk.* "Why not? You will only get in the way and get hurt."

Jake clenches his jaw. "What is your plan, then?"

I ball my fists and shove them in my pockets. "If I tell you, you won't follow it," I bite. "So you and Sara need to get downstairs before someone gets hurt."

The pain in Jake's eyes is unmistakable. He takes a deep breath before opening his mouth. I cut him off before he can say anything. "Sara," I start. "You need to get to the basement."

She looks at Jake, then back at me.

"For him, for me. Jason will be down there and you already know that Jake is indestructible.

"Adam," Colton says. "People."

I swear under my breath and usher Jake and Sara down the hall. "Get downstairs," I hiss and run back to the living room. Colton stands behind the wall, peering through the window from the side. Four men walk up, holding guns. There is an unmarked van parked further down the road, hidden in the trees. How did I miss the van? I stand on the opposite side of the window and watch the men. They have strange face masks on, thick, black ventilated pieces of cloth secured around their mouth and noses. Two of them start circling the house while the other two walk up the steps to the front door. I flex my hands, gathering my magic, breathing in the oxygen around me. I focus on a spot of wood on the porch, feeling its grain and flammability from here. Before I have the chance to let my magic loose, the man closest to us grabs something from his pocket and hurls it at the window. It lands with a crash, spraying glass into the room. Colton and I duck, turning our backs to the window. When I look at the object, I see a small, circular ball roll in, spraying green smoke from it.

No, not smoke. Gas.

I meet Colton's eyes and we run. "Jake!" I shout, covering my mouth and nose with my shirt. I run down the hallway, towards the basement where Jake and Sara should be. I find them by the door. Jake has Sara behind his back as he stares at me.

"What?" He asks.

I crash into them. "Get down, cover your mouth and nose," I say. I can already feel the effects of the gas making me sluggish.

*Not yet.* I gather my magic again and use the gas in the living room. I focus on the furniture and the air coming in through the window. And then I release it. Explosions rock the house and we crash into each other, Colton sliding into the wall before falling to the ground. Jake covers Sara with his body and I crouch next to them. The gas ignites, along with its drugged and chemical properties, clearing the air of any threat while hopefully keeping the men outside until I can get Jake and Sara to safety. When the explosions are done, I hear muffled swearing from the other room.

"Thought that would work, didn't you, 732?" A man's voice shouts. I hear the crunching of glass. "We were prepared for a trick. We were told that you like to end fights before they start. We planned for that."

I look at Colton, but he's got his eyes trained down the hallway. I follow his gaze to the end of the hallway to see a figure rounding the corner. He's dressed in all black and has his gun raised, pointed straight at us.

"Unfortunately for you, I have orders to collect only one of you," he says. "So I suggest you listen carefully."

# CHAPTER FIFTY FIVE

# JAKE

Sara grips my arm as I shield her from the man in front of us. Adam crouches between us and the man in black. It's the same man who ambushed me at my work weeks ago. The one who wants to take me back to Robert Caulder.

"I'm here for 54," he says. "Come with me and nobody gets hurt."

"No," Adam says. "Nobody is coming with you."

*Adam, careful.*

The man tilts his head to the side before firing his gun at us. Sara shouts and flinches behind me. The shot hits the wall in-between Colton and us, leaving a hole in the wood. "That was a warning. Come with me, or the next one goes in your friend over there." The man aims his gun at Colton.

Adam goes very still. I can see his hand flexing behind his back. He's using his magic. But what is he going to do with it?

"I'm going to give you to the count of five to get over here," he says. His finger rests over the trigger. Colton stays still, eyes trained on the gun pointed at him.

Adam stands up slowly, hands in the air. "I'll go with you," he says. "Leave Jake alone, and I'll go with you."

The man shakes his head. "I'm sorry, Caulder specifically wants 54. Only him, really," he says. "Adam-" My words are cut off by someone grabbing me from behind. I am pulled away from Sara. She grabs at my arm, shouting my name. I struggle with the person behind me, trying to get free of their grip and clawing at their arm. My gut sinks when I feel a chain slip around my neck. "No," I whisper. "No!" I shout this time, grabbing at the chain that is locked around my neck.

Adam turns around, eyes going wide. Someone creeps up behind him, a silver chain in their hand. "Behind you!" I say to him, still struggling with the person holding me. I get an arm free and shove my elbow into their face. Stubbornly, they hold on.

Too late. The man sneaking up on Adam grabs him and pins his arms to his sides. Adam growls and headbutts the man. The man grunts and drops Adam. He turns around, arms held loosely at his sides and fingers twitching, gathering magic.

"Stop!" The first man says. We both turn towards him. The man has a hand in Colton's hair and a gun pressed to his head. Colton has a bloody nose, but a fire still rages in his eyes. "Everybody stop and the boy lives."

Adam freezes and meets Colton's eyes. They hold each other's gaze for a while before Adam says, "Lower your gun and I'll lower my magic."

The man laughs before pressing it harder against Colton's temple. He winces but doesn't make a sound. "Lower your magic?"

A warm, golden glow surrounded my brother, shrouding him in a cloud of deadly sunlight. He smirks. "I'm sure you've heard of the... destructive properties of my magic," he says. "I'm not sure you want to see what happens when I ignite the very air you're breathing." Adam's fingers twitch and the golden light surrounds the man. "Lower your gun, and I'll lower my magic."

The man slowly lowers his gun, angling it towards the floor. The glow fades.

"Leave," Adam says.

The man smirks. "Not without 54. And, seeing that we have him, we'll be going now." The man raises the gun and points it at Adam. "No tricks and I won't shoot."

Adam glares at the man. The person holding me drags me towards the front door. I struggle to rid myself of the hands holding me. I lock eyes with Sara still huddled on the ground. She has a hand on her belly and is moving to get up.

The man starts to drag Colton with him. Adam steps towards them, hands out.

A gunshot fills the room. Adam throws up his hands and a small yet powerful explosion forms in mid air. When the light clears, Adam is standing there, his arms covering his face.

"Jake?" Sara says.

I look at her and see red covering her chest. "No, no, no nonononono," I say. "Sara, hold on!" I shove out of the grip holding me and rush to her, catching her as she collapses. I press a hand to her bleeding chest. "Sara, look at me."

Her beautiful blue eyes find mine. They are filled with tears. I feel hands grabbing me. I shove them off and try to heal her, pressing my palms to her wounds. My magic flares, but can't make it past the silver chain around my neck.

"Get this off me!" I shout, my eyes flicking around the room. None of the men move. I feel more hands on me. "I can heal you; just hold on," I say to Sara. She grabs my hand and puts another hand on my cheek. She gives me a weak smile.

"I love you," she says.

I blink back tears. "Don't say that like you're dying," I whisper. "You'll be okay." The hands start to pull me away. I fight against them, my magic roaring in my veins. "Sara, please!" I grasp her hand as the two pairs of hands finally pull me to my feet. "No! Let me heal her! Please!" I cry.

"You're magic is reserved for Robert Caulder alone, now," one of the men hisses in my ear.

I fight against the men, throwing punches that don't land. Adam rushes to Sara's side, putting pressure on her wounds. He strips off his own shirt and uses it as a makeshift rag.

"Sara!" I shout as the men drag me down the hallway, over broken glass, and out the front door. They shove me into the back of a van and chain me to the seat. I pull against the chains, trying to get out. Trying to get back to Sara.

The doors close. A moment later, I feel movement and the van is pulling away, leaving behind the house, Adam, and Sara, our son still in her womb.

# CHAPTER FIFTY SIX

## COLTON

I feel Sara's blood still oozing out of her wounds underneath Adam's shirt. Adam had me take over so he could get Jason. The basement door opens and then Jason is there, kneeling next to her. Adam is close behind him, eyes frantic. I meet his eyes, shaking my head slightly.

"She's dying, Jason," Adam says, his voice cracking.

He nods and scoops her up in his arms. Her eyes flutter open and she gasps. Her hand strays to her belly. "Keep breathing, Sara," Jason says. "We're going to take care of you."

Sara nods and leans into his chest.

"Colt, go with him," Adam says.

I nod and stand up, wiping my hands on my pants as I follow Jason out. He lays Sara in the back seat. I slide in next to her, holding the shirt on her wounds again. She reaches out and grips my hand weakly.

"I'm here. We've got you," I tell her.

She smiles weakly. "Thank you," she breathes.

Jason starts driving, the truck rolling over any obstacles in our way. "Ten minutes," he says. "You can make it ten minutes."

* * *

"Help!" I shout, running into the hospital. I run through a waiting room full of people and straight to the front desk. What a sight I must be with blood staining my clothing and hands. The two women at the front desk snap their heads up. One of them stands.

"Young man? What's wrong?" She asks.

Jason follows behind me, carrying Sara in his arms. She's pale and her blonde hair is stuck to her neck with sweat and blood.

"She's dying and she's pregnant," I say.

The second woman nods and picks up her phone. The first woman makes her way from behind the desk. "Follow me," she says, pushing open doors. We follow her through hallways and past nurses rushing this way and that.

"What is her name, age, and relation to you?" she asks me as we rush down hallways.

"Sara Harrison, twenty three, she's my Aunt," I say.

"How did this happen?"

"A freak accident in the kitchen," I lie.

“How far along is she?” She asks.

”Eight and a half months? Maybe a week or two more.”

The woman nods and rushes us into a room. There is a team of nurses and a few doctors waiting for us. “Lay her here,” she says. Jason lays her on the table. I give her hand a squeeze.

“You‘ll be okay. There are doctors here,” I say to her as they roll her away. Her eyes barely flutter in response. “Please be okay,” I whisper. Jason puts a hand on my shoulder.

“I’ll show you the way to the waiting room,” the woman says softly.

I nod and we silently follow her down the hallways. “Here are the restrooms if you need them.” she says.

“Thank you,” Jason says.

Hours later, Jason and I sit in the waiting room, our clothes still covered in Sara’s blood. People have come and gone, speaking in hushed tones. Some of them leave with their families, others come and go one at a time. Nurses walk by, some with baskets, others with monitors on wheels. I am pacing behind the chairs where Jason sits when a nurse walks in and calls my name. I freeze and turn towards her. Jason stands, and we follow her into the hallway. She waits for the door to close before speaking.

"How is she?" I ask.

The nurse takes a deep breath before answering. "Mr. Rosen, Mr. Roames, I'm sorry. She didn't make it through surgery," she says softly.

Cold floods my body. "What happened?" I ask.

The nurse presses her lips together. "There was shrapnel embedded in her chest; it had punctured a few arteries and one piece had hit her heart. The doctor said he was surprised that she was able to make it here."

*Adam's explosion that blocked the bullet... it scattered when he hit it.* "And... the baby?" I whisper. Blood pounds in my head.

The nurse smiles with tears in her eyes. "A healthy baby boy. Five pounds," she says.

I feel tears slip from my eyes and Jason claps a hand to my shoulder. "You were able to save him," he whispers.

She nods.

"What will be done with her body?" I ask. *What would we do with her body? Put it in the back of the truck with a newborn in the backseat?*

The nurse looks at us sadly. "We will keep her body here for a few days until funeral arrangements can be made," she explains.

I nod, looking to the ground.

"Would you like to see him?" the nurse asks.

Jason nods. "Yes, please," he says.

The nurse nods and leads us down the halls to the nursery. There is a sectioned off part of the room she leads us to. In the small room are two nurses and a baby in a small bed. The nurses smile when we walk in. "He's doing well!" The nurse next to the small bed says. "Is there a name you have picked out for him?"

I nod. "Grant Harrison," I say, repeating the name Jake had told me when I asked a few days ago.

The nurse scribbles the name down. The first nurse steps closer to me. "Mr. Rosen, I wanted to ask you about the incident," she says.

I nod, fear building in my chest.

"What we found in Sara, it looked like fragments of a bullet," the nurse says. "Was this a domestic violence kitchen related incident?"

I shake my head no. "We made a mistake with the pan. Had it on too high of a heat. It blew apart and Sara was right there." A flimsy story, but hopefully, it will hold.

The nurse nods again. "I wanted to make sure. The baby is healthy and ready to go home. Is there family he'll be with?"

I nod again. "Grant will be under my family's care," I explain.

She smiles. “Wonderful.”

# CHAPTER FIFTY SEVEN

## JAKE

The chains cut into my wrists as I tug against them. The van started moving hours ago, taking me further away from Sara and closer to Robert Caulder. Unlike the other times I've ridden in the back of one of these vans, there is no Handler to watch me. I must not be considered 'dangerous' enough for Caulder to spare one on me. I grunt as the van goes over a bump and I am pitched forward. The belt around my waist keeps me on the bench, but does little for my top half. The chains rattle and sway. I know if I can get my wrists free of the cuffs, I can figure out a way to get out of the rest of the chains. I wiggle my wrists, putting pressure on my joints to try and slip out. I hear a pop and sharp pain shoots from my hand up my arm. I clench my jaw to keep from crying out as I try to slip my wrist out. My magic rushes to heal the broken joint and I am too late in wiggling my wrist out. The joint heals and I am still stuck in the cuffs. I let out a shout of frustration and throw my head backwards. I've got to get out of here so I can get back to Sara. I can heal her if I get free of these horrid chains and retched silver one around my neck.

The van eventually stops moving. Light blinds me when the doors open. My eyes are still adjusting when the

Handlers roughly unlock me and pull me to my feet. I stumble out of the van and onto the patterned pavement. I look up and see Robert Caulder's mansion in front of me. The Handlers march me forward, up the beautiful stone steps and through the large wooden door. Before we get deep into the house, I am shoved into a small bathroom.

"Clean yourself up," one of them says and he stands in the doorway with his arms crossed.

I glare at him but turn to the sink. My bloodstained hands leave marks on the handles as I turn on the water. I wash off Sara's blood, watching as it flows down the sink. I dry my hands and wipe off the blood on the handles.

When I'm done, the Handler grabs my arm and pulls me out of the bathroom. They drag me up the spiral stairs and into the study where the man who now holds my life in his hands waits. I feel my body start to shake. Behind the desk sits Robert Caulder. His hair is thin and his skin looks gaunt, but it's him. He smiles darkly when he sees me.

"54, what a surprise," he says in a weak voice. Despite his frail form and airy voice, he still sends shivers down my spine.

I don't respond.

He waves a bony hand at me, beaconing my forward. The Handlers shove me towards him and I catch myself on the desk. The cup that sits near the edge rattles with the force of my weight.

"It seems that you have forgotten your manners, boy," he says. Caulder waves me forward again. I slowly make my way towards him, a pit forming in my stomach with each step. This is the man who bought me and my brother, and countless others, for labor. The man who whipped my brother multiple times. Who tortured me under the title of 'training'. Who shot me, hunted me down, and brought me here. Who ripped me away from Sara as she bleeds out on the floor, and our son who I'm not sure will survive the day. The Handler forces me to my knees in front of Caulder.

The man in front of me reaches around my neck and unlocks the silver chain. His hands are cold and send shivers down my spine. He pulls the chain away and holds out his arm.

"I took your advice," he starts. "I had it removed, but I haven't recovered from the surgery." He holds out his skinny arm. "You know what to do."

I look at his pale arm and grit my teeth. "No," I rasp.

Fire burns in Caulders eyes and he backhands me. I catch myself against the desk leg and push myself up. My cheek stings and throbs, but I refuse to let him know that it hurts. Despite looking frail, he still hits hard.

"You belong to me, 54, and you will do what I say," he says.

I glare at him.

"You were never returned. This contract here," he pats a pile of papers that rest on his desk, "is still valid."

"Technically, I died, so it is void," I say. "You can't keep a dead Worker around."

Caulder grips my chin with surprisingly strong fingers and pulls me close to him. "I believe you are still breathing," he seethes. He releases my chin and holds out his arm. "Do it."

I glare at him and clench my fists. Behind me, I hear a Handler pull out his taser. Caulder nods and he jabs me with it, sending a jolt through my entire body. I clench my jaw shut and refuse to make a sound.

"If you don't, I'll send my men back to that house and get your brother. We'll see how well you cooperate with his safety on the line," Caulder whispers.

"You wouldn't dare," I whisper. "You can't control him or his magic. It's too dangerous." *He doesn't know about Sara.*

"We'll see about that," he says. He holds out his arm again. "I'm not asking, 54."

*He's serious about Adam.* I think. Slowly, I raise my hand to his arm and close my eyes, feeling my magic flow into him. His body is a wreck, broken and battered. I let my magic heal all the tears and the weak bones and muscles. There is so much damage done that I can't heal it all right now. Healing what I can today uses all I have. I'm gasping for air and covered in sweat when I pull my hand away. Caulder takes a deep breath and flexes his hands. He already looks stronger; his skin has more color and his face looks less sunken. He nods to the Handlers.

"Take him to his lodging," he says, picking up a pen and turning his attention to the papers in front of him. "I want to see him again tomorrow."

I glare at him as the Handlers pick me up and drag me out of the office.

"54," Caulder says right before we leave the study. The Handlers pause and I look at him over my shoulder. He's smiling. "Welcome home."

I look away, feeling a chill run through me. *This is not home. This is hell.*

My lodging is a small, concrete room in the basement of the house, illuminated by a fading light in the center of the ceiling. It has a single cot with a random assortment of bedding lying on it and a toilet in the corner. There is a shower near the toilet with a small sink nearby. A small trunk sits at the foot of the cot. They've chained my ankles to the middle of the floor, giving me enough room to reach the toilet and shower, but not the door. They put the silver chain back on. I pace the length of the chain, hearing it scrape across the ground with each step I take. My hands shake from overuse of my magic. I've already tried to slip my feet out of the cuffs around my ankles. The attempt left my skin raw and irritated. I welcome the sting on my skin. Without my magic to heal me, the small scrapes are still there, despite my attempt happening nearly an hour ago.

The door squeals as it is pushed open. The man who kidnapped me stands there with a Handler by his side. He smirks at me, the scar across his eyebrow raised.

"How are you adjusting to your new quarters, 54?" he asks me.

I straighten my spine. "What are you doing here?" I ask, ignoring his question.

The man steps into the room, looking around. He lets out a low whistle. "I'd say it's pretty bland. It could use some decor, maybe a nice rug to go under the bed?" He watches me. "I thought I'd pay you a visit after all the trouble I went through to get you here." He sits on the bed. It groans under his weight, just as all cots do. "How is Robert doing? They brought you straight to him without going through proper protocol."

"He's cruel as always," I say. "How did you find me?"

The man smiles. "My good friend Jan Klarke had suspicions about you after your little "accident". He reached out to me and I started investigating." The man crosses one leg over the other. "Jake Harrison, son of Maria and Grant Harrison. But there were no hospital records of your birth. No school records. Nobody in town remembered you growing up. So, how is it that you had lived in Kansas your whole life, yet there are no records of you actually being there? That's when I reached back out to Jan and Rebren paid your work a visit. We knew then that you were someone trying to hide something. The night I found you confirmed everything I needed to know when your broken nose stopped leaking blood unnaturally fast. It was a matter of figuring out where you'd gone after that, but traffic cameras aren't hard to get access to when you've got the police on your side." He smiles at me.

My heart pounds and I can't seem to breathe right. "Jan figured it out," I whisper. "He knew for months."

The man nods. "He asked me to bring you in after hours. It would look terrible for his company if I'd come for you during store hours. Bad publicity for him. I'm sure you understand."

I lean up against the wall and raise a hand to my head. "Why didn't you follow me home, then?" I ask, meeting his eyes and lowering my hand.

The man tilts his head. "Good question. I was tempted to, but I did promise you that I'd leave the woman out of it and I figured following you to your home would only drag her into it." he pauses. "Although, she did end up getting involved. I do hope she survives, I really do, 54."

I feel my heart pound at his words and I grind my teeth. "Why didn't you let me heal her?" I growl.

"You belong to Robert Caulder. Anyone else needs his permission for you to heal," he says simply.

I can't look at him. "You fired the shot that killed her," I state.

"Yes, but your brother caused the bullet to fragment and scatter. So, whose fault is it really?" he asks, standing. "It's been a pleasure, but I do have a payment to collect and a job to get back to. Enjoy your time here, and welcome back to where you belong." The man walks out of the door and closes it, the lock echoing in the stone room.

# CHAPTER FIFTY EIGHT

## ADAM

My magic swirls uncomfortably underneath my skin as I box against the standing punching bag in the old barn. Sweat drips down my back and I breathe in the musty air.

The sound of the gunshot echoes in my ears and the blood soaking Sara's shirt burns in my mind.

Hit with the right fist, then the left in quick succession. Don't forget to cover your face.

I let out a grunt as my fists connect with the bag, the sound echoing in the large barn. The birds in the rafters sit and watch. If only I had jammed the gun before he could shoot instead of simply blocking the bullet.

One, two, three, come around with your leg and knock your opponent over. Don't forget to breathe.

I should have gotten them to the basement first and then checked on the intruders. Sweat drips into my eyes and my breath comes in quick pants. My arms burn and I feel my knuckles bruising underneath the tape.

Right, left, duck. Be light on your feet, putting most of the pressure on the balls of your feet.

I should have, I should have, I should have. More blood on my hands, more life lost because of me. My heart thunders in my chest, pounding to the same rhythm as my fists. A frustrated shout bubbles up from my chest and echoes through the barn. The birds let out startled hoots and fly away, escaping through the cracks in the roof. I collapse against the bag, using it to support my weight, and gasp for air.

No matter how hard I try, everyone I try to save ends up in chains or dead. Jake ended up with a bullet in his chest, and the rest of the Workers were still stuck in their same place, locked in chains. Sara is bleeding from a wound because I couldn't get her to safety, and Jake is dragged away in handcuffs and a silver chain around his neck. 1048 dead, his body smoking. Brandon's whole right side was covered in burns. I close my eyes and feel sweat, or is it tears, drip from my nose onto the bag.

"Knock knock," Jackson says, his voice dragging me from my spiraling thoughts.

I push away from the bag and start unwinding the tape around my hands. There are sweat marks on the bag from my body.

"I wanted to check on you," he says hesitantly, hovering just inside the doorway.

"I'm fine," I say curtly.

I hear him kicking at loose rocks on the ground. The sound of stone rolling against wood clear as day behind me.

"You're certainly fine in boxing," he states. "But I know you box when you're upset."

I drop the tape and sigh deeply, letting my head fall backwards until I'm staring at the patchy roof. "I've got so much blood staining my hands," I whisper. "Jake, 1048, a couple of Handlers, now Sara… it's my fault."

Jackson's soft footsteps get closer and closer as he slowly walks up to me. "All you did was block the bullet."

I shake my head. "I should have jammed the gun before he fired it. I should have gotten them to safety sooner. So many things I could have done differently… I had control over the situation this time. I could have *stopped* it." I feel tears burn my eyes and I blink them away, looking down. "She's dead and he's gone because I couldn't stop them."

Jackson puts two hands firmly on my shoulders and pulls me into him, wrapping his arms around me. The tears are falling freely now and I lean against Jackson, letting my head rest on his shoulder. "The men… I couldn't stop them," I cry.

"Nobody expected you to," Jackson whispers, rubbing small circles on my back. I wrap my arms around him and sob.

"She's dead and I've lost him again," I gasp out. "I couldn't, I couldn't…"

"Shhh," Jackson soothes in my ear. "Just breathe."

My breathing comes in ragged gasps and I struggle to fill my lungs before another sob wracks my body. I clutch at Jackson's shirt, trying to hold onto something to stop me from falling into that numbness again. "Please," I whisper.

"I've got you," Jackson says softly. "I've got you."

My breathing steadies and the tears stop flowing. The pain in my chest sits there, no longer threatening to swallow me whole but taunting me. The numbness starts creeping in and I bury my face in Jackson's neck, trying to hide from it. "I don't want to disappear again," I mumble.

"I know it hurts," he whispers. "And it's okay for it to hurt. Loss hurts."

I breathe in a shaky breath. "I don't know how to stop the numbness," I admit, whispering it. I'm suddenly aware of the exhaustion that seems to go down into my bones.

Jackson is quiet for a long moment. "You find purpose," he says.

I slowly shake my head. "I can't help anyone. It ends the same."

"You don't have to save anyone right now," he says. "But there is someone who needs you."

I lean back, looking him in the eye with a confused look. "Nobody *needs* me, Jackson. I need everyone else."

He gives me a knowing smile. "Do you trust me?"

I let out a long breath. "Who is it?"

Jackson lets me go, patting my shoulder before walking to the door. He holds it open for me, motioning me to go through. As I pass, he hands me a bottle of water. "Hydrate before you get a headache."

"Did you have this the whole time?" I ask before taking a long drink.

He smiles. "I set it by the door on my way in." He leads me back to the house, past people in the yard. Allivane is gardening around the planters along the edge of the yard, Connor is by her side, and Ben is talking with Fredrick as they walk. Jason's truck is back in the driveway, as is Abby's gray car. Jackson holds open the side door, the one that leads into the kitchen. We pass Ashley and Heather who are baking some bread product on the large table.

"Hey, Adam, Hey, Jackson," Heather says, waving at us with a flour covered hand. Her blonde hair has come loose from her braid and some strands fall around her face.

I give a small nod in return.

"Afternoon, ladies," Jackson says. "It's looking good!"

That gets a smile from both of them. Ashley figured out early on that she loves cooking and is found most days in the kitchen.

We exit the kitchen and Jackson leads me to the living room. With the help of a few of the older men, Jason repaired the broken window and ruined furniture quickly. On the new couch sits Abby and Jason. Colton stands next to them, leaning against the wall. Abby has a bundle of blankets in her arms. All three of them look up when we walk in.

"How is he?" Jackson whispers, crouching in front of Abby. He stares at the blankets.

"Sleeping," she whispers back. She meets my eyes and gives me an encouraging smile. "Come meet your Nephew, Adam."

The numbness and the pit of pain are driven back by an invisible force, awe and wonder quickly taking their place. I make my way to the couch and sit in the small section next to Abby, staring at the bundle of blankets. A newborn baby is breathing deeply, a teal pacifier in his mouth. I hesitantly reach out and brush a hand lightly over his head. Tears of a different kind pool in my eyes as I stare at the newborn. Abby gently moves the sleeping bundle into my arms.

"Adam, meet Grant," she says.

I cradle little Grant in my arms, holding him close. He's so warm and so soft. "Hi, Grant," I whisper, blinking back my tears. He's so innocent, so pure. I look at Jackson, who is smiling.

"I told you to trust me," he says. "He needs you, Adam. Until we can get Jake back, he needs you."

I look back to Grant, sleeping in my arms, and nod.

"We will get him back," Colton says, determination written on his face. We lock eyes and I nod, feeling that same determination build up inside me, replacing the numbness. "I've got a few ideas, but they're going to take time and a whole lot of work."

Getting Jake back from Robert Caulder won't be easy. We'll have to do something we've never attempted before with nobody inside and only a small group of us. I nod once more, meeting each of their stares with equal fire.

"What do you have in mind?"

# END OF BOOK ONE

Made in the USA
Columbia, SC
01 May 2025